———————— ★ ————————

"You've got one hell of a story here, and you don't even know it. You've got a story here that folks have been trying to piece together for decades."

The intensity of her stare made him uncomfortable. Her words made him feel even more uncomfortable. They sounded like the ravings of a madwoman. He was cautious. "I didn't get the impression that Hollingsworth was *that* interesting."

"I'm not talking about Hollingsworth," she said, "although I know he's in the middle of the woodpile someplace. I'm talking about her and her clan."

"Her?"

Impatiently she said, "The woman in the portrait— Kathleen Day Baker."

———————— ★ ————————

"A complex, engrossing plot and highly recommended."

—*Mysteries By Mail*

KATIE'S WILL

TOM MITCHELTREE

W🌐RLDWIDE.

TORONTO • NEW YORK • LONDON
AMSTERDAM • PARIS • SYDNEY • HAMBURG
STOCKHOLM • ATHENS • TOKYO • MILAN
MADRID • WARSAW • BUDAPEST • AUCKLAND

KATIE'S WILL

A Worldwide Mystery/November 1999

First published by Write Way Publishing, Inc.

ISBN 0-373-26328-7

Visit us at www.worldwidemystery.com

Printed in U.S.A.

KATIE'S
WILL

ONE

HE CLIMBED DOWN out of the Siskiyous, dropping two thousand feet from fir-packed mountains to the sun scorched, yellow grass of the Rogue River Valley. Ahead of him was Ashland, Oregon, a forgettable town except that years before it had embraced the Bard of Avon and now housed one of the finest Shakespearean theaters in the nation. Good skiing and a small college added to the town's interest, enough so that Paul Fischer promised he would return to it as he whizzed by on the freeway in his leased Pontiac.

In the distance, beyond Medford, he could see Table Rock and Lower Table Rock pushing up from the valley floor like two harvested mountains cut off flat near the base. West of there would be Jacksonville nestled up against the lower hills of the Coast Range. The valley itself was a big scoop out of the Crater National Forest.

The vast expanse of sky above and the heat trapped in the valley below were oppressive, the second threatening to peel back the vinyl roof of the car and do worse to the top of his head. He had gotten the idea he would not need air conditioning in a car in fog-shrouded, wind-swept San Francisco. He had two sets of clothes stained with sweat and one extensive heat rash to remind him that he had been wrong. People were sent to hospitals with temperatures he had seen in the last two days.

He felt in the ache of his bones and the throb of his muscles the distance he had traveled. He was weary, but not so much from the miles journeyed as by the transition in his life this trip represented. It was meant to be a plum shared with his wife for years of dedication and patience; only, as irony would have it, the patience wore thin before the plum was ripe. Now he was left to unravel the mystery of one man's life without understanding the puzzle of his own.

A few miles down the freeway he turned off at Central Point. He found Hanley Road and followed it west. Jacksonville would be in the corner of the valley where rolling hills made a gentle transition to the mountains that stacked up behind them.

He sank back into the seat of the car and slowed down. He was in no hurry. Hurry had made a blur of the last fourteen years of his life. Degrees were to be had and articles and stories to be published. Choice teaching positions were taken as stepping stones to Harvard and Yale. He earned a Ph.D. with honors from a top school. Finally he won a lush grant from a mid-western school to write a biography about an illustrious graduate with enough money for Paul to take a year off to travel out west before making a bid for one of those major-league teaching jobs. Unfortunately, in the rush, he had fast-danced himself right out of a wife.

To his right, houses clawed their way up distant hillsides, not quite reaching the crests and not yet spreading to the roll of peaks behind them. A house stood out from the rest like a sparkling white gem displayed on green velvet. He had to crane his neck to catch a glimpse between trees and houses of the Victorian manor a mile or two away. He was a little surprised to find such an opulent home set in its own small forest in a valley that had not been known for its wealth since the gold rush days. Someone had held on to his money.

By the time he pulled his car into Jacksonville, he was ready to pour himself out of the front seat and sit like a puddle in the shade until he no longer felt like someone's dinner popped from a microwave. He hated excessive heat almost as much as he hated excessive cold. Give him 80 and a slight breeze any day.

He wanted to hate Jacksonville, too. He wanted to kick up dust with the toe of shoe, spit, and scoff at the place with eastern superiority, except the town was quaint in a New England way. He liked it as soon as he stepped out of the car. The town smelled of baked dirt, old leather, and grass clippings left to dry in the hot sun. The air was heavy with these odors, giving the dust a taste as he imagined the old west would taste.

He stood in front of a two-story, brick building, once a courthouse, and now the Jacksonville Museum. Above the arched windows and the tall, white columns and near the peak of the portico roof was a small plaque on which was the date 1883. Although he had seen a hundred buildings like it in the south, he knew the residents here would be proud of this one because it was a rarity in the Northwest.

He was not ready to climb the steps to the large, double doors through which would begin a good six months of research on a subject that would thrill few but the moneymen behind the project. Paul tugged down his necktie another notch and unfastened a second shirt button near his neck. He knew that his New England formality would not do out west, but he had yet to break himself of the habit of dressing for every occasion. He turned away from the museum and locked his car. He wanted to walk around the town and get a feeling for old Harry Hollingsworth's territory before he went to work.

He traveled from one California to the next: from the state to the street, the main thoroughfare down the center of Jacksonville. Down these four short blocks he saw many of the original buildings that had been erected during the days of wealth when the town had been the booming gold capitol of Oregon. Still standing proud and worn were the U.S. Hotel, the Beekman Bank, and the Masonic building. Their days of glory had come and gone, but they wore their wrinkles with pride and refused to be put to rest. He turned around and walked back down the street. He would have time later to push his nose into every corner of this town. Right now he needed to put on his best, smiling face and make himself welcome at the museum.

In the museum he would find bits and pieces of the life of Dr. Harry Hollingsworth, some of it in writing and much of it in medical equipment he had left behind, but Paul would not find the bits and pieces of life that would make good reading in a book. No, he would have to kick the slats out of Jacksonville to do that, and even then, he wasn't sure what he would have.

He climbed the steps of the museum and entered through the double doors, feeling confident that he would end up with a worthwhile book. Old Myrtle Lee, the first curator of the Jacksonville Museum, and then Mary Hanley after her, had done their jobs well. They had pursued the history of the town in every attic and every closet of every home that had historical importance, and they had brought it back to rest securely in the museum. He knew he would not have to find history here; he would just have to write about it.

To make it easier for him yet, Hollingsworth still had a home somewhere in town. Many of the houses of his patients, most of the landmarks of the town in which he lived, and most of the streets and roads he had traveled were still in place. Finally, to top it all off, two of his grandchildren still lived in the area. This was going to be a piece of cake. He was a little embarrassed to be paid so much money to write the book.

On the second floor of the museum he looked through the top of a glass-enclosed case at a row of Indian arrowheads. As he drew back to move on the next case, he saw a reflection of himself. Unprepared for this vision, he saw himself for an instant differently than before. The sight was only moderately encouraging. His eyes were blue, his complexion nicely browned, his features square and masculine. These elements worked together pleasantly enough, but a permanent five o'clock shadow and dark circles under his eyes bit into what might have passed for handsomeness to give his face the first bloom of middle age to come. He shivered.

Since no one was around to see him, he took stock of himself in the reflection. His light brown hair was short and thick with only a few strands of gray here and there. His teeth were incredibly white, so much so that they saved his last ties with youth and made him seem younger than he was, despite the other clues that said otherwise.

He stood up straight, tired of the image that he saw. There was not much he could do about it now. At six foot, one hundred-eighty pounds he was not physically imposing, but he was in good health and good shape, owing that to moderate exercise that included walking and weightlifting. Although he did not consider himself to be handsome, he felt attractive enough to say that he was satisfied with the cards dealt to him. They could have been a lot worse.

He finished his tour of the second floor and walked to the staircase at the front of the building. The steps dropped to a landing and then split into two staircases that curled back down to the main lobby. He followed the curve to the left and concentrated on his feet as they tapped their way down the marble steps. He was halfway down when, for no reason, he looked up. He stared into eyes that kicked the wind out of his lungs.

She was an incredible creature. Her eyes were a brighter blue than any eyes should be, almost as if the painter of her portrait had invented a color that did not exist, that could not exist, even if it did glow on his canvas.

They were bold eyes set wide on the face and round with expression. They seemed to say that she was interested in him and him alone. A slight twist to the lips suggested the amusement she felt because he, like a fool, stood there thunderstruck. The tilt of her head made it clear, though, that he was not the first to feel this way. She had an arrogance in that tilt that suggested she expected nothing less of him than stunned surprise.

He sat down on the steps. Here, hanging on the wall was a portrait of a woman who embodied his conception of perfect beauty. Her perfection was such in his mind that even the strands of long, blonde hair that had escaped from those piled on top of her head were just the right touch, just the way the woman of his dreams would have used a slight flaw to underline her perfection.

He sat and stared and then finally shook his head. The clothes she wore in the portrait were turn-of-the-century. In the same moment he had found his dream girl, he had lost her. He smiled. His wife had told him that he would be better off with another woman. If this was the best he could do, he had no reason to file for a divorce.

As he rose, he felt a rush of warm air sweep over him, and he swore, just for an instant, there was a hint of perfume in it. He smiled to himself as he slowly descended the stairs and went to the office door under the stairwell. This was no time for him to develop the mind tricks of a fiction writer. His knock was answered by an attractive woman in her fifties or sixties. He introduced himself.

"Hi," he said. "I'm Paul Fischer, and I'm here to make old Harry Hollingsworth roll over in his grave."

The woman stood in the doorway for a moment, sizing up Paul from head to foot. She did not smile, and when she did speak it was with a marked lack of enthusiasm. "You're too damned young and too damned good-looking to do the job right. You write letters like an old man who has lived in a library most of his life. Come on in." She turned around and walked inside the office, leaving the door open to him.

He followed her into the small, cluttered office, feeling obligated to defend himself. "I'm sorry if my letters gave you the wrong impression," he said. "I'd like to tell you that I'm a child prodigy, but the truth is I worked my butt off to get where I am, and I got there fast because I'm a pretty smart fellow."

"We'll see about that," she said. She pulled out a chair from an old oak, roll-top desk shoved against one wall, its small shelves and cubbyhole over-flowing with papers. She waved a hand and said, "I don't apologize for anything, including this mess."

Mess might be a kind word. The room was stacked to the corners and halfway up the walls with artifacts, books, and papers. A flintlock rifle leaned in one corner, its butt resting in a box filled with China plates. Near the desk a patchwork quilt was folded neatly and placed on the seat of a ladder back chair. The woman removed the quilt and motioned him to the chair.

She said, "Every time someone empties out an attic the junk ends up here until I can figure out what the hell to do with it. Some of it's good and some of it's garbage. There're times I wish they'd sell it off instead of bringing it here. How many rifles does a museum need, anyway? By the way, if you haven't figured it out yet, I'm Nora Ryan, the curator here."

"You have nothing to apologize for, even if it *did* cross your mind to do it." She stared at him through round, owlish, rimless glasses.

She was one of the few older women Paul had met who was able to wear her hair cut for a younger woman and get away with it. In her black skirt and vest, white blouse with ruffles, and gray tweed jacket, she was a good-looking woman. She had a look to her face that suggested she knew it.

Reading his thoughts, she said, "I'm sixty-five years old and don't look it. If I dyed my hair I could pass for a young forty. That's harder than hell on a woman who has accepted the fact that she's sixty-five."

"You don't look a day over forty," he said, not knowing what else to say to a woman as aggressive and intimidating as she was.

She snapped back, "And you don't look a day over twenty-five."

He decided to counter aggression with aggression. He learned long ago that older women who were curators or librarians practiced the art of intimidation as a defense against what, he did not know, unless it was being curators and librarians. "I'm working on being older. In fact, I'm a lot closer to forty than you are."

She sat down in the chair to the desk, saying as she folded her hands in her lap, "Yes, son, but you're on the wrong side of it. What do you need? You didn't come here from Pennsylvania for nothing."

"In your letter you said you would help me with my research on Harry Hollingsworth," he said.

She pointed to a door at the far end of the room. "Hollingsworth's in there. At least what I've got on him is in there. The family keeps some of the records themselves. Although the doc and his patients have been gone for a long time, you're going to find that doing research on him will be sticky. Relatives of both the doc and his patients still live in the area, and they may not want private medical records of their kin made public. Some of these folks had a hell of a time being good Victorians."

"I assure you, and the community for that matter," he said, "that I'm only interested in the good doctor and the fact that he left medicine with his marvelous invention, the pill."

She laughed sarcastically. "That's the poorest excuse to glorify the old man that I ever heard. He wasn't the least bit interested in contributing to medical science, only in making his own life easier. And, as I understand it, he wasn't even the first to put medicine in tablet form."

He laughed, too, because he knew how close to the truth she was. He confided in her, "Yes, but the other two doctors who share credit for the invention of the pill didn't go to the school for which I'm writing this biography."

She tilted her head to one side and gave him a look that was both shrewd and wise, because the round glasses and her oddly shaped eyes made her look like a gray-haired owl. She pursed her lips before she said, "They gave you fifty thousand outright and another twenty-five for research. You also get a cut of the book and the right to market it any way you can once the university press run has petered out. I'll give you all the help I can as long as a big chunk of that research money ends up in the museum coffers."

He knew from her first letter that a deal would have to be struck with Nora. She kept the financial picture of this museum in good shape even in the worst economic conditions, a tribute to her wily way with money. If he was going to bargain with her, he would have to play down the size of his grant. "I'm still supporting a wife and two kids, a home for myself, and my research. That money's not going to stretch very far."

She slapped her hands on her knees and laughed gleefully. "Listen to that boy spin a yarn," she said. The smile disappeared from her face, and she pointed a finger under his nose. "Fifty thousand will pay your bills nicely for a year, and fifteen thousand will more then cover your research expenses.''

"Twenty five thousand," he corrected her.

The finger still waved under his nose. "Fifteen thousand. Ten thousand goes to the museum."

This time his laugh was sincere. "Let's be reasonable," he said. "That's a pretty steep price for the use of your files."

She dropped the finger and learned forward to stare into his eyes. "You've got one hell of a story here, and you don't even know it. You've got a story here that folks have been trying to piece together for decades. You got a story, if you can break it, that'll put your book on the top of the charts and leave it there. Ten thousand is a spit in the bucket compared to what's out there if you do this right.''

The intensity of her stare made him uncomfortable. Her words made him feel even more uncomfortable. They sounded like the ravings of a mad woman. He was cautious. "I didn't get the impression that Hollingsworth was *that* interesting ''

"I'm not talking about Hollingsworth," she said, "although I know he's in the middle of this wood pile someplace. I'm talking about her and her clan."

Now he was sure the woman had a screw loose. "Her?" he asked.

Impatiently she said, "The woman in the portrait, Kathleen Day Baker.''

He let the name bounce around in his mind for a few seconds, and then he decided it was too formal. The woman in the painting was definitely a Kate, not a Kathleen. "My grant's for a book on Hollingsworth—''

She interrupted him. "Hollingsworth will lead you to the Bakers, and then you'll be back begging for information on that woman. I know. There's been a dozen of us who got hooked on it, but we dead-ended. We need your new blood, and you'll give it, too, because a good biographer knows a hell of a story when he sees it.''

As beautiful as the woman might have been, he knew he had a business deal that had no room for her in it. He tried to let Nora Ryan down gently. "If I find out anything interesting about the Bakers in my research, I certainly will share it with you, but I'm here to do a book on Hollingsworth. Your help will definitely be worth some money to the museum. Perhaps we should talk about that figure at a later time.''

She leaned back in her chair and smiled at him smugly. ''You sit there cock-sure of yourself and think that. When you come crawling back the price just might be twelve grand.''

He got up and edged to the door. ''If that story really is out there, I'd probably be willing to pay twelve thousand for it.''

She shook her head. ''Poor sucker, you don't know what you're in for. Come back tomorrow and get started.''

He smiled, waved, and left the room certainly more curious about the history of this town than he had been when he had first arrived. He wondered what kind of secrets might be buried in this unlikely spot that would make for best-selling reading.

Just before he opened the front door to leave, he again felt a rush of warm air envelop him in the cool chamber beneath the stairwell. He stepped quickly outside. In the heat a chill crawled up his back. Caught off guard by these strange currents, he hurried to his car, assuring himself that he had run into another of those peculiar women who had spent too much time trapped in the past, surrounded by antiquity, so that she believed that every little, dusty fact was a pearl. Comfortable with that idea, he ignored the second whiff of perfume that seemed to follow him from the museum.

TWO

HE DID NOT return to the museum the following day, or the next. Instead, in his own words, he burrowed in.

He spent Wednesday searching for a place to live. He could have moved into an apartment, but that was not what he wanted. He was looking for a house with enough room in it so that his two boys could come out before the end of summer and spend time with him. Time with his boys had become very important to him now.

He could not believe his fortune when the real estate agent showed him the house he could get on a six month, renewable lease. The cottage was located on an old, narrow asphalt road called Shady Lane. The little lane was lined with trees so that the agent's car seemed to turn into a tunnel as they approached the house. The house itself was set well back from the road, encircled by a drive. At the front of the property was a beautiful rose garden filled with a dozen or more varieties of the flowers, each in its own square of soil that was surrounded by manicured lawn.

Behind the roses, across the drive, was the house, which sat in the middle of its own perfect lawn. After his tour of the property, he compared the house to a New England cottage. The house was white with a green roof, and it looked as if it had been built in the 'twenties or 'thirties. He had probably seen hundreds of homes like it before, but he had never noticed them because they were not placed in such a perfect setting.

A six-foot-high hedge on the left hand side of the property isolated the house from its neighbor. An orchard extended so far behind the property and to the right that Paul could not see anything through it but more trees. The agent had pointed out fruit trees to him. There were Bing, Royal Ams, and Black Republican cherries, Yellow and Red Delicious apples, and Bartlet pears. The owner of the orchard, the agent said, did not object to the people in the neighborhood picking fruit for their own use, as long as the neighbors were considerate about it.

Since the front of the property was lined with trees and bushes, and then the roses, the house sat in the middle of a marvelously isolated garden, a beautiful piece of land cut off from the rest of the world. It seemed to Paul to be the perfect place for a writer to do his work.

There were other advantages to the house as well. The land belonged to an old couple who finally tired of keeping up the grounds. They walked away from the property to move into a retirement village. They had left behind most of their furniture in the house, and most of the tools in the workshop and garage. The only thing they asked of the person who leased the place was that he maintain it well. Paul agreed to do that, although he was a brownstone man who had little experience with yards. Laughing, the agent assured him that rose bushes and grass were hard to kill.

The house had three bedrooms. The boys would have a place to stay. At the back of the property was a small barn, perfect for boyhood adventures. Finally, the capper to the deal, was a small guest house located next to the garage behind the main house. Perhaps, he thought, if he presented it just the right way, he could convince his wife to come out and visit him when the boys came.

By Friday morning he was ready to face Nora Ryan. And, as soon as he stepped into the museum, he discovered that she was ready for him. She met him in the entry.

"Well," Ryan said, her hands planted firmly on her hips as she blocked his way, "the great biographer has finally decided to return. I've had to alter my plans for the last two days while I waited for you to come back."

He was at fault, he knew. He could have called her at any time in the last two days, but he had not felt like it.

He would see more than enough of this woman in the next six months to a year. He was in no hurry to start seeing her now. He said, "I had to find a place to live and to move in, and then I had to get a telephone installed and the electricity hooked up. I've been spoiled by apartment living for too long; I've forgotten how much trouble it is to move into a house."

She threw her head back and made a loud sound with her tongue. Having done that, she wheeled around and walked into her office. He followed her.

Inside she asked, "Where'd you get a place to live?"

"Somewhere between here and Medford on a little drive called Shady Lane."

"Is that over by Oak Grove?" she asked.

"I think so," he said.

She nodded. "That's a good area. If you get too close to Medford, you'll find some folks there who'll want to wine and dine you because you're a writer. If you stay in Jacksonville, you'll find a group who'll want to write history for you, the way they see it. Hide out in Oak Grove and maybe you'll get this book written halfway decent."

He stopped in the middle of the room and crossed his arms. He decided it was time to lay down the law for Nora Ryan. He said, "I think I'll do all right on this, Nora. The reasons I got the grant are I have a good background in this period of history, a good reputation as a teacher, and an equally good one as a researcher and writer. I can also distinguish a good story from a bad one: I know when someone is feeding me a line of shit, and I know when someone is trying to use me socially."

She threw back her head and again made that sound with her tongue. Then she said, "Personally I'm not sure you know shit, but maybe you'll prove me wrong. Come on," she added, "follow me."

She led him to the door in the back wall of the office and unlocked it for him. Behind the door was a storage room, long and narrow, and dark, despite artificial lighting overhead. He noticed immediately that the temperature in the room was more comfortable than it was in the office and museum, both of which were not air-conditioned and were uncomfortably warm on this hot day.

"Climate controlled," she said, again reading his mind. "The humidity in the room is kept constant, too. We have too many old documents that are on their last legs to fool with the weather around here. It costs as much to keep this room just right as it would to air-condition the whole museum."

He only half listened to her, awed by what he saw. Most of the room was divided into a series of long rows of high shelves, each of the shelves crowded with books, old brown folders tied with strings, or storage containers about the size of shirt boxes standing on end in neat formations. Each section of shelving was marked with a code number.

Compared to the mess in the office, the neatness of this room was a surprise in itself, but there was even a greater surprise here for him. On a desk in one corner of the room was an IBM computer with a CD ROM and a laserprinter. It was an impressive piece of hardware to find in the back room of a museum of this size.

Nora interrupted his thoughts. She said, "You don't know how hard it is for an old lady to learn how to use one of those damned things. I swear computers are meant to kill man, not to make his life easier."

"I'm impressed," he said.

"Don't be," she snapped. "Winters are long here, tourists few, and time heavy on an old lady's hands. I've got nothing better to do for six months of the year but to play with that damned thing."

"Do you mind if I use this?" he asked.

"Not at all, as long as you don't mess it up, and you pay for any materials used."

He walked to the table and lightly ran his fingers across the keys of the computer, listening to the peculiar rattle they made.

Nora Ryan had her head back again, staring at him from under her glasses when he looked up at her. He realized he had been silent for several seconds. He asked a question that had been playing at the back of his mind since Tuesday to fill the void. "Why would I want to write about Kate Baker?"

Nora slowly lowered her head and smiled broadly. "I was waiting for you to ask that. Did you see that big, white house on the hillside when you came in from the freeway?"

He nodded. "It looked Victorian, but I wasn't close enough to it to tell for sure."

"Probably one of the finest examples of Victorian architecture outside of San Francisco. That's the Baker place. There hasn't been a soul living in it for years, but there's a fund that spends more than a hundred thousand a year to keep it up inside and out exactly the way it was the day it was built."

"Is it a museum?" he asked.

She chuckled. "Nope, not at all. It sits on private property, and it's guarded round the clock so no one can get near it."

"But why?" he asked. "That seems like a waste."

"Don't ask me. I haven't been able to find out. Let me tell you a little about the Bakers. Kate was the real beauty, but Emily and Elizabeth were pretty, too, only they were dark like their mother. Those three beauties were filthy rich, owning half the valley at one time. And they were all well-educated and brought up with social graces." She smiled even more broadly. "And," she continued, pausing for just the right dramatic impact, "all three of them died old maids, never married, a one of them." She tilted her head back to look at him from under glasses, the look on her face as smug as could be.

He did not want to give Nora the pleasure of a reaction from him, but damn, as hard as he tried he could not help but say, "I find that hard to believe. Any man would've been a fool not to want to marry someone like that Kate."

"There must have been a valley full of fools then," she said. "Not one of those gals married, and there's not a person in this valley living who can tell you why. Those ladies took their secrets with them to the grave, and I'd give an arm and a leg to know what they were."

"I would be interested in knowing what they are, too," he said to himself. To Nora, he added, "If I find anything interesting in my research, I'll let you know."

She let out a horselaugh before she wheeled around and walked from the room, throwing back at him, "I'm counting on it."

It took him several hours to familiarize himself with the computer system and with the information stored on the hard disk. He discovered that the museum had an extensive collection of papers that belonged to Doctor Hollingsworth. The doctor was a fastidious man who'd kept copious notes about his life, his family, and his practice. He also was not one to throw anything away; it appeared that hundreds of his possessions were either on display in the museum or stored away in one of several storage rooms on the grounds, everything from his medical bag to the presses he invented to make tablets. Enough original material existed to justify a photograph section in the biography. Paul felt confident now that he would produce a handsome book for the medical school.

He used the computer system to take notes, printing a hard copy of listings and files that would be of interest to him. After several hours in front of the terminal, he was ready to get out from under the artificial lighting in the room. The thoughts of sunshine and food were too strong. He decided to break for lunch.

He shut down the computer, turned off the lights in the room, and closed the door behind him. Mrs. Ryan was not in her office. He walked out into the lobby. She was not there, either. He shrugged. He thought she might be able to recommend a place for him to eat lunch. As he was walking out the front door, he paused long enough to look back and stare into the eyes of Kate Baker. He felt a little twinge in his chest and laughed. It would be just like a man without a woman to fall in love with a portrait, he thought.

He found a small café on the corner of the ell that was the heart of Jacksonville. He ate a sandwich at a small table near the front of the café. The waitress was friendly when she took his order, but for the most part people in the cafe paid little attention to him. He took his time and ate slowly, not at all in a hurry to get back to the museum. The events of the last few months had taught him a lot about loneliness, enough so that he was no longer excited about locking himself away in the back room of a museum.

Outside the window of the café Jacksonville was a town standing still. He imagined it was much like it had been when both Hollingsworth and the Bakers lived. The dust, the heat, and the wilted grass were the elements of all summers past or present. The people now were only a little less naive. No, it would be easy to slip back into time here; it would be easy to imagine Kate Baker walking up the street, a shopping basket hanging from one arm, and that smile on her lips. He sighed.

He paid his check and left the building, moving from the comfort of the café into the thick heat of mid-afternoon. He had worn a sports coat and tie, and again he felt over-dressed in the July heat. He took off the coat and tossed it over his shoulder. He loosened his tie, unbuttoned the top button of his shirt, and rolled up his sleeves while he walked down the street toward the center of town.

He walked slowly back to the museum. The warmth of the sun and the earthly smell of the town were overwhelming. He felt closer to nature than he had for a long time. He had spent so many years with his face buried in books or his body firmly planted in the middle of concrete campuses, that he had lost touch with the feel of the earth.

Here in this thinly populated valley in the heart of the western wilderness he felt...different. He laughed. Different, he said to himself, but not necessarily better.

Back in the museum he found Mrs. Ryan in her office. He smiled and said, "You have done a marvelous job with your inventory. I'm finding it quite easy to locate the things of interest to me."

She was at her desk, looking over a document in front of her. She lifted her head briefly to acknowledge his return and then glanced back at the document. She said as she continued to read, "Thanks. Don't overlook the papers left by Hollingsworth's son, Jeff. Also, Mary Day Baker and the doctor were friends, and she left an extensive journal behind that we have."

He leaned in the doorway and stared at the back of Mrs. Ryan's head. "I thought the Bakers were a mystery," he said.

Without looking up she said, "The Bakers were too prominent for too long to be a complete mystery. A lot of material about them was left behind, but you can bet your boots that what we've got is the well-censored, sanitized version. Since there is no way to get to the records left in the house, we'll have to accept the version they left behind." Her words were clipped and her head did not lift from the document in front of her. She made it clear to him that she was too busy for this conversation.

"Thanks," he said, walking quickly from the doorway, past the desk, to the back room. On his way by the desk he glanced over her shoulder to see what she was reading. He waited until he was inside the room with the door shut behind him before he let out a short, low laugh. Mrs. Ryan was deeply engrossed in the major league baseball box scores in the sports section of the local newspaper.

Three hours later he sat before the computer, his elbows on the top of the table and his chin resting on his crossed hands. His face was an unnatural white, almost the color of marble, caught as it was in the dull glow of the computer screen and the bright, fluorescent light from above. He held his pose for several minutes. It appeared that he was staring at the monitor, but he was not. He was lost in time, and his mind was a century away. He would have been surprised to find that he was breathing a little faster than he normally did.

In just three hours of research, he had lifted a veil and caught a glimpse of...of what? He let his left hand drop to his thigh and placed the forefinger of his right hand between his teeth, chewing on it softly, unconsciously.

He read the quote again. "There is no greater grief and unhappiness than the grief and unhappiness that Elizabeth and I have given each other." He found these words written on the back of a sheet of paper that belonged to Charles Hollingsworth. A box was drawn around the words in thick, heavy pencil.

He had found another quote that was just as cryptic, only this time the writer was Doctor Hollingsworth himself. He said of the Baker girls, "Silas has given them greed, and Mary has given them unrealistic purpose. No good can come of this."

Finally in one of the last entries of her journal, Mary Day Baker had written, "If I have done right, why do I feel so much trepidation? What have I done to my girls?" Someone at some time had tried to erase these words so that they were only a faint trace on the page.

He shut down the computer and removed a disk from one of the drives. Before Nora had left for the evening, she stopped in and told him how to lock up before he left. She wasn't going to wait up all night for him to finish. She had also told him that he could take home some of the documents if he left a list on her desk of what he had. He gathered up the materials he wanted to take with him over the weekend and left the room, making sure all the doors were locked behind him.

He was too preoccupied with his thoughts to notice how late it was. He drove home in darkness and had to stumble about between garage and house because of it. When he finally did get inside and turn on some lights, he did not bother to fix himself something to eat. Instead he went into the dining room where his laptop sat on the table and turned it on.

He began to write a few minutes later, when the computer was warmed up and he had the documents spread out on the table around him. He told himself that he was really writing about Doctor Hollingsworth, even if the first sentence did begin: "She was at one with the pain..."

THREE

SHE WAS AT ONE with the pain, removed now from her earth and as close to a metaphysical world as she could be. Then, another spasm crushed the breath from her body and suffocated her until it eased enough for her to suck in air between her clenched teeth. She panted in precious air and then the next contraction started the process all over again.

Yes, she thought, when she could think again, many women do forget the pain between children, but it all floods back at once and builds like the horror in a Gothic romance. An idea about women and suffering played in the back of her mind, but she had to let it go when the next contraction enveloped her in its vice.

The doctor stared down at the woman on the bed, fascinated by her struggle, that, in this light and this setting, seemed almost poetic. She lay in the middle of a cherrywood bed, its hand-carved headboard rising nearly to the ceiling, framed by white lace and white cotton, her pale and beautiful face surrounded by a thick spread of dark, curly hair. A single lamp burned next to the bed on a marble-topped stand.

He had never seen a woman fight the pain of birth the way Mary Day Baker fought it. She arched her back, she twisted from side to side, and she sucked in her lips until her mouth was no more than a thin, white line below her nose, but she never made a sound, and, except for her lips, her face was a calm mask.

When he had come to deliver her first child eight years before she had set out for him her rules of birth. She had said, "This childbirth is between the three of us: me, you, and the baby. I don't want an audience, and I don't want Silas up here, either. I lick my wounds and do my suffering alone."

He cleared a spot on top of a linen chest near the bed and placed his instruments next to the porcelain bowl, its pitcher already full of boiled water. He poured water into the bowl and carefully washed his hands, using the homemade soap his wife had put into the "baby bag," as they both called it. He checked the two sets of forceps, one with sponge tips and one without. He then carefully ordered splints, cotton, and bandages so that they would be in easy reach. Finally, he unfolded a rubber sheet and moved to the bed. He folded the covers back until they slipped off the end of the bed, and then he worked the rubber sheet under Mary. He left her nightgown in place for now, preserving her dignity as long as he could.

Other women in labor would insist upon being surrounded by females and demand the nightgown be left in place right through the whole darned thing. "The thought," he blustered to himself. They probably wanted the child delivered blindfolded, too. He was indignant. After all, this was *1890* and Oregon was a progressive state, and he was a married man of forty and an experienced doctor at that. Such modesty should be of another era, he thought.

"If all women could be like Mary," he mumbled as he took a cold, wet towel and wiped the moisture from her forehead. She was beautiful. She was gracious. He laughed. She was rich. She cared about her body and her health, and she wasn't the least bit shy about a doctor examining her to make sure it all worked. "If you want to buy a good horse you've got to open its mouth and check its teeth," she would say.

Mary twisted on the bed again. Doctor Hollingsworth frowned. Her body needed to be in good condition, he thought. She had been excessively tired and anemic during this pregnancy. Mary had a history of long labors and high blood loss during childbirth, and that was when she was fit.

He sat on the side of the bed and waited. He had to do all the work for some women when it came to birth, but not for Mary. She did it all herself, needing him only to wrap up the loose ends. She was quite a woman, Mary Day Baker. She had risen from a servant in New York City to the queen of the Rogue River Valley. It was a shame, he thought, that she had to make the journey with Silas Baker.

The expectant father stood on the front porch with one foot on the railing. He rested his right elbow on the raised knee and occasionally dipped his head down to the stem of the pipe in his right hand. He was not a demonstrative man, come frost, drought, or childbirth. He would pass the vigil on the porch, in the fading light of a July day, staring across the land that was his. He accepted the fact that the land was not his for as far as he could see, but it was through no fault of his own. If he could have gotten it, he would have.

What he had was given to him by the will of God. The will of God had given him a lot. To the east his land stretched to the railroad tracks eight miles away. To the south his fields pushed against the city limits of Medford. To the west he could stand on his land and see clearly the streets of Jacksonville. To the north... He spit over the railing into the flower beds that fronted the porch. To the north he had built the house in a grove of trees on a shelf of land about a hundred and fifty feet above the floor of the valley. The hills continued to rise behind the house until they folded into mountains. He owned a little land above the house, but, except for the water it brought him, he considered it to be worthless. He wanted flat land that he could plow and plant until it produced money crops. He smiled. Money crops had made him rich. He owned half the valley. He lived in a beautiful house. He had a lovely wife. And soon, he would have a lovely son.

Outside the bedroom door a child knelt, her ear pressed against a carved panel of mahogany. She was her mother in miniature, her hair thick and dark, and her eyes light green. And she was pale like her mother, but she was no duplicate. Those people who blurted out how much the mother and child looked alike, immediately checked themselves. Something was different about the two. While both of them had pleasant features, the mother's were fine and the child's were not. Emily Baker's face was chiseled more, so that the jaw and the nose were sharp lines instead of gentle curves, giving her a dark and brooding appearance. She was a dark and brooding child, a product of her appearance.

She knew that the odds were against her this time. Elizabeth, the picture of equanimity, so calm that her life slipped by almost unnoticed, had proven to be little competition for her father's attention. First born, Emily had carved out a spot in his heart, although no one carved out a spot too deep there. Her hold on him was tentative because of that, and she feared the threat the next child might bring to her position in the family. She could handle another girl. She could not stand the thought of a boy, a son for a father who craved nothing more.

She pressed her face against the cool wood and whispered, "Let it be a girl. If it is a boy, make it dead."

Elizabeth Baker slept the restless sleep of a four-year-old down the hall, thrashing about in the muggy heat of this July night, mumbling indistinct words, and occasionally shuddering as the shadow of a nightmare flickered across the edge of her undefined consciousness. She did not fear the arrival of a brother or sister. She did not fear rejection from her father. She feared the night; she feared the shadows; most of all, she feared Emily. An image of Emily was the only thing of substance that took shape in Elizabeth's mind when she woke up in the night. Emily was the embodiment of fear.

Elizabeth was prettier than her sister, perhaps even prettier than her mother. She had inherited all of the intricate features that made her mother so beautiful, but she also had borrowed heavily from her father so that she had his brilliant blue eyes to go with her dark hair, and she had his robustness of shape that contrasted sharply with her mother's almost frail figure.

Her mother's frail figure was being tested tonight. The long, crushing contractions controlled her mind and her body so that there was nothing left to her world but pain, the pain of a body trying to turn itself inside out. She lost herself in the pain; she succumbed to it. The center of her world was her womb, and all the energy in that world flowed toward it, pushing, ejecting its core.

Lips in, arch, twist... The doctor watched, concerned now because the continuous contractions didn't seem to be doing their job. The baby was still not in the birth canal. The labor pains had started early in the morning, and now it was past ten at night. Mary was visibly weaker and did not look like she could keep this up.

Outside, a moon full and pale rose into the night, casting a dim light across the valley. Silas stepped from the porch and walked across a broad stretch of lawn to the edge of the rise and looked down into the valley. His land was a patch quilt of grays and blacks, of crosshatchings and stripes. The wheat and hay fields were gray, the alfalfa black under the light of the moon. Filbert, walnut, apple, cherry, pear, and peach orchards criss-crossed in rows. Columns of vegetables could just be seen in the distance, set on the flat, most fertile part of the valley. Getting water to these fields was a challenging task, but he had overcome the problems with a series of small canals controlled by gates that sent it to different parts of his land, and by an irrigation ditch that bisected his property. Above the house he had dammed a creek and made a pond from which to draw water during the summer when the streams ran dry.

He was proud of his accomplishment, as he would be proud of this boy to be born. In the hills above the house hundreds of his cattle grazed. To the east of the house was a huge dairy herd. He provided beef and dairy products to much of the valley. His fruits, vegetables, and some of his meat were shipped by train both north and south. The nuts were sent all over the country. He smiled at the thought. He had an empire that continued to creep out into new markets. The only thing he needed was a son to give it to. He turned and stared at the light burning in the second-story window. He would have that son soon, he thought.

The baby arrived at dawn, long after Silas had curled up on the porch swing to fall asleep, long after the doctor had decided that he could not save both the mother and child. Mary had given birth to a healthy, screaming baby, larger than the ones that had come before it, lighter and more like Silas than the other two. In fact, the only characteristic the child shared with the siblings was her gender. Mary had given birth to another girl.

He took his time cleaning up both mother and child. Freshly scrubbed, wrapped up warm and secure in her mother's arms, the baby quieted down and quickly fell asleep. Mary tried to hold the baby as best she could, but the effort was too much, and she had to lay the child on the bed next to her. She was very weak.

Hollingsworth knew that the crisis had not passed for Mary. She was still bleeding heavily, and despite his efforts to stop the flow of blood, he knew that her race with death would be a close one.

He sat down on the bed beside her and put a hand on her forehead. Stroking her hair gently, he said, "The baby's fine, but the mother is not doing well. You've had twenty hours of hard labor and you're worn out." He paused, struggling to find the right words that would not panic her. Finally, he said, "I'm having a little trouble with the bleeding."

Her eyes flicked open for a second and then closed, the eyelids too heavy to be held up in her weakened state. She spoke softly, but distinctly so that he did not have to lean down to hear her words.

She said, "I do not think I could do this again." Her face was a death mask white except for the bold, dark circles under her eyes.

He took a cloth from the linen cabinet, soaked it in the bowl of water, and used it to wipe the sweat from Mary's face. Her hair, so beautiful when this began, now lay in strings around her face, wet with sweat.

Hollingsworth said, "There can't be a next time, Mary. This one has nearly killed you; another one surely will."

She ran her tongue around her lips before she said, "You mean if this one hasn't already done the deed."

"Yes," he said quietly, "if this one hasn't already done the deed."

"Is it a girl?" she asked.

He nodded and then realized that her eyes were still closed and she could not see his face. "Silas will be disappointed," he said.

The expression on her face did not change, but the lips were sucked in for just an instant. He had seen this look of hers often, and he knew it to be one of resolve. Mary Day Baker was a woman of deep resolve. "Then I guess I can't die. Someone will have to protect Kathleen from her father's disappointment."

She was a women who could will such things, one who could turn inward and deny death. At times it seemed as if she could do almost anything from will but give her husband a son.

Silas was awakened. He was told the news bluntly by the doctor before he had a chance to clear the sleep from his head and feel the full impact of his own disappointment. The doctor said, "It's another girl, Silas. She'll have to be your last child. If Mary lives, and I think she will this time, another child would be sure to kill her."

Silas said nothing to the doctor. He glanced back at the house before stepping down from the porch and walking across the lawn. He did not stop at the edge of the rise. He carefully worked his way down the slope until he reached the bottom. He followed the irrigation ditch through a pear orchard until he reached a clearing on the other side. Here an acre of corn had been picked, the stems cut, and the soil plowed under so that it lay rich and black in the early morning sun, fertile and ready for the next crop.

Silas stared at the ground, for the first time feeling how useless it was to him because it would pass from his hands some day and there was no way to control with the assuredness of blood relations the kinds of hands that would dip into it and strain the earth with their fingers.

No tear would come to his eyes. No anger would flush his face. No depression would stoop his shoulders. The disappointment would be buried deep inside, behind a cool exterior. But he knew damage had been done, permanent damage that would be fatal.

He unbuttoned the fly of his pants and relieved himself on the rich, fertile dirt.

FOUR

NORA RYAN yelled at him from the length of the hallway that bisected the lower floor of the museum. "It must be a great life when you don't have to show up to work until eleven in the morning." There was a cutting edge in her voice that told him that she wasn't joking.

He smiled and waved. He did not give a damn what Nora Ryan thought of him or his working hours. She was a convenience to his work, but not a necessity. "I have been working," he yelled back, "but not here." He let himself into the office and then into the record room.

He had just warmed up the computer and booted in a disk when Nora came into the room. He expected curiosity to get the best of her. She wouldn't let him do this project without keeping a close eye on it.

She asked, "And just exactly where might you've been working on this book if it wasn't here?"

For the fun of teasing this nosy woman he might have made her drag the information out of him, but he did not want to waste the time. He said, "I drove over to the library at Southern Oregon State College. They have a lot of information over there that I'll be able to use."

Nora nodded. "That's one good place to look." The statement suggested there were other places to look as well, but she did not elaborate. Instead, she said, "Your wife called."

Paul blushed. In order to hide the rush of emotions he felt, he simply said, "Oh."

Nora stared at the back of his head for several seconds before she said, "She asked that you call."

Paul nodded.

She added, "I got the feeling that all is not right between you and your wife."

"We have some things to work out." He began banging on the keyboard of the computer, bringing up one file after another without taking time to look at the information that appeared on the screen. Nora Ryan got the message that the subject was closed and walked from the room.

He did not want to deal with people today. He chose to deal with facts and figures, instead. He decided to find out what it was about Jacksonville, Oregon, that made Harry Hollingsworth abandon the comforts of San Francisco to come to this dangerous piece of territory.

He found out that the site where the town is now located was a quiet corner of the earth prior to 1850. Only a few trappers and French adventurers had spent much time in the Rogue River Valley before then because of the unfriendly nature of the Kelawatset Indians who once massacred fifteen men in the famous mountain man Jedediah Smith's traveling party.

Courage, though, then as now, was directly proportional to the amount of profit to be made. Between 1850 and 1851 gold was discovered in Jackson Creek, a small brook that meandered below the base of the hill where the old pioneer cemetery was now located at the north end of town. The next year Rich Gulch was struck, a main find of gold in a creek not far from where Oregon and California Streets now crossed. Within a year a tent city had sprung up, housing several thousand miners. The first log cabin was built shortly after that.

By 1860, Jacksonville had become the largest and the oldest town in Southern Oregon. By 1884, miners had removed an estimated thirty million dollars' worth of gold from the surface of the land and had burrowed underground, honeycombing the underside of Jacksonville with shafts and tunnels. The diggings brought a large population of Chinese laborers to the community to help in the mines. Another population of gamblers, thieves and prostitutes soon moved in.

In the year 1869 a freak thunderstorm sent a flood of water racing down from the mountains that washed away much of the mining equipment along the creeks in the area. The flood was followed by a wind storm that leveled many of the surrounding trees. These events seemed to mark the beginning of the end, as if signs from heaven. Although gold mining remained an industry for ten more years in Jacksonville, it was a steadily declining one after the storm. The boom ended and Jacksonville, a town without purpose, lingered near death.

Harry Hollingsworth came to Jacksonville the year after the storm. At the time, he moved into a thriving community with no permanent doctor, professional men having been scared away from the town by its rough and rowdy mining camp reputation. His timing was perfect. Jacksonville had become a peaceful village in desperate need of a doctor.

As Nora had suggested, Paul's research into Hollingsworth kept bumping into the Bakers. His research documented Silas Baker's rise to prominence in Jacksonville history. Baker was an ambitious and single-minded young man who came to Jacksonville from the east with the expressed purpose of getting rich. He arrived in town in 1860 at the age of twenty. Silas learned quickly that the easy pickings in the gold fields were long gone and only those claims with a heavy investment of men and equipment were turning out a steady flow of gold. He went to work for one of the mining companies for a very small percentage of the take. After two years, he took his savings and headed back east.

He proved to be an excellent businessman. Eight months after his departure, a ship sailed into the Umpqua River at Scottsburg, laden with supplies purchased with Silas' earnings from the gold fields. He hired a mule train to pack his goods over the mountains to Jacksonville. With a good eye for luxury, Silas brought the town the types of fashionable goods that the residents could not get outside of San Francisco. Starved for the niceties from the outside world, Jacksonville residents bought out one mule train load after another. Silas became rich.

He made two important decisions during this time. While in New York to purchase his own ship to cut down on transportation costs, he married Mary Ellen Day, a servant girl to one of the richest families in New York City and the sister of the man he hired to captain his boat. They knew each other only a brief time before Silas proposed and Mary accepted. He was in a hurry. She was anxious to take a trip anywhere.

Mary Day Baker would return with Silas on the ship and make the grueling trip over the mountains to Jacksonville without a word of complaint. She was a strong-willed woman, a fact that Silas may not have noticed in his haste. Although she was never to return to the east, Mary was New York-born and, in a sense, New York-bred by her association with the wealthy, and that would influence her attitudes for the rest of her life.

The second important decision made by Silas was to buy land. Every indication in the material that Paul read was that Silas Baker's only major purpose in his life was to buy land and make it produce. He would end up owning half of the valley around Jacksonville and Medford before there was no more land for him to buy.

Paul stored this new information on a disk and made a hard copy on the printer. While the printer hummed out its lines of copy, he leaned back in his chair and faced the obvious. Once again his research had turned up more about the Bakers than it had about Hollingsworth. He appeased his conscience by noting that at this point in his research there was no way to determine what would be valuable and what would not be. The truth was, of course, he was heading in the wrong direction, and he knew it.

He put the disk into his leather briefcase and the hard copy in a file that he left in the room. He never kept both records of his research in the same place, for safety's sake. He shut down the equipment and turned off the lights in the record room. In the office he found Nora Ryan sitting at her desk.

"Hello," he said. "Have you got a minute?"

She did not appear to be doing anything except waiting for him to come out of the room. She spun her chair around and faced him. "I have a few minutes," she said.

He put his briefcase on the top box of a stack of three and carefully rested his right elbow next to it, shifting his weight until he was comfortable. He asked, "How much help can I expect from you?"

One eyebrow shot up on Nora's face. "None without asking for it."

He smiled. A certain, steady reasoning always seemed to be behind Nora's answers. He said, "I'm beginning to see the limits of information available to me. I thought you could tell me if I've missed any sources."

She nodded her head vigorously as she said, "I knew it wouldn't take you long to find that out. With the info you've got, you have the makings of a real boring book."

"I'm beginning to see that," he said.

She looked at him over the top of her glasses, measuring him in some way. For such a pleasant looking woman, he thought, she was disconcertingly intimidating. "Crack the Baker story and you will crack the Hollingsworth story. I tell you, the two families are connected at the hip."

"I'd feel a lot more comfortable about my research if I knew that were true," he said. "The Bakers are interesting, but I'd hate to think I used up my research money on a dead end."

She puckered her lips and then folded her hands across her stomach. She held this pose for several seconds before she said, "Three attempts have been made to write about the Bakers. None of them got very far."

"Ah," he said, not really surprised. If he found the Bakers interesting, he was sure others had, too.

She had a self-satisfied look on her face, as if she had just told him something he had not wanted to hear. "Yes," she said, "they didn't get very far because the information they needed is either locked away with the Hollingsworth kin or in the house on the hill."

A thought flashed through his mind. He put it in words. "And you were one of the ones who tried."

She smiled broadly now. "Of course I tried," she said. "I'm no fool. I know a great story when I see one."

Now he laughed. "Think you see," he said. "Until the information is dug out, you won't know if there is a great story or not."

"That's right," she said.

"Do you have any suggestions?" he asked. "Or is this project really going to be as hopeless as it sounds?"

She stood up and took a step toward him, examining his face closely. She said, "Not hopeless, just impossible." After a pause, she added, "You might just be good looking enough to pull it off, though."

"That's a rather nebulous quality," he said. "How is that suppose to benefit me?"

She stood back, her arms crossed on her chest and a look of satisfaction on her face. "Yup," she said, "that face just might do it. The woman who handles the Baker estate, the lawyer, is about your age, smart as a whip, and single. She's not a bad-looking woman, either."

He laughed. "I see what you're getting at. Forget it. I'm a married man."

She pursed her lips and looked over the top of her glasses. "Not very married, I suspect."

Despite his every effort not to, Paul blushed. He could not think of an appropriate response, so he asked, "What makes you think that?"

She smiled and ignored his question, saying, "The only way you're going to get to those records is to romance your way to them. I tried everything else and that woman wouldn't give me the time of day."

He wondered what Beth might have said to Nora Ryan about their marriage. It wasn't like her to talk about such things to strangers. And if she hadn't said anything, were their marriage problems so transparent that someone like Nora could read them on his face?

"I won't be romancing anyone while I'm here," he said, "but, if you have some information I can use, we can talk about a contribution to the museum."

She turned back to her desk and pulled open the large bottom drawer on the right side, saying as she did, "It will cost you money and then some, for my help." She removed from the drawer a small manuscript inside a blue folder. She held it out. "That's as far as I got after five years of trying."

He reached up to take the manuscript from her, but she didn't let go of it. Impatient with games, he was tempted to jerk it out of her hand. "All right," he said, "what's the 'then some'?"

The sound of her voice suddenly became intense and urgent. She said, "You promise not to quit until you find out what went on inside that house." All of the softness was gone from her features and her eyes were riveted to his. And then, in a blink, she smiled and laughed self-consciously. "I can't stand the thought of dying and not knowing what those crazy women did to each other." She looked up at him again from over the top of her glasses and smiled sheepishly.

Later, as he was driving to his house with the folder sitting on the car seat beside him, he reminded himself that good a researcher must be suspicious by nature. To accept something at face value is to see it the way the presenter wants it to be seen, but not necessarily to see it the way it really is. Mrs. Ryan might be a nice, curious old lady, but he doubted it. More than likely she had dead-ended on her book and she was looking to him to get the information she needed to get started again. He did not open the folder until he had washed the dinner dishes, cleaned up after himself, and made a strong cup of coffee. Then, relaxing on the living room sofa with his feet on the coffee table, he placed the manuscript on his lap and turned back the cover. Inside was a large photo of the three sisters.

He sat in silence for several minutes, unwilling to turn to the next page. They were so incredibly beautiful that even a picture taken over eighty-five years before did not diminish their loveliness.

The photographer must have realized the precociousness of his subjects. This was not one of those stale, forced, posed, turn-of-the-century portraits. The women were standing on the front porch of the house on the hill as they smiled at the camera. They all wore long dark skirts that came down to the tops of their shoes and light-colored blouses tucked into high waistbands. Emily and Elizabeth had their thick, dark, shining hair piled high on their heads, giving a certain Grecian quality to their looks. Kathleen wore her hair long and loose, the blonde strands thick around her face. The two darker women smiled at the camera; Kathleen flirted with the lens. While the other two fit Paul's image of Victorian women, Kathleen seemed too bold, too strong, and too modern for the times.

Emily appeared to be the least sincere of the group. The smile on her face looked forced: There was a certain gravity in the fact that her blouse was buttoned to the chin, and, while Elizabeth had her arm around Emily's waist, Emily had both of her arms behind her back.

Of the three, Elizabeth seemed the most innocent. Her face was honest and her expression serene. Paul thought he would like her best of all three as a person. He imagined that both men and women would like her best.

Kathleen would have tugged at the heartstrings of any man who laid eyes on her, but he doubted if other women would have liked her much. If she looked at men the way she looked at the camera, no woman could be sure of her man in Kathleen's presence. Standing there with a seductive smile on her face and one hip thrust toward the camera, she must have been a handful for any man hamstrung by the lingering, strict morality of the Victorian Age.

He turned the page and began to read. Two hours later he understood why Nora Ryan had given up. Like his research on Hollingsworth, she had failed to find the information to bring her subjects to life. None of the writing lived up to the expectation created by the photograph inside the cover.

The phone rang and he was startled by its sound. Its ringing echoed through the quiet, empty house. He slid down the sofa to answer the phone, which sat on the end table near the fireplace.

"Hello," he said.

"I've been waiting for you to call me," the voice on the other end of line said.

He took a deep breath and answered in a voice that was overly polite, "I'm sorry. I told you how I feel about calling you."

"That's foolish," Beth, his wife, answered. "It won't hurt you to talk to..."

"Your lover," he said without the rancor he sometimes felt. "It will if I can't be nice, and I know I can't be nice."

"Are you settled?" she asked, changing the subject.

He leaned his head on the back of the couch and shut his eyes. The pain he felt threatened to strangle the words in his throat. He forced them out so that they almost sounded normal. "How are the kids?"

"They miss you," she said.

"Can I talk to them?"

"They're in bed, Paul. Another time. If we can arrange a time for your calls, I'll have them there to answer the phone."

He nodded. Beth had always been reasonable, right up until the end when she had changed so dramatically, so suddenly that no one could believe it had happened. Even now, six months later, many of their friends were still trying to deny the fact.

"How about two your time on Sundays?" he asked.

"That would be fine." She was silent for several seconds, and he could hear her breathing in the receiver of the phone. It had quickened slightly before she asked, "Have you made a decision about a divorce?"

"No," he said.

"You owe it to yourself to get one," she said.

"You're welcome to get one," he said, testily. "I won't stand in your way if that's what you want."

She let out a long, slow breath, and then said, "You know I don't know what I want. I don't know if I'm sick, or if I've been sick all along, and now I'm on my way to getting well."

"What does your counselor say?" he asked.

"She says I've got a lot to get out before I'll know the answer to that."

"And you couldn't stay with me and do that?"

"No," she said. "I've been unfaithful to you."

He nodded his head, too choked to speak. Rather than let her hear the tears in his voice, he reached over and dropped the receiver back on its cradle.

He slept fitfully that night, waking to the image of the sisters dancing in a circle around him, their smiles hiding some dark secret that their eyes could not completely obscure. He tried to push them from his mind so that he could go back to sleep, but Kathleen would not allow herself to be put to rest. The thrust of her hip, the tilt of her head, and the glow in her eyes beckoned him, taunted him. And then the image became Beth, and he knew he would not go back to sleep.

In the dining room he sat down in front of his computer, turned on the printer, and then turned on the machine itself. The letters on the screen slowly came into focus, notifying him that the computer was ready for use. He opened the blue folder next to him and looked again at the picture of the girls. He began to write.

FIVE

MARY WALKED FROM the parlor, through the formal dining room, to the ornately carved, swinging door that led to the kitchen. She stopped for a moment to examine the gleaming brass plate on the door. In the next room she could hear the giggles of children. Mary reached out with her fingers and ran several streaks down the brass plate before pushing open the door.

The children sat at a large, square table at one end of the roomy kitchen. They took their meals here before their parents ate in the formal dining room. Three women were in the kitchen with the children: Mable, the old, silent cook; Silva, the spinster housekeeper; Chin, the young Chinese girl who came in each day from Jacksonville.

Mary addressed Chin. "Polish the brass today," she said. "It's a disgrace. I'm not sure why we pay you as much as we do."

Chin bowed slightly and remained silent. All of the women in the kitchen were intimidated by Mary. Although they each did their jobs well, Mary was never satisfied by their work, and, although they kept the house spotless, Mrs. Baker never thought it clean enough.

Mary stopped at the table to examine her three daughters. Emily, the darkest of them, was prim and fastidious even in the middle of her meal. She was a delight to her mother, the only one of her children who did not object to the clothes she was told to wear, or, went to her music lessons without a complaint. It was sometimes hard to remember that she was only twelve.

Nothing could dampen Elizabeth's spirits. There was something about her cheerfulness that seemed to make her glow. Although she was as dark as Emily, this glow made her seem much lighter. Both had pale complexions, but Elizabeth's seemed healthier. Both had black hair, but Elizabeth's shined.

And then there was Kathleen. Mary's eyes stopped on the blonde child. Most women she knew had a special feeling for their last child, a certain soft spot for them. Not Mary. It seemed that Kathleen had been given to her as some kind of curse.

Mary's eyes flashed and she exclaimed, "Kathleen Day, what have you got on?"

Katie smiled up at her mother and said boldly, "I'm wearing breeches, mother. It's not fair that only boys get to wear trousers."

"She took them from my drawer," Elizabeth said.

"And Ellie stole them from my drawer," Emily added.

"Heavens, Emmy," Elizabeth countered, "you out-grew them years ago."

"Perhaps I did," Emily snapped, "but you've no right to take them from me. They were a gift from father."

The thought of the trousers still made Mary angry. Silas and she had agreed before the first child was born that she would be free to dress, religiously train, and educate the children the way she saw fit. The way she saw fit stringently paralleled the upbringing of children in the best families in New York society.

When Kathleen was born, Silas bought Emily a pair of pants and took her on horseback with him while he tended the land. A quiet battle of sharply spoken words behind thick oak doors continued between husband and wife over the issue of the trousers. Silas said he would have to teach one of the girls the duties of the land since he had no son, and that meant she would have to wear trousers. Mary said none of her daughters would ever wear a pair of pants. The battle was still unresolved.

Mary said, "Kathleen, go to your room and take off those pants immediately. I'll not have my daughters looking like boys."

Kathleen slid down from her chair and stood on the floor, looking down at her handiwork. It had been necessary for her to roll up the legs of the pants and then find a belt that would cinch them up tight enough for her small waist. The idea that her mother did not appreciate her efforts angered her.

Kathleen looked up from her pants and smiled, a hard, cold, willful grin. "I don't think I will, mother. Our dresses are not very good for play."

Mary's anger was slow to rise until it got momentum. When it got going though, it could out-race a locomotive. "You'll do as I say," she shouted, "or I'll have a large dollop of that stubborn Irish blood of yours."

"I don't think I will," Kathleen insisted, her little fists balled in tight knots that rested on her hips.

"Mable," Mary screamed, her face red as a lobster, "get me a wooden spoon!"

Mable did as she was told. She was too old and too indifferent to the children to interfere. Only Chin might be foolish enough to put herself in the squabbles of mother and child, but even she knew better than to step in when Mary was this angry. Mable placed the spoon in Mary's hand.

With little ceremony, Mary walked over to Kathleen, picked her up by the back of her pants, and brought the spoon down hard a dozen times on her small bottom. Silence reigned in the kitchen when she was done. Mary lowered the child to the floor and looked down at her. Katie's bright blue eyes stared back, unblinking, with only a hint of a tear in them.

"You'll change your clothes now," Mary said, barely in control of her voice.

Kathleen did not respond at first. She seemed determined not to let a sign of her pain slip out. Finally, she said, "I don't think I will."

Mary dropped down and grabbed the little girl by the shoulders and began to shake her. "You'll go to your room and stay there. You'll not eat for the rest of the day, and if you come down again in the morning in those pants, you'll never eat again, ever!" She let go of the child and sat on her haunches, breathing hard, her eyes wild with anger.

The next morning in the kitchen Mary expected to find all in order. She had checked on Kathleen late the night before and found her asleep in bed. Katie had removed the trousers and put on a nightgown.

Emily greeted her mother with, "I don't think you beat her enough." Elizabeth was giggling behind her hand. Kathleen sat at the table eating the last piece of toast, stuffing it quickly into her mouth. She was naked.

"Kathleen!" her mother shouted. "Females are never seen unclothed in public. Ever!"

"She ate two helpings of everything," Elizabeth offered. "She's prepared for another day in her room."

"I'll get the wooden spoon for you," Emily volunteered happily.

Mary put her hands on her face and slowly shook her head from side to side. After a moment she said, "That'll not be necessary. Chin will take Kathleen to her room and dress her, and then the two of us will go to church to pray for her poor, devil-plagued soul. Afterward, we'll ask Doctor Hollingsworth to give her a purge so that she doesn't get sick from stuffing herself."

Kathleen grasped the bottom of the chair with both hands, ready to fight these drastic consequences. She could handle a beating; she could handle a day in her room; she could handle two hours in church. But the thought of a dose of the doctor's worst medicine gagged her.

Chin, who had a great deal of experience handling the willful child, simply picked up Kathleen, chair and all, and carried them both upstairs. She knew that a wrestling match would ensue and that overpowering strength and pure determination would ultimately win out. Then, Chin would have to change her own clothes and clean up. As she laboriously lifted the chair and child up the stairs, she hoped that Katie would change her ways before she got much bigger.

After Mary returned from Jacksonville with the contrite child sitting stoically beside her, she retired to the bedroom, leaving the girls in the care of Chin. Never fully recovered from the birth of Kathleen, Mary had to seek out long hours of rest each afternoon to make it through the day. She would rise again before dinner to oversee the evening activities of the family, but she would retire again early in the evening, even before the children. She would not see Silas again until after dinner.

On this day, like all other days of the week, the afternoon meant freedom for the girls. They were not allowed to attend the public school in Jacksonville; instead, they faced a steady stream of tutors each day to teach them reading, arithmetic, music and art. Mary was not satisfied with this rudimentary education. She insisted that Silas have textbooks imported from the east, and that he hire an instructor from San Francisco to teach the girls Latin, history, and philosophy.

Except for a few weeks in the summer, the girls took instruction each day of the week from eight in the morning until one. They were given an hour for lunch before an hour and a half of music lessons. The two older girls alternated between the organ in the parlor and the piano in the living room. Katie had yet to begin music lessons, but she had proven herself to be precocious enough to begin school. At the age of four she could already read and write.

By three-thirty in the afternoon the girls were free, at least until dinner time at six when they would have to eat and then do their lessons. Usually Elizabeth and Kathleen were left to play together while Emily joined her father. She would spend time with him in his office or have her horse saddled for a tour of the ranch.

Today Emily offered to join the girls in play. Elizabeth was suspect, but she kept her opinion to herself. She knew that Emily did not think much of her or Katie, and she rarely wanted to be with them unless it was to her advantage.

"I'm thinking of taking a hike in the woods" she said. "One of the hands said that there's an old mining shaft just over the hill and I want to see it."

It was late summer and already a chill was in the air. Mary objected to the children going into the woods during this time of the year because the rattlesnakes would still be out.

"Did you ask mother?" Elizabeth knew the question would make Emily mad, but she was one to make sure things were done properly.

Emily gave her a cold look, something like the one their mother gave them. "We're only going over the hill," she said

Her sense of caution gave way. Elizabeth was also not one to stand up to pressure. She said, "As long as it is not too far."

The hills behind the house were the bottom steps of a series of rises that would climb ten thousand feet to Mt. Pitt and the Umpqua Forest. The laurel, oak, manzanita and madrone trees on the hills would give way quickly to the pine trees that stretched across shallow valleys and rising slopes.

The girls followed a path that traveled along the winding route of the creek and led to a dam made of logs, which controlled the flow of water to their father's fields. The pond behind the dam was not large, but it was deep. The water flooded a ravine and crept up the sides of the two steep slopes. Their father came up alone occasionally to sit in the shade of the trees and fish for the trout he had stocked in the pond.

From the pond they followed a deer trail until they reached the top of another hill. They looked down into a small valley carpeted with a thick growth of cedar and fir trees. The ground beneath the trees was deep with layers of decayed needles and branches, so thick that the earth was spongy and their steps became more difficult. Once or twice Elizabeth had to stop and pick up Katie to carry her past spots that were too rough for her tiny legs.

They climbed through this valley, over a rise, and into the next one, and then into the one after that, each time going a little higher. Elizabeth was becoming concerned. The sun dipped low in the western sky, too low for them to go much farther and be back before dark. She voiced her concern to Emily.

"Emmy," she said, "it will be dark soon. You said it was just over the hill."

Emily ignored the remark for several minutes, resolutely trudging forward. She said, finally, "The shaft is just ahead of us, where the hill climbs."

"It's already too dark to see anything. I think we should go back," Katie said.

"Don't be silly," Emily snapped. "We've been going in a circle and the house is just over the rise."

Elizabeth considered this for a moment, finally deciding that it did not make much sense. Katie expressed the doubt Ellie felt. She said, "If we're so close to the house, why'd we have to walk so far?"

Emily did not answer. She led the girls to the base of the slope and made a big display of searching the area along it. The search proved futile. "I don't understand it," she said. "The shaft's suppose to be here."

"Well, it's not," Katie said.

"We must get back. It's getting dark," Emily said. She walked them away from the slope and then stopped near a dense thicket of trees. "Wait here. I've got to relieve myself."

Elizabeth felt a flutter of fear. She wanted to push on before they lost the light, but she knew well the lessons of modesty taught to them by their mother. One's toilet was a secretive business, shared with no one.

Emily disappeared into the trees and was quickly swallowed up by the shadows. When the sound of her footsteps had ceased, Katie said with conviction, "She's left us for sure."

Elizabeth knew well enough that Emily was sometimes cold and cruel, but she didn't think her sister would abandon them. She shouted, "Emily!" There was no answer.

After a half an hour of searching, Katie was the one to ask, "Do you suppose a bear got her?" The idea seemed like a nice one to her. Emily deserved to be done in by a bear.

Elizabeth took Katie by the hand and led her back to the steep slope. She said, "I'm sure that if we can see the house from the top, we'll be able to use its lights to guide us back. We must tell someone that Emily disappeared."

At the top of the rise they found another valley, its center a deep, black pool filled with trees. The house was not in sight.

Two hours later, Emily stood within the enveloping arms of a willow tree near the dam. She watched with interest the lights that moved like plodding fireflies back and forth across the fields below. She would like to have stayed under the tree a little longer for effect, but already one of the lights had separated from the rest and begun to climb toward her. She squatted down and rubbed her hands in the dirt beneath the tree and then reached up to streak her fingertips down her face.

Satisfied, she stumbled from beneath the tree and cautiously worked her way down the incline toward the light, whimpering softly as she walked.

"Daddy," she cried, "Daddy!"

The light paused, then it moved in her direction. When it reached her, the lantern was lifted up, and she could see her father's face. She threw herself at him and wrapped her arms around his waist.

He stood quite still and did not return her hug. When she stepped back from him, he asked, "Where are the other two? Your mother's fraught with worry."

Emily recognized the quiet anger in her father's words. He did not like his evenings disturbed and he did not want his children to be an imposition in his life. She knew she must be careful of what she said. "I don't know," she said. "We were separated and I couldn't find them again."

"Where?" he asked.

"Higher up in the woods," she said, a little afraid now because of the coldness in her father's voice. She thought he would be glad to see her; now she wasn't sure. "Elizabeth said there was a mine shaft for us to see."

Several men in the search party joined them. Silas looked up the hill into the darkness beyond the glow of the lanterns. "I'll not ask one of my men to break his leg in this darkness because of the stupidity of my children. I'll find them in the morning."

The men were careful to exchange looks only when they were sure Silas could not see their faces. He had a reputation of being cool to most and frigid to the rest, but even these men who knew him did not believe him to be so cold as to leave two little girls out in the woods all night.

One of the men voiced the concern of the rest. "I wouldn't mind going up and looking for them, Mr. Baker," he said. Several other men nodded agreement.

"You'll do no such thing," he snapped. "Their mother spends a fortune having silly ideas put in their heads and this is what she gets for it. The girls will get a good scare and their mother will have a good fret. It'll do them all some good." He grabbed Emily by the arm and dragged her down the incline.

Each of the men slowly turned and followed, afraid to defy their boss.

ELIZABETH WAS TERRIFIED. The night was filled with one, long, continuous chorus of sounds that she did not recognize, sounds that were more intimidating to her than the wild pounding of her own heart. The only noise that gave her comfort was the soft murmur of Katie's voice as the little girl sang and hummed all the tunes and songs that she had learned by heart.

While Ellie's fear prevented her from talking, the sound of her own voice frightening in the echoing emptiness of the night, Katie provided a running monologue between songs. "I don't know that sound, but I'm pretty sure it's not a bear. I would think a bear would be our only worry. I should like a bear to eat Emily."

The damp, cold air seeped through their thin dresses and penetrated the surface of their skin. The two of them curled close together beneath the shelter of a towering pine. Hours after fear had given way to desolation, they fell asleep, first Katie and then Elizabeth, who was mesmerized by the rhythmical breathing of her little sister.

AT THE HOUSE Silas Baker stood his ground in the doorway of his wife's bedroom, refusing to back down from Mary's tirade. He told her that she had raised willful children and now it was coming back to haunt her. That was her problem. The one child he had taken under his wing had found her way back.

"You sent the men home?" she asked, incredulous. Her face was so pale that the skin looked transparent. She swayed on her feet.

"They'll have learned a good lesson by morning," he said.

A hammer on a horseshoe could not have duplicated the metallic click to her words as she spat back at him, "You go get those girls now, Silas, or I'll kill you." Her eyes were wide, and she looked crazed enough to do it.

"If you want them, you go get them. It's your spoiling that makes them do such foolish things." He had just enough time to step back and brace himself before his wife flew across the room and slammed her fists against his chest. There was little force behind the blows. She slid to the floor.

He carefully disengaged his feet from the tangle of arms and legs and walked from the room. Over the years this scene had repeated itself several times. When Mary became over-wrought, she fainted. He sent for Mable to put his wife to bed.

Emily cowered behind the door of her bedroom, her ear pressed to the wood to hear the exchange of words between her mother and her father. She did not know what caused the greater part of the fear she felt, the knowledge of what she had done or the conviction that her parents would find out about it.

ELIZABETH WOKE just as the first sliver of dawn rose above the mountains to the east. She was terribly cold. She had wrapped her thin little body around the chubby ball that was her sister. Her neck was stiff and her arms and legs moved sluggishly, making her reluctant to draw back from the one spot that offered warmth. She did, though. She felt a sense of duty to her sister. If she did not get Katie home safely, who would? Certainly not Emily. Not even her father.

She tugged Katie to her feet and held her up under the arms, rocking her gently as she whispered, "Come on, Katie, time to get up. We must get back home before mommy gets worried."

Wisps of fog floated between the trees. Their skirts became wet as they brushed up against foliage laden with morning dew. Both girls shivered in the cold, their bodies no longer able to produce enough heat to fight the chill. Elizabeth's teeth chattered noisily.

When they reached the rise by the dam, tears filled Elizabeth's eyes. There had been a faint hope left in her heart that she would find her father leading a band of searchers to look for them. Instead, there was not yet any movement on the ranch as everyone still slept.

They slipped in the back door of the house and were met in the kitchen by Chin. The servant worked quickly to get them out of their damp clothes and into a warm bath. She kept them in the tub for a long time, rushing from the kitchen with more hot water each time the bath cooled. She brought them hot chocolate to sip and cooed softly to them in a language they did not understand.

She had them fed and tucked in bed in warm flannels before Silas came downstairs to take his breakfast in the study. When Chin was sure he was in a good frame of mind, not dangerously cranky as he often was in the mornings, she told him that the girls had returned on their own.

"I see," he said. "Send for the doctor."

Chin was an Oriental beauty with long, black hair who could speak English perfectly. The expression on her face was always calm, even now, when she did not approve. She said, in her quiet voice, "I think the children will be well."

"The doctor's for Mary," he said. "I'm sure she'll have a fit that will keep her in bed for a week once she wakes up."

Upstairs, Emily slipped out of her room and quietly walked down the hall to Elizabeth's bedroom door. She turned the doorknob slowly, noiselessly, and entered the room. She could see Elizabeth in bed with her back to the door, obviously asleep. Next to her was a tiny, inverted exclamation mark, the period the head of Katie. The covers were around the little girl's head so that the features of her face were in shadows, except for the brilliant blue eyes that stared out at Emily.

The stare was so intense and so cold that Emily felt a shiver work its way up her spine. She thrust her chin out and said, "What are you staring at?"

Katie's small voice said, "You're mean."

"What did I do?" Emily demanded to know.

"You know what you did."

"Prove it," Emily said, feeling a little uncomfortable. "No one will believe what you say. You got lost."

"You got us lost on purpose, and I don't care if they believe me or not. We both know it's true, and we both know you're mean." The blue eyes stared out from the covers, unblinking.

The statement seemed so ominous, so threatening, that Emily glanced around the room to make sure that the voice was coming from Katie. She was just a baby. What could she understand?

In the end, none of the children were punished for the adventure. Mary believed the fright they had received was punishment enough. Silas disagreed, believing that Elizabeth should be whipped for leading the others astray, but he did not push to have his way. He had no need to see how mad he might make Mary.

As for Elizabeth and Kathleen, they did learn a lesson from the episode: that was the last time they let Emily into their play. And it was the last time as children they trusted her.

SIX

PAUL FISCHER sat in a small, over-stuffed rocking chair and balanced a cup of tea in his lap. Across from him in a heavily padded wingback chair sat Alma Parsons, better known to the members of the Hollingsworth family as Auntie M. She was the last living child of Charles Hollingsworth, Doctor Harry Hollingsworth's only son, who also became a doctor.

She sat across from him quietly, expectantly, a peculiar, lopsided grin on her face. Alma was seventy-four years old and looked older. Like many old people who were not long for this world, she was as lopsided as her smile.

Paul tried again to explain to her what it was he wanted. The first explanation had done nothing to change the smile on her face or to encourage a response from her. He said, "I'm writing a biography about your grandfather. I find that the information in the museum isn't complete enough for me to write about Doctor Hollingsworth and do him justice. I understand that you have some private material that might be of help to me."

She was so slow to respond that he thought he was going to have to repeat himself for a third time. Finally she said, "Why would you want to write about him?"

The question startled him. He blurted out, "It's an honor to have a biography written about you."

"I shouldn't think so," she said.

Again he stared across the space between them at the twisted smile on her face. "He made a major contribution to medicine," Paul said.

"You mean those pills?" she asked. "From the size of the molds he used I'm surprised he didn't choke half his patients to death."

Paul was at a loss as to what to say. He had assumed that these people would be glad to have someone write about one of their relatives. In fact, the youngest member of the family he had contacted, Jeff Hollingsworth, seemed delighted about the idea. Unfortunately,

Auntie M. was the family matriarch and controlled all the historical material relating to Doctor Hollingsworth.

He should have expected something like this from the beginning, he told himself. Alma lived in a small, single-story, white frame house, with green shutters on the sides of the windows. The yard was surrounded by a neat, white picket fence. The lawn was perfect, and the flower beds were overflowing with a wide array of glorious flowers that seemed to be oblivious to the heat. He knew that a perfectly old, perfectly helpless, perfectly harmless, little old lady lived here who hadn't had a thought drift through her head in years that dealt with more than a rose pedal *or* a blade of grass.

"Your grandfather's contribution to medicine was significant and the medical community now wants to remember him," he said, speaking a little louder and a little more slowly to see if that might help their faltering communication.

It seemed to work. Alma did not take quite so long to answer this time. "Pooh!" she said.

"Pooh?"

"Exactly," she said. "He never thought much of what he did about the pills. In fact, he was glad that some other fellow came along and figured it all out so he wouldn't have to be bothered. The only thing he wanted to do was make his doctoring easier."

"Now see," he nearly shouted, "that's just the kind of information that would make this biography interesting. If I had access to his records, I could write a really good piece on him." He nearly rolled his eyes thinking about the way he was talking to this woman who looked like a dried-up prune.

"You won't get them," she said.

He got the same sinking feeling in his stomach that he'd gotten when he first opened up the gate to the picket fence. "Them?" he said.

"Yes," she said. "The records."

"By denying me access to your grandfather's records, you are denying him a place in medical history," he said.

Her laughter sounded more like a dry, hacking cough. When she stopped, there was a little spittle at the corner of her mouth. She dabbed at it with a handkerchief she had wadded in her lap, and then she said, "The man has been dead and buried for over a half a century. By the time your book is published, I'll be occupying a plot of ground not far from him. Medical history won't mean much to either one of us.''

He kept himself from pleading, although the temptation was there. He now realized that he had underestimated Auntie M. She was feeble, all right, but not feeble-minded. He said, ''It may not mean much to you, but think of the proud heritage it would leave for the rest of your family.''

''I suspect you'll write your book regardless,'' she said, ''and they'll still have their heritage.''

''We're talking the difference between a few hundred books sold and many thousands; the difference between obscurity or a place in history.''

She said, ''It sounds like we're talking about you and not the doc. You won't get the records.''

He took a long, deep breath and asked calmly, ''Why not?'' He understood that researchers hit these kinds of snags. If there were no difficulties like this, anyone could write a biography. These types of problems were what ultimately made a biographer great.

Her head seemed to drop to the right on its own accord. She left it there as she said, ''Because there's information in those records I don't want you to know.''

He tried to explain. ''A competent researcher knows how to use discretion,'' he said. ''If we're not trustworthy, we'd never have access to information.''

She laughed again. ''Trustworthy my foot,'' she said. ''I've been reading books all my life. I know just as well as the next person that you hone in on a tasty morsel and turn it into a headline story to titillate your readers. Making a horse pill isn't going to turn a book into a best seller. You want your celebrities to be deviants; you want to glorify their perversions. You want to convince people that the only truly successful people are the mediocre ones just like you, and that all the rest are abnormal or insane.'' She ended this tirade in a coughing fit that lasted for several minutes. Paul went to the kitchen and brought back a glass of water for her, quite aware now that Auntie M. was far sharper and far more adamant than he had first suspected.

He was tempted to excuse himself and leave, but he knew he

would not get what he wanted that way. Instead he pushed ahead and asked, "What could the doctor possibly have done that needs to stay buried fifty years after his death?"

She righted her head, but one corner of her mouth continued to sag as her smile returned. She said, "My grandfather, my father, the whole lot them." She stopped herself. After thinking for a moment, she continued, "We'd have a lot better chance of being proud of them if the records were left unpublished."

"Would you at least answer one question for me?" he asked, beginning to feel exasperated. He didn't feel like he was being denied something important to his research; he felt just the opposite. Old Auntie M. was undoubtedly trying to keep hidden some family skeleton that wouldn't mean a thing to anyone today. He had run across the same thing a dozen times before.

"Probably not," she said. "What is it?"

"Would you tell me what your records cover, so I know what I don't have?"

She thought about this for some time. Evidently she decided the information was harmless. She said, "Grandfather kept a private journal. He kept records in it he thought too personal for the more public records."

Paul almost laughed. Again he had underestimated Auntie M. Doc Hollingsworth's private journal probably had information in it about a lot of skeletons from a lot of family closets. More out of his own curiosity than anything else, he asked, "Is there information in it on the Bakers?"

Her eyes met his. They seemed to mock him. "Bitten by the Baker bug, are you?" she asked.

"I haven't been bitten by any kind of bug," he said defensively. "I notice that the names of Baker and Hollingsworth seem to show up together in a lot of places."

The coughing fit seemed to have sapped some of Auntie M.'s strength. She slumped a little in the chair and her head rested on a lace antimacassar. She was slow to respond again. "Yes, yes," she said, her words trailing off. "The Bakers had more than their share of skeletons to hide…"

"You must have known the sisters," he said. "What were they like?" His tone changed, although he was not aware of it. The new softness in his voice seemed to stimulate a change in Alma. Her head rolled to one side, and she closed her eyes as she looked deep into her past for memories. She held that pose while she spoke slowly about an age gone by.

She said, "The paintings and photos do not do them justice. They were the most beautiful women this valley has ever seen. I remember how we girls used to hate them so because, even though they were much older than us, they still managed to turn the boys' heads when they walked by. They had been trained in dance and music by some fancy people their mother brought in, and they had a grace to their movements that was the envy of all.

"Kathleen was the real beauty in the lot. She was physically different from the other two. I didn't think her features were as fine, but her personality made up for it. She was friendly and approachable; the other two were not. I think Elizabeth was the shy one, but not shy enough for her own good. She got mixed up with the wrong people and didn't have the experience to know the difference.

"Emily was her father's girl. I never did know him; he died before I was born, the mother, too, but they still talked about him when I was growing up and nothing nice was ever said about him. I don't know how a man can stimulate so much hate that it follows him years after he's dead, but Silas Baker did it. Emily seemed to want to copy him. She worked hard to be hated." She turned her head toward Paul and opened her eyes. "The little information I have about them isn't going to answer many questions. The answer to their mystery is up in that house, and you're not going to get it."

"Why do you think Elizabeth got mixed up with the wrong people?" he asked.

"Leave me alone, now," she said, rolling her head back to one side and closing her eyes again.

He excused himself, leaving the woman sitting in her chair with her eyes closed. By the time he had returned to where he had parked his car, he was whistling. When he first applied for the grant to write the book on Hollingsworth he'd felt excited. He hadn't felt that way since, not when he faced the reality of a long, routine, boring research assignment. But now he knew he was wrong. This was going to be a challenge. The excitement was back.

That morning he had planned to go to the college in Ashland to search for more historical documents, but that plan had been changed by a phone call. Jeff Hollingsworth, a great grandson to Harry, had phoned to learn more about Paul's project. It did not take much coaxing on Paul's part to find out just what Jeff wanted. He wanted to know how much money a book like this might mean to the family.

Paul had been honest about it. If he wrote a book about Dr. Hollingsworth from records that were available to the public, he wouldn't owe the Hollingsworths a penny. On the other hand, if private records existed that were vital to the success of the biography, a percentage of the book could be assigned to the family in exchange for the use of the information, or he could buy the information with his research funds.

That was when Paul learned about Auntie M. The few descendants of the doctor had long ago left the valley. The Hollingsworth clan was diluted by marriages and the relatives spread all over. Auntie M., a sister in Portland, and Jeff were all that was left of the immediate family.

Paul started his car and drove east, heading for the freeway that would take him to Ashland. Poor old Doctor Hollingsworth, he thought. He would be disappointed to know that the best his son could do was to produce two children who didn't amount to much. Jeff's dad had died in a hunting accident. Auntie M. had married young, taught school for forty years, and retired to the little white house. She had not given birth to any children. Her husband had died from a heart attack a few years before.

Jeff managed an appliance store in Medford. His sister was a housewife in Portland. Whatever special providence that had been assigned to this family had been limited to the elder Doctor Hollingsworth. Perhaps some of it had been passed on to the son. Paul would not know that until he searched the records in Ashland.

After finding little information at the college in Ashland, he returned to Medford and did two things before returning to his house: he stopped off at a photograph studio and arranged for copies of the photo of the three sisters from Nora Ryan's transcript to be reproduced. The quality of the original was excellent, so he asked that the copies be enlarged, and he asked that Kathleen be isolated from the original and a separate photo of her be made. Then he stopped for a hamburger for dinner.

At the house he found a letter waiting for him from his wife. He stuck the letter in his shirt pocket, put a tape in the stereo, adjusted the volume so that it blocked out the world beyond the interior of his mind, and poured himself a large glass of wine. He made himself comfortable on the sofa and pulled the letter from his pocket, leaving it on his lap unopened while he stared at it and drank the wine.

He might have sat that way all night, wondering about the contents of the letter without the desire to open it, except the phone rang, snapping him out of his trance. He picked up the receiver and cradled it between his shoulder and chin while he poured himself another glass of wine.

"Paul Fischer," he said.

"Miz Livingston." The voice was soft and pleasantly female, but the tone was businesslike.

"Miz Livingston," he said, non-commitally. The name meant nothing to him.

"Miss Pamela Livingston," she said. "I'm the attorney who is in charge of the Baker estate."

He took a long drink from the glass of wine before putting it down on the end table. Here he was, trying to put distance between himself and the Bakers, and now they were pursuing him.

"Mrs. Ryan mentioned that a woman handled the estate, but she didn't mention your name. It's interesting that you should call; I was just looking at a photo of the three sisters."

A short pause passed before Miss Livingston responded. "I appreciate your interest in the sisters. They were quite lovely women and each talented in her own way. I understand that you're doing research for a book about Doctor Hollingsworth, though."

"That's true," he said.

"Good. Although your prime interest is in Hollingsworth, I think it only fair to warn you that all materials pertaining to the private lives of the Bakers are in private hands, and they're copyrighted. Any use of that information would be in violation of the copyright laws that I'm sure you, as a researcher, are familiar with."

"Let me correct you if I may," he said, keeping in check a slow, burning anger. "Any use of the materials would be in violation of the copyright laws. The information, if arrived at from another source, would be available for my use."

These were just the kind of legal roadblocks he found in research that aggravated him the most. People complained because writers did not present the whole truth, yet this was the thing that kept them from the truth. He added, "That's an interesting precaution for some folks who've been dead for a long time."

"The Bakers wished to protect their right to privacy, even after death," she said.

"Just what was it these people did that made them go to such an extreme to hide it?" he asked.

"I couldn't tell you that," she said. "We, too, honor the privacy of the estate."

Sarcastically, he said, "I suppose the estate is going to gobble up Alma Parsons' records, too." As soon as he said it, he knew he shouldn't have.

"We're working on that," Pam said.

Now that they understood each other, Brian was ready to end the phone conversation. Pamela Livingston could disappear back behind her legal interpretations, and he would disappear behind his. His were a little different from hers: These folks were part of public domain, part of its history; therefore, rightful subjects of a biography. "Thanks for the information," he said, dismissing her.

"Before you hang up," she said, quickly, "I do have information that's part of the estate that refers to Doctor Hollingsworth. Public access to this information is authorized in the will, and you're welcome to stop by the office and see it. Our address is in the phone book: Waiters, Williams, and Livingston."

As long as he still had her on the phone, he decided to ask the one question whose answer would free him to deal with just the Hollingsworth biography. "Why is it the ladies never married?" he asked.

"The Baker sisters?" Her question was rhetorical. After a few seconds, she said, "If you're looking for a scandal in that, forget it. They simply chose not to marry."

"Women today choose not to marry," he said, "women back then did not. That any one of these beautiful women didn't marry would have been a shock, but that none of them did suggests...suggests..." He was at a loss for words to complete the thought. He simply could not imagine these women not married during a period of time when morality damned near demanded that they be married.

"Suggests what, Mr. Fischer?" she asked.

"I don't know," he said, lamely. "I just can't imagine it."

"I'd like to comfort you and provide you with an easy answer to that, Mr. Fischer, but I was always told that they didn't want to marry, and that was that. I do suppose it's rather peculiar, now that you mention it."

"Isn't there some answer to that in the records they left behind?" he asked.

She laughed. "The Bakers were very bright women. They didn't trust their desire for anonymity to a lawyer, regardless of the reputation of the firm. In the study of their house is a large, steel, impregnable safe, rather ornately done, I might add. Silas Baker kept it in his office. The girls had it moved up to the house, and they deposited whatever memories they wanted preserved in it—along with the combination. I couldn't tell you what was in the safe, and I certainly couldn't tell you how to get into it."

"And I suppose there's nothing of importance just sitting around the house," he said.

"The house is pretty much the way it was when the last sister died in the 'fifties, except that all of the smaller items have been locked away. If we were to have a thief up there, he'd have to bring a moving van with him to take anything of value. No personal papers are lying about."

"I thank you for the information," he said. "I'll stop by to pick up what you have on Hollingsworth." On a whim, he asked, "When I do stop by, I couldn't take you out to lunch, could I?"

"That will depend on my schedule. Check with my receptionist when you come in. I'll let you know then."

"Okay," he said. Once he had put down the receiver he chuckled to himself. He was sure that if he didn't pass inspection with the receptionist, he would not get a lunch date.

He would like to have returned to his wine and let the evening pass at a leisurely pace, but once again his interest in the Baker sisters was stimulated. He knew it was a waste of time, and he was bein' drawn away from more important research, but once again he v enticed to his computer and once again he sat down to write r

on a story he knew would never be completed. And, deep in a corner
of his mind, he knew that as long as he sat in front of the computer
to write, he could delay the opening of the letter from his wife, delay
the reading of something he didn't want to face.

He was dragged back to the present only once, when he glanced
up from his computer to see the image of man standing in the shadows just beyond the French doors. Or at least he thought he had seen
a man. When he finally realized what he had thought he'd seen, the
image was gone. He glanced up once or twice again, but after that
he was too deep in the story of the sisters to remember an image that
might not have been real.

The man was still there, though, deeper in the shadows, staring
intently at the writer at work.

SEVEN

KATIE STOOD below the dam and listened to the rush of water that flowed an inch over its top and dropped in a clean shiny sheet to a small pool below. Giant ripples radiated away from the foamy water at the bottom of the dam. She imagined them to be great tidal waves crossing a peaceful ocean to reach an unsuspecting people on a far shore.

Across from the dam the pool emptied down a stone chute to the hand-dug irrigation ditch below. Although Kathleen liked this spot because it was natural and noisy, she enjoyed the stretch of canal from the dam to the orchards below almost as much. Her father left this part of the ditch alone. Below he had his workers clear the irrigation canal of weeds and grass, leaving banks of slick black mud. Gates bisected the canal in dozens of places and miniature canals spread out in all directions. She found that too artificial to appreciate.

She walked along the ditch, pausing now and then to turn over a rock to see what was under it. She liked to push the bugs she found to make them move. She felt like she had the power to push whole, tiny worlds into action.

Each day she would find something new in the rich, thick grass along the canal. Only yesterday she had found a rattlesnake sunning itself on a rock in the tall grass. She had tapped at it with a long stick and the snake had sluggishly slipped off the rock and disappeared into the grass, still too chilled by the early spring air to protest with a rattle of its tail. She wouldn't be silly enough to bother a snake in summer when it might be shedding, or when it was warm enough to strike out like lightning.

Her father killed the snakes. He had a collection of rattles in a giant glass jar in his office. The jar was half full. She was not fond of snakes herself, but she sensed that something was wrong with the way her father persecuted them. He was known to take a whole day to track down and kill a snake he had spotted in the fields or orchards.

The canal water slowed down by the house as it crossed the ledge of land carved into the hillside. Her father had built a series of locks to take the water down the two hundred feet to the valley. From her bed at night she could hear water pour over the locks. It was sweet music to her, mixed in with the sounds of spring such as the croaking of frogs or the slap muskrats made when they slid down the muddy banks into the water. In the summer the sounds would disappear as the water level dropped. The water would only flow when her father went back up the hill to the dam and opened its floodgate to fill the irrigation ditches below.

She wandered away from the ditch toward the house. She didn't want to go in just yet while sunshine was still left in the fading light. She sensed, even at the age of eight, that this complexion of hers, trimmed with all its light features, made her different from her two sisters. They ran from the sun and hid themselves in darkened rooms. Usually, long after their lessons were ended, Emily was down at the office with father, learning how to keep the books, and Elizabeth was in the parlor, practicing music. But not Katie. No, not Kathleen. She always longed to be outside, even in the winter when it was cold and rainy.

She crossed the lawn and stopped at its edge to look at the valley in fading light. Sometimes she wanted to walk down the slope, across the fields and orchards, to the lights of the small city of Medford. She would like to go there by herself and see the store windows and watch the people. It was not easy being a sister to Emily and Elizabeth. It was not easy being a Baker. Bakers stuck together and did not need other people. That was the lesson her father was teaching her. In a way, her mother was saying the same thing.

Elizabeth stood in the front doorway of the house and shouted to her sister. "Katie, Emmy says you're to come in now and clean up for dinner."

Katie wrinkled her nose. "Time to get ready for dinner," she mimicked the voice of Elizabeth. "Time to get ready for bed," she continued as she walked into the house. "Time to eat breakfast. Time to do your school work. Who'd have thought that Emily would become my mother?" The change had been gradual, but decisive. Kathleen's mother withdrew into her bedroom to stay. She seemed physically capable to the girls, but she insisted that her health was far too fragile for her to waste it outside the bedroom. Doctor Hollingsworth still paid his visits faithfully twice a week and stayed for an hour or two, although he seemed to feel that he could do little medically for Mary. She would never be as strong as she had once been, and she had let this knowledge color her outlook on life. Instead of being frail, she decided that she was weak and sickly. Instead of deciding to do what she could with life, she decided to do as little as she could. Instead of focusing on her needs, which were more desperate, she chose to direct her attention to the needs of her daughters.

The formal dining room was next to the parlor. It could be reached through large double doors from the entrance hall, by French doors that opened onto a portico, or from the kitchen through a serving door. The girls were no longer allowed to go through the serving door or to spend much time in the kitchen. Mother insisted that the kitchen was no place for girls of their position.

Katie thought all of that was foolishness and told her mother so, but such outbursts only got her a good scolding and time in her room so she didn't see much point to saying it twice. When she walked into the dining room both Emily and Elizabeth were already seated. Katie took a seat near the head of the table.

Emily waited for her to sit down before she said, "Ladies do not come to the table dressed like that."

Katie ignored the comment. Emily was wearing a long black skirt that came nearly to the floor and a pale yellow silk blouse with a matching yellow bow at the collar. Elizabeth wore a black skirt and a plain white blouse. Katie wore what she normally wore, a gray calico wrapper that stretched from the floor to high on her neck. The fact that it was fitted at the waist kept if from being little more than a sack.

"You don't need Sunday-go-to-church clothes to eat," Katie said, matching Emily's icy stare with one of her own.

Emily usually got her way with most things. She had some kind of inside track to her mother that Katie didn't understand, and she was the only one of the three who their father could tolerate for any length of time. But this was one battle Emmy would not win. Silas himself thought that dressing for dinner was foolishness, and if the subject was brought up to him, he would rage about it. Before Emily could respond to Katie's remark, Silas threw open the double doors from the hallway and trudged into the room. He went directly to the head of the table and sat down.

Immediately, the kitchen door opened and Silvia came into the room to serve Silas. While their father was being served, Emily led the girls in a brief prayer of thanksgiving. She had to hurry through it because she knew that if she wasn't finished before the food was on her father's plate, he would begin to eat, a fact that seemed to undercut her authority to lead prayers.

Tonight Silas did not dive silently into his food as he normally did. Instead he looked at the two older girls on his left and then at Katie on his right. "Why is it," he asked, "with a dozen chairs at this table, you have to crowd me so?"

Katie turned her head away from her father so he could not see the little smile on her lips. Emily was the one who arranged the seating and insisted that the girls sit loyally at the feet of their father. Although she didn't understand why, Katie already knew that her father was not much interested in any of them and only tolerated their presence and little more. If he had had a bad day, as it appeared he had today, the tolerance fell to the wayside.

"It's because we enjoy your company," Emily said. She said it so well that for a moment Katie thought she was going to get away with it.

She did not. Silas snapped back, "Bullshit."

Emily rocked back in her chair as if she'd been slapped. Elizabeth turned white and concentrated on her plate.

Katie smiled at her father and asked, "What is bullshit, father?"

"Kathleen!" Emily shouted across the table.

Silas pondered his youngest for a moment and then decided not to pursue the issue. He had much more important things to talk about.

He picked up a fork and waved it at each of the girls. "This land is Baker land, and it belongs to Baker blood. It'll be yours someday, and you make sure it stays Baker land."

Emily nodded her head forcefully. "Of course we will," she said. "This land will always be Baker land."

Katie had heard this statement from her father many times before. She always wondered what it was that made him feel like he had to say it. Today, she asked, "Why wouldn't this always be Baker land?"

His laugh was more of a snort. He said, "They know they can't take it from me in a fight, but they think they can steal it."

Elizabeth focused on her plate, carefully dividing each of the servings into a space of their own. When she completed that, she began to eat the cream corn. She would finish that and then move on to the potatoes and from there to the meat. And she would never look up. She was afraid that if she did look up her father would notice her presence and actually direct some of his anger at her. She could not cope with anger.

Emily followed her father's every word. She believed that everything he said was really directed to her, another part of her education that would enable her to carry on the tradition of the ranch after her father died.

Katie finished her mashed potatoes. She could eat anything else cold, but not potatoes. Then she asked, "Who are *they?*"

"Those damned city councils they've got," he shouted. "The one in Medford and the one in Jacksonville. They're trying to steal some of my land."

"They can't do that," Emily said with conviction.

"How can they do that?" Katie asked, curious about this strange relationship between her father and towns that could lead to thievery.

"By making up laws," he said, shoveling a fork full of potatoes into his mouth.

Katie thought about that. She decided that some piece of information must have been left out. She tried to explain that to her father. "If it's thievery, I shouldn't think they could make up a law to protect it. If they do make up a law, I should think that the land must not be yours the way you think it is."

Silas slammed down his fork on the table and sat upright in his chair. His face turned crimson. The two older sisters stared at Katie with their mouths open.

"I'll be damned to hell," Silas shouted. "I knew those teachers were anarchists and this proves it. They've turned one of my own against me, swayed her empty head and filled it with hogwash."

Katie sensed the insult more than she actually understood it. She too sat upright in her chair and slammed her fork on the table. She said "They call it reason, father, and it's quite distinguishable from hogwash. I don't think you'll be able to keep your land if you continue to blame its loss on my teachers.'' She put her hands on her hips and waited for the abuse that was sure to come.

She didn't have to wait long. "God gave with one hand," Silas shouted, "and He took away with the other. He gave me land, and then He gave me daughters. Daughters! You're only as good as what you've got, and when you let someone take that away from you, you're not worth horseshit. I made Baker a name to fear in this valley; you three are sure to make it the butt of all jokes.''

"No, father," Katie said, "I'm sure that Emily will mind your land just the way you would.''

Emily sputtered, started to say something, and then thought better of it. If an insult had been buried in Katie's words, she wasn't sure what it was.

Silas sat in thought, his fork pointed at Katie. She was the peculiar one of the lot. Unlike Emily, who worshipped the boots he walked in, or Elizabeth, who ran from him in fear, Katie was the only one to stand up to him. He might have swept the others aside and embraced this girl, more like him than the rest, if her mother's liberal ways had not left their mark. Katie had no feeling for land, only a sense of right and wrong. A man wouldn't succeed if he sat back and waited for justice.

"No matter how they twist the law to suit them, the fact is that I've this land and they want it. The land is mine," he said, quietly now, but from deep inside of himself so that the words filled the room. "No man'll take it from me.''

Katie cocked her head to one side. She wondered whether or not another question was worth another outburst. Curiosity decided the issue. She asked, "Why do they want your land?" she asked.

Instead of becoming angry again, Silas leaned back in his chair and relaxed. If he didn't explain the truth to his daughters, they'd never get the facts right. He said, "Jacksonville has never forgiven me for blocking the railroad.''

"But Jacksonville has a railroad," Katie said.

"Yes," he said, leaning against the table again, "but they only have a spur connecting them with Medford, and they had to go miles out of their way to get that because I wouldn't let them cross my land. They'd have had a major depot if it weren't for me, and now that they've got their city limits pushed to my land, they figure it's time to get even.''

Emily decided she had let her little sister out-shine her long enough. She asked a question of her own. "Can they take your land, just like that?" she asked.

He continued to look at the blue-eyed child so composed and serious in the solid, ladder-back chair that dwarfed her. "They have the power to annex the land and buy it out from under us," he said.

"At fair market value?" Katie asked.

"What?" Silas asked, awed now by the intelligence of this little girl.

"Mr. Williams explained fair market value to me in mathematics," she said. Mr. Williams lasted a year before both Emily and Katie out-distanced his knowledge of the subject.

"Fair market value's not the issue," he said. "If they cut the first slice of the pie, they'll get the rest in time."

He returned to his meal and did not continue the conversation. After dinner he left the dining room and disappeared into his study for a cigar. He had a lot to think about. Today he had discovered which of his girls could best run the ranch when he was gone.

Monday morning, Katie awoke with a sense of anticipation, or was it a sense of foreboding? She expected her father either to have it out with all of her teachers or to have another of those scenes with mother that was only slightly muffled by the bedroom walls. As she sat in the parlor, doing her lessons, her head was tuned to every sound within the house. She knew it was only a matter of time before her father came strolling in and the excitement began.

Two momentous events did happen that day, but neither Katie had anticipated. The first was more surprising than the second, although not by much. At two o'clock Silas strolled into the house. He had missed lunch. Katie thought that he must have been brooding in his office, preparing for the scene she was sure would follow. He had waited until now because the lessons were over for the day and the girls would be free to be sent away.

He came into the parlor and said, "Get your britches on and come with me." This was not an unusual request. He still took Emily out with him on occasion to survey the land.

Emily nodded and said, "Yes father."

"Not you," he said. "I'm speaking to Katie. It's time for her to learn the ranch."

Emily flushed bright red. She couldn't keep the anger from twisting the features on her face, turning her beauty into a mask of hatred. "She's not allowed to wear britches," she shouted. "Mother said." She knew as soon as she said it that this was a foolish thing to say, but she was too hurt to think of anything else. Her father was betraying her.

"Your mother doesn't know a barn from a cow's ass," he said. "Get your britches on, Katie."

Katie did as she was told. She didn't think much of the idea. These were the very same britches that had gotten her in so much trouble once before, although now they finally fit her and she didn't have to roll up the pants legs. When she came down, her father was pacing in the hallway and Ellie was standing in front of the closed doors to the parlor. The look of terror on her face suggested that Emmy was behind the doors, in a rage. Katie could hear the older girl's sobs of exasperation coming from the other room.

"I'm ready, father," she said. As they left the house, she shouted back to Ellie, "If I were you, I'd run hide for a while." When she glanced back again she could see the back of Ellie's skirt disappear through the door to the kitchen.

Katie braced herself for the onslaught when she returned to the house. Emily, she was convinced, would be waiting to pounce on her as soon as she walked through the front door. She considered a trip around to the back of the house to enter through the kitchen, where she could linger until her father returned. She almost changed directions, too, and then she decided she wouldn't alter her life because of fear. Emily might be able to intimidate Ellie, but she wouldn't do it to Katie.

She marched up the front steps and across the porch, making as much noise as she could. She threw open the front door. She stood in its opening with her hands on her hips and defied Emily to attack. What greeted her was the second great surprise of the day. Emily waltzed out of the front room just ahead of a tall young man. The boy looked vaguely familiar to Katie, but she couldn't place him at the moment. Emily solved the problem by making an introduction.

"Charles," Emily said, "this is my little baby sister, Kathleen.

Kathleen, this is Charles Hollingsworth, Doctor Hollingsworth's son.''

Katie remembered now. She had seen him once or twice in church when she was younger, although she had never known his name. He would sit in the back with other boys and girls his age and not always be attentive to the sermon. She wondered why he was here.

"Shut the door behind you, silly, and come in. You'll let in the flies," Emily said.

Flies were not a problem in early spring, Katie knew. She wondered if Emily was trying to make a fool of her or something like that. She shut the door and followed the two back into the front room.

Katie took a seat in one of the wingback chairs near the marble-faced fireplace. She watched her sister very carefully. Emily was predictable. Vengeance was a religion with her. An excessive display of affection or friendliness would only be a ploy to prepare for her next assault. Katie had learned the hard way that Emily was not to be trusted, and she had discovered no cause since then to change her mind.

Instead of sitting quietly and trying to intimidate with eye contact, Emily flitted about the room in a whirl that made Katie dizzy to watch. Instead of speaking with a cold, sharp voice, she bubbled nonsense from her lips. Instead of being critical of her sisters, she sang their praise. Katie listened intently, awed.

"Kathleen is a marvel. Even father says so," Emily said. "She has such a grasp of numbers and all those scientific things that just don't mean a thing to me at all. I wouldn't be surprised if she's a prodigy.'' She had to stop because the speech had made her breathless. She did not seem to be aware that she was behaving strangely.

Charles turned his attention to Katie from a point near one of the front windows where he had chosen to stand and watch Emily. He said teasingly, "Say something clever for me, Katie."

"Are you lost?" Katie asked.

Charles smiled. "Why should you think that?" he asked.

"I can't imagine anyone coming here intentionally to see Emily," Katie said.

The flash of anger in Emily's eyes lasted just long enough for Katie to see it. Emily said, "You just never know what she'll say."

Charles laughed good-naturedly. Katie liked his appearance. He was tall and slender like his father, yet he looked strong, even powerful. His hair was brown and the features of his face were either square or straight. The eyes were brown and they had the same warm, friendly look to them that his father's had. The first impression he created was of a nice, pleasant, friendly, caring person. She knew that he was going to be a doctor like his father just by looking at his face.

"I suspect," Charles said, a smile on his face, "that sisters have the same kind of relationship with each other as brothers and sisters. I've a younger sister who might have the same attitude toward me as Katie seems to have toward you."

"We really are close," Emily insisted. She was not quite good enough an actress to make the statement convincing.

"To answer your question, Katie," Charles said, "I rode out with my father. I specifically came along to see Emily. We once went to school together, and I suspected then that she might grow into someone quite beautiful. I was right."

Katie was mesmerized by the transmogrification her sister had undergone. She actually blushed and paled at the same time, a seemingly impossible accomplishment unless one paid close attention to the ear lobes and the throat. These two spots were quite white on Emily.

Emily struggled for something to say. Finally, after two false starts, she said, "Charles has been in Iowa for the past two years studying to be a doctor like his father. In two more years he expects to return to Jacksonville permanently to practice."

None of this information explained Charles' presence to Katie. Even if he thought Emily to be pretty, he certainly must know something of her personality. Unless he was a fool, how could he overlook that particular flaw in her character and still want to see her? As far as Katie could tell, other than sprouting a few new pieces of anatomy, her sister had become meaner in the last few years, certainly not nicer. Not nice enough to attract the attention of a boy like Charles.

She made that point to him. "One visit with Emily should be all that it takes," she said.

"All that it takes for what?" Charles asked. Katie seemed to amuse him because each time she spoke he smiled broadly.

"To decide not to see her again," Katie said.

"Katie!" Emily snapped.

Charles interrupted her. "But you're wrong, Katie," he said. "I've asked her to sit with me in church on Sunday."

"And he has asked me to write to him when he returns to school," Emily said.

Katie shook her head and got up. She felt sorry for Doctor Hollingsworth. It must be hard to have a child who was mentally incapacitated. "I don't think she can keep up the farce forever," Katie said, leaving the room, "so there may be hope for you yet."

KATIE'S RELATIONSHIP with her father changed dramatically. She was removed from the classroom for the summer and placed in Silas' care. She spent nearly eight hours a day with him as he carried out his duties as land owner. He explained the books to her and the flow of money that was non-stop. He dictated to her his system of shipping and storage until she could repeat it by heart. He taught her all that he could about planting crops and about the conservation and nutrition of soil. She learned quickly, but she was only just going on nine and her learning lacked enthusiasm. She wanted so much to be out in the fields or along the irrigation ditch, poking and prodding instead of studying.

Emily was too preoccupied with Charles Hollingsworth to pay much attention to her sisters. That didn't mean she had forgotten. She was well aware that her father had shifted his attention away from her to Katie. She even suspected, rightly so, that he saw in Katie a better manager of the family affairs than he saw in her. She did not resent that, not as long as Charles was a part of her life. If she could imagine herself the wife of a successful doctor in Portland or Seattle, why concern herself with the much more difficult role of running the family empire? Ultimately her share of the ranch would mean a comfortable living for her and her husband.

Charles Hollingsworth did not have any long-term plans. He might have laughed out loud if Emily had shared her dreams with him, but he was too nice of a person to do that. He found Emily to be nice enough. She was certainly attractive. But neither of these traits were reason for him to fall madly in love with her. Considering the cold and aloof character of the father and the withdrawn nature of the mother, he wondered what that mix might mean to Emily in the future.

Time suspended the issue of their relationship. Early in August he packed up his bags and left for medical school without making a commitment to Emily. She read into this that she had been a pleasant diversion for the summer, but not the stuff that made for permanent relationships.

She accepted his departure from her life with poorly disguised anger. It gnawed at her insides and demanded a victim to appease it.

As KATIE BEGAN to understand the operation of the ranch and her father's routines, she found mysteries in his life that she didn't understand. She was aware now that her father slipped out at night two or three times a week. That stimulated her natural curiosity, but not as much as did the relationship between her father and Chin. She had only discovered in the last year that Chin did not live on the ranch. The daughter of a family who came to work in the gold fields, she had remained in Jacksonville after her mother had died and her father had returned to his ancestors in China. She lived in a little log cabin in the foothills between the Jacksonville cemetery and edge of the Baker ranch. Each morning she would follow a well-worn path through the hills to the Baker house to arrive before the sun came up. Each evening she would return in the dark after the girls had been put to bed for the night.

Katie understood little about the relationship between husbands and wives, or men and women. She measured the behavior of others against her own behavior. For that reason she could never understand what Chin did in her father's office each morning when she took him his brunch and Katie was sent away. Katie decided one day to investigate, to climb into a hayloft across from her father's office and spy on the two of them through the front window.

Ten minutes later she had Elizabeth in tow, dragging her from the house to the barn. Poor Elizabeth had a difficult time with the ladder to the loft. The barn was huge, its peak rising nearly forty feet above the ground. The ladder was narrow, straight up and down, and its rungs were a little loose. Katie scampered up the ladder without a hitch, but Elizabeth hugged it for dear life, slowly pushing herself up step by step while keeping her eyes closed. She wouldn't have put herself through this if she had felt the need to prove her little sister wrong.

Katie had already swung open the loft door and was standing near the edge of the opening. "Good, they're still doing it," she said, pleased because now Elizabeth would see that she hadn't lied. Below, just over the top of the curtains that blinded the lower half of the window, she could just make out the naked backside of her father and below him on the sofa the much smaller shape of Chin, also naked.

Elizabeth stopped three feet from the edge of the door, frozen in her tracks. She put a hand to her mouth and said, "Oh, Katie, what've you gotten me into?"

"Hush," Katie whispered, "father might hear you."

"I hope not," Elizabeth moaned. "I don't know what they're doing, but I'm sure I'm not suppose to see it."

Katie wrinkled her nose. Her sister's timidity irritated her. She didn't know what her father and Chin were doing, either, but she doubted that it was anything to be feared. Chin didn't impress her as being very brave.

Elizabeth moaned again and said, "I know I'm not suppose to see this, and I don't know how I'm going to get down."

"You'll get down the same way you came up," Katie said.

Both girls were watching Chin and their father. Neither noticed the arrival of Emily until she spoke.

"Why are you spying on father?" Emily asked.

Elizabeth slapped a hand to her chest and sat down with a thud on the floor of the loft. Katie glanced back at her sister and said, "Go away, Emily. You're not invited to join us. "

"Join you in what?" Emily asked.

"None of your business."

Emily turned to Elizabeth and stared down at her, a cruel smile on her face. "Join you in doing what?" she asked again.

Already frightened enough, Elizabeth could not tolerate the threat in Emily's voice. She blurted out, "Katie wants to know why Chin and father are in his office—naked."

Emily stared across the way, paled, and then flew into a rage. "Get out," she screamed, kicking at her sister on the floor. "Get out of there, now!" She reached down and grabbed Elizabeth by the arm and dragged her toward the ladder.

The terror she felt because of her sister easily overcame the fear she had of heights. Elizabeth scampered down the ladder as fast as she could go, and when she reached the ground in the barn, she took off running to the house as fast as her legs would carry her.

Katie ignored them both. She had come to the loft for a purpose, and she wasn't going to leave until it was satisfied. She was tired of the way Emily tried to intimidate them all the time. She was not afraid of her sister.

"Get away from the door," Emily yelled. "Now!"

"Be quiet or go away," Katie said. She took a step closer to the edge and stood on her toes to get a better look.

It happened so quickly that she never could say with complete confidence that Emily had pushed her, although she never doubted that she had. Emily insisted that when Katie stepped close to the edge, she reached out to grab her little sister and pull her back to safety. Instead, they had bumped and Katie had lost her balance.

All dreams of flying like a bird or floating like a cloud came to a swift end as the ground came at Katie so fast that she had little time to do more than put out an arm in front of her. She heard the bone in the arm snap before the impact of the fall knocked her senseless.

Lesser falls had killed bigger people. Katie should have died that day. Nothing broke the thirty foot fall to the ground. She landed on her head, the only cushion her badly broken arm and a few inches of loose soil. But she did not die.

While Katie lay in a coma, one morning Silas trudged along the irrigation ditch to the dam as he did almost daily in the summer. A summer that had held so much promise took a nasty turn. Temperatures soared over the hundred degree mark. The heat had ruined his plans to conserve water. The fields were dry, and he now had to use the dwindling supply of water behind the dam.

That was aggravation enough, but not as irritating as the time he had wasted. He had spent nearly five months educating his youngest daughter about the ranch's operation, and now the clumsy child had fallen from the barn loft and landed on her head. Doctor Hollingsworth was not sure if she would live, and he doubted that she would be normal if she did recover. The time spent educating her had been a loss. He didn't easily accept loss.

The small pond at the base of the damn was dry. Silas walked across it to the dam itself. He and his men had cut great timbers and squared them to form the face of the dam. They sealed the cracks between the logs and buried the ends in the banks on either side with dirt and rock. A sluice gate had been left centered on the bottom of the dam. A plate held in place by water pressure closed the gate.

Silas needed only to climb the face of the dam to the top and turn a metal wheel there to lift the gate open. He found his favorite footholds and pulled himself to the top.

When he lifted his face over the top of the dam, the rattlesnake that had been sunning itself there struck without the traditional warning from its rattles, burying long fangs deep into Silas' neck.

Silas let go of the timbers and fell back on the dried mud of the pool. By the time he regained his senses the rattlesnake was already out of sight. The picture of him sitting there like a fool might have been comic if it were not for the two stinging holes in his neck.

He sensed that it might be ironic for a man who hated and killed snakes the way he did to die from a snake bite. And he knew he was going to die. He went to the house, sent for the doctor, called Emily to his room, and took to bed. Three days later he was dead.

A week later Katie emerged from her coma. Doctor Hollingsworth called it a miracle that she suffered only a concussion and a number of broken bones.

Katie was both sad and disappointed when she learned of the death of her father. She wanted so much tell him her version of her fall.

EIGHT

PAUL GOT UP from the dining room table and walked into the living room. The letter from his wife was still on the coffee table unopened. He picked it up before he sat down. He opened it.

Ten minutes later he wadded up the letter and threw it toward the fireplace. He picked up the phone and dialed his home number. After several rings, the other woman answered.

"Let me speak to Beth," he said.

A long silence was followed by the muffled sound of voices behind a hand clamped over the telephone receiver. Finally, Beth answered. "Paul?"

"Yes, Paul," he said.

"It's late," she said.

"I'm sorry. I just read your letter."

"Oh."

"Oh?"

"It took you long enough to read my letter."

"I've been busy," he said. "Writing," he added.

"Too busy to read my letter," she said quietly. "And you say you love me."

"Isn't that just it," he said, "before, you claimed I didn't love you. You're full of contradictions, and I still don't know what the hell is going on." He leaned back on the sofa and put his feet on the coffee table. He didn't expect much of an answer from her.

"I'm enjoying the luxury of being contradictory," she said.

"Do you want a divorce?" he asked.

"If you want to do that for you, I think you should," she answered again, as she had answered a dozen times before.

"Let's not worry about me, the aggrieved party. Just answer the question."

"I told you before," she said. "I don't know what I want. I need time to figure that out. I know I'm being selfish and a bitch, but if you don't want to file for a divorce that's what you get."

"And what do I get in the end?" he asked. "What's my reward for patience? Does my wife come back to me, to be faithful until another skirt attracts her?" He was sorry he said it as soon as the words came out.

"My psychologist tells me that anger's good. But I'm ahead of you there," she said. "I was plenty angry before I left you. Tears are good for you, too," she added. She was very quiet, even in her anger. He knew she was in bed, not quite awake, and that the other woman was beside her, probably on his side of the bed.

"That makes us even. We're both plenty angry."

"Divorce me," she said.

"Is it over?" he asked.

"I don't know," she said.

"Do you want a divorce?" he asked.

"I don't know," she said.

"Is there a chance we might get back together?" he asked.

She waited before she answered. "Maybe, but not the way it was."

"And how would it have to be?" he asked.

"I don't know," she said. "I wouldn't be seeing a psychologist if I had all the answers."

This conversation was a repeat of several they had had before. He decided to end it. "How are the boys?" he asked.

"Call them on Sunday and find out."

"Okay."

"And next time read my letters at a more reasonable hour if you plan to call."

"Okay," he said. The phone clicked dead.

Monday morning, after a restless weekend, most of it spent thinking about his wife, he got up late and took a long, hot shower before dressing in his best suit. Today he would see Pamela Livingston and try to dig out some more information on Hollingsworth—and on the Bakers.

Medford was a contrast of old and new, each mixed with the others so that aged stucco might be framed on each side by sheets of glass. Pamela Livingston's law firm was located near the city center on an open lot that included parking space. The building was large and stately, the natural wood exterior stained a dark brown. The long, gently sloping, multi-gabled roof was covered with a brown Spanish tile.

As Paul walked through the front door of the office building into a reception area, he decided that the architect had found a perfect combination for the law firm. The building reflected both traditional design and modern interpretation on the outside.

Inside, the same theme existed. The interior walls were plastered over and painted off-white. The carpet was wine-colored. In contrast, the chairs in the lobby were over-stuffed and classic in design, matching perfectly two antique end tables and an early American armoire.

He gave his name to the receptionist and asked to see Miss Livingston. The woman behind the desk made a brief call and then told him to take a seat in one of the chairs.

An older woman, more conservatively dressed than the receptionist and carrying a file folder, stepped from a doorway in a hallway to Paul's right and walked toward him. When she reached his chair, she said, "I am Miss Livingston's secretary. She asked me to give you this folder. She also said she'd be free for lunch in about fifteen minutes if you'd like to wait."

Paul stood up and took the folder from the woman, smiling. He said, "I would like that."

The secretary returned his smile and said, "I'll tell her." She walked back to the office.

Beggars can't be choosers, he told himself. He had suffered far greater indignities in his quest for research material than going out to lunch with a lawyer. In order to find out how much a sacrifice he was making, he walked to the reception desk. He stood there for a minute before the young woman there noticed him.

"Can I help you?" she asked.

"I haven't met Miss Livingston before. You couldn't tell me something about her, could you?" he asked.

The receptionist laughed good-naturedly. She said, "You're going out to lunch with her, and you want to know what you've gotten yourself into."

"Exactly," he said.

"Well," she said, leaning over the desk and speaking more softly, "Pam is thirty, unmarried, and good at what she does. Not that it matters, but she's also one good-looking woman, so I don't think her looks will ruin your lunch.''

Their conversation came to a quick end when the front door opened with a whoosh of air and a well-dressed man walked into the room. His stride was confident, and he was noisy, chattering almost as soon as he opened the door.

''Is that woman going to go out to lunch with me today?'' he asked. ''She owes me that. She beat my butt but good in court again.''

''I'm sorry, Mr. Owings,'' the receptionist said. ''She already has plans for lunch. She said to tell you no, even if you begged.'' The woman sounded very sympathetic.

Owings glanced around the room until his eyes settled on Paul. He raised one eyebrow and tilted his head toward him. ''Is that the lucky son-of-a-gun?'' he asked.

Paul was not sure if he liked Owings or not. The man was over forty, but he had a strong, healthy look to him of someone much younger. His hair was gray, long, and wavy. His blue eyes were clear, and they danced on his face as his expressions changed. Physically he had a certain appeal to him, but the brassy cockiness of the man turned Paul off.

''Hopeless?'' he asked, rhetorically. Of Paul, he asked, ''Would you consider making this lunch a threesome?''

''Mr. Owings,'' the receptionist chided, ''she said she would see you at the club at ten in the morning for tennis. You're not to interfere with her lunch plans.''

He laughed easily. ''You tell her I'll not have her beating me at tennis after she beat me in court this morning.'' The man whirled around and was quickly out the door, his laughter still filling the room after he left.

Paul said to the receptionist, ''Friendly fellow isn't he?''

''Don't let him fool you,'' the woman said. ''On a tennis court or in a courtroom he has a killer instinct. He's the district attorney.''

''I'll try not to have to do business with him,'' Paul said.

A few minutes later a call came through to the desk that sent Paul back to Pamela Livingston's office. The receptionist walked him back to the doorway where the secretary waited for him. The older woman led him to another door inside her office and opened it for him.

Paul walked into the room, glanced at the woman standing behind the desk, and surveyed the furniture, looking for a place to sit. Suddenly he snapped his eyes back to the woman and stopped in the middle of the room.

After several seconds of silence the woman tilted her head to one side and asked, "Are you not feeling well, Mr. Fischer?"

He was not. The shock twisted his stomach into a knot. "How the hell is it you look almost exactly like the photo I have of Katie Baker?" he blurted out, still too dumbfounded to do more than stand in the middle of the floor and stare at her like a fool.

"Not many people still remember the Bakers, so few make the connection," she said. She was wearing a dark, two-piece suit and had on under it a frilly white blouse with a high collar. With her hair piled high on her head she could have been Katie Baker seventy years ago.

"There has to be a connection," he said. "I don't believe in reincarnation."

"Let's start over again," she said, walking out from behind her desk and offering him a hand. "I'm Pam Livingston, the lawyer, and you're Paul Fischer, the writer."

He shook her hand. Her fingers were warm and soft, and he let them linger in his hand for a second before he let go. "Correct. Paul Fischer, the writer. Now, are you going to tell me about the connection?"

"There's a nice restaurant down the street if you'd like to walk with me," she said. She picked up her purse from the desk top and walked to the office door. He had little choice but to follow.

When they were out on the sidewalk, she offered an explanation. "Actually, Katie's eyes were more blue than mine and her hair was a little darker. She wasn't quite as tall as me, either."

Although it was difficult to estimate because she was wearing high heels, he guessed that Pam Livingston was about five-feet, seven-inches. She had a nice shape that tennis evidently kept well-conditioned.

Even with her high heels on, Paul was taller than Pam, but he was not in the same kind of condition. Weightlifting kept all his parts from sagging, yet it did little for the wind. He would not want to meet Pam on a tennis court.

As they approached the restaurant, he reminded her, "You still haven't answered my question."

She didn't answer right away. A waiter met them at the door and directed them to an isolated table in the back of the combination restaurant and bar that was decorated like an old English pub. Again, in this setting, Pam Livingston seemed to melt into the past and become Katie Baker. The similarity was uncanny, so much so that coincidence could not be the explanation for it.

After they had been seated, she said, "I'm surprised your research didn't turn up the information. Silas Baker had a brother, Timothy. Grandfather Tim came to the valley long after Silas had become wealthy. Tim had a ranch, too. He never got rich, but he did get married. And, unlike his brother, he produced offspring that produced offspring. Katie is a cousin of mine. Livngston is my step-father's name."

For some reason that he couldn't explain at the moment, he found her explanation unsatisfactory. He didn't pursue it, though. Instead, he changed the direction of the conversation while they ordered their meals. "As fascinating as I've found the Bakers, I'm really interested in Harry Hollingsworth. What can you tell me about him?"

During the meal she told him what little she knew about the doctor. She explained that her side of the family had little to do with either Silas' family or the people of Jacksonville. Everything that she knew about the doctor was in the file she had given Paul.

Suddenly, she waved her fork in the air and gave it a slight twist as she said, "If you don't back off the book you're writing about the Bakers, I'll have to consider an injunction to stop you." He found himself looking into the eyes of a hard, seasoned lawyer.

He smiled. "Have you ever heard about the first amendment, counselor?" he asked.

"I'll do what I have to protect the wishes of my relatives," she said.

He smiled again. "That's very loyal of you," he said. "By the way, I'm writing a book about Dr. Harry Hollingsworth."

"That's bullshit," she said, without a blink of the eye.

He did not blink an eye either. "And so's your threat," he countered.

During the long silence that followed, he chose the opportunity to finish his lunch. What she failed to realize, he told himself, was that a good teacher was a master actor who could play a variety of roles, even ones that contrasted sharply with those played by an aggressive lawyer.

Like a skilled gambler, she exposed part of the cards she was holding to see his reaction. She said, "You've been to the museum in Jacksonville, to the college in Ashland, and to the courthouse in Medford. In each of those places you not only gathered information about Hollingsworth, but you also gathered information about the Bakers. That doesn't suggest to me that you are writing a book solely about the good doctor."

He responded immediately with, "The lives of the Bakers and the lives of the Hollingsworths overlapped."

She responded quickly with, "And that includes a trip to a photo studio to have a picture of my three cousins copied and enlarged."

"Handsome women every one of them," he snapped back. "You don't have a photo of yourself I could add to my collection, do you?"

"Why the fascination with the picture?" she asked

He laughed. "When was it a crime for a man to admire beauty?"

She put down her fork and relaxed. In that pose she looked even more like Katie Baker. She said, "I want a cup of coffee and just a few more minutes of your time."

"Fine with me," he said.

A waitress came to the table and cleared it. After she had returned with coffee for each of them, Pam began the conversation again.

"I don't know a great deal about the lives of those women," she said. "My grandfather and his brother were not close. Silas pretty much kept everyone out of his life, including his brother and his own daughters. Tim Baker said it was for the best. He said that the few people who did come into contact with the Bakers were doomed to unhappiness."

"What did he mean by that?" he asked.

"I don't know," she said. She qualified her statement. "I allowed myself to get into an unfortunate situation. As a relative of the Bakers I'm just as curious about their lives as you are, but as an attorney who handles their estate, I must satisfy myself with the terms of the will. Ethics keep me from prying."

"I wouldn't think that trying to find out something about your heritage would be prying," he said.

She smiled; her face was more lovely than he wanted it to be. After all, she was the one keeping him from information he needed. It was ironic that she would have Katie Baker's beautiful face.

"We each define our terms in our own way," she said.

"What do you think about the will?" he asked, dropping a bit of a bombshell, considering that no one else seemed to have come up with the will in their research. He was curious to see if the Baker in her or the lawyer in her would answer this question.

He expected her to ask: which will? To his surprise, she said, "I'm surprised Nora Ryan never found that when she was doing her research. Nora really is a bright lady and a competent researcher, but the will was an inexcusable oversight on her part."

"What can you tell me about Mary's will?" he asked.

"The estate has been trying to remove her will from public records for years. Unfortunately, once something becomes a public record, it seems to stay a public record," she said.

"Are there other wills for me to find?" he asked.

He was now able to distinguish the difference between the smile that came from Pam Livingston and the one that came from the attorney. He got the second one this time. "No, the Bakers hired smarter lawyers after that. Any other wills are registered with the county, but the details of them are kept a secret of the law firm. Only those people who might have a legitimate claim against the estate have the right to access these wills."

"You still haven't commented on Mary's will," he said.

"When Mary Baker died the terms of her will were unusual," she said, the attorney's smile still on her face.

"That's your statement?" he asked

"That's my statement," she said. "Would you like to walk me to my office?" she asked. "I have an appointment soon."

She paid for their lunch. He offered to pay, but she insisted. As they walked into the office parking lot together, he noticed a yellow Mercedes which contrasted with the subdued tones of the other cars parked there. He said, "I bet that car is yours."

"What makes you think that?" she asked.

"It looks like the kind of car a young female executive on the way up would get for herself," he said.

They stopped beside the car. She said, "Yes, it is my car. I'm rather proud of it. Not too many single women in Medford can afford one."

He thought of saying something sarcastic about materialism, or feminism, or something along those lines, but decided against it. He didn't need to antagonize this woman, especially if she held the key to more information about either Hollingsworth or the Bakers.

He said, "Thank you for lunch. I owe you one. I hope before I leave the valley we will be able to do this again." He offered her a hand and then said goodbye. She disappeared into her office building, leaving behind just a hint of perfume vaguely familiar to him. He walked away, still impressed by the Kate Baker in Pam Livingston.

TWO DAYS LATER he was once again in front of his computer, writing a book he swore he would not write. He might have stopped the book after his lunch with Pam Livingston, but a trip after that to the University of Oregon library in Eugene and the Oregon State library in Salem changed those plans. Once again he found valuable information too important to pass up.

NINE

"CHARLES HAS ASKED her to marry him," Elizabeth whispered as she trotted up the stairs behind Katie. "He asked Emily!" Her voice pleaded for understanding. This was traumatic, a disastrous event that she hadn't foreseen.

"Hush," Katie said. "You're talking nonsense." They reached the landing and walked down the hall to the back room. When their father died, Emily moved from the back room to her father's room. Katie moved from the small nursery to Emily's room.

She walked to one of the windows in the back of the room and stood quietly, looking outside while she waited for Elizabeth to join her. Ellie closed the bedroom door and rushed to her sister. She said, "I tell you, it's the truth. I heard them, just a few minutes ago, in the parlor." She peeked around Katie's shoulder so that her sister could see clearly the distress etched on her face. "He isn't waiting for me to grow up. What am I to do?"

Katie found it disgusting to have a sister a whole four years older than herself who had to come to her for advice. Elizabeth, it seemed, was totally unable to make up her own mind about anything.

"You're sixteen; Emily is twenty. Charlie is twenty-two or three. I'm afraid you've been defeated by the numbers," Katie said. She was quite fond of numbers. They often made great sense to her when they seemed to mean little to anyone else.

"But what does that have to do with anything?" Elizabeth asked, truly afraid she was missing something monumental. It was understood that baby Kate was something of a prodigy.

"It means," Katie said, "that Emily is of marrying age and you aren't."

"I will be soon enough," Elizabeth moaned.

"Not soon enough for a young up-and-coming doctor. Right now Emily's the peach among the pears in the valley."

"Don't be disgusting," Elizabeth said. "You can't believe anyone would take a second look at Emily. I mean, we're talking about Emily. God only knows what all that adds up to.''

Katie looked down to the slight twist to her right arm that had not been there on the day Emily shoved her from the loft. Although most people would not notice there was something wrong with the arm, Katie was aware of it. She could still do most things well, but when it came to the delicate maneuvers involved in sewing or piano playing, she was forced to rely on her left hand. She knew first hand what a relationship with Emily added up to.

"Our sister is very pretty," Katie said. "And she manages the largest and most successful ranch in the whole state, a good part of which will be included in a dowry should she marry. Quite a few men could forgive Emily her flaws, considering her worth.''

"Not Charles.''

Katie considered that. She thought Elizabeth might be right. Charlie was happy being what he was, an assistant to his father until he took over the family practice someday. Charlie had little interest in ranching and showed no inclination toward fancy living. No, she was sure that he was pure blind stupid in love. Locked away in a medical school for years, he never got to know Emily except for her letters and during those short visits home. He had an awakening in store for him.

"You're right," Katie said. "He must have some dumb reason like being in love with her.''

Elizabeth stamped her foot and cried, "Don't say that. No one could ever love Emily.''

"Actually," Katie said, thoughtfully, "Emily's not incompetent. I've kept a close watch on the books, and she's doing all right by the ranch. She isn't bringing in a great deal of money, but she isn't losing any, either. Considering the gigantic cash reserves father built up, that leaves us all in good shape, thanks to Emily.''

Elizabeth marched to the door, shouting over her shoulder, "Now you're defending her. I'm the one being abused.''

Katie turned to stare at her. Elizabeth could be so dramatic at times; it was impossible to decide if she was truly feeling abused or not. This time Katie decided that she was not.

"You're being silly," Katie said. "You want to go to Willamette University and study music. You said so yourself. Charlie isn't going to wait for you to do that, and he's not going to marry you and then send you off with his blessing.''

Elizabeth stopped with one hand on the doorknob. She wondered if she should do something to warn Charlie before he let this thing go too far. No man deserved to be married to Emily.

Down the hall the sound of a small dinner bell could be heard. Katie opened her door and waited until she was sure that the others had gone to the dining room. Then she walked down to her mother's room, entered and shut the door behind her.

She no longer liked to come into this room. Something happened here about the time her father died that she didn't understand. She, of course, was in a coma at the time, so she didn't find out about his death until later. Since that time her mother had turned her bedroom into a tomb, a boiling hot one at that. She kept a fire going at all times, and she had heavy, black curtains hung over the windows so that little light came in the room and even less fresh air. The hot air hung in the room around the big bed like an invisible stone that seemed to keep her mother pressed to the sheets.

Her mother rarely left the bed. She sat on it, propped up like a queen in pure white silks, dictating to any audience she could coax into the room. Katie and Elizabeth stayed away, but Emily was up here as often as she could be. For some reason, neither Doctor Hollingsworth or his son came to see Mary anymore. If she needed a doctor, she had one come from Medford.

When Katie walked into the room she found her mother sitting on the side of the bed, her feet dangling a few inches above the floor. ''Help me,'' she said. ''I want to move to a chair closer to the fire.''

The room smelled as if her mother were dead already, Katie thought. She wondered what the room might smell like in another thirty years. Her mother was only in her early forties, and she showed no inclination to leave the room that had been her home for nearly twelve years.

Katie helped her mother off the bed and gave her support as she slowly shuffled the few feet to a chair that was shoved up close to the fireplace. She lowered her mother into the chair and stepped back from the fire. Katie couldn't understand how her mother could stand such heat, yet the woman seemed on the verge of edging even closer to the flames once she was in the chair.

"I'm cold," she said. "I hate winters."

The statement seemed absurd to Katie. Winter in Southern Oregon was mild, a fact that had enabled her father to make a fortune from ranching. Certainly the rain and fog could be unpleasant during this time of the year, but it hardly ever snowed and the only true danger to the ranch was a late frost in the spring that might harm the fruit crop. Her father had always lavishly praised the weather in the valley.

"A woman my age should not be this cold," she said.

"Is there anything else I can do for you, mother?" Katie asked, always polite to the woman. Although she had begun to resent the years of indoctrination she had undergone in this room, she could not bring herself to treat her mother in any other way. She didn't know if it was because she feared Mary, or if it was because she was afraid the woman was so weak that any resistance to her idealism might cause her to collapse.

"What's going on downstairs?" her mother asked.

Katie moved to the opposite side of the fireplace, away from the heat. She could see her mother's face clearly from here. With each flicker of the flame in the hearth the contrast between her mother's ageless beauty and her premature aging could be seen. When the flame was brightest, her mother seemed terribly old, almost frail like a dried leaf held awkwardly in rough fingers. When the flame died, the shadows in the room softened her features and that alabaster skin looked healthy again and full of life. Regardless of what the flames did, the eyes remained dead. They had died some time after her father was buried. Katie wondered if her mother had held out some romantic notion until the end that he would come back to her and drag her from this room back into life, and when he died Katie wondered if the dream didn't die, too.

Katie answered her mother's question. "According to Elizabeth, Charlie is asking Emily to marry him."

The eyes flickered into the life for a second and then the eyelids lowered and extinguished the flame. "She cannot marry him," Mary said. "He's not good enough for her." Katie noted that the second statement was made with much conviction to it. She wasn't surprised because they had been told time and time again, with passion, that few men would be good enough for them. Mary said again, "She can't."

"Elizabeth will be happy," Katie said.

Her mother glanced at Katie, one eye squinting down on her. The youngest daughter knew that her mother didn't approve of her precocious nature. She wanted intellectual daughters, not intelligent ones. "Why will Elizabeth be happy?" Mary asked, resigned to the fact that she would have to ask the question whether she wanted to or not. Katie rarely volunteered information.

"Elizabeth wants to marry Charlie, herself," Katie said. She expected the same response from her mother about the idea of marriage.

Mary stared at the flame, lost in thought. When she did answer, it was to the fire and not to Katie. "That might not be so bad," she said.

This was more than Katie could let go by unchallenged. She said, "But you just said he wasn't good enough for Emily."

Mary looked up from the fire and seemed to be surprised that Katie was still in the room. She didn't owe Katie an answer, she knew, but she decided to give her one anyway. There must be no misunderstanding about this later on. These three sisters would need each other very much in their futures, and it wasn't right for a mother to drive a wedge between them, especially when that wedge was a man. She said, "I doubt that Elizabeth will ever be able to care for herself. To put her in the care of a doctor might be the best thing for her. Charles' father certainly served me well at one time."

Her mother was in a strange mood today, more talkative than she normally was. Katie took advantage of it. "Why doesn't Doctor Hollingsworth come here anymore?" she asked.

She expected her mother to become angry, or at least to become impatient with her, as she usually did when Katie pried. Instead, tears gathered along the bottom of her eyes until they overflowed and dropped to her cheeks. The tone of her voice softened as she said, "The choice was his, not mine. Go find Emily and tell her I wish to talk to her as soon as young Charles leaves."

Katie left the room confused. She began to suspect that there were things in this family that she didn't understand at all.

Emily and Charles had gone to the parlor after dinner. Katie was not brazen enough to walk in, although there was not much danger of facing one of Emily's tirades if she did. Emily was a different person when Charles was in the house. That did not mean, though, that her memory was failing her. She could and would get even later.

Katie leaned one ear against the door and held her breath. She could just make out the words being spoken inside. There was excitement in Emily's voice as she said, "I know just the house."

"It's not far from my father's office," Charles said.

A hand touched Katie's shoulder and she nearly let out a cry. Elizabeth leaned against the door beside her sister.

Katie whispered angrily, "Don't do that again. You quit sneaking up on me."

"What are they talking about now?" Elizabeth asked, speaking a little louder than Katie liked.

Katie put a finger to her lips and said, "Quiet. They're talking about a house."

Elizabeth nodded. "She said she would marry him. They plan to live in a house in Jacksonville." She seemed remarkably calm to Katie, considering that only moments before Elizabeth was sure that her life would be over if Charlie didn't marry her.

"You don't seem upset anymore," Katie said.

"I'm not," Elizabeth said. "I was listening at the door when you were talking to mother. I know for a fact now that mother will never let Emily marry Charles."

"Don't be so sure that will stop Emily. She had never been one to let other people tell her what to do, especially since father died. In fact, she's getting quite good at bossing people around on this ranch," Katie said. She was being so emphatic that she failed to keep her voice down. The parlor door swung open suddenly and the two girls tumbled into the room.

Emily stood in the center of the room with her arms crossed. Charles was poised with his hand on the doorknob, chuckling. "Sneaks," he said.

"We just happened to be walking by," Elizabeth said.

"That's the only way you can learn anything in this family," Katie said.

Charles laughed but Emily did not. The look on her face suggested it would be a good idea for the two younger sisters to make themselves scarce that afternoon.

"What did you hear?" Emily asked. She scraped off just enough of the edge to her voice to hide the cruelty that was usually just beneath the surface of her words.

"That you plan to get married," Katie said.

Emily's chin rose a little in the air as she said, "That's right."

Katie asked, "If you marry, who'll run the ranch?"

Emily smiled now. Katie never trusted this smile because it meant that revenge was not far behind. She said, "That's your problem, not mine. I consider one third of the ranch to be mine. I plan to sell my share so that Charles and I will never have to worry about money."

For a man who was about to become rich, Katie thought, Charles seemed indifferent to her statement. He said to Emily more than anyone in the room, "I'm sure that's something you'll have to work out with your mother. The estate is in her name. Besides, my practice will make all the money we'll ever need in life."

Katie's brain flew quickly over the other implications in Emily's statement. This sacrifice for marriage seemed grand to Katie, considering that Emily ran the richest ranch in the state. Emily, a girl who enjoyed power over other people, was giving up a great deal for a marriage to a man who was nice, but certainly not made in the image of the perfect gentleman portrayed to them by their mother over the years. As long as Charles was in the room to act as a buffer between them, Katie decided to ask some pointed questions.

"You don't mind defying father's wishes?" she asked.

Emily stared at her sister, unblinking and unsmiling. "What's that supposed to mean?"

Katie said, "Father left specific directions in the will. The land is not to be divided unless the ranch is in financial distress."

Now Emily smiled. She said, "That's what father gets for dying too soon. If he had had his way, little Katie would be running the ranch. He was grooming her for the role when he died. He didn't think I could do it. He was wrong," she said, defensively, a little break in her voice that suggested deeper emotions. "I've done a good job with the ranch. Katie will get her chance someday, but with only two thirds of the land. If she's as good as father said she was going to be, she won't need my part of the ranch."

"Just which part is your part?" Katie asked.

"The part closest to Jacksonville," Emily snapped back.

Now Katie understood. It had taken her years to be in a position to do it, but Emily was finally ready to get even with her father. He had turned his attention to Katie just once and Emily had never forgiven him for it. By dividing the ranch and selling off her share to the people of Jacksonville, she could get back at her father not once, but twice. Pushing Katie off the loft was just the beginning of her vengeance. "I don't think mother's going to like that," Katie said.

Emily paled. "You'll not tell her a thing."

"I watch for you over my shoulder, now," Katie said to Emily, "so I won't be caught off guard again. Twice was enough. I'll do whatever I wish to do."

Emily blushed. She struggled to keep her tongue in cheek. She said with strain, "You're a sniveling brat. Fortunately mother recognizes that fact. That's why I have her ear and you don't."

There was truth to that, Katie knew. Emily was the one who ran things around the ranch, and even her mother was not oblivious to the implications behind that. They all had to cater to Emily at one time or another to make sure that their needs were met. Katie went through Silva most of the time, avoiding the unpleasant task of having to ask her sister directly for anything. Silva made sure that Katie's needs were buried secretly within her own budget items.

Elizabeth took advantage of the one moment in her life when she actually was in a position to cause Emily anguish for once. She said, casually, "I don't think we have to worry too much about this marriage. Mother just said that she would not allow it, that Charles was not good enough for you."

Emily crossed the distance between them quickly and slapped Elizabeth so hard that it knocked her sister to the floor. She bent down to hit her again, when Charles grabbed her arm and pushed her back.

"Emily!" he said. The look on his normally affable face turned stone hard. "We don't need your mother's approval for marriage, and we don't need your money. And we especially don't need this."

He reached down and helped Elizabeth to her feet. Surprisingly, the middle sister was smiling. Her satisfaction far out-weighed the pain she felt.

"Mother did say she wanted to see you," Katie said.

For a moment Emily met Charles' gaze. She broke the eye contact quickly and walked from the room, saying as she left, "I think you should leave now. I will see you tomorrow."

Charles looked at the two younger sisters, nodded his head knowingly, and walked from the room as well. Katie closed the door behind him and turned to Elizabeth. She was going to admonish her sister for her lack of tact, but she never got past the smile on Elizabeth's face. She started to giggle, and then both of them broke into laughter.

Precocious, a prodigy to some degree, wise beyond her years: despite these marvelous traits, Katie was still a child of twelve and many mysteries in life had not revealed themselves to her just yet. Whatever happened upstairs between Emily and their mother was one of those mysteries.

The first part of the argument that followed was clear to everyone in the house. Neither Katie nor Elizabeth had to rush upstairs to press their ears to the door. Emily's high-pitched cries filled the house, shrieked through the heating vents, and rushed up and down chimneys. Mary's voice, though not as sharp or as strong, followed Emily's, deep water over large boulders following fast water over a rolling river bed.

First Emily pleaded with her mother, and then she became defiant. "You'll no longer tell me what to do, mother," she shouted. "Charles and I will be married because he's a good man, more than good enough for me."

Mary's reply was firm and to the point, the one hammered home year after year for the benefit of each of the girls. "There are gentlemen in the world with dignity and means who have more to offer in life than all the young doctors in the world. They know wealth and they know position. They can turn this ranch into a single, perfect pearl in a string of pearls. They can give you more in life than you can possibly imagine for yourself here. Wait for one of them. Don't waste your life on Charles."

Emily's response was quick and equally to the point. "Those kind of men live a world, a universe, away from this stupid little valley. The chance of them coming to me is so small that a needle in a haystack would seem a pillar next to it. I have Charles in hand now."

"Don't be foolish," Mary said, a calmness in her voice now that showed more strength than any of the girls suspected that she had. "We can manage the ranch for a year or so. I'll send you to San Francisco. There's a fine finishing school there for young, wealthy

ladies like yourself. They can give you the social graces you still lack
and then they can introduce you to society. You'll find a handsome,
wealthy young man who'll take you by the hand and lead you into
a new world, a glorious one.''

Emily changed her tactics. She began to play on Mary's weakness.
''Wouldn't that be marvelous, Mother,'' she said, the anger still obvious in her voice. ''I'll leave a dunce behind to take care of your
very extensive needs, and I'll leave a child behind to run a financial
empire. I suspect I shall return from San Francisco as a lady and find
all I left behind has gone to dust, including my mother.'' By the way
Emily said the last words, it was clear to Katie a threat was buried
in them.

Mary's voice was still firm and her resolve was unshaken. She
said, ''You'll not marry Charles.''

Katie jumped as she heard the sound of something heavy hit the
bedroom floor above her. She rushed from the parlor and headed up
the stairs. No telling what Emily might do, even to their mother. She
could hear Emily's words clearly now that she was out of the parlor.

''Don't let your bitterness ruin my life, too,'' Emily screamed.
''Just because you couldn't have your doctor doesn't mean I cannot
have mine.''

''Watch what you say,'' Mary said angrily. Katie and Elizabeth
arrived at the bedroom door at the same time, just as their mother
swung her arm about and slapped Emily across the face. The porcelain pitcher and bowl that Mary had knocked off the bedstand as
she got up were in pieces on the floor.

Kate was surprised. All her life her mother had been little more
than an invalid who needed to be helped from bed to her chair. Now
she stood erect and strong in front of her daughter with no sign of
her weakness showing. If she were really so strong, Katie wondered,
why should she want to spend her life in this room?

''Watch what *I* say?'' Emily spit back, one hand rubbing the red
glow on her left cheek. ''Watch what I say,'' she screamed. ''The
games you played turned Chin into a whore, father into a whore-
monger, and you into...into a drugged wastrel. Look at you, Mother.''

The arm swung again, and again Emily took the blow and held
her ground. ''You don't know what you're talking about,'' her mother
shouted.

"I know about the doctor; I know about the morphine; perhaps you would like to tell me about the rest," Emily sobbed.

Mary looked over her shoulder at the two younger girls in the room. She said, now calm and controlled, "Please leave us. Emily and I have many things to discuss." The girls left the room and the door closed behind them.

They sat in Katie's room for two hours and waited for their mother's door to open again. Whatever words were said in there this time were said so quietly that none of them drifted down the hall. In fact, none of them even drifted to their mother's door. Elizabeth walked down several times to put her ear to the wood, but nothing came of it.

Katie suspected that when the door opened, their lives would be changed. A struggle for power was going on in there, a struggle that only one woman would win, for now. If Emily won, their father's dream would be gone, but then they would all be free to live their own dreams. If their mother won, the status quo would be preserved, for now. But Katie suspected that a great price might be paid for that. Her fears were confirmed when the door opened.

Emily came out of the room, her cheeks still wet with tears. She looked somehow older than a few hours before, and for once in her life, she even appeared to be vulnerable.

Emily turned back to her mother and said, "You'll pay a dear price for this on earth, and then a greater price in hell."

Their mother's voice drifted from the room, weaker now and less sure. "I've always known I would."

THEIR LIVES did not change drastically, as Katie feared they would. But they did change. Emily packed her bags and left for San Francisco within a few weeks. A lawyer in town was hired to monitor the finances of the ranch, and one of Silas' most loyal workers was elevated to the position of overseer. Elizabeth was put in charge of the household, and Katie was to continue to monitor the operation and finances of the ranch.

Elizabeth proved adequate at her job as long as she let Silva do most of the work and let Katie make most of the decisions. Katie, the mere child, maintained that fine eye for financial details. She kept the lawyer and the overseer honest. In fact, much to his embarrass-

ment, the overseer often found himself knocking at Silas' office door
to ask the little girl dwarfed behind the desk her opinion of the decision he was about to make. Rarely did Katie offer poor advice.

A year and a half later, Emily returned with little fanfare and even
less communication in the interim. Almost immediately after she got
back, Elizabeth was shipped off to the same finishing school and
Emily took back her control of the family affairs. Katie was allowed
to be a little girl again, although she still monitored the books in her
father's office, and now Emily found it necessary to stand outside the
door to wait the chance to ask for advice, for in the year and a half
she was away, Katie had tripled the ranch's profits.

TEN

AWAKENED FROM a deep sleep, Paul rubbed a hand over his eyes before he answered the phone and asked, "Who the hell is this?"

"Jeff Hollingsworth," the voice said.

"Jeff," Paul said, recognizing the voice now, "Do you know it's three in the morning?"

"Auntie M. died last night," Jeff said. "I've got the material she had on Doc Hollingsworth."

"I was sorry to hear about Auntie M.," Paul said.

"She had a massive stroke; she died in minutes," Jeff said. "If you want to use the material she left behind, we've got to make a deal."

"I'll be home this afternoon," Paul asked.

"I'll be there at six." The phone went dead.

Paul returned to bed, but he couldn't get back to sleep. Much later, after a shower and breakfast, he sat down in front of his computer just as the sun was about to rise. Two hours later he was interrupted by the sound of his doorbell.

He expected to find Jeff Hollingsworth standing outside his door, too eager for a profit to wait for Auntie M. to turn cold or for night to fall, but instead of Jeff, Paul found himself standing face to face with Pam Livingston as he swung open the door.

She smiled at him and said, "Hi. I was just jogging by and I thought I'd stop in and say hello." She was wearing a jogging suit, but it was obvious that if she had been jogging, it was at a pace that wouldn't produce a drop of sweat or force a hair out of place.

"Shady Lane is a dead end, and even at the break of day, it's harder than hell to find. Why is it that I doubt that you just happened to be jogging by?" he asked, opening the door wider to let her in.

"So I lied," she said, sweeping into the living room and whirling in a circle to take in the inside of the house. "This place is a real find," she said. "Is that a guest house out back?"

"Yeah, it is," he said. He was waiting for an explanation for her visit, although he vaguely remembered that she wasn't one to volunteer information until she was ready.

"If the owners ever want to sell the place, let me know. I wouldn't mind having it for myself. It has a lot of potential. Have you got any coffee?" She marched from the living room toward the kitchen. She never got that far. The pile of documents on the dining room table and the glow of the computer brought her to a halt.

Following behind her, Paul smiled to himself. First of all, he was delighted to note, that even in sweat pants, she had a marvelous shape, and, more important to him at the moment, not one damned thing on the table was about the Bakers. All of the research material was about Hollingsworth. He was still smiling when he entered the kitchen to get the coffee.

"How do you drink your coffee?" he asked.

"Black," she said. "If I put cream and sugar in it, I'd be tripling the poison."

He brought them both a cup of coffee, sliding hers across the table and then pulling out a chair for himself. As he sat down, he asked, "You wouldn't be going through my papers, would you?"

She dropped on the table the stack of papers she had in her hands, saying, "I didn't know that writers were so sensitive about their work."

"And I always thought that good lawyers were less obvious than this," he countered.

"No," she said. "Some good lawyers are very obvious when it suits their needs."

"Looking for anything in particular?" he asked.

She took a sip of coffee before answering. "Just curious," she said.

He would be interested in having a photo of Pam Livingston in black and white to see just how much she resembled Katie Baker. Right now she looked like a near duplicate as she sat in the early morning light that filtered through the dining room windows.

He decided to shoot from the hip and see what would happen. He said, "If you are looking for the material from Auntie M.'s estate, I don't have it."

She took another sip of coffee and then asked, casually, "What do you know about that?"

He said, convincingly, "Jeff Hollingsworth called me about the papers, asking if some kind of deal could be made for them. I told him the truth. If something was in them that I could use about Doc Hollingsworth, I'd be glad to get my hands on the material. If nothing was, then I wasn't interested. I'm not writing about anyone but Hollingsworth."

She leaned an elbow on the table and said, "I've got that material wrapped up."

"I figured as much," he said.

She stood up. "Good," she said. "I'm glad we both understand that." She moved toward the front door.

He followed her, asking, "Was that the only reason for this visit: to make sure I didn't have those papers?"

She turned around and laughed. "I guess so," she said. "Sounds kind of cold and calculating, doesn't it?"

At that moment Pam Livingston was absolutely beautiful, and she looked strong and fortified against the world. She was so pretty that he felt a little twinge in his chest and a slight turning in his stomach.

"Yes, calculating is a good word," he said.

She smiled as she said, "This account brings in a lot of money for our firm. I wouldn't want to lose that."

"Money is something we all understand," he said.

She walked to the front door and let him open it for her. She turned and offered him her hand, saying, "There's a dinner and dance at the racket club tomorrow night. Would you care to join me?"

"I'm a married man," he said, feeling a bit foolish.

"If I remember right," she said, "you're legally separated. Just how legally separated are you?"

That was a question he hadn't considered. He had been too busy trying to figure out the cause of the separation to consider its significance. He answered as honestly as he could. "I think of myself as legally separated; my wife considers herself divorced."

She nodded, satisfied with his answer. "It's obligatory that you arrive at the club in a Mercedes. I'll pick you up. Will eight be okay?"

He had been so long removed from anything resembling a date, he was a little flustered by this invitation. He asked self-consciously, "What should I wear?"

"Oregon formal, not East Coast formal. A sports coat will do."
She left, running gracefully across the lawn to her car parked in his
driveway. Her strides were long and easy; she moved like a good
runner. He shut the door and returned to the table.

"Well," he said to himself, "don't you feel like a jerk? You just
lied to the nice lady who asked you out to dinner."

He spent the day at his computer, writing eighteen more pages for
the biography about Hollingsworth. He was in the kitchen cooking
dinner after finishing writing for the day when the phone rang. When
he answered it, Nora Ryan's business-like voice greeted him. "Paul,
this is Nora Ryan."

"Hello, Nora. What can I do for you?" he asked.

"I've come across an interesting find. Something I think you'd like
to see," she said.

"What's that?" he asked, noting a hint of excitement in Nora's
voice. She didn't impress him as someone easily excited.

Nora would not be hurried. She continued, "Nancy Simpson, Guy
Simpson's youngest daughter and her husband—of course she's not
a Simpson now, she's a Lanier—bought a piece of land up the north
hill from Jacksonville. They plan to build a house there, as soon as
honest folk can afford to build a house. To make a story short, this
last weekend they were walking their land—it's real overgrown up
there—and, back in a grove of trees just thick with berry vines, they
found an old cabin. It's only a one-room affair and it sits kind of
down at one end, but it seems to have weathered the years fairly well.
They came to the museum and asked me about it. I m sure of it: it's
Yo Chin's place."

He played with the name for a minute before it meant anything to
him. Then it dawned on him. "The Baker's Chin?" he asked.

"That's right," she said.

"Did they find anything of interest in the cabin?" he asked, doubt-
ing that anything of Chin's would survive this long.

"They didn't get into the cabin," she said. "Nancy's husband,
Bob, said he'd be glad to fight his way into the cabin if he had help,
but that the vines were too much for one man."

"Let me guess," he said, "you volunteered me to help?"

"Well," she said, "you wouldn't expect an old lady to go up there,
would you? This is snake season."

"I'm not any more fond of snakes than you are," he said.

"You're right," Nora said. "Besides, even if there were anything of value left in the cabin, it's probably all in Chinese. It wouldn't do you much good."

He almost said something about his college background, and then he stopped himself. Nora did not need to know that he had studied both Chinese and Russian extensively during his years in school. Both languages had served him well, allowing him to tackle research papers that most students couldn't attempt. He had impressed a lot of professors that way.

He said, "I'd best not leave a stone unturned. When does this Bob fellow want to go up there?"

"I told him you'd meet him at the museum at eight in the morning," she said.

Paul felt a little bit like he had been manipulated by a pro manipulator. "Okay," he said.

"I'll see you tomorrow morning," Nora said just before she hung up.

He ate his dinner in solitude in the breakfast nook in the back corner of the kitchen, contemplating the significance of these potential sources of information. Hollingsworth's papers would certainly be of value as far as the biography was concerned. But since the doctor died in 1920, at the age of seventy-four, it was unlikely that his papers would unravel the mystery of the Baker sisters. After the doctor's death, the sisters would still live another half a lifetime.

Chin's cabin would be no more than a passing footnote in his biography. He might take a photo or two and probe around inside it, but the poor Chinese girl was of little significance to his research. After the death of Silas Baker, she seemed to have withdrawn into the woodwork at the Baker home, probably too afraid of Emily to raise an eyebrow in protest against the harsh treatment she had there. She had evidently become so quiet that there was nothing in Paul's records to explain what became of her.

His thoughts were interrupted by a knock at his front door. He carried his dinner dishes to the sink and dropped them off on his way to the door. When he opened it, he was greeted by Jeff Hollingworth, who pushed his way into the room, a large box under his arm. Paul shut the door behind them.

"I wouldn't be surprised if that damned lawyer is having me followed," he said, dropping the box on the coffee table. "Just to be safe, I carried this stuff out in a trash can last night and then sneaked it into my car this morning. I Xeroxed the whole thing over at the college library in Ashland. You owe me forty-five bucks for that."

"I think you might be a little paranoid," Paul said, lifting one flap of the box to peak inside. "Pam Livingston doesn't impress me as someone who has people followed. I talked to her this morning. I'm pretty sure she hasn't got this material locked up in a contract, or she'd have been over to get it by now. Make her lay her cards out on the table, and whatever you do, don't make any contract with her retroactive to your aunt's death or this stuff will be worthless to me."

Hollingsworth paced nervously back and forth between the kitchen and dining room. He talked as he walked. "I hope I'm not being stupid about this. I'd hate to lose the five thousand dollars she's offering. I've struggled all my life trying to get ahead and haven't made it. I sure could use that money."

Jeff Hollingsworth looked a lot like Charles at about the same age. At thirty, both men were tall, slender, and a bit stooped. Their sandy hair was fly-away and their eyes had a permanent exhaustion built into them. Charles looked that way because he was over-burdened with work. Paul guessed that Jeff looked that way because he was over-burdened with debt.

"If you play your cards right," Paul said, "you can get the five thousand from Pam and probably a few more from me. Now, go in the kitchen and pour yourself a cup of coffee and give me some time to go through this material. If it's worth anything, I've already got a deal worked out for you."

Hollingsworth nodded and strode into the kitchen. The simple act of pouring a cup of coffee seemed to require a great effort, Paul thought, if the noise from the kitchen was any indication. He shook his head. Jeff looked like a middle-aged man rushing into old age with all sails unfurled, all guns blazing, oblivious to the fact that he was heading toward a rocky shore full speed ahead.

But, Paul said to himself, the man was orderly and thorough. The papers in the box were carefully duplicated, kept in order by page number, and set in alternating stacks to show division by relationship.

Paul would be able to go through the papers quickly and decide if there was anything of interest for him.

When Jeff returned from the kitchen, Paul said, "You seem to have done a good job of this."

Jeff stopped long enough to stare at the box for a moment. He nodded and began pacing again. "Alma's great treasure," he said. "She had the papers stuffed in a couple of old dress boxes in the attic. It took me most of the night to go through it and put it in order and half the day to make a copy of it."

"Did you see anything of interest?" Paul asked, curious whether or not any of this meant anything to Jeff besides money.

Jeff answered sarcastically. "All of it's top notch stuff, worth millions. I don't know what the hell you're looking for. To me it's all old news about the long dead. That kind of gossip's no good unless you can make somebody's ears burn with it. "

Paul nodded, only half listening to the other man. The material had most of his attention now. He asked, "What are you going to tell Pam about this?" he asked.

"I'm not going to tell her shit," Jeff said. "I figure whatever happens between the time Alma died and she gets this stuff is none of her damned business."

Paul did not say anything for several minutes. He was locked into the material, completely. He felt like he had just dug up a box in the backyard and found it full of gold. Information in these papers would blow open the Baker story, and a number of items made Doc Hollingsworth far more interesting than he had been. He put the papers back in the box and walked over to the dining room table. There he had a check and contract made out to Jeff Livingston. He filled in some figures and then walked back into the living room, handing the papers to Hollingsworth.

Jeff looked through the contract quickly and then asked, "What's this going to be worth in the long run?"

"I can't guarantee you an amount beyond the check for a thousand dollars," Paul said. "That's yours to keep, plus a percentage of my profits. If you sign something with Pam that keeps me from using this material, the thousand dollars comes back to me."

Jeff nodded and then scribbled his name on both copies of the contract, returning one copy to Paul. "You know that check will clear Livingston's desk before it clears the bank, don't you?" he asked.

"That will be her problem, not ours," Paul said. Jeff folded the contract and put it in his coat pocket. As he walked to the front door, he said, "I'm having a sale on TV sets down at the store. Stop by and I'll make you a real good deal." He opened the door and let himself out.

Paul picked up the box of papers and headed for his computer. He needed to get as much of this as he could on disk before morning. Pam Livingston might try to have this material impounded and tied up in court so he couldn't use it, at least until after a trial. A clever lawyer could keep this stuff out of his hands for years, even if he did have a legal right to it.

Paul had a portable scanner. The first thing he did was scan each page he thought valuable into the computer and then save it both on his hard disk and then on a floppy. Later he would print out a copy and store both it and the floppy in a safe deposit box. After that, Pam Livingston could do anything she wanted.

THE NEXT MORNING, after only a few hours of sleep, Paul climbed the front steps of the museum and walked through the double doors. Nora Ryan was waiting for him in the doorway of her office, a peculiar smile on her face.

She turned and beckoned him into her office with a wave of her fingers. Inside she stopped short of her desk and pointed to a young man sitting near it. "Paul," she said, "this is Bob Lanier. He's going to take you up to the cabin."

Lanier was a young man, probably no more than twenty-five, Paul figured. He was dressed in jeans, a work shirt, and logger boots. He looked the part of the hardy, northwest stock of people. He was broad-shouldered and muscular. His dark hair curled tightly on his head and a tuft of fur peaked above the open neck of his shirt. Despite a black mustache and a five o'clock shadow, his bright blue eyes let the boy in him show through and saved him from looking much older than he was.

"I'm glad to meet you," Paul said, offering the boy a hand.

Bob got slowly to his feet, wiped his hand on his pants, and offered it to Paul. They shook.

"You didn't exactly come dressed to work, did you?" Nora commented.

Paul looked down at his clothes. He was wearing an old pair of slacks, some loafers that would no longer hold a shine, and a flannel shirt. By his standards he was wearing work clothes, but he admitted that they didn't compare with Bob's. "These are the worst clothes I have," he said.

She shook her head and exchanged a look with Bob Lanier. She said, "I don't know about these Easterners. They've still got too much British in them." She pulled a ring of keys from one of the slots along the top of the roll-top desk. She selected one and held it out to Paul, saying, "In the back of the carriage shed is a storage room. Inside you'll find some old work clothes and boots that belong to the caretaker. You'll need to wear them where you're going."

A half an hour later he knew she was right. They had a short, silent, dusty ride to the plot of land in Bob's old pickup. Near the road to the cemetery Bob turned the truck down a gravel track that wandered east along the base of the hills. Ten minutes out of town, he turned left onto little more than a dirt path and bucked the truck up a long slope until he reached a level spot near the tree line. Bob stopped the truck and got out.

The boy wasn't much for speech, and when he did talk, it was to the point. "This is the front of our land," he said. "We got to clear it ourselves to save money."

The rolling slope in front of them had been cleared long ago and was now thick with yellow, summer wheat. The neat, orderly stalks of wheat ended where Bob's land literally tumbled down a steeper grade. Earth slides, rolling rock, and falling trees had worked their way down to the edge of the field.

Noticing the expression on Paul's face as he looked at the mess, Bob explained, "It's not as bad as it looks. As I clear the slope, I push the stuff down here where I can burn it. Up above the land levels out on a shelf. We'll build our house up there."

As they worked their way up the slope, Paul could see where the boy and his wife had started to reshape the land. The worst of the debris was at the bottom of the slope, like Bob had said. Where this had been cleared away the hill had been terraced and the rock from the soil used to build retaining walls.

The work of the Laniers had not reached the shelf. Here tall weeds and thick patches of vines choked the ground under a thin spread of trees. Paul spotted the cabin before Bob pointed it out to him. Berry vines deep in one corner of the shelf of land humped up high over head and actually spread out into the branches of a large cedar tree. The point of the cabin's roof could just be made out beneath this tangle. He could see why the place would have gone unnoticed for so many years. The lot of land itself was out of the way, and the cabin was buried under the bushes and trees.

"We got two things to worry about," Bob said. "Those vines will rip you up pretty bad if you let them, and," the boy grinned, sheepishly, "the snakes like it up here."

Paul looked around on the ground, suddenly feeling a chill in a morning that promised to be hot. "What kind of snakes?" he asked.

As he walked over to a tall fir tree, Bob said, "The only ones you got to worry about are the rattlers. They're pretty shy as long as you don't step on them." To Paul's surprise, Bob jumped up and grabbed a lower branch of the tree and pulled himself from the ground. In a minute he was fifteen feet up in the branches. Suddenly, a canvas duffel bag dropped from the tree and landed nearby with a metallic crash. Bob followed it down, lowering himself from a branch back to the ground.

As he opened the bag, Bob said, "These are my tools. Keep them in the tree to save me having to haul them up the hill."

Two hours later they had cut a path through the vines to the cabin, using the razor sharp machetes from the canvas bag. During that time Paul had prided himself on the fact that he had not passed out from exhaustion, a real temptation after the first hour in the hot weather, and he had not cut himself to ribbons on the vines, thanks mostly to the clothes Nora had given him. He had seen one snake, but did not identify it. Instead, he kept his eyes closed and waited for it to go away. He figured that was better than screaming at the top of his lungs and running down the hillside like a fool. .

He survived the ordeal by following Bob's lead. The boy paced himself as he worked, and he didn't worry about snakes, figuring that they were more afraid of him than he was of them. Right or wrong, this attitude allowed them to reach the cabin in a reasonable time and to clear away debris so that they stood in front of the door, ready to open it.

"You never know what you're going to find in something like this," Bob said. "There's sure to be some Black Widow spiders and maybe a nest of snakes. Once we get the door open, don't go rushing in."

Paul didn't need the warning. He would be happy to go inside once Bob had cleared the way and said it was okay.

One tug of the door not only opened it, but brought it crashing down in pieces at their feet. Although the logs from which the cabin was made were still in reasonable shape, the timber for the door, the window frames, and the roof were rotted away. The cabin was little more than a shell, except for one section of roof that still offered protection overhead. Years of droppings from the cedar tree had built up a thick mat that kept one corner of the cabin dry. Here the wood was weathered, but preserved, and a length of loft was still intact overhead.

Using a long board from the door, Bob poked around inside the cabin, knocking away thick masses of spider webs and probing in the tangle of weeds that grew up from the cabin floor. Satisfied, he went inside.

Paul followed him. The cabin was tiny, no more than twelve by fourteen feet. Because little debris was on the ground, it was clear that the floor had been made of dirt. If anything of Chin's had been left here, it was long gone; the cabin was empty. Time had wiped it clean.

"It doesn't look like we're going to find much here," Paul said.

"No, it doesn't," Bob agreed. He took the stick and gave the section of loft a shove. The whole thing buckled and crashed to the ground. The two men turned and looked at each other. There, at their feet in the middle of the rotted boards, was a tin box wrapped in decaying leather.

AN HOUR LATER the box sat on the desk in Nora Ryan's office. Closing the lid of the box, Nora said to Paul, "It always amazes me what people keep that they think is so valuable it has to be hidden away. There's not one thing in there of any monetary value."

"For a minute I thought we had a real treasure here," Bob Lanier said. "I was kind of disappointed when I saw them hankies."

Paul smiled. He knew that the lace handkerchiefs were not of much value, even if one of them did have the Baker monogram on it. Nor were the two faded, brown photos of Silas Baker much good. Other photographs of Baker had survived in much better shape. But both Nora and Bob were wrong: there was one priceless possession in the box, and he had it in his hand.

"Do you suppose someone around here can figure out what that means?" Nora asked. By "that," she meant the book in his hand whose mother-of-pearl cover still gleamed bright white despite the years.

"If Bob will let me take it with me, I'll see if I can find someone to translate it. I don't imagine it's going to be easy. I doubt that Chin was very well educated. Much of the writing in the diary is probably a mix of English, Chinese, and original symbols that won't make much sense to anyone."

Paul watched the expression on Nora's face as she stared at the diary. A little bit of lust was there. He could tell that she didn't want to let the book out of her sight, but she was helpless to do anything about it. Bob had already agreed to let Paul have the book before they got to the library.

"Yes," Nora said, not taking her eyes off the book. "Of course, I might have a contact or two at one of the universities who could tell us something about the diary. If you'd leave it with me, I might be able to expedite matters."

"Give me a couple of days with it first," Paul said, "and then we'll see."

The woman looked at him with a hint of anger in her eyes. She started to say something and then thought better of it. Instead, she said, "Don't forget to leave your work clothes here."

He took this as an invitation to leave from a woman who was disappointed in him. He wondered if she knew about his language background in Chinese. If she did, she could certainly figure out that he had no intention of sharing the contents of the diary with her. He was sure that he would find in these the makings of one hell of a book, and he wasn't about to give her a chance to write it first.

She walked him to the front door. As he was going down the steps, she asked, "You will get the diary back to me, won't you?"

He patted his pocket where he had put the diary and said, "Just as soon as I'm done with it."

He was halfway down the walk to the street when she yelled after him, "Didn't I notice something in the background information you sent me that you had studied several languages?"

His stride only wavered a little. He smiled for just a second before he turned around and said, "Yes." He continued to walk backward down the sidewalk.

"Chinese wasn't one of them, was it?" she asked.

"I studied Chinese a little bit," he said.

"How much is a little bit?" she asked.

He couldn't resist. He turned around and picked up speed as he said, "Only six or seven years."

If Nora Ryan said anything to him, he didn't catch it. He was intent upon getting away from her, so much so that he took a course away from his car, which was parked in front of the museum. Nora could corral him if he headed toward it.

HIS EVENING WITH Pam Livingston was pleasant. The restaurant in her athletic club was just a shade nicer than most of the chain restaurants he had been in, and the food was no worse. The facilities of the club were adequate, including covered tennis courts, several racquetball courts, and an indoor/outdoor swimming pool.

They kept to themselves. She did not bother to introduce him to others in the club, including Chuck Owings, who waved from across the restaurant.

After dinner they had a drink and danced in the lounge to a live band that he considered to have a modest talent. Four hours after she picked him up, she delivered him to his doorstep. Two things about the evening surprised him. First of all, not once during the evening did the topic of the Bakers come up. And second, just before he got out of the car she leaned over and kissed him lightly on the lips.

He might have had pleasant dreams, reliving that kiss, but as soon as he entered the dining room, he thought for a moment they were not quite the way he had left them. Finally, he smiled to himself. He was becoming paranoid. First he thought he saw someone outside his window watching him, and now he thought someone had gone through his papers.

As satisfied as he might have been with the explanation, he had a restless sleep that night with no pleasant dreams.

ELEVEN

THE THELMA TITTLE School for Girls in San Francisco was located at the base of Knob Hill, high enough up for a view of the bay only slightly obstructed by the commercial buildings in the downtown area. The school building was a four-story Victorian manor that had once belonged to a family made wealthy by shipping and made poor by a typhoon that swept through Southeast Asia and sank the family fleet.

Nineteen prim and proper young ladies occupied the top two floors of the house, living together in relative peace since most were from wealthy families of good name who knew the importance of social graces. The twentieth girl occupied a small corner room by herself because she tended to be less concerned about social graces, and because she was suspected of doing the unthinkable.

None of the girls were quite sure what the unthinkable was. Girls of good families were protected from such thoughts by a society that tended to ban anything in print that might suggest the unthinkable. That, of course, did not keep the nineteen girls from spending a great deal of their time thinking about the unthinkable, whatever it was. The twentieth girl kept her thoughts to herself.

Kate Baker had been tempted on more than one occasion to straighten out the girls. Raised on a ranch where animals cared little about propriety, she had a pretty good idea of what the unthinkable was, but even she was impressed by the enormity of the effort to keep the subject secret. She could not bring herself to be the one to let the other girls in on it.

For good reason. At seventeen she still wasn't clear about the relationship between what the animals did in the farmyard and what people did in the bedroom. She did know that only a year before she had developed a new, disconcerting function of the body that no one could adequately explain to her, and that this function was absolutely disgusting to her because it sometimes interfered with her normal pursuits. But somehow she knew that this function, the barnyard, and the unthinkable were all tied together.

Her classmates suspected Kate of partaking in the unthinkable. Kate was innocent, but the fact that she took long walks each afternoon and sometimes disappeared down the drain pipe in the middle of the night was enough to make her suspect in their eyes. If they had bothered to ask, Kate would have been glad to tell them that she took a trolley each afternoon to a small college near the center of town and attended two medical classes that happened to interest her far more than the pedantic, boring, endlessly repetitious classes at the girls school that dealt with walking, talking, standing, sitting, eating, dressing, etc., etc., etc.

In the evenings, when she could get away undetected, she walked the streets of San Francisco, climbing the hills of the city, or trudging down to the docks to absorb the mysteries of the ships that landed there from all parts of the world.

She was not foolish. She knew enough about the unthinkable to know that a girl was not safe alone in San Francisco at night, so she took precautions. She bought trousers and boots, an old seaman's sweater, and a heavy coat with a high collar.

With some effort she could wrap a band of cotton around her chest to flatten the embarrassing bulge of her breasts and hide her female shape in baggy clothes. With her hair pinned up and hidden in a stocking cap and a hint of coal dust on her face to suggest a growth of beard, she could walk freely about the city after dark without being disturbed. She bought a pipe and stuffed it in one corner of her mouth, and after much observation on the docks, developed a sailor's shuffle that kept her leaning a little to port. No one guessed that she was a female, and if they did, she had that loaded derringer in her right pocket that she had taken from her father's desk drawer before she was sent to school.

If it were not for these two escapes, she didn't think she could survive another day in school. Even though Elizabeth had come through it with little apparent damage, and Emily seemed to be changed by the experience not at all, Kate was sure that she was going to turn into something porcelain that would forever have to be dressed and posed by other people. Even though she only had six more months to go, she wasn't sure she could make it.

Secretly, and it had to be a secret, she was proud of what she had accomplished. In the year and a half she had been in San Francisco, she had taken a number of courses in mathematics and science that were the first steps toward a position in medicine. She had every intention of becoming a doctor.

How she was going to accomplish this goal was still a mystery to her. Course work was no problem. Even some of the classes at the girls' school would help her to get into a medical school. No, the problem lay first with her mother and then with Emily, who now ran the ranch with the same kind of iron fist that their father had used. Because their mother's health was failing steadily, Mary had completely turned the reins of power over to the oldest, and now Emily made the family decisions. Even if Mary said it was a good idea for Kate to go to medical school, an unlikely thought at best, Emily was sure to put a stop to the idea. She controlled the purse strings of the ranch and could stop anything she didn't like, independently of her mother.

Kate's only hope was that she would come into some money of her own, and one day, after returning from one of her "long walks," there was an indication that maybe that could actually happen. Pinned to her bedroom door was a letter from Emily. As always the contents of the letter were brief and to the point:

Kathleen,
Mother's condition has worsened. I do not want to alarm you, but there is some question about an immediate recovery, if there is to be a recovery at all. I will not ask you to come home now, although I think it would be wise to realize that your stay at the school might be cut short. If that is the case, I doubt that you will have the opportunity to return to finish your classes. I hope you will not be too disappointed.

Yours truly,
Emily

Kate threw the letter onto her desk and bounced down on the bed. She suppressed a giggle, and then let it out anyway. She decided she should have her laughs now, before she went home. She wouldn't be disappointed to leave the school, and she doubted very much if her mother's condition was as serious as Emily suggested. Instead, she imagined that her older sister was itchy to get Kate back under her thumb again and this was a good excuse for doing just that.

A red-haired girl stuck her head in the doorway and asked, "Kate, could you help me? I stuck a needle in my finger while trying to sew on a button."

Kate climbed off the bed and took the offended finger in hand to give it a thorough examination. She led the girl to the wash basin on her dresser and cleaned the area around the small wound.

"You let that dry in the air, Sara," Kate said. She moved to her bed, stooped down and withdrew a bag from under it. She removed a small linen wrap from inside the bag which she used to put a bandage over the hole made by the pin. The end result was something small and neat that stopped the bleeding and comforted the victim.

"You're good at that," Sara said.

"Thank you, miss. Just as soon as I become a doctor, you can become one of my first patients."

Sara looked at her friend with her head tilted to one side, her pose suggestive of the perplexity she felt. "How can you say that?" she asked. She was fascinated by Kate's visions.

Kate sat on the bed. "That I'll be a doctor?" she asked.

Sara nodded. "Exactly. Women can't be doctors."

"Don't be silly," Kate said. "Women are doctors; there's just not enough of them for most people to know about."

Sara sat down next to Kate. She was one of the few girls who came to see this strange girl from Oregon. Sara was conscious of that, so much so that she usually left the door open behind her when she came into the room. Kate had an air of sophistication about her that was far beyond what was good for a young girl, and that scared Sara.

Sara shuddered. "Think what doctors have to do. The things they have to do—to men."

Kate laughed. "And just what is it they have to do to men?" she asked, delighted by the blush on Sara's face.

"Don't make fun of me," Sara said. "I couldn't imagine what they do to men."

Kate suppressed a laugh. It was her ability to poke fun at such things that had earned her the reputation she had. She was sure that an anatomy class would explain a lot to her. As it was, the information she possessed was only a little less vague than the information possessed by the rest of the girls.

"I'm not making fun of you," Kate assured Sara. "Did you ever think that a woman doctor might just serve only women?"

Sara had not considered that, and she was quick to admit it. "What a wonderful idea. The thought of having to see a man about my body has always terrified me. Seeing a woman wouldn't be so bad." She laughed. "Of course I'm not sure I know that much more about my own body than I do about a man's."

Kate couldn't admit the same. At first she justified it in the name of scientific discovery, the exploration of her body. But science could not account for the fact that certain parts of her body when touched in a certain way caused definite pleasure to be experienced.

Kate sighed. "And I have so much more to learn. I hate wasting my time in this awful school when I could be learning to do something that would be of use."

"Is that why you slip out at night?"

"Yes," Kate said. "And when are you going to go out with me at night? There's a whole world out there you haven't seen yet."

Sara flopped down on the bed, bouncing once or twice before settling on her back. "The idea knocks me off my feet," she said, laughing. She used the laughter to hide her fear. The idea of being caught slipping out terrified her.

"I may have to go home soon. This may be your last chance to go."

The laughter died in Sara's throat. Despite her fear, she really did want to go with Kate and share her adventure. "Okay," she said, "but promise we won't get caught."

Kate laughed. "Of course we won't get caught."

The five women who ran the school were no fools. They would make several checks on the girls before the night was out. Thelma Tittle had not established a reputation for such a fine and reliable school by letting her girls run wild while they were in her care. No, she guaranteed their innocence when they returned home.

Kate did not look so innocent at this moment. She had removed her dress and petticoats and replaced them with the dark gray pair of trousers and the black, high neck sweater. She had climbed beneath the covers to hide while the bed check was made, and then, when she was sure it was safe, she had climbed out, lit a small candle on her dresser, and proceded to shadow a beard on her face, pin up her hair, and darken and thicken her eyebrows with bootblack. With her black stocking cap pulled low on her brow and the collar of her sailor's jacket drawn up high on her neck, her disguise was complete. Darkness became her final friend, obscuring enough of her female characteristics to allow her to get by with her charade.

As soon as Sara squeezed into her room, Kate knew she was going to have a problem. Sara was no great beauty. In fact, her square features, pale complexion, and bright, red hair were not particularly appealing at this stage in her life. Too much awkward child untempered by cultured woman remained to give her much hope for great things. Unfortunately, those were just the characteristics that were almost impossible to disguise, even in men's clothing. Instead of looking like a man in her disguise, she looked like a younger girl. Her face was so pale that any attempt to suggest a beard looked absurd. Even the attempt to put bootblack on her eyebrows proved comic. The red stuck through the black that surrounded it.

Kate shook her head. "I think you're hopeless," she said. "I guess the best you can do is keep your head down and stay in my shadow any time we're around men."

Kate expected a total disaster. She was sure that Sara would be too afraid to crawl through the window to reach the drain pipe and ivy they would use to get to the ground. But to her surprise, Sara made it down without a slip or a squeal, although she was quite pale when her feet touched the earth.

Kate decided that their first adventure together should be a short one. She planned a simple trip to the downtown area. She enjoyed a walk down the streets now that they were cleared of debris from the recent earthquake and fire of 1906, and she found the skeletons of buildings yet to be rebuilt fascinating in the night sky and fog.

Sara chattered throughout the tour given to her by Kate. Instead of being afraid, as she expected to be, she found herself awed by the beauty around her. If there was one thing they shared in common, it was this appreciation of the artistic. The same things that appealed to Kate's sense of artistry also appealed to Sara's.

An hour later, Kate said, "I think we should go back to the school now. We don't want to over-do your first night out."

Sara would hear nothing of it. "No!" she said. "It has taken me this long to build up my courage; I don't want to ruin it now. I want to see the waterfront."

"The longer we stay out, the better chance we have of being caught," Kate warned. With two of them gone, she figured the risk of being caught had doubled.

"You've never been caught," Sara pointed out. "Besides, I stuffed my bags and clothes under the covers just like you do, and no one will be able to tell the difference between me and those things if they do a bed check."

Kate did not want to argue. She loved to visit the docks at night. "Okay," she said.

Kate planned a relatively safe tour. She took them down Market Street to Fisherman's Wharf where they would be just two more sailors wandering about at night. Kate had learned from her adventures that she must skirt Chinatown because that was dangerous even for men at night, and she must avoid the Latin Quarter on Russian and Telegraph Hills because she wasn't sure she could trust the colonies of Italians, French, Spanish, and Portuguese who lived there. Sometimes their feuding spilled over into the streets and anyone could get caught up in it.

The excitement of the evening seemed to fuel the spirit of adventure in Sara. The more she saw, the more she wanted to see. She said, "No one has paid the least attention to us. Let's keep going."

Kate said, "That's right, no one has paid the least attention to us." She kept the sarcasm from slipping out. Almost everyone had turned to stare at the funny looking man with the high-pitched voice, and more than one had pointed at them after they had passed.

Sara grabbed Kate's right arm in both her hands and pleaded, "Take me to the Barbary Coast."

The thought made the blood drain from Kate's face. North beach was one of those places she had put off limits to herself, not because she didn't want to see it, but because even she didn't have the courage to visit that one section of San Francisco that had a notorious reputation. Her first instinct was to say no. Later she wished she had.

"Only if you promise to keep your mouth shut," Kate said.

They needed only to follow the Embarcadero around Telegraph Hill, and they would walk through the heart of the Barbary Coast.

The girls were not allowed to walk here even during the daytime with chaperons because of the danger associated with this side of town. Kate found that peculiar, considering the short distance between Knob Hill and the waterfront. She often wondered if the value system of one class of people from the next could degenerate in such a short space.

Tales of horror that drifted up to the school from the Barbary Coast seemed to confirm that the degeneration did indeed take place. Hardly a day went by when another murder wasn't reported, or another sailor discovered missing, or more obscene behavior found behind another closed bar door.

They kept to the ocean side of the street and stayed out of the light. Although their journey was only to be a few short blocks before they worked their way back to Market Street, Kate felt a surge of panic halfway into the trip. There was much more noise and movement here than she had imagined. A steady stream of men wandered in the streets going from bar to bar, or from pier to bar and back. They found it more and more difficult to stay out of the way, sometimes being forced into the flow of traffic where they could be scrutinized easily by those who passed. Kate drew little attention because she was well practiced in the art of deception, but Sara kept drawing attention to herself either by her mannerisms or by the comments she'd make.

At one point Kate whispered, "If you don't shut up, I'm going to pull your tongue out of your mouth."

Sara snapped back, too loud again, "Did you see that horrible looking man in the doorway of the bar? He only had one leg and he was throwing up on the peg attached to the stump of the other."

Kate had seen the man, and she had caught a glimpse inside the bar, clearly seeing the bare breasts of a waitress as the woman crossed the room. Worse yet, she had even seen a hand reach out and squeeze one of the breasts. She decided that they must hurry on.

As they walked past a recessed doorway, a hand reached out and grabbed Sara by the arm. First Sara and then Kate, who had her other arm, was jerked to a halt.

A big man moved out of the shadows and smiled at them. "Can I buy you fellows a drink?" he asked.

To keep Sara from swooning and dropping to the ground, Kate

took a thick fold of flesh on her friend's arm and pinched it as hard as she could. Sara let out a yelp.

The big man looked down at the arm in his hand and then felt it up and down. He said, "Your friend is a scrawny one, isn't he? Has he been sick?"

"Very," Kate said, trying to make her voice deeper. She tried too hard and coughed several times. When she recovered, she said, "He has the plague."

"Jesus Christ!" the man exclaimed, pushing Sara away from him. "Get him off the Coast."

A number of people had taken an interest in the scene, far too many to make Kate comfortable. She grabbed Sara's arm again and dragged her across the street. She knew it was the wrong direction to be going, but there was little choice. They had to get out of the light and away from these people. She pulled Sara onto a pier and led her out over the ocean.

"Where are we going?" Sara asked, still so frightened that her words stuck in her throat.

"We're going out on a pier for awhile, until those men back there forget we exist. And then we're going to hurry back the way we came and get out of this part of town. I never imagined it would be like this."

"Like what?" Sara asked, now feeling terrorized.

"You're a pain, Sara," Kate said.

They turned right onto a smaller branch of the pier, away from the schooners and yawls that seemed to feed a steady stream of seamen into the town. Here the catboats, sloops, and cutters were tied up and few people passed them in the dark. They walked until they came to the end of the pier where a thin railing separated them from a drop into the black waters fifteen feet below. They leaned against the railing and looked back at the city. San Francisco was not the city of lights it had been since the earthquake. Much of Nob Hill still remained dark, as did the heart of Market Street.

Kate turned to Sara and said, "After the earthquake I wanted so much for the city to be the same again. But it's not. There's still a smell of fire, and the reconstruction has been very, very slow."

"What a time to be romantic," Sara said. "You want to wax poetic about lights of the city while we're trapped in the worst part of the town. Try thinking about getting us out of here.'' She pulled the cap from her head and shook out her hair.

"Don't take that off," Kate said. "What if someone sees you?"

The warning came too late. Two men emerged from the shadows. One of the men said in broken English, "Give money."

The smiles on the faces of the men showed white, white teeth. The dull shine of long knife blades could be seen in the dim light. Kate reached in her pocket and felt the cold steel of the little derringer. She pulled it out and pointed the gun at the men. Neither of them moved.

"Run fast," Kate whispered to Sara. "Don't stop until you get back to the house."

According to Mrs. Tittle, women were not meant to be brave. That was one lesson that Sara had learned well. She dashed past the two men.

Kate put her back against the railing and began to move along it toward the pier. Neither man moved. She had hoped that they would turn and run when they saw the gun, but they had not. They turned their bodies to follow her progress. She soon would reach a point where she would have to squeeze by them.

They came at her so quickly that she nearly did not have time to react. Like a fool, she had not bothered to cock the weapon. When she did finally cock it and point it again, the nearest man was only a foot away. She pulled the trigger.

The gun was small, the caliber light, and the noise it made no more than a pop. At first she thought nothing had happened; the man had stopped advancing toward her, a smile still on his face. It took her a moment to understand: there was a dark chip in the middle of the row of his white upper teeth; the man suddenly collapsed to the wooden deck.

The other man did not pause. He was on her in an instant. She threw up a hand and deflected the plunging knife as their bodies crashed to the pier. The knife stuck in the wood. The man sat on her with one hand held to her throat while he used the other to try to pull the knife free. It stuck fast.

The moment of terror had passed for Kate. While the man struggled with the knife, Kale calmly measured her options. She still held the gun in her hand, but it was useless. She would have to rotate the double barrel around to fire the second shot; she wasn't sure she could do that.

The sailor pulled his hand away from her throat so that he could use both hands to extract the knife from the wood. Kate reached her left hand around and twisted the barrel in that instant, simultaneously, the knife came out of the wood and lifted high overhead, and then the knife came down and the gun went off.

The bullet smashed into the man's heart and jerked his body about ever so slightly so that the knife blade sliced through the soft part of Kate's left shoulder instead of through her throat where it had been aimed.

The sailor collapsed and began to thrash about spasmodically. She threw him off and got up. The gun flew over the railing and Kate took off running as fast as she could, hoping beyond hope that the hot, sticky blood flowing down her arm would slow.

She pushed her way through the crowd as she ran along The Embarcadero, drawing attention to the strange-looking sailor who seemed to be fleeing from the direction of two small pops, recognized by the Barbary Coast regulars as gun shots. Few paid attention. Death was a big part of the people who lived on the north beach.

Kate did not stop running until she came to Fisherman's Wharf. There she slowed and quickly blended into a late-night crowd that still milled about on the streets. She went all the way down to Van Ness before turning left into the city center. There she walked slowly in the shadows and let the panic ebb from her body. It was replaced by the dull throb of pain in her shoulder. She slipped into a dark doorway and pulled back the coat from the wound so that she could see what damage had been done to her.

She probed the wound with her fingers, wincing in pain as she did so. The cut was deep, but not very long, because it had cut across the rounded hump of tissue on the outside of her shoulder. She had lost some blood. The heavy sweater she wore under her coat had absorbed most of it. The coat itself showed no signs of blood and none of it had trickled down to her fingers. She decided that the wound was not severe, and, once it was cleaned and properly bound, it would heal itself. She didn't want to explain to a doctor how she had received the cut, so she was determined to treat herself when she got back to her room.

The thought of her room brought to her a new set of worries. What had become of Sara? If the girl was still wandering about San Francisco, she could be in more danger. Kate would have to find her.

She pulled a handkerchief from her coat pocket, wadded it up, and stuffed it between the wound and the sweater. By pulling her coat tight across her chest and buttoning it, she could put pressure on the wound and stop the bleeding. She stepped out of the shadows just as a man and woman walked by. The couple was startled by her sudden presence, and they hurried down the street away from her. Kate walked on until she reached California Street and then she turned left again. She would reach the school from the back side.

When she saw the school she knew she was in trouble. All four stories of the house were ablaze with lights. She pulled off the stocking cap from her head and used it to wipe the blacking from her jaw and eyebrows. She pulled the pins from her hair and let it fall back to her shoulders. At least she would go in looking like a woman. She stuffed the hat in a pocket and walked up the steep set of stairs to the front porch. As soon as she reached the front door, it swung open and she stood face to face with Mrs. Tittle. The expression on the older woman's face was surprisingly calm.

Mrs. Tittle said, "Please come with me to my office. I certainly do not want the other girls to see you looking like that."

Once inside with the door closed, Mrs. Tittle pointed Kate to a chair while she took her position behind her desk. Kate was glad that the office was cool. She was afraid that if it had been stuffy in here she might have passed out.

Mrs. Tittle said, cautiously, "Sara has given us her version of this evening. Would you like to give us yours?"

Kate slumped in her chair. She didn't know where she should begin. Could this woman survive the truth? "It was a foolish thing to do, and entirely my fault. I made Sara go with me," she said. "The Embarcadero..."

Mrs. Tittle interrupted her quickly. "Perhaps I could refresh your memory if I told you Sara's story. Unlike yourself, she did not have the courage to return by way of the front gate. She climbed the ivy and returned to her room before we knew she was back." The woman paused and stared down at her hands. Finally she said, "I am having the ivy cut down tomorrow." Kate nodded her head in agreement.

The ivy would have to go. Mrs. Tittle continued, "Sara told us that she had worn a plain dress and you had worn seaman's clothes, and the two of you wandered around Fisherman's Wharf as a couple, for several hours. She said that she became nervous and left first. She did not know what became of you."

Sara had more grit than Kate imagined. She could obviously lie with conviction if she had to. Kate would not have given her that much credit. "I don't think she has told you the whole story," Kate said, ready now to face the consequences of her actions.

Mrs. Tittle would have none of it. She interrupted, saying, "She told me the only version of the story I want to hear. She will be punished severely, of course, but her reputation will be saved, and, with the time we have left with her, we will try to mold her back into the lady she should be."

Now Kate understood. "Hear no evil, see no evil," was Mrs. Tittle's motto. If she could put on blinders, she would. "What about me?" Katie asked.

Mrs. Tittle pulled open her desk drawer and removed a slip of paper from it. She placed it on the desk top. She said, "Your fate, it appears, seems to be tied up in many ways with this piece of paper. This telegram came for you this evening, the one I was delivering personally to your room when I found you gone. That, of course, led to a bed check, which led to the discovery of Sara's absence." She slid the paper across the desk toward Kate.

Kate stared at the yellow message folded over so she could not read the words. She was afraid to pick it up. "What does it say?" she asked.

Mrs. Tittle seemed to enjoy this moment. This was her only chance to take revenge against a recalcitrant child. "This message will change your life forever. I cannot say whether it will be for the good or the bad. I do know that it will save you from the humiliation and punishment that you have coming to you. I do believe, despite the bad news, it may be a life-saver for you, but I am not sure you deserve to be saved."

Kate reached over the desk and picked up the telegram, unfolding it so she could read it. The message was simple, as only Elizabeth could make it. It read: COME QUICKLY. MOTHER IS DYING.

"I offer my condolences," Mrs. Tittle said. "Of course you will

have to return home. Because of this illness and its possible consequences, you will not be able to return to the school, which is what
I will tell the others.''

"I'm sorry," Kate said. "I never wished to harm you or the
school.''

Mrs. Tittle remained calm. She leaned forward on her desk and
said, "A lady is expected to behave in a certain way in our society.
Always remember that this is a man's world, and you were not meant
to lead the way. If you learn that lesson, your life will be a happy
one. If you fail to learn it, your life will be a misery." With that she
got up and left the room. Kate got up slowly and walked to her room
by the back staircase. She would need time to dress her wound, to
clean up, and to pack.

THREE HUNDRED MILES to the north another decision was being made
that would effect Kate's life: Behind the closed, double doors that
opened into Mary Day Baker's bedroom the drama of death was
being played out to its last act to a small, but appreciative audience.
Emily paced majestically back and forth across the room at the end
of the bed, speaking boldly and defiantly to the gaunt figure propped
up by her halo of white pillows. Mary's body was failing her rapidly,
but her mind was still sharp, though there was little she could do to
avoid the assault of Emily's words, who was having her final say,
spilling out her final accumulation of bitterness.

She said, "The lawyer will be here in a few minutes and we'll
work out all the final changes in the will to the way I want them."
She stopped for a moment to measure Mary's reaction.

Mary shook her head slowly and whispered, "It's not fair."

"Fair!" Emily screamed. "Fair! Where was the fairness years ago
when Charles asked me to marry him? Where was it then?" she
demanded.

Mary closed her eyes, and said, "I explained."

"You can explain it to the devil," Emily said. "He'll have a great
laugh. At my expense."

"You can't do this to your sister," Mary said.

Emily dropped her hands to the footboard of the bed and leaned
her body against it. She seemed to collapse slightly, using the footboard to hold herself steady. "My sisters," she said softly but with

the same bitterness as before. "What have they done to deserve one inch of this land? What have they done? Elizabeth, despite your best efforts to educate her, is a simpleton. And your lovely daughter Kate should have been born a man. She has always wanted to wear pants and ride horses. Forget about them. Think of me. At one time I wanted nothing more than to be the wife of a simple country doctor and do nothing more than cook his meals and raise his children. But what did I get? I got a gigantic ranch to run that puts me in pants and on horses. I have to bury my nose in account books half the day. I have to ramrod reluctant men to get them to carry out my orders. Trained well to be a woman, you and this ranch have turned me into a man. Me, who wanted so little. I just wanted to be loved by one man completely and not have to share that love." She broke into tears.

Mary was too weak to reach out to her injured daughter, but her heart reached out to her. Tears rolled down her cheeks as she whispered, "I'm sorry. I should have sold the ranch when Silas died and given you your money when you came of age. I was being selfish. I did not want my world to change."

In despair, Emily waved her arms to encompass the room, the house, perhaps the whole valley. "This is all I have left now, and I'm not going to give it up. Father had a dream; I'm going to make his dream come true and you're going to help me."

"It's not fair to your sisters," Mary insisted again.

"You had a vision for all of us. You wanted us to be ladies, to marry well, and to live a Christian life. How are you going to insure that now that death is so near?" Emily demanded. "Like everything else you're going to defer that to me. But with you gone and the girls given their money, neither you nor I will have a hold on them. They can go off and live as they like, marry whatever riffraff their money will attract."

Mary thought of that and winced. She would like to hold on just a little longer—until she could shape all their lives. The cold she felt in her hands and feet told her she did not have that time. She might have just enough time to meet with a lawyer.

"What do you want?" Mary asked.

Emily was quick to answer. "I want everything left to me. I'll support the girls until they are married. Once married they must live on the ranch and continue to work the land as partners in order to share in the profits. If they choose to leave the ranch, they will lose all claim to it." She paused to see her mother's reaction. Mary had closed her eyes and was listening. "If I do not approve of their future husbands, they will not be able to live on the ranch, and they'll not have a claim to it."

Mary shook her head no. "That's too much," she said. "I'll not make them slaves to your bitterness."

"You promised me," Emily shouted.

Mary responded quietly. "I said I owed you. I do. But I don't owe you the souls of the other girls."

"You ruined my life," Emily said.

"And you continue to ruin it," Mary snapped back. She opened her eyes and spoke clearly. "They have been trained well, and I trust they will make good choices in marriage, but there is the ranch to think of. If they're to live on the ranch and share in the profits after marriage, I think it wise that you have the right to approve of their husbands. That means I'll sign the ranch over to you. But if they don't chose to live with you, Emily, I'm going to make arrangements for a yearly allowance so they don't have to. They'll not be bonded to you. I'll want them to continue to practice their religion. If you should die first, the property is to go to Kate. Those are my terms."

Emily considered what her mother had said. It did not give her absolute control over her sisters, but it was enough. In fact, it was more than she expected. "I can agree to that," she said.

Tears trickled down Mary's cheeks. "I'm sorry I'll not live to see the grandchildren, but I know there will be many. Eventually the ranch will have to be divided among them, but not until the three of you are gone. The Baker Ranch is to stay in the family. The property can be sold only under the gravest of circumstances, and only if our lawyer and the three of you agree."

Emily objected to that. It made some of her control dependent on the other girls. "I should be able to make those decisions alone," she said.

"No," Mary said.

Emily sensed that she could not win this point, so she tried for another that might work just as well to her advantage. "If either of the girls leaves the ranch unmarried, they should not be allowed to return.''

Mary stared at her daughter. There was a coldness in her eyes that suggested that love was a thing of the past for her oldest. ''The girls will always be welcomed back to the ranch. I'll not give you the means to drive them away. And as long as they're on the ranch, you'll support them to the same degree that they've been supported in the past. Now get the lawyer up here.''

Emily had to be satisfied for now. She knew that she hadn't gotten everything that she'd wanted, but she had gotten enough. Later she would find the loopholes in this agreement that would give her the control she wanted. She left the bedroom with a smile on her face.

THE TRAIN RIDE to southern Oregon was slow. The train crawled up the side of the mountains, hissing great clouds of steam as it managed the hump between Oregon and California. An hour later, when the train pulled into the station at Medford, Kate was exhausted. She had been unable to sleep.

The sight of Elizabeth was a muted shock, like another blow to a body already stunned by too many blows. The long black dress, the small hat with the black veil told it all. Kate had arrived home too late.

TWELVE

PAUL GOT UP early and moved to the dining room table and turned on the overhead light. He decided he would get some work done as long as he was awake. He was still in the process of translating Chin's diary. Progress was slow. He had to dust off the cobwebs from the Chinese he had stored in his brain where it had remained unused for several years. He had studied the language specifically to do research into the poetry of Ezra Pound. The combination of Chinese and Pound had served him well, each together making excellent subject matter for dozens of projects, term papers, and reports.

Pound's poetry and Chin's small, neat characters ordered in the diary of Chin were two different things. Pound wrote in the vernacular of the elite; Chin wrote from humbler origins. Pound spoke the metaphors written in the sky of Chinese mythology. Chin spoke a basic language of earth, a language bastardized by foreign exposure. It would take Paul some time before he learned Chin's language so that he could read her diary easily.

He learned from the diary that she had maintained a long-time sexual relationship with Silas Baker. She had not started the affair. He attacked and raped her one day when Chin had brought him his noon meal. The pattern had repeated itself again and again over the next two years. The physical relationship was constant, either in Silas' office, or occasionally at her cabin on the hillside. Sometimes Silas would slip out at night and go to Chin's cabin.

Chin seemed to accept this as the fate of a Chinese girl left behind in a foreign country. She had had little feeling for Silas Baker. She could do no more then live day by day, deeply dependent upon the small amount of money she made from her job with the Bakers. Silas gave her extra money, which she saved judiciously, but he never gave her enough to make a break from the family.

Once again Paul bent his head over the diary and began to read, keeping paper and pen handy to write down symbols that were confusing to him so that later he could go back and try to figure out their meanings through context. Several hours later this exercise was interrupted by the ringing of the front doorbell.

He did not consider his appearance until he opened the door and stood face to face with Pam Livingston. He had not shaved in two days; he wore an old green T-shirt with bleach stains down the front; his comfortable jeans hung on his hips without a belt to hold them up; he stood in the doorway in his bare feet. Pamela looked at him from head to feet and back to head again. She smiled.

"I think I should have called first," she said.

He swung the door open wide to let her in. As he shut the door behind her, he said, "Go fix coffee while I go fix me."

"I don't usually take orders from men," she said, walking into the living room.

He had already turned down the hallway to his bedroom before he answered. "Suit yourself," he said "I'm still going to fix some for me."

"Since you put it that way, of course I'll fix the coffee," she said.

He could hear Pam in the kitchen while he was in the bedroom looking for clean clothes. For a moment he felt a great sadness. He missed being with a woman. It wasn't just sex. He missed the hours of lying in bed with a woman, feeling her warm, smooth skin pressed against his. He missed the smells of a woman. He missed a woman's quirks. Most of all he missed the company.

He showered, shaved and made himself presentable in tan cords, a pin-striped shirt with a button-down collar, and a brown, V-neck sweater, too warm for the weather. He managed to ruffle the Ivy League look just a little by pushing up the sweater's sleeves. When he returned to the kitchen he found more than coffee waiting for him. Pam had rummaged through the refrigerator and cupboards and gathered together enough ingredients to make fresh biscuits to go with eggs and sausages.

"I didn't see any breakfast dishes, so I figured you hadn't eaten yet," she said, sounding apologetic.

"I didn't know that lawyers could cook," he said.

"Despite the fact that people think we live on whiskey and part of the take, we actually do eat," she said cheerfully.

He sat down in a chair near the computer and let her serve him. She put his plate down in front of him and hers across from him before returning to the kitchen to pour them both a cup of coffee. She came back and sat down.

"Why don't you get this computer off the table?" she asked. "You're not going to do much candlelight entertaining with all this junk here."

"I eat romantically by the glow of the flickering computer monitor. You don't know how that drives women wild," he said.

"A computer desk doesn't cost that much. I'll get you one if you like."

He glanced at her out of the corner of his eye. "That's very nice of you," he said. "How is it I rate so highly?"

She pushed back in her chair and met his eyes with hers. She held the stare for a second before she said, "I think it's time we talked about your wife."

"I think I've pretty much told you the basics about that," he said.

"No," she said. "You've left out some key information. You haven't said whether or not you love the woman, and you haven't said if you hope to get back together again."

He placed his fork on his plate and leaned back in his chair. Although he continued to stare across the table at Pam, he really did not see her. He looked beyond her, into some distance that still remained murky. He had spent so much of his time reacting to events, he had not had time to think about the future.

After some thought, he said, cautiously, "I don't know the answer to either one of those questions. Actually, I doubt if it matters what I think. My wife has been calling all the shots."

Pam nodded and smiled, as if she had expected an answer like that. "Are you angry?" she asked.

"Any man would be angry if his wife left him for another person," he said. "The fact that my wife left me for another woman only confuses the issue, but it doesn't change it."

They ate in silence for several minutes. Pam concentrated on her plate and whatever thoughts that had triggered this conversation. Paul was sure they would finish their breakfast in silence when Pam said suddenly, "I'm interested in you."

He waited for a moment for an explanation, but it didn't come. He was forced to ask, "What does that mean?"

"I'm courting you," she said, blushing slightly. "I'm not much fond of being bold, but you don't trust me farther than you can throw me, and you're so locked up in your own problems that you can't see beyond them.''

He nodded his head and slowly absorbed what she had said. When it was clear, he asked, a little incredulously, ''Why me?''

She smiled. For the first time he noticed a touch of shyness hidden behind her confidence. She said, ''You yourself seem to have fallen in love with Kate Baker just from a glance at a picture. I've had the pleasure of your company, as well as an impressive file of background information to sway my opinion. You're a handsome, intelligent, highly educated, and momentarily available man. A single woman who has yet to meet the man of her dreams is entitled to take an interested look, isn't she?'' Again she stared boldly into his eyes.

He laughed. That was the kind of honesty he admired in Kate Baker. ''What about Chuck Owings?'' he asked.

''Chuck Owings is a perfect example of why I'm interested in you,'' she said. ''A thirty-year-old professional woman who has never been married finds a limited number of romantic prospects in a town the size of Medford. We have men who are divorced, like Chuck, we have those who claim they'll get a divorce just as soon as you go to bed with them, and then we have those younger men who'd be happy to service an older woman. Forgive me if I show an interest in an intelligent, educated, and available man who rolls into town.''

He nodded, not knowing what else to do. He wasn't sure if he saw himself in the same light as she saw him. Handsomeness was in the eye of the beholder, intelligence nebulous. He had known brilliant men who could split atoms but not carry out a successful shopping trip to the grocery store. And he didn't know if he was free. He might be legally separated, but he certainly wasn't emotionally free.

She interrupted his thoughts, waving a fork at him as she said, ''But, I didn't come to talk about such things. I came to invite you to play racquetball with me this morning. If you beat me, I'll let you take me to lunch.''

He was glad the conversation had shifted. ''And if I don't beat you?'' he asked.

''You can still take me to lunch,'' she said.

''Do I get a minute to think about it?''

''Sure,'' she said. ''Oh, there's one more thing. This afternoon I'm

going to make my monthly inspection of the Baker house. I thought
you might like to come along.''

He finished the last of the food on his plate before he allowed
himself to answer. Only one answer was possible, but he didn't want
to appear to be too eager to give it. "I thought the Baker Estate was
closed to the public,'' he said.

"The estate is closed to the public. It's not closed to the law firm,
nor is it closed to any of the Baker relatives, nor is it closed to anyone
who takes an interest in the house from a historical stand point. I
assume the book you're writing on the Bakers is going to have something to say about the house—from an historical stand point, of
course," she said.

He did his best not to flinch, but he couldn't say for sure how he
reacted to her statement. As calmly as he could, he asked, "What
makes you think I'm writing a book about the Bakers?"

"I'm still keeping track of your research, but I know that any book
about the Bakers will fail because there is too much information that's
unavailable.''

He sipped his coffee. He understood that she had most of the cards,
even though she didn't know what they were. She had confidence
from past experience that she was going to thwart his efforts to write
this book. She could afford to humor him.

But, a tour of the Baker house was a tour of the Baker house. Of
course he would take it. He said, "I'm a lousy racquetball player.
I've never considered myself a great lover. I get excited about some
obscure thing written by mostly unknown writers. I haven't proved
to be very good at extended relationships, and I don't know what the
hell I'm going to do about my marriage. If you're really serious about
courting me, keep all those things in mind.''

"Sure," she said, smiling brightly. "Most of the men around here
think they're the world's greatest lover and have never read a book
by even a known writer. In fact, most of them think Hemingway is
an actress.''

He nodded. "Let's go play.''

"Good," she said. "I bought you a pair of sweats on the way
over here. We can stop at a store along the way and you can get
yourself some court shoes.''

He threw an arm over the back of his chair so he could face this woman. He still expected deception from her, but he let his guard down just a little. He would trade off a little deception for the pleasure of her company. A lonely man could afford to bargain.

She stared back at him and said, "I'm not as easy as you think. Our relationship will have to be set up in freshly poured concrete before you get me into your bed. Right now you're carrying a bucket of sand and I'm carrying a bucket of water. A few ingredients are missing, and we have a lot of mixing ahead of us before we can start talking about concrete."

He liked the metaphor. "Wouldn't it be a lot easier to buy a tube of super glue?" he asked.

"Come on, cowboy," she said. "If we're going to get this relationship on the move, we've got to get started."

She was a tough racquetball player, both coordinated and skilled. He could match her coordination, but she had him when it came to skill. Racquetball was not his game. He might have played a competitive game of tennis—ten years ago. He was satisfied with his effort, though. She didn't walk all over him. She worked hard for her wins.

He stayed with her until about the fourteenth point, and then she sucked down deep and went after him. He did the best he could. He dove for the ball. He used the back wall, the side walls, and the ceiling. He played close to the front wall and forced her into mistakes. He dropped a few lucky serves into the back corner where she couldn't dig them out. In the end, she still won. She won because he was a lazy English teacher turned full-time writer, who had never hefted a racket unless it furthered his career. When it came to a winning edge, he didn't have it. His shots fell a few inches short when he didn't have a few inches to spare.

She won five games straight, none by more than five points. He was dead tired by then. She showed signs of wear herself. They had mixed their first handful of sand and a ladle of water.

As they walked off the court, she draped an arm around his shoulder and leaned on him. Still breathing hard, she took a deep breath and said, "You play a mean game. I can't believe you haven't played this before."

He was aware of the heavy breathing, the breast pressed against his side. Something deep inside stirred, something that he thought might be dead. He said, "Games like this do little more than remind me that I'm getting older."

They both ducked down and walked out the tiny door in the back of the court. They stood in a hallway that led to the locker rooms. She leaned into him and kissed him lightly on the lips. He stepped back from her. She smiled at that and turned around, walking toward the women's locker room, twirling the racket from the cord she had attached to her wrist.

He leaned against the wall and watched her disappear, fighting the flame inside that flickered, that threatened to spark and run wild. In the locker room he showered and dressed. She was waiting for him in the clubhouse where they had agreed to have lunch together.

After the meal, she directed him to the freeway. He made the short hop to Central Point and then exited on Hanley Road. Instead of continuing to Jacksonville, she had him turn right about halfway there and drive toward the hills. He could see the big, white house between the trees occasionally, but for the most part the view was obscured. Only one spot on Hanley Road offered a good look at the house.

Time was bound to change everything. He remembered from his research that the trees that now blocked the view of the house were just saplings when Kathleen was born. Now they were full grown and clothed luxuriously in leaves that had the slightly wilted look of late summer. The trees dominated now, instead of the house. He wondered what Silas Baker would think of that.

The road rose up, climbing into the hills. He came to a stop where the road joined with one that ran through the hills, stretching toward the freeway in one direction and Jacksonville in the other. He turned left.

He had driven about three quarters of a mile down the road when Pam said, "Slow down or you'll miss the drive."

She wasn't kidding, either, he soon found out. The drive was little more than a dirt track cut through the thick forest that came up to the highway's edge. He eased his car from the road to the track, concerned that his vehicle might not survive what looked like a rough journey.

"Relax," Pam said. "There's an asphalt slab under all the fallen leaves and branches. We put the mulch there ourselves to discourage people from driving down here."

She was right. His car glided over the ground as he followed a winding route through the trees. He swung the car around a curve and slowed. High, cast-iron gates hung between square, thick, brick posts. A twelve foot fence made from iron bars spaced closely together disappeared in either direction from the gate.

"I think that's meant to discourage visitors," he said.

"There's a lot you can do to protect a monument when you've been left millions to spend on security," Pam said.

He stopped the car in front of the gates. He stared up at the formidable barrier before him. Each bar in the fence was in the shape of a spear, the head of it pointed toward the sky. The tips of the spears were sharp.

"Just exactly what is this a monument to?" he asked.

"Beats me," she said, opening the car door to get out. "The will simply said this house was to be maintained forever as a monument. You'll have to wait here while I go to the gate. A sophisticated electronic system has to be over-ridden or we'll have half the police in the valley up here."

A heavy-gauge steel box was attached to the right brick post. She used a key to open it and then punched in an elaborate code on a keyboard inside the box. He was too far away to make sense of the code she used, but he could see lights inside the box change color, first from red to green, and then from green to blue. She seemed satisfied with the blue and closed the box.

From there she walked to the gate, and, using another key to unlock it, opened it up. She motioned him to drive through. After she closed the gate, she rejoined him in the car.

"That's pretty elaborate," he said. "Has anyone ever broken in here?"

"Several people have tried," she said, "but no one has actually gotten in the house before the police arrived."

"What's so valuable inside the house that needs this kind of protection?" he asked, slipping the car back into gear and driving onto the grounds of the estate. The road was clear of debris once inside the fence.

Pam's face seemed to be transformed by the new setting. He noticed it around her eyes at first. No matter how broad her smile, the corners of her eyes were drawn down by tensions she couldn't hide.

Here, in the dark, hooded serenity of the tall firs mixed with the low scrub oak and laurel, she relaxed and her eyes smiled, too. She seemed more beautiful now to him, much more like Kate Baker than ever before.

She leaned her head against the back of the seat and turned to him. Suddenly a light came on in her eyes and she said, "You asked me a question, didn't you?"

He laughed. "Yes, I asked what was so valuable inside the house to warrant this kind of security."

"Surprisingly," she said, "not enough to risk getting caught trying to steal it. Silas Baker didn't invite many people into his inner world, so he put on a display for those on the outside looking in. He wanted them to see a giant house, huge barns, and fields and orchards that stretched as far as the eye could see. Inside the house the furnishings are comfortable, but they are now rather common antiques with no unusual value attached to them. I suppose if you could strip the house clean and sell everything for top dollar, you might make a hundred thousand out of it. A thief could expect probably twenty percent of that. Not much incentive to over-ride one of the most sophisticated security systems this state has ever seen, one that cost far more than the thief could get."

He had to agree with that. He doubted that twenty thousand dollars was worth jail and the small odds of not getting caught. He continued to drive, catching only a few glimpses of the house through the thick forest on the estate before he was suddenly upon it. He stopped the car under a carriage port that extended from the side of the house. The road continued around a circle to the left until it rejoined itself at the back of the house.

Pam pointed to her right and said, "This was the entry most often used by visitors." Steps climbed up to a covered porch. A bank of French doors opened into the house. "Behind the doors," she said, "is the formal dining room. The few visitors who came here ate in the dining room and were either entertained in the den or in the parlor, depending upon whether or not they were Silas or Mary's guests. The girls weren't allowed to have many guests when their parents were alive, and not much entertaining took place after their mother and father died."

He climbed out of the car and shut the door. He wasn't ready to go inside yet. He wanted to get back from the house and have a good look at it first.

"Do you mind if I walk around on the outside for a few minutes?" he asked.

"Not at all," she said. "We have time before I have to go. I want to go inside and open all the windows and doors and air out the place. That's one of the chores I take care of each month."

"Who'd suspect a lawyer's life to be so difficult," he joked.

"Some things about the job aren't glamorous," she said, climbing the steps to the porch.

He walked down the drive in front for about a hundred and fifty feet until it met a low fence similar to the one that surrounded the estate. He was surprised because he didn't see how this fence would offer much security. He walked toward it.

When he reached the fence he understood why it stood only four feet high. The face of the bluff on which the house sat had been carved away. A concrete retaining wall had been poured so that the house and yard now sat on a long, rectangular shelf with a forty foot drop straight down to the hillside below. The reason he had not noticed this from the road was that the concrete had been painted in earth tones to blend in with the surrounding hillside. He turned around and looked at the house.

He could see that its large size was in part illusion. The ornate overhangs typical of the Victorian period made the house appear to be larger than it was, much like the overhanging fenders and bumpers on cars in the 'fifties had made them seem huge by today's standards. That didn't mean that the Baker house was small, but it wasn't a mansion. Paul had seen houses similar to it in San Francisco, and he was sure that Baker had copied the design from there. The right front of the house was a tower that reached higher than any other part of the building. It was capped with a witch's hat turret. The front porch curved around the tower. The door at the top of the steps probably opened into the hallway where the tower more than likely contained a spiral staircase. At the other end of the porch another door opened into a room that Paul knew from his research was the parlor. Behind that was the dining room. The roof of the porch was supported by hand-carved posts and the railing was made of finely-turned spindles. Every eave, every arch, every piece of trim had complex, hand-carved designs on it, so much so that the house appeared to be overdone, almost gaudy. Arched windows spiraled up the tower on the outside.

The left side of the house stuck out beyond the porch. Tall, curved bay windows climbed to the second story. Again small pillars separated each window and intricately carved supports jutted out at the top to brace the roof above the bay.

The house was three stories tall, but the third was built into the eaves and rafters of the roofs, so that only small gabled windows appeared at the top. This was where Mable and Sylva lived out their lives when they were not working in the kitchen or cleaning the house.

As he walked back toward the house he counted the chimneys. He could see four. The parlor and the dining room shared one. Another ran up the left side of the house, near the front for the formal living room and the bedroom above it. The chimney in the back went with the kitchen. This was the one that connected to the fireplace in Kate's room.

The front door of the house opened and Pam stood in it. "What do you think?" she asked.

He stared at her without answering, transfixed by her beauty and by how much she looked like Kate Baker in this setting. Finally he said, "The house has been well-maintained. It looks new." He climbed the steps and joined her.

"It would take a million dollars to duplicate this place today. Up-keep alone would be unreal. I keep that in mind when I fantasize about living here."

A strand of hair had fallen across her face. He reached up and pushed it back. They were standing very close to each other, and he was aware of it. He said, trying to redirect his thoughts, "You really love it here, don't you?"

She looked into his eyes. She was not staring into them, but searching carefully to see what was there. The searching did not make him uncomfortable, but her nearness did.

"I guess I'm a Baker at heart," she said.

That was the wrong thing for her to say to him at that moment. He might have resisted his impulse if she had said anything else. He reached a hand behind her neck and pulled her face to his and kissed her lips. She didn't resist, and a pleasant fullness to her lips told him she was enjoying herself. He held the kiss a little longer than was decent. If she minded, she didn't say so after they separated.

Again her eyes searched his. "Romanticism and Victorianism go hand in hand," she said. "You can't stand on this porch without wanting to kiss someone and feel guilty about it."

He chuckled. "Sorry," he said, "but I refuse to feel guilty."

She took him by the hand and led him into the house. "I think we had best look at the house and not at each other," she said.

The house was elegantly designed inside. The rooms on the lower floor had twelve-foot ceilings and the rooms upstairs had nine foot ones. Most of the rooms had a fireplace. The ones on the lower floor were fronted with marble. The upper floor fireplaces were of brick. Each of the rooms, from the formal front room to the small parlor, had entries with double doors. The doors on the downstairs rooms were either handsomely carved or had inserts of stain glass or etched glass. The double doors on the upstairs bedrooms were plain in comparison. He stuck his head into the tiny alcove rooms on the third floor. They could not hold much more than a dresser and a bed, so he knew that the life of a servant for the Bakers had not been a grand one. Emily certainly wasn't one to let the help share the living room.

Three rooms drew him to them. The parlor was small, almost square. On the floor was a Persian carpet and on the one wall that did not have a door or window built into it, hung an oriental tapestry. A painted and lacquered Japanese screen was folded into one corner. A small fireplace, offset from the center, was on the same wall. A collection of chairs and a settee, copies of an early French design, filled the rest of the room. Only a small writing desk against one wall suggested the room was used for anything but conversation. A candled chandelier hung from the ceiling. It was much too intricate and ornate for the tiny room.

In the entry the curved staircase spiraled to the second floor and then, ironically he thought, continued its graceful climb to the maids' rooms. The twisting stairway did make the inside of the tower especially impressive, considering that the rest of the room was sided by decorative double doors and leaded glass windows.

The living room was depressing, he told Pam. She agreed. Dark panels of wood covered each wall, the only visual relief carved inserts in each square of wood. The floor was covered with a large parquet pattern. Carpeting helped to relieve some of the monotony of the room, as did a white ceiling and the white marble on the fireplace. Most of the furniture in the room was made of rich wood covered with dark velvet.

He liked the study. It was large and comfortable. The back wall and the end wall toward the center of the house were lined with bookshelves which contained an impressive collection of books. Again this was part of Silas' facade. Most of the books still had stiff pages and unbroken backs.

A huge, oak roll-top desk was located against one wall and next to it was the famous safe that Pam had mentioned. He pointed it out to her. "So this is it," he said. "The answer to all mysteries lies inside."

She walked up to the safe and patted it. The steel box was taller than Pam, and its double doors looked formidable despite the large combination dial on one side and the thick handles used to open them.

"I honestly don't know what lies behind those doors," she said. "The safe could be empty or it could be stuffed full of gold for all I know."

"And you're not the least bit curious to find out?" he asked.

"Not the way you are," she said.

She was making fun of him, he knew, but he let it go. "Why don't we blast this open and find out what's in it?"

She spun away from the safe and walked out the double doors. From the other room she shouted, "You're welcome to try. Just remember, I warned you about the security system."

"Yes you did," he said. While she was in another room, he stayed behind and wrote down the make of the safe and its serial number.

The last room of the three was his favorite. This was the one that belonged to Kate as a child, the one at the back of the house that now looked onto a full growth of trees that had not been there in her youth.

As he stood in the doorway of the bedroom, Pam explained to him, "Kate always remained in this room when she returned to live in the house. The other bedrooms are much nicer than this one, but it was her favorite. Elizabeth moved into her mother's bedroom, and Emily remained in her father's."

The room was simple enough. At one end was the fireplace that connected with the ovens in the kitchen below. At the other end was a queen-sized cherrywood bed, its headboard rising six feet to a top that was carved with Gothic swirls that were almost gargoyle-like. The bedstand, matching mirrored dresser, and chest of drawers were topped with marble. The wood frame around the mirror had the same carved gargoyles as the bed.

"I'm trying to feel her in this room, but I don't," he said.

"Aren't you ashamed of yourself for falling in love with her like that?" she asked. She was sitting in a winged-back chair by the fireplace, a peculiar smile on her face.

He breathed deeply of the room. It smelled of Pam Livingston. Or was he smelling Kate Baker? He smiled at the thought. Of Pam he asked, "Jealous?"

"Maybe a little," she said. "I'm here now, and she's long dead, but I still don't seem to be able to compete with her."

He shook his head. "You mean I won't quit trying to write about Kate, which means you lose out, right?"

"No, I mean I think you're in love with her, and I can't compete with that."

He smiled to himself, thinking about what she said. A little of it might be true, but not much. He was still a flesh and blood person. He said, "I don't have my love-life sorted out, yet." He walked from the room.

She caught up with him on the porch and took his hand. "Let me introduce you to your lady love. She sleeps over here."

An iron fence surrounded a square of ground in the far corner of the yard. Inside the square were five graves, each with matching headstones. The five Bakers lay in the square beneath the marble. He leaned against the fence and looked at the graves in silence.

Finally, Pam nudged him. "We have to go now." He nodded his head and followed her to the house to help her close it up again.

THIRTEEN

THE TWO OF THEM were a common sight on a warm summer day as they rocked together in unison on the boarded sidewalk in front of the doctor's office. For old Doc Hollingsworth these hours of relaxation were his reward for years of hard work and long hours serving the needs of the people of Jacksonville. For his companion, Kate Baker, these hours were another opportunity to pick the doctor's brain about medicine.

Since her return from San Francisco she had been his voluntary assistant, managing his office when he was on calls, taking care of minor emergencies herself, and always studying the medical books he had stacked in his office.

Kate was just what the doctor needed. Harry and young Charles had not done well in practice together. The boy wasn't content with a small town practice, preferring instead to seek out well-heeled patients in Medford or to spend his time at the college in Ashland teaching and lecturing. Two years before Charles had moved into a house of his own, set up a small office in it, and then opened a much larger office in Medford. Although he made himself available to patients several afternoons a week in Jacksonville, most people still preferred to come to Doc Hollingsworth instead.

Doc had fewer patients now. While Medford grew, Jacksonville continued to lose population. Harry Hollingsworth's practice began to shrink as well. He didn't mind. He was growing old and he needed more time for himself.

Kate needed as much time away from the ranch as she could get. Hampered by the terms of the will, she fought a battle with her sister over the control of their lives. Although the battle still continued, it was clear that Elizabeth had surrendered to Emily. She remained on the ranch, a prisoner of inaction. Kate plotted and planned. Now, in 1910, she was twenty and ready to become her own woman.

Harry leaned back in his rocking chair and closed his eyes. He was still a handsome man in his sixties. His deeply tanned skin contrasted nicely with his iron-gray hair. Although he was forced to wear glasses now, they seemed to illuminate his bright blue eyes and added an extra sparkle to them that suggested vitality. He was still an active man, but now he no longer had to prove his worth or that he was the last defense against disease. No, now he could lean back in a chair, relax and enjoy life. He was at peace with himself.

His companion was not. She was restless and eager to go despite her attachment to this old man and her love for this valley. She wanted more from life than what she had, and she felt she had a debt to pay. Still vivid in her mind after three years was the fact that she had once taken a life. Now she wanted to do something to save it. She felt the time was right to discuss that with Doc Hollingsworth.

She leaned back in her rocker and closed her eyes, saying as she did so, "I think it's time I made a change."

For years he had served Mary Baker well as a friend and advisor. He knew it was only a matter of time before he would fill the same roll for the girls. At least for Kate and Elizabeth. Emily sought no one's help.

"If it's nursing you want," he said, "my alma mater's a good one."

The chairs creaked for several seconds before the reply came. Although the words were measured, the emotion behind them still came through. Kate said, "I want to be a doctor." She held her breath.

Hollingsworth continued to rock in his chair for some time while he considered his response. He knew that the wrong word from him could crush a dream or fuel an unrealistic fantasy. When he finally spoke, with warmth and compassion, he made the truth a little less brutal. "I think you would make a marvelous doctor," he said. "You practically run my office now, and you know as much about medicine as I do. But, Kate, it's not time."

She knew what he was talking about. They had often discussed it. Society had taken the strong will of women that had been needed to conquer this wild country and broken it, turning females into helpless beings, good for little more than proper socializing and ornamental decoration. He had already been told by a dozen men in town that fresh Kate Baker had been given too much rein; she was beginning to forget she was a woman.

"I only have one life," she said. "I could waste it waiting for the right time."

He chuckled. When it came to logic, Kate had been given an extra dose. Only the truth would do for her. He kept his eyes closed and continued to rock as he said, "There's no room for women in medicine. Not many schools will teach them to be doctors and not enough patients will go to them to support the ones who are physicians."

Kate stopped her rocking and turned in her chair to look at the doctor. Despite the promise to herself to remain calm, she couldn't suppress the passion she felt. "Oh, Harry," she said, "I don't just want to be a doctor, I want to be a surgeon. I want to save people with my hands. I want to heal. If I stay here and continue to do what I'm doing, I'll suffocate."

Harry opened one eye and looked at her. He raised his eyebrow as he looked at the beautiful child next to him. Why someone as pretty as this would want to do something as messy as surgery was beyond him. But he knew what passion denied was, and he knew compassion. He said, "Well, I've been looking into that. Nothing to do with you, of course. I was thinking more about Charles. You know, wondering what it might have been like if he had thought of surgery." He was lying, of course. Charles was only interested in money now, not surgery.

Three years of working with this girl left few mysteries about her desires, even if she thought she'd hid them well. He knew what she wanted long ago. He had hoped this fire would burn itself out, but it hadn't. He continued, "Yes, if Charles were interested in surgery, he'd have had a lot of places to choose from. Now, if Charles had been a girl, he'd not have those choices. No, he'd have to get out of the country to do that."

"How far out of the country?" Kate asked.

Doc Hollingsworth opened both eyes now as he felt one of Kate's hands tighten around his forearm. "England will train a woman to be a doctor," he said, "but they're reluctant to give them a license to practice. No, the best place for you to become the kind of doctor you want to be is in France. There's a couple of medical schools in Paris that would serve the purpose."

She couldn't keep the excitement out of her voice. Both of her hands tugged at the doctor's arm. "Paris! How fine that sounds. I'd love to go to Paris."

He nodded his head, believing that he too would like to go to Paris if he were her age. "Well, that's a powerful dream, but a trip to Paris would take a lot of money. It would take you four years to become a doctor, licensed to do surgery, and then most countries wouldn't accept the license. First you'd have to pay for those years, and then you'd have to stay in France to earn a living, and, even though medicine is a universal language, you'd have to learn French."

Kate's enthusiasm did not waver. "If I had to worry about every step along the way, I'd never get out of bed in the morning to go to the kitchen. First I need to get myself to Paris, then I need to get into a medical school, and finally I'll worry about my future after that."

"Those are nice thoughts, Kate, but don't forget about Emily. She has other plans for you."

Kate jumped from the rocking chair. "Emily be hanged," she said. "I've worked around her for years, and I'll do it again." She leaned down and kissed the doctor on the forehead.

He watched her hop down from the sidewalk and run down the block. In a few minutes she'd be in her carriage rushing full tilt back to the ranch, afire with this new plan of hers. He hoped he hadn't said the wrong thing. He wanted to give her enough hope to get her through until the realization of the impossibility of her dream sank in. Maybe he'd given her too much hope. He closed his eyes and continued to rock.

AFTER TURNING OVER the buggy to one of the ranch hands, she walked from the barns up the road to the house. It was afternoon and she knew where to find Emily. Her sister retired to the parlor for tea at this time.

Without ceremony, Kate threw open the double doors of the parlor and strolled into the room. Since she would only have the satisfaction of this moment once, she wanted to make the most of it.

Emily, sitting on the sofa in the room, glanced up from her book only long enough to say, "Close the door—from the outside."

"Emily," Kate said, "I've come to say goodbye." She stood in front of her sister with her hands on her hips.

Emily carefully moved a cup and saucer from her lap to the table next to her chair. She then returned her hands to her lap and folded them there. "And just where is it you propose to go?" she asked.

Kate was disappointed. She had expected an explosion. No matter. If her first statement didn't get the desired reaction, her next one would. "I'm going to Europe to study to be a doctor," she said.

The expression on Emily's face changed slightly, but only enough to suggest a hint of a smirk. Emily said, "I thought Elizabeth was the only one in the Baker clan subject to silly dreams."

Kate strode into the room and took a seat across from her sister. She knew that Emily would bait her, but she wasn't going to respond to it. She answered calmly, "A woman has as much right to be a doctor as a man—more so, considering how few of us are doctors as compared to the number who are men."

Emily waved her hand as if to dismiss the whole topic of conversation. "Don't be a ninny and be misled by those female rabble-rousers. A woman's role is well-defined and it doesn't include doctoring."

Kate leaned forward in her chair to make her point. "But it does include managing a large ranch and running a business, doesn't it, Emily?"

Emily did not miss the implication. "Don't try do be clever with me. This position was thrust upon me by mother. I would just have soon been a married woman living a different life from this."

Kate had a difficult time imagining that. Emily seemed to take a great deal of pleasure from her role, especially when it came to bossing other people around, men and women alike. Married life would not have afforded her that pleasure.

"I don't think it really matters," Kate said, "what you think is a woman's role. I've saved enough money to get me to Europe and have an income guaranteed to me by mother's will. I shall not need your approval."

Emily smiled suddenly and said, "But you have my approval. I will make arrangements to send your yearly allowance wherever you want."

Kate leaned back in her chair and stared at her sister. This was not what she expected. Emily should be fighting her on this every step of the way. "You seem eager for me to go," Kate said.

"Pooh," Emily said. "Eager's not the word. I know you're not very happy on the ranch, and if this seems to satisfy you, so much the better."

Kate crossed her legs and folded her arms, taking time now to stare across the room at her sister. At twenty-eight, Emily was only slightly less beautiful than she was at eighteen. Time had done little to change the features of her face, except now a slight shadow ran down below her cheek bones. The shadow made her face look more mature without making her look older.

If her looks had not changed much in ten years, neither had her character. She was still a hard, unloving woman who saw her sisters as charges instead of flesh and blood relations.

She was not one to give up something or someone unless it benefited Emily to do so. Just exactly what was it, Kate wondered, that Emily would achieve if her youngest sister left? "Of course, I do worry about the operation of the ranch if I'm gone," Kate said. "You've left the financial management of it pretty much up to me over the last few years."

"I managed while you were in San Francisco; I will manage with you in Europe. I may hire someone to run the ranch for me, or I may pass that responsibility on to our lawyers. You're not indispensable," she said, smiling broadly.

The smile convinced Kate that Emily had something in mind. She decided that she had best do some checking before she left. Kate stood up. "I still have to write some letters and make some contacts," she said. "I don't imagine I will be leaving for a while."

Emily nodded her head "Please leave me alone," she said. "I wish to finish my tea in peace."

After Kate had shut the doors behind her, Emily remained immobile in her chair for some time boiling with two conflicting emotions. One had its core in fear, the fear of losing control of one of her sisters. The other was rooted in revenge. With Kate out of the way, she knew she had a chance to break the terms of the will and get rid of her sisters once and for all. She knew she'd never be happy until she had the ranch all to herself. Once she had that, she could plot its growth, figure a way to expand it, and continue her father's quest for dominance in the valley.

For Kate the next two weeks were a whirlwind. Doc Hollingsworth had expedited matters by going to Medford and sending a cable to the French counsel in San Francisco. A representative of the French government was able to confirm by return cable the existence of a small medical school in Paris that admitted foreign students, regardless of their gender. The next class was to form soon.

Kate delayed a confrontation with Elizabeth as long as she could. She was sure that the news of her departure would be a blow to Ellie. She was startled when Elizabeth's response was, "I think that's nice that you can get away," and put her nose back in the book she was reading while lying on her bed.

Kate stood in the bedroom doorway and stared at her sister for nearly a minute. Finally she said, "I don't think you heard me right. I'm going to be leaving for Europe in a few weeks to become a doctor."

Elizabeth marked the page she was reading and closed the book, placing it beside her on the bed. She was wearing a long, flowing dress, brightly colored, that clung to the curves of her body. When she rolled on her side on the bed, folds of material gathered around her.

She propped her head up on an arm and said, "I heard you just fine. I've always thought you'd be leaving on some fine adventure someday. Have you told Charles?" Charles Hollingsworth had taken a strong interest in Kate ever since she had returned from San Francisco.

Kate moved into the room and sat on the end of the bed. For a moment she felt like a little girl again, coming in to sit on her mother's bed for an evening visit. Elizabeth looked more like their mother than any of them, especially now, lying in bed.

"I was afraid you were going to be upset," Kate said.

"I will be upset," she said, smiling. "But not as upset as Charles will be."

Kate laughed. "Poor Charles. Twice burned. Next time he will know not to seek love at the Bakers."

The smile flickered briefly on Elizabeth's face. Kate did not notice the change. If she had, she might have learned something about her sister that would have surprised her; Elizabeth had become a marvelous actress over the years. She had learned to play the role of the dutiful sister, loving and generous, to display competence in the household, while all the time suppressing a burning, romantic passion seeking fulfillment. At the heart of that passion was Charles Hollingsworth, a man who had shown only a modest interest in her until Kate had returned from San Francisco.

"Yes," Elizabeth said. "Perhaps now he has learned his lesson." Yes, she thought, perhaps now he will know he was meant for me.

Kate put the fingers of her left hand on her cheek and shook her head. Poor Charles, she thought. He had wanted so often to propose and she wouldn't let him. Ever so patient, he thought he had enough time to wear her down. He'd be heartbroken. To change the subject, Kate said, "You can come and visit me. Wouldn't it be marvelous to stroll the streets of Paris arm in arm and see the sights? I shall miss you." She would, too. She loved Ellie.

Elizabeth wasn't listening. She was too busy dreaming what it would be like with Kate gone and Charles all to herself. He would have eyes for her then. He would want to be alone with her as he now wanted to be alone with Kate. He would see what a marvelous wife she would make for him.

Two days later when Kate stopped by Charles' office to tell him of her plans, again the reaction was not what she expected. Sitting in a chair behind his desk, he leaned back in it and roared with laughter. He made no attempt to control it until he was through, and then he sat upright in his chair and said, "That's the stupidest thing I've ever heard. What crazy notions has my father been putting in your head?"

Kate was indignant. She snapped back at him, "If it's a crazy notion, it's entirely one of my own."

Perhaps it was the thought of losing another Baker. For whatever reason, Charles Hollingsworth for the first time in their relationship made no effort to be a gentleman. He stood up and leaned over his desk and unloaded his feelings. "It's both crazy and stupid. No decent woman would think of crossing the Atlantic alone, even if it was to join a convent. No lady in her right mind would consider becoming a doctor. No God-fearing female would consider living on her own. You've sinned thrice in your thoughts, and I suggest you run along to church and beg for forgiveness."

Kate's mouth dropped open. She stammered out her reply. "I'm not talking about some dark dream I had," she said, "I'm talking about my immediate plans for the future."

Angry now, Charles slammed a fist on the desk top and shouted, "Bullshit! What you need is a good whipping and a few-months tethered in the kitchen. Your father did us all a disservice when he tried to turn you into a boy."

Kate had used her charm and beauty to get what she wanted from men, to work around their prejudices against women, and to serve her own needs. Because they deferred to her beauty, they never confronted her with their true feelings. Not until now. Now she was seeing what men truly felt about her. She was shocked. She too became angry. "Are you suggesting that I shouldn't become a doctor because I'll never be as good at it as a man? Is that what you're saying?"

"What I'm saying to you, Kate, is that there's no need for a woman in medicine. You can go off to Europe and waste your time becoming a doctor, but for no purpose. You'll starve to death before you'll have a practice that will pay your bills. Listen," he said, softening his stance, "you've already been trained to be a lady. Marry me and you can be a wife and a mother of my children. If it's medicine you want, my practice is growing and I can always use the services of a nurse. Throw out those silly notions of yours and do what God planned for you."

Kate drew her mouth into a tight line across her face, turned on her heels and stomped out of the office. Despite a dozen attempts on Charles' part, Kate refused to see him again before she left.

FOURTEEN

"MODERN TECHNOLOGY," Paul said to himself. "Wonderful inventions." With that he completed the phone connection through the modem in his computer to an educational information service that linked together library computer banks for most of the universities in California. For a modest fee and the price of a phone call, he had more information available to him than he could use in a thousand lifetimes.

This was the next step in his quest for information about both Hollingsworth and the Bakers. If this failed to pan out, he still had the Library of Congress and a similar information network for the East Coast schools.

When he was linked to the network, he typed in Harry Hollingsworth's name. Although most home computers and business computers displayed information on their screens almost instantaneously after the request for it was made, computer links like this could not do the same. It could take this massive computer several minutes to search each of its banks of information linked together by phone wire over thousands of miles.

Paul did not bother to read what was on the screen. He scrolled through it to find out its length, and then he sent it to the printer to have a hard copy made. He did not bother to store it on a disk because it was just as easy to boot it in through the modem as save it.

The information on Hollingsworth printed out eleven pages. Impressed by that, Paul typed in Kate Baker's name. He didn't expect much if anything on her. He was surprised two minutes later when the screen filled with information. He found himself staring at a research paper entitled, "Women Doctors During World War I." He fed the information into the printer. A half an hour later, nearly fifty pages of printer paper piled onto the floor in front of the coffee table. He was still folding the paper into a neat stack when his phone rang.

"Let's talk," Beth said.

He carried the phone with him into the kitchen to get a cup of coffee as he said to his wife, "Okay, let's talk."

She said, "I know I'm being selfish. I know that you don't understand. I know that I'm being unfair to you. But, if you still love me as you say you do, you must be patient. I need time out. I need to get my feelings in order."

Returning to the sofa, he stared down at the printed papers on the coffee table without really seeing them. "I'm not opposed to giving you time," he said. "We've known other couples who heeded that and it did their marriages a lot of good. On the other hand, I don't know of too many marriages that survived an affair very well."

"It's not an affair," she said.

"You mean there's no sex involved in this?"

"No," she said, cautiously. "I didn't say that."

"So there's sex and there's love, but it's not an affair," he said, fighting back the anger that was rising in him.

"Sex is not important. It's not a driving force like in an affair. I don't expect you to understand this, but I'm safe with Denise."

"Try to explain it to me. I'm going to need to understand if I'm to be patient about this."

"I'm not sure when it began," she said. "I've felt like I've been suffocating for years. I tried so hard to be the perfect mother and wife. I volunteered for work in the schools and in church. I kept a spotless house. I tried to meet your every whim. And then I got mad. The more I tried to please you, the more I felt cheated. This was my life I was wasting by serving your needs. What about my needs?"

He interrupted her to say, "That's when we decided it was time for you to finish your degree."

"I know, I know," she said. "You were really good about that. You watched the kids and did a lot of the chores around the house. But I got a little taste of freedom when I was out of the house and at school. Suddenly I was someone who was rewarded for good work with good grades, and who was respected for the opinions I held. I wasn't just 'mom' or 'dear,' I was someone worth something."

"God," he said, shaking his head, "you sound like we never appreciated a thing you did. Isn't it obvious that the boys and I love you? Isn't that good enough? What the hell can Denise do for you that we can't?"

"She doesn't put any pressure on me," she said.

"I don't understand," he said.

"She doesn't make any demands of me," she said.

"Oh," he said. He still didn't understand. How could two people live together and not make demands on each other? He asked, "Just what kind of commitment have you made to Denise?"

"I haven't made any commitment to her," she said.

"Isn't she afraid that you'll come back to me?" he asked.

"She understands the risks. She understands my need to be free right now," she said.

He leaned back on the sofa and put his feet on the coffee table. "It sounds to me like you really do want it all. You want Denise, you want the kids, and you want me waiting in the wings."

"I told you I was being selfish."

"Yeah," he said, "that's one thing you certainly have learned to be. Maybe you'd better tell me what it is you want so we both know what it is."

"I want to put my life in order," she said.

"That's fine for you, but it puts my life in disorder."

"Do what you have to do," she said.

"And you will do what you have to do?"

"Yes."

Without considering the implications, he blurted out, "I'm dating someone." He wanted to hurt her the way she was hurting him.

"Do what you have to do," she said and hung up the phone.

He put down the phone and picked up the computer print outs. The last thing he wanted to do was to think about Beth.

FIFTEEN

ELIZABETH GIGGLED. Deep in the shadows of the front porch she snuggled against Charles Hollingsworth's chest. She closed her eyes and let the warmth of his body spread over her, and then she felt a different kind of warmth inside flash-flood through her. She tilted her head back and waited for his lips to find hers. And then the front door opened.

"Elizabeth. Come in the house now. You'll catch your death of cold."

"How considerate of her," Charles whispered, the frustration he felt obvious in the sound of his voice.

Elizabeth found his lips and kissed him quickly. She anticipated the opening of the front door, as it had opened so many times before. Regardless of where they tried to hide from her, Emily seemed to know just the right moment when to spoil their intimacy.

"I have to go in now," she said, gently separating herself from Charles' arms.

"Can't you just once ignore her commands? She has no hold on you," he said, his frustration giving way to anger. Emily ran this courtship with a firm hand, worse than her father would have done it. The days of the week that they could see each other were set. Their hours together were limited. The time alone they were granted was almost non-existent. Elizabeth was nearly twenty-eight-years old, he himself already in his thirties, yet a proper courtship best suiting children was demanded of them. He knew Emily was behind the delay, perhaps as a way of getting even with him for some past sin, although he didn't have a clue what that might be. Emily, afterall, was the one who had dropped him.

Elizabeth put her hands on his chest and let them linger there for a moment. In truth, she was torn. Yes, she would like to stay there in the shadows with him uninterrupted by Emily's meddling. On the other hand, she was very much afraid of what might happen if she did stay. She turned and rushed to the front door.

"I have to go inside," she shouted, and then she slipped through the door and shut it behind her. She would like to have stood there with her back against the glass of the door, illuminated for Charles to see, hoping against hope that he would finally break down and rush after her. If only he would do that, she thought, scurrying up the stairs.

But, of course, he would not do that, and that was why Emily had so much power over them. Until Charles proposed marriage to Elizabeth, she had to remain in her sister's good graces. With Kate gone for so long she was left at Emily's mercy, and God knew she had little of that. No, she dared not make a false move or Emily would find a way to leave her homeless and penniless, despite what Kate might say. Elizabeth was sure of it.

She had just swung open the doors to her bedroom when she heard Emily's heavy footsteps on the stairs. She quickly shut her doors and hoped that Emily would pass by her room, but that was not to be the case. Her older sister rarely failed to stop by after an evening with Charles. She seemed to have a mission in life to deliver a threat each and every time Elizabeth saw the doctor.

The doors pushed open and Emily walked in. Elizabeth waited for her, seated on the end of her bed with her hands folded in her lap. To her surprise something landed in her lap next to her hands. It was a letter.

Elizabeth looked up at Emily and the question on her face was answered before she asked it out loud. "It's from Kathleen," Emily said.

Finally, after years, Elizabeth's mail was delivered to her unopened. Convinced that neither Kate nor Elizabeth was going to be a threat to her rule of the ranch, Emily no longer paid much attention to their activities. Evidently the only thing she considered to be a threat to her dominance of the estate was the relationship between Elizabeth and Charles.

"Well?" she asked.

Elizabeth shook her head no. Once again Charles had failed her. "No, he didn't ask me to marry him," she said.

Emily shook her head slowly, as if she were looking at something quite pathetic. "Why do you waste your time?" she asked.

"I'm not wasting my time," Elizabeth whispered. "You've chased away every other man. This is better than nothing."

"I knew you'd say something stupid like that," Emily said as she turned around and walked out the door, slamming it behind her. She dare not let herself say more than that.

Although she did not know it, Elizabeth did hold Emily's fate in her hands. If Elizabeth could finally manage to marry Charles Hollingsworth, Emily could wrest away another third of the estate for herself. Unlike the fortune hunters she had chased away, Charles was too much of a gentleman to marry for wealth. He would insist that he and Elizabeth live away from the ranch, even if that meant losing Elizabeth's share of it. Until that marriage took place, Emily was no closer to realizing her goal to have the whole pie than she had been when Kate left.

Elizabeth rolled over onto her stomach and tore open Kate's letter. Unlike the first two years she was gone, Kate rarely wrote now. Nearly four years away from the ranch had given her new friends and new interests. Satisfied that Emily would do no more harm than she normally did when Kate was present, she no longer worried about the fate of the middle sister. Elizabeth was a little hurt that her baby sister could so easily desert her.

She read the letter once, twice, and then she went back and read it again. Kate was so busy that she did not have time to write often, making her letters precious to Elizabeth. Often she thought these pages of neat, carefully formed words were her only contact with a sane world. She set the letter aside and rolled onto her back to think about what her sister had said. Once again her words were not comforting. Her letter read:

My dearest Ellie,

I know I promised you I would be home just as soon as I finished my schooling, but what good is it to have spent years becoming a doctor if I cannot practice my skill? In his letters Doctor Hollingsworth assures me that the valley is not ready for a woman doctor. Here, in the poorest parts of Paris, men, women and children alike beg me to make a visit. I am the only care they get.

I shall return to my lovely Oregon just as soon as I can, I promise you. No, I have not forgotten my sisters, nor have I forgotten my homeland. Although I have missed you dearly and have been homesick often, I know I have a great mission in life to carry out. As a doctor I can do so much good for so many.

I cannot give you a date for my return. True, I am not making much money from my efforts as a doctor, yet my allowance from home more than pays my way. Uneasy times in Europe have made their currencies unstable and ours worth much more. For that reason I actually live much better now than I did when I arrived.

I would love for you to come to stay with me. I doubt that Emily would miss you any more than she has missed me if you were to leave. I can't say the same for Charles, but the truth is that perhaps distance would make the heart grow fonder in his case. As it is, he doesn't seem to be inclined to change the relationship between the two of you, if I read your letters correctly. A trip to Paris might do you good, but I think you should consider that carefully. I am a very busy woman right now trying to establish a practice among the poor, while still studying surgery at the medical school. I wouldn't have much time for you, I'm afraid. Also, Europe is in turmoil at the moment and there are rumors of war.

It's all so silly. I'm not sure what it is about but all of these old, supposedly sophisticated and stable countries seem to delight in making the most absurd accusations against each other. One of the doctors at the medical school insists that it is all about money, as he says everything is about, and this will not end until one country takes what it can from another or gives up trying. Nonetheless, these could be dangerous times, and I don't encourage you to come for a visit. Still, I would love to see you.

You always were the great romantic, my sweet Ellie. This time your imagination far out-distances the truth. Although a fellow student or two may have shown an interest in me, as well as one or two doctors, I'm afraid I haven't been very cooperative. Although France has proven to be quite liberal and the medical school here in Paris has encouraged women students, the fact is a woman still has to work twice as hard to receive half of

*what a man receives. Many of our men graduates move into
lucrative practices after graduation. We women are left to serve
the poor, assist the faculty, or train nurses. Only a few women
doctors have made their mark in Europe and that's mostly in
the charities. I understand it's much worse in America.*

*I shall not give you any more advice about Emily. You've
proven yourself to be a survivor. I even suspect you probably
know how to handle her by now. As for your question about the
providence bestowed on her by mother, I can't answer that. I
don't know what hold Emily had on mother, any more than I
understand why she thinks it right that she have all at the expense of the rest of us. I suppose there are secrets there that we
don't want to know. Usually, secrets are far more important to
the people who hold them than they are to the people who are
excluded from them.*

*I must go now. It is after midnight and I have just returned
home after delivering a baby. The girl was stillborn and the
mother died shortly after the birth. Such is the fate of the poor,
and such is the fate of the woman doctor. The family I left behind
in grief now believes that mother and daughter would have lived
if a male doctor had been there, once again failing to realize
that their malnutrition, lack of cleanliness, and poverty are their
enemies and that a man would have not done any better. Tomorrow I have surgery in the morning and my rounds in the
afternoon, once again continuing my crusade against habits that
encourage disease.*

Write me. Your letters mean so much.

I love you,
Kate

Elizabeth rolled over on her stomach again and read through the
letter. "That's it," she said to herself. "My wonderful little sister had
the answer, as usual." She hopped off the bed and walked out of her
bedroom.

She paused outside of Emily's bedroom door. She hated entering
the room. In here Emily had become more and more like their mother,
at night dressing in a white silk nightgown and surrounding herself
in bed with white linen. Elizabeth knocked on the double doors.

"What do you want?" was the reply.

Elizabeth opened the door and walked a few steps into the room. She wouldn't walk all the way in because she had a fear, which she was sure was unreasonable, that she would never leave the room if she slipped too far into it.

"I've made up my mind," Elizabeth said. "I'm going to Europe to join Kate."

Emily paused only a second to think before she answered, "Good. The two of you are well-suited to each other. I'll pay your way over, give you some extra to settle in, and arrange for an allowance to be sent to you."

"Your generosity suggests you will be glad to see me go," Elizabeth said, feeling a little hurt despite the fact that there was little love between them.

"Of course I will miss you," Emily said, with little sincerity. Her eyes looked past Elizabeth to the door.

Elizabeth turned around to see what Emily was looking at. Margaret, the latest in a long line of servants, was standing in the doorway with a tray containing tea and a late snack. Margaret waited patiently in the doorway for the conversation to end.

Elizabeth turned back to Emily, realizing that their conversation had ended for the time being. She would like to send the servant away and continue their talk, but she knew Emily would never let that happen. For some reason beyond Elizabeth's understanding, Emily was especially nice to Margaret. That was out of character. After Kate left, Emily had hounded Chin unmercifully until she was found one day by her young daughter, hanging from the rafters in her tiny cabin, a victim of her own hand. A dozen other servants came and went, all quitting because of the harsh treatment they received from Emily. But not Margaret. From the beginning something was different about her. "Go away now," Emily said. "Go back to your room and don't disturb me again."

Ellie walked past Margaret and left the room. The servant smiled kindly to her as she walked by. As Elizabeth opened her own door she heard her sister's door shut and the lock turn. It would be several hours before it opened again and Margaret returned to her own room. In a way it disgusted Elizabeth that her sister could have a friendship with a servant when she couldn't even have one with her own sisters.

TWO NIGHTS LATER Elizabeth left Charles leaning against the railing of the porch while she walked down the steps and across the lawn to stand in the dark and stare at the lights of Medford. Poor Charles, she thought to herself. He had just been told that he was going to lose another Baker, that Elizabeth was going to join her sister in Paris.

Joining her, he put an arm around Elizabeth and drew her close to him. She could just make out the shape of his face, but not enough to give her a clue to his thoughts. The tension in his body suggested he had come to a decision. She held her breath.

"I want you to marry me," he said.

She let the breath out slowly. She had taken a risk to get him to say those words. The thought of traveling to Europe alone had been terrifying. The thought of staying there even worse. She did not know what she would have done if he hadn't asked her to marry him.

Suddenly she couldn't hold in the joy she felt. She pushed away from the startled Charles and rushed across the yard, screaming gleefully, "Emily, Emily!"

She was hurrying up the front steps when Emily opened the front door, saying, "What on earth?"

Elizabeth grabbed her sister and spun her around, laughing as she said, "Charles has asked me to be his wife." She jumped up and down, jostling Emily as she did.

Emily separated herself from her sister and stepped back. She was waiting for Charles with arms folded when he walked up the front steps. "Congratulations," she said, the words ice from her mouth.

He smiled. For the first time in his relationship with Emily, he felt a moment of triumph. Emily was obviously not happy that he had proposed, and he was delighted. "Thank you," he said.

The two of them stood face to face, their eyes locked. "This is a surprise," she said. "I was expecting to deliver Elizabeth to a boat, and now I'm to deliver her to a church. Fortunately I was already preparing myself to do without her."

Charles shook his head slowly side to side. "Dear, dear Emily, you won't have to do without her. I think it will be wonderful sharing the estate with you. We can use profits from the ranch to build our own house just next to yours."

Emily, the pale daughter of a pale, pale mother turned translucent. For a moment she even wavered a little unsteadily on her feet. She was not looking into the face of a man delighted to be betrothed. She was looking at the smirk of a man who was about to get revenge. She saw in Charles a challenge to her that neither of her sisters could mount. Already she was planning how to defeat it.

Charles saw in front of him a woman who was afraid, as well she might be. She had been sure she would drive off her sister one way or another. The last thing she expected from Elizabeth was resistance. And the last thing she had expected from Charles was vengeance. She had been manipulating for years and had taken control of the ranch and the Baker fortune away from her sisters. Well, if she could play that game, so could he. He would make those years of patience on his part pay off for him. He would get himself a Baker, then he would get the fortune, and then he would end up with half the valley. The people in the valley would admire him as they had never admired any man before.

SIXTEEN

PAUL HAD RUN UP an impressive phone bill trying to crack the Kohlier safe in the Baker house. Well, not exactly crack the safe. He had hoped to trace it through its serial number, find out who insured it, and then see if he could get an inventory of its contents. He knew it was far-fetched to think he would stumble across this kind of information in a computer bank, but he'd always believed "you never know what you'll find unless you look."

Unfortunately, his plan wasn't working very well. He had pursued a hundred different entries and had yet to follow one to Kohlier Safes. He was stymied. In frustration he typed into the computer, HELP, and pushed enter.

The computer responded with: *What can I do for you?*

He smiled. Many computers and programs had help modes. Most did not have such a casual response as this one did. He typed into the computer: I cannot find anything on Kohlier Safes.

The computer did not answer immediately. Hooked to a vast network of information, he would have to wait for an extensive search before he was fed a response. Paul expected to see an *"insufficient data"* message flash on the screen. Instead, a lengthy message appeared. It read: *Look under category San Francisco; sub-category business; sub-category manufacturing; sub-category history; subcategory suspended operations; sub-category safes; sub-category Kohlier.*

Simply retyping this message into the computer would not get the desired response. Instead, the process was laborious. First he punched in San Francisco. He was shown a long menu that he had to scroll up the screen to read. When he reached Business on one menu, he found a numerical code next to it.

He punched in the code and was shown another menu. He kept up this process until he reached Kohlier Safes.

Fifteen minutes later he had read all there was to read about Kohlier Safes. He knew the history of the business, the biography of the owners, and the date they stopped manufacturing safes. In this section was a menu of model numbers for the various safes manufactured by the company. Punching in the model number of the Baker safe, he was shown another menu. One of the choices on the menu was Serial Numbers.

Serial Numbers gave him the information he already had. He discovered that number 17834 was purchased by Silas J. Baker about the time that Kate Baker was born. He hit the Clear button and M at the same time, backing up to the menu. Nothing else on the menu showed much promise, except a category marked Codes, one that appeared on all of the menus he had seen. He punched that in to see what it was.

At first it did not look helpful. The screen filled with a series of file codes intended for computer operators who wished to add to the files already on record. He was familiar with all of them except one: Rec 10922. He stared at that for a long time. He wondered what that meant. He began returning to the menus, searching each to see if there was a category in any of them that said Rec. He didn't find it until the very last, after he had scrolled through a long menu listing items for San Francisco. He coded into Rec and waited to see what would happen.

Nothing happened. On the blank screen in front of him a cursor flashed. I'm back to where I began, he thought. He typed in Kohlier Safes. The screen showed a question mark. He typed in the number 10922. The screen flashed OK. He thought for a moment and then typed in again, Kohlier Safe. Again he got a question mark. Something played in the back of his mind. A five digit number preceded the information about Kohlier. Since he hadn't written it down, he had to go through the process of working his way back through the menus.

Ten minutes later he was staring at the "OK" on the screen. He typed in the new five-digit number and waited. Suddenly a list of numbers began to scroll up the screen. He had to hit the break button on his keyboard to stop the scrolling and to read the numbers. They made little sense to him.

The first group of numbers began with 01, and, when he let the list run through to the end, it stopped at 1267. After each of these numbers was a dash and a group of ten numbers.

He tapped the bottom of the table with his thumb and stared at the end of the list. He could feel his excitement building, but he dared not get his hopes up. In front of him, he was pretty sure, was the list of combinations for all Kohlier safes. Somebody had done a sloppy job of protecting them, but what could you expect in a computerized world run mostly now by kids under thirty? The last Kohlier safe was made in 1910, so who would expect these combinations to need much protection?

Again he sat and thought. He knew enough about computers to know that a logical mind was at work when this information was input. A logical approach would identify these codes for him.

He returned to the Kohlier menu. He decided to check the Serial Number category again, hitting the category for names because it came up first on the menu. Since the serial numbers listed the names of the owners of the machines, he figured that the names would lead him back to the serial number category. Instead, he was looking at an alphabetical listing of all the owners of the Kohlier Safes. On the left hand side of each name was a number, 01 through 1287. To the right of the name was another number, again 01 to 1287, only this time randomly assigned. Silas Baker, number 924, was also number 311. Five minutes later a return to Rec provided Paul with the combination to the Baker safe.

It shouldn't have been that easy, he thought, unless the programmer had intended it to be that way. More than likely whoever put this information into the computer had not envisioned a dedicated researcher with computer knowledge and a need to know a combination for a Kohlier safe entering the system, so he had not used a tough code to protect the combination.

He disconnected the modem and shut down the computer. He was just stuffing the paper with the combination in his shirt pocket when he heard Pam Livingston call out, "Anybody home?"

"Come on in," he shouted, as he quickly shuffled papers dealing with Hollingsworth on top of the ones about the Baker safe.

She was wearing a dark, three-piece suit. She also had her hair drawn back and was wearing glasses instead of her contacts. She had explained to him once that this was her courtroom wear, necessary because neither judges nor juries seemed to trust a female lawyer who looked too attractive. The more school-marmish she looked, the better chance she had of winning her cases.

"I have only a few minutes, but I thought I would stop by to see how things were going," she said as she walked into the dining room.

"Things are going fine," he said. He noted the phony lilt in his voice and shook his head.

"How's the book going?" she asked. She held his gaze.

He knew which book she was talking about. Trying not to give anything away, he asked, "How strong is your resolve?"

The smile remained but the eyes were puzzled. "How so?"

"I was just wondering," he said, "if you'd really like to know more about the Bakers if the information were to prove embarrassing for the family name. Then again, I wondered whether or not you even cared. After all, this is no more than a job for you."

She considered what he said before she answered, "I care some, but yes, it is mostly just a job."

"Then, say, if you could get into the Baker safe to see what was in it, you wouldn't really want to."

The smiled faded "No," she said, shaking her head. "I wouldn't. That's a funny thing to say."

"Like I said, I was just wondering."

"We would have a much better relationship if you did less wondering, especially when it's about the Bakers. Let me remind you that I can and will bring legal action against you if you continue to work on that book."

"I heard you the first time you said it," he responded, more sharply than he had intended.

She got up, a shadow crossing her face. "Sometimes I think the one thing that got us together might just be the thing to keep us apart."

He knew what she was talking about, so he didn't bother to answer. He was well aware that his "wondering" could lead to a choice between a relationship with Pam and a book about the Bakers.

The shadow that had drifted over her face disappeared, once again replaced by a smile. In the driveway, he grabbed her arm before she could open her car door and pulled her to him. The kiss was briefer than the last, but it seemed to reassure her.

"Thanks, I needed that," she said.

He nodded "It really was my pleasure," he said.

After she left, he returned to the house more confused now than he had been. He knew he could symbolically wad up the combination of the safe and throw it away, but that would be pointless because he could just as easily get it again. But he promised himself that he wouldn't try to use it. He still had more he could write, and then if the book came to an end, it came to an end. Right now he needed a woman in his life more than he needed the Baker book.

He walked back into the dining room and turned on the computer. Once again he began to write.

SEVENTEEN

"YOU FORGOT," she shouted, "there are many things I can do, including making a decision that you're not a suitable husband for Elizabeth, so don't tell me what I'm to do."

Charles smiled through the outburst. When Emily had finished her say, he calmly replied, "There's no reason for hysteria, Emily. We're not talking about taking the ranch away from you; we're talking about sharing the management of it. I've been over your mother's will quite thoroughly, and it doesn't say anything about you 'ruling' the ranch. You've been a marvelous manager of the ranch to date, but once Elizabeth and I are married we will be able to relieve you of some of that burden."

She was furious. She saw through his little ploy. He was out to grab control of the ranch away from her. "No," she said. "I'm not going to let you do that. I'll stop the marriage first."

Charles laughed at her. "Don't be pathetic, Emily," he said. "Your mother was no fool. She outlined quite clearly in the will cause for you to object to a marriage. Sorry, but I don't fit into that outline. I'm breaking your hold on this ranch and on your sister, and there's not a damned thing you can do about it."

Emily sputtered. She wanted to shout something that would deny that, but nothing came to mind. Basically Charles spoke the truth. Finally she said, "Well, we'll just see about that."

She whirled around and ran from the parlor. He could hear clearly her heavy footsteps as she stomped up the stairs. He smiled.

Emily waited for Margaret in the upstairs hallway. The oldest sister, the one so strong and unbending, rushed into the waiting arms of the servant and sobbed on her shoulder.

Margaret pulled the other woman to her and kissed her hair. "It's okay," she said, patting Emily on the back. "It's okay."

"But it's not okay," Emily cried. "He's going to take the ranch away from me."

"No, no, no," Margaret cooed comfortingly. "We won't let him do that. We'll stop him.'' She wrapped an arm around Emily's shoulder and led her to the bedroom. She shut the door behind them.

Elizabeth waited outside on the front porch, terrified by what was happening inside the house. Charles seemed to have changed overnight, one moment showing no interest in the estate and the next deciding that control of it was the most important thing in life. It was as if it had become a crusade with him. He was determined to knock Emily ''off her throne,'' as he put it.

Elizabeth was sure that no good could come of it. If she and Charles married, her husband and sister would wage constant war against each other. If the marriage did not go through, her sister would spring back at her, sure to take vengeance for the threat Charles had been to her power. She paced the porch, wringing her hands, and called out into the evening, ''Kathleen, where are you when I need you.''

NINE THOUSAND miles away, Kathleen Baker was leaning against a wall of the Hotel Claridge in Paris, crying softly to herself in the late night air. The last thing from her mind at that moment was Elizabeth. Instead she was mourning briefly a young English soldier who had just died in her arms, a victim of sepsis and an early casualty of the First World War.

She did not fully understand the events that had changed her life so dramatically. She knew that bitter feelings had been smoldering in Europe for a decade, and then suddenly it had all sprung into flames. England, France and Russia were at war with Germany, Austria-Hungary, and Turkey. When Dr. Elizabeth Garrett Anderson had organized a Women's Hospital Corps to serve both allies, Kate quickly joined. They moved into the newly built luxury hotel and turned it into a hospital. Casualties began to arrive within a short time.

Their first patients were not the most seriously wounded, but they were victims of something more insidious than bullets or bombs. They suffered from sepsis and tetanus, from gas gangrene and shock, and they died in incredible pain, and they died in incredible numbers. Kate's first significant experience as a doctor and a surgeon was marked by failure as patient after patient died. She was wise enough to know that no doctor could do a better job under the circumstances, but each death took another nick out of her heart.

She wiped her eyes on her sleeve and pulled out a handkerchief to blow her nose. When she was sure she had calmed herself, she walked back into the building. The patients who still had a chance to live must not see her cry.

She was met inside the hotel by Becky Muldoone, the best thing that could happen to a doctor. She was a competent, caring, and sympathetic nurse, absolutely loyal to Kate Baker. Given the chance to choose the doctor she wished to serve, she picked Kate. Her explanation was simple. She chose the best doctor in the hotel.

"Come on, honey," she said. "You've been on the floor twenty hours straight and your feet want a break. You take a nap and I'll wake you if you're needed."

Kate hugged Becky and rested her head on top of the nurse's head. Short, plump, and decidedly unattractive, Becky Muldoone had been given an over-sized, loving heart to make up for her physical failings. Men who wouldn't have given her a second look on the street fell passionately in love with her in the hospital because of her goodness. Becky accepted their admiration for what it was, a bi-product of war, and devoted herself to her only two passions in life. First, she wanted to be the best possible nurse she could be. And second, she wanted to find the best possible man she could—for Kate Baker.

Kate pushed away from Becky. "I really should take a look at my patients. If I'd been there sooner I might have saved the Dobbins boy."

"Don't be foolish, Kate dear," Becky said. "The boy was doomed the moment his stomach filled with shrapnel. You couldn't have done a thing for him and you know it. That you cared was all you could give him."

Kate nodded her head, aware once again that Becky's logic was often better than her own. "Okay," she said. "But make sure that I'm up by dawn."

Becky watched the doctor walk away and mumbled, "Ah, but dawn's such a short time away and my baby needs her sleep. She's going to take the bloom off the flower too soon if she's not careful."

While she stood in the lobby of the hotel, the front doors swung open and a tall, handsome man strolled in, especially impressive because of a long cape he had draped over his shoulder. Dr. Angelo

Ferrano always made it a point to check his patients on the way home from an engagement with his latest conquest.

"My gorgeous Nurse Muldoone," he said, "when am I going to have a consultation with your incredible Dr. Baker?"

Becky laughed. "Just as soon as you take me to bed, doctor. After that I'll gladly open the way for you to meet my doctor."

Angelo stopped and kissed Becky's hand. "I'll put you in my appointment book."

"My, my," Becky said. "You really must be desperate."

"Don't look at it that way, my rose bud. Think how beautiful your doctor is, and how I would need to prepare myself first to reach such dizzying heights."

"And we all know what you plan on doing once you get up there, don't we, doctor?" she said.

He laughed. "Follow me around," he said. "I can't get my nurse either in bed or out of it when I'd like to. If you're nice to me I might settle for second best and sweep you off your feet."

Becky might have felt insulted if the doctor wasn't so charming. No exciting man in her memory had ever rated her as high as second best before. She smiled and followed the doctor toward the stairs that led to the patients' rooms.

Nurse Muldoone did not have to sacrifice her body to protect Kate Baker from the Italian doctor. Within a few months it became clear that the hospital could not find enough fuel to heat the building during the winter. Dr. Garrett Anderson packed up her staff and moved it by train to Chateau Mauricien, a deserted villa at Wimereux. By that time the Italians had joined the allies and Dr. Ferrano was recalled to his native country.

The work was harder in the villa. Away from Paris fewer doctors attended to the wounded, but there were not fewer wounded. Kate and the other doctors worked eighteen hours a day without relief, every day. As always Becky Muldoone worked at Kate Baker's side.

One fine morning in early spring Kate sat on her bed in a small alcove room in the attic of the villa. The sun filtered in through a window at the end of a gable and surrounded her on the bed. For the first time in months she did not feel like bounding out of bed to see her patients. She was tired, so tired that she did not believe she could move from that spot.

She was sitting on the same spot when Becky stuck her head in the room to see what was wrong. "Bless me, Lord, is that my Kate Baker sitting in her bed clothes yet?" she said, bringing a hand to her chest and showing an expression of mock surprise on her pudgy face.

"I'm too tired to move," Kale said.

Becky came into the room and shut the door. "Then crawl back in bed and go to sleep," she said.

"I can't," Kate said, trying unsuccessfully to push herself from the bed. Instead of getting up, she lost her balance and ended up on her back.

"Your body's trying to tell you something, darling," Becky said. "You can't go at this pace forever. I want you to crawl back in bed and I'll cancel your duties for today. You've covered for enough doctors to give them time off that you need not feel guilty."

"It's not the doctors, it's the patients that make me feel guilty. I can't expect them to schedule their injuries around my day off."

"They'll have to," Becky said. "There'd be a lot more unfortunate patients if my doctor were to collapse and not be able to help anyone. You get back in bed."

She was too tired to argue anymore. She climbed back under the covers and was asleep as soon as her head hit the pillow. When she woke again, the sun still bathed her bed, but she felt more rested.

"I only needed a few minutes," she mumbled to herself. She threw back the covers and dropped her legs over the side of the bed. Her mind felt fresher, but her body seemed to ache more than it had. She wondered if she might not be coming down with something. Becky answered that for her a few minutes later when she stuck her head in the door again.

"She lives," the nurse said.

"Of course she lives," Kate answered. "In fact she only needed a few minutes of sleep and now she's ready to go back to work."

Becky laughed. "Of course that's all she needed. A few minutes—short of twenty-four hours."

Kate lifted her head from her hands and her mouth dropped open. "Twenty-four hours! I've been asleep that long?"

"You certainly have, dear. And you did very well. Tossed, turned, talked in your sleep, snored. I was very impressed. I always suspected you could sleep like the rest of us if you gave it a try.''

"What about my patients?" Katie wailed. "They'll think I've deserted them."

Becky shook her head. "Care waits for no special doctor," she said. "Those that needed it were happy to get care from whoever was there. Those that were well enough to think of something other than themselves were delighted that you took a break before a breakdown took you."

"Well, I've had my sleep, and now I can go back to work." She stood up slowly, stretching muscles stiff and sore from too much bed rest.

Becky came over and pushed her back down on the bed. "No you don't," she said. "I've arranged for you to take another day off, so there'll be no working for you today. Besides, it's gorgeous out and you need some sun."

"I can't leave my patients that long," Kate protested.

"You don't have a choice." Becky's tone changed. "I've been putting off telling you this, because I know what it'll mean, but I guess I've got to say it now. Dr. Anderson is turning over the hospital to the French and is returning to England. She has a chance to set up a five-hundred bed hospital in Bloomsbury, England. Of course she wants us all to go with her."

Kate sat upright, angry. "As what?" she demanded to know.

"As a doctor, of course," Becky said, and then lowered her voice to say, "if it can be arranged."

Kate stood up and put her hands on her hips. "If it can be arranged? Doctor Anderson knows she's one of the fortunate ones to be licensed to practice in England. She also knows I won't have a chance at it. The best I can be in England is a glorified nurse. I didn't work this long and hard to do that."

"Perhaps in your own country," Becky said, afraid of her own words. The last thing she wanted was to be separated from Kate.

"I'll have to face that someday," Kate said, "but I want years of experience behind me before I do. I won't give anyone an excuse to turn me down. Right now, though, Europe is the only place in which I can practice, and I'm not going to leave it."

"For the time being," Becky gently said, "you don't have a

choice. The French are treating us as a unit, and we all have to go together.''

Kate's anger quickly spent itself. She had already realized that a woman had few rights in a war zone. ''When are we to leave?'' she asked.

''We stopped taking patients today. As soon as they are treated and shipped out, we will go,'' Becky said.

Kate walked to the alcove and stared out the window. ''I'll have to think of something,'' she said.

Becky could not hold it in any longer. She blurted out, ''But we'll still be together at Bloomsbury.''

Kate turned and smiled. ''I hadn't planned to doctor without you, Muldoone,'' she said. ''I just need to figure where that's going to be.''

Becky looked relieved. Suddenly the expression on her face changed. ''Oh,'' she shouted. ''I forgot.'' She dug in her pocket and pulled out a letter. ''It's from your sister.'' After Kate had read the letter, she asked, ''Is it something serious?''

''Oh, quite,'' Kate laughed. ''Elizabeth is to marry soon.''

''Oh,'' Becky said, sounding disappointed. ''But you already knew that.''

''No, I knew she planned to marry, but in the Baker household plans tend to get changed by mysterious powers. To be honest,'' she said, ''I'm surprised these plans didn't get changed as well.''

AT THE BAKER RANCH Emily continued to maneuver the final pieces in place to see if she could alter Elizabeth's plans. She was adamant now. Charles Hollingsworth would not do as part of the family. He was too dangerous.

Charles, on the other hand, was finally relaxing his guard around Emily. At first when the engagement was announced, the two of them were in a constant clash of wills, but that gradually began to change. Emily seemed to have backed off from the battle and was now pleasant to him. Charles had been suspicious in the beginning. Now he accepted her treatment of him as natural. After all, he had been her first love, and she was bound to hold some hard feelings about that, especially now that he was about to marry her sister.

Late in April, while out on his rounds, he stopped by the ranch in the afternoon to see Elizabeth. He was met at the door by Margaret, the servant, who told him that Elizabeth had gone to Medford to do some shopping, but Emily was in her room and would be glad to see him. Put that way, he felt he could not excuse himself without stopping in to say hello to the oldest sister.

Margaret led him to the bedroom door and then discretely disappeared as he knocked. Emily told him to enter. He felt a little chill of anticipation as he turned the doorknob. He had not been in this bedroom since Mary Baker died. He was curious to know if Emily lived much as her mother had, as Elizabeth once suggested. Inside the room he was disappointed to discover that the similarities were not apparent.

Although Emily was stretched out on the bed, surrounded by white, and a fire glowed in the fireplace on this sunny but chilly day, the room was not at all oppressive as it once had been. The curtains on the windows were thrown open, and the room had been lightened additionally by the use of brighter colors. Emily had chosen peach and cream colors for the walls and carpet, and she had either removed or covered as much of the dark paneling in the room as she could.

Charles was so surprised by the change in the room that he was left speechless for a moment. Emily asked, "Is something wrong, Charles?"

"No, no," he said quickly and blushed. "It's just...well, it's just..."

Emily pushed herself into a sitting position with her back to the headboard of the bed and smiled. "What you mean to say," she said, "is that you expected my bedroom to be different. What was it you imagined?"

"I hadn't imagined anything," he said, defensively. "The last time I was in this room it belonged to your mother."

"Oh, yes, mother," Emily said. "She did keep the room dark, didn't she? I was tempted by that once. Something was comforting about this room when it was dark and warm, like it was a refuge from the cold realities of life. Mother was never very good with reality, but that wasn't a trait she passed on to all of us."

Charles ignored the implication of that statement. It was obvious that both Kate and Emily were the practical ones in the family, and

Elizabeth was the romantic, not a trait highly valued by the other sisters.

"I'm surprised to find you in bed," Charles said. "Are you not feeling well?" He felt more comfortable with Emily if he kept their conversations related to an area he understood.

She patted a spot next to her on the bed and said, "Please sit down. For a doctor who must spend a lot of time in women's bedrooms, you certainly look uncomfortable in mine."

He came over and sat down. "For many reasons," he said, "I find it difficult being impersonal about you, Emily. We do have a history together that I do not share with my other patients."

She smiled and said, "Yes, the future might have been different at one time. But it wasn't to be," she added. He thought she looked a little wistful.

For a moment the years disappeared and he felt again the desire he once had for Emily. He kept it in check, of course, because he was an honorable man, but the old question came back to nag him. The time seemed right to get an answer. Taking one of Emily's hands in his, he finally asked, "Why did you break off our relationship? I thought back then that we were very much in love and very much meant for each other."

She stared into his eyes for a moment before gently pulling her hand from his and sliding off the bed. She walked to one of the windows and stood with her back to him. He looked at her there and sucked in a sharp breath of air. The light from the window turned her nightgown transparent, and he could see the beautiful shape of her body. He felt like he should jump from the bed and run from the room, but the vision in the window mesmerized him so, he could do nothing more than sit and stare dumbly, waiting for her to answer.

Her voice was so tiny and so frail when she answered him, he could not believe it came from Emily. She said, "You don't know how much I loved you—how much I wanted you then. Or," she said, throwing her head back, "how many times since then I have wanted you."

"Why then?" he asked, both words sticking in his throat before he forced them out. She turned around in the light and his heart thundered in his chest.

She stared across the room at him for a long time, clearly struggling inside for the right words, for the right actions. "I can't tell you now," she said in a whisper. Then, suddenly she rushed to him and threw herself into his arms on the bed.

"Oh, Charles," she said, burying her head in his neck, "I know it's wrong, but I want you so much."

He was too startled to say anything, and too aware of the warm flesh pushing against his body, separated by only the sheerest of materials. The passion he felt moved to his throat and threatened to strangle him. A reasonable man might have been able to resist Emily, he thought, if one of her hands had not moved to the buttons on his vest and begun to undo them.

For all the passion that filled the room before he made love to her, the act itself was like wading upstream against a strong current. She seemed to fight him all the way, and then, when it was over, lay back with a satisfied smile on her face.

He was not sure if he was the first, but something wooden about the way she made love suggested that she had not done it before.

He dressed with his back to her, a little ashamed of himself. At first he felt the need to clarify, and then he was at a loss for words to do that. He said lamely the only thing he could, "I guess this changes things."

Emily's voice was flat and cold, nothing like it had been only moments before. If she were not still lying naked on the bed, he might have turned to look at her. "It certainly does," she said.

"We'll have to tell Elizabeth," he said.

"About this?" she asked. The way she said the words, she seemed to be mocking him. He turned to look at her.

Since he had never made love to a virgin before, he didn't know what to expect from one. He knew, though, that the hate he saw in Emily's eyes was not the right response.

He blushed. "Not this," he said. "We can't tell her about this. We'll have to tell her about us. I know it will hurt her, but she must know."

"You don't know how many ways you can hurt her, but you can rest easy about this. I have no intention of her knowing about us because there isn't going to be an 'us.'"

He was confused. Again he turned to look at her, and again he looked up those pale white, naked legs and beyond, and he stopped himself. Turning away, he said, "It is noble of you to protect your sister this way, but I can't possibly marry her now, not after what we've done. It's only right that we marry."

Emily's short, harsh laughter exploded from her lips. When she stopped, she said, "You fool. There's no Emily for you, and there's no Elizabeth for you, either. You're done with the Bakers." This time she laughed again, longer and harder.

He turned to stare at her. Slowly he was beginning to understand. She had done this deliberately to break up the marriage with Elizabeth. "You won't get away with this," he said. "I'll tell Elizabeth the truth: how you seduced me to come between us. She'll believe it because she knows how incredibly cruel you are."

Emily brought a hand to her face and squeezed her lips shut to stop the laughter. She twisted her head back and forth until she suppressed it. Finally, she said, "You still don't understand."

Angrily Charles shouted, "I certainly do understand!"

Emily sat up and pointed a finger at him, the smile gone as her lips curled on her face. "You stupid idiot," she screamed, "that son-of-a-bitch father of yours made love to my mother. The reason we didn't get married, brother, is because that's illegal in this state—as is incest."

His lips moved but nothing came out. The thought was too horrifying to believe, yet a message at the back of his brain said it was true. His father had spent too much time with Mary Baker for him to believe that they had a normal doctor/patient relationship.

She got up on her hands and knees, and like a dog about to attack, snapped at him, "He probably would have fathered us all if he'd gotten the chance, but Silas finally became suspicious. He made sure the servants never left them alone together for any length of time, and he took on the task of fathering his own children after that. Unfortunately, to the day she died, mother never was quite sure who Elizabeth's father was." She smiled wickedly and asked, "How does it feel to make love to your sister?"

Charles never had a chance to answer that question. Just then the bedroom door swung open and Kathleen Baker walked in. From the hallway Margaret explained weakly, "I tried to keep her out."

Kate stopped and put her hands on her hips. "My, my," she said, "I can't wait to hear the explanation for this."

EIGHTEEN

THE PHONE RANG. At this time of the evening, after ten, he was sure it would be Beth calling to ask about the boys. The phone was still on the dining room table next to the computer. He picked up the receiver.

"Hello."

"I thought we had an agreement," the voice snapped. "I haven't seen you for weeks, and I'm beginning to suspect that you're onto something."

He smiled. Nora Ryan would never be one to beat around the bush, he thought. "Hello, Nora," he said. "How have you been?"

"I've been neglected."

"I'm sorry," he said. "I don't have much to tell you. I'm still waiting for a translation of the Chin diary. Until I get that, I will continue to work on the Hollingsworth book."

He knew that lies didn't come much bigger than that. He had finished the Chin diary a week before, and, of course, he was still working on the Baker book, pausing to work on the Hollingsworth biography only when he dead-ended on the other. He hadn't had too many dead-ends lately. With the Chin diary, the information about Kate in Europe, and the Hollingsworth papers, he discovered that he had enough pieces of the puzzle to put together big chunks of the picture. Pieces of information that had seemed meaningless to him two weeks ago, now made the greatest of sense.

"Why don't I believe you?" Nora asked.

He was confident that she was fishing. She might be able to keep track of his movements in the valley, but she certainly would not know what kind of information he picked up on his computer through the information service.

"I wish I had something to hide, Nora. That would mean I'm a lot further along with my research than I am," he said. He found he enjoyed lying to Nora Ryan. He got the feeling that she hadn't been lied to enough in her life; that she had done most of the lying.

"I still don't believe you," she said.

She must figure that everyone works the way she does, he decided. He wanted to laugh but thought better of it. Instead, he wanted to sound contrite as he said, "Okay, okay, you caught me. I did come up with one thing."

A harsh laugh came from the other end of the line. "I knew it. You Easterners come in here and think you're dealing with a bunch of stupid hicks. What is it?"

He told her about the thesis that contained information concerning Kate's years in Europe. He finished with, "I'll bring you a copy tomorrow and let you look at it."

"You're damned right you will," she said. "I'll expect you first thing in the morning." The phone clicked as she hung up.

"Yes, and it's been nice talking to you, too, Nora. Feel free to call and accuse me of anything you like anytime you like." He laughed and hung up the phone.

He turned back to the computer. The amber letters on the screen stared back at him, waiting for him to add more to their legions. He had been putting the finishing touches on some background information about Mary Baker when he had been interrupted by Nora's call. He now typed in the rest of it and then reread what he had written.

What he had written so far answered some of the questions, but not all of them. He knew that Emily had turned to Margaret for love, yet that did not explain why the other two never overcame their unhappiness and found love and marriage. As he was considering that, the phone rang again.

"Hello," he said.

"Hello to you, too."

"This wouldn't be a gorgeous lawyer making an obscene phone call, would it?" he asked.

"You wish," Pam said. "Actually, I've got some good and bad news for you."

"It's late. Hit me with the good news first."

"I have to break our dinner date this weekend."

"You're kidding," he said. "If that's the good news, I can't wait for the bad."

"I'm sorry," she said, "but something has come up. I've got to go up to Diamond Lake for the weekend to meet with clients. They want to take care of their wills, work out a property agreement with a neighbor, and write up the terms of a lease. I'm going to be really busy or I'd ask you to go, but...let me sweeten the pot. It's suppose to be hot this weekend, which means the Baker house will need to be opened up. I was hoping you'd do that for me.''

It came as a wave of nausea, but he knew that it wasn't being driven by illness. She was offering a suicidal man a loaded gun, forcing him into a moment of truth. "I'm surprised you'd trust me to do that," he said, careful not to show the emotions he was feeling.

She laughed. "I made sure you didn't have any safe-cracking in your background.''

He tried again. "I thought you were trying to discourage me from this Baker research.''

"That didn't work," she said. "I decided the best thing was to let you keep digging until you ran out of information and then gave up.''

The numbers to the safe's combination were spinning in his head. He realized that if he refused to do this for her, she would want to know why. He wasn't sure he could provide an explanation that wouldn't make her suspicious. He decided that the only thing he could do was agree and then deal with the ethics of that later.

"Okay," he said. "I can do that.''

"Great," she said. "Listen, if you like, I'll notify the security people that you're going to be up there for the weekend. It's kind of nice under those trees when the weather turns hot.''

"Sure," he said. Why not? He asked himself. Why not make this a real test for him, one he couldn't possibly pass given a long weekend?

"Wonderful. Why don't you have lunch with me tomorrow, and we'll make plans?''

"That'll be fine," he said.

"I'll pick you up tomorrow, then.''

"Tomorrow," he said.

After he hung up the phone, he stared at it for a long time. Although he suspected it was guilt, he wondered why he felt that she knew about the combination to the safe; that she was setting this up as a test of his feelings for her? Since the beginning, despite the protests, it seemed as if Pam had been facilitating his research.

He managed to get some work done before the phone rang again. He was sure when he picked up the receiver that this call would be from Beth. He was right. She had gone two weeks without making contact with him. That was about her limit.

"I thought this would be you," he said.

She was silent. She had become cautious in this last year, thinking out each of her responses before she said them. That irritated him because it implied that the spontaneity that had existed between them for so many years had become a victim of the separation. Without that, he couldn't imagine them ever getting back together.

And then she answered. "I saw a lawyer today. She tells me I should be able to get the kids and a handsome settlement if we divorce."

"Really," he said. "You were unfaithful to me, whose only crime seems to be inattention, and you deserted me for another woman for an unnatural relationship, and now the court is going to reward you handsomely for doing that. If that's the case, I'm sorry I wasn't unfaithful to you, an alcoholic, and a brute. Then I might have been able to get it all for myself."

"You always manage to twist things to suit you," she said.

He lost patience. "If the only reason you called was to be abusive, then let's just hang up," he said.

"That's not why I called," she said quickly.

"Then what do you want?"

"I want to know more about the woman you said you were dating."

"If you remember the terms you insisted on in the legal separation," he said, "we are free to pursue other relationships without consequence should we decide to divorce. Even if Pam and I were having an intimate relationship, which we're not, it has nothing to do with you, and, you couldn't introduce it in a divorce proceeding, anyway."

"I wasn't thinking about that," she said, her phone receiver certainly covered with frost by now, he thought. "I was thinking about the boys. Should we divorce and you two marry, I want some indication of the kind of mother she would be to the boys."

"Well," he said, "she won't expose them to any kinky relationships." He was sorry as soon as he said it, even more so when he heard Beth's soft sobs on the other end of the line.

"God damn you," she said. "Don't twist the knife. I know this is not natural, and I'd stop it if I could do anything about it, but you must understand some people feel this way, and they can't do anything about it."

"I know that," he said. "I'm just not convinced you're one of them. If I were, we'd be divorced by now."

"Then why can't you convince me?" she asked, the tears still in her voice. "No matter how I look at it, I keep coming back to one thing. I love Denise."

"Then let's call it quits," he said.

"No," she snapped. "No," she said more softly. "Please, not yet. I need more time." The anger dissolved inside of him. It always did. Another emotion was bigger than his anger, his hurt, his disgust. He still loved the woman, and he hadn't yet found the switch to turn that off.

"Are you in love with Pam?" she asked.

"No," he said. "Not yet."

"Then please wait." Again there was that long pause. "I still love you," she said. "I never stopped loving you. I just needed a love that didn't hurt so much."

The tears started running down his cheeks, and he had to fight to keep his voice from cracking as he said, "I have to go now. I'll call you in a couple of days." He hung up the phone.

The next day he and Pam worked out the details for the weekend over lunch. After they had finished eating, he mentioned Beth's phone call. "She seems to be concerned about our relationship," he said.

Pam laughed. "She's not the only one. I get the feeling that no one owns a chunk of you at the moment."

"You don't own people," he said. "If I've learned anything this year, I've learned that. No, you have a tenuous lease on their emotions and that's it. Fail to nurture that and you end up with a broken lease."

"Prosaic," she said. "How do you get one of those leases?"

He reached over and pushed back the hair on her face and stroked a cheek with one finger. "You're a terrific person, Pam," he said. "If I haven't fallen all over myself for a chance to touch your feet, it's because I'm emotionally traumatized at the moment. But I'm beginning to get over it, so let me warn you that you may no longer be safe in my company.''

She said little as she drove him home. After she had parked at the back of the house, she turned off the ignition and leaned over and kissed him on the lips. When she pulled away from him, she said, "Are you ready for some trauma treatment? I've got the rest of the afternoon free.''

"What does trauma treatment include?" he asked, already aware of and afraid of the answer.

"I want to make love to you," she said.

Naked, she was more beautiful than he could believe. She was lithe like a fashion model, only her body was more sinuously rounded and full, built more to please the eye of a man than the eye of a woman. The sight of her hovering over the end of his bed without her clothes was too much for him. Something snapped inside of him. He meant to be slow and gentle with her, but the passion took over as if the long months of celibacy had stored up a power he could not control. He made love to her once, and then without pause, he made love to her a second and a third time. He might have made love again if she hadn't whispered to him breathlessly, "If you don't stop, I think I'll explode.''

NINETEEN

IN THE END, there was no explanation for the obvious. The expression on Charles' face had been an answer in itself. For once, Emily could not hide the naked truth, so to speak. Kate laughed at her own pun, but there was no humor behind the laughter. Becky Muldoone, sitting to Kate's right, looked at her quizzically, but knew enough not to ask any questions. Kate rarely spoke of her family, and, since her return from a visit to the states, did not speak of them at all, although she was sure they occupied Kate's thoughts.

Kate and Becky had been traveling for nearly a week. They had left Paris at the end of April, less than a week after Kate had returned from America, to cross France and Italy by train. Near the boot heel of Italy they would catch a ferry to take them to Albania, and from there they would reach Northern Serbia by any means they could. Upon her return, Kate had volunteered to help Doctor Elsie Inglis set up three military hospitals to treat the wounded and to fight an outbreak of plague that infested the area.

Kate needed the challenge at the other end of the trip to erase the memory of her brief visit home. How perfect it had been to catch Emily in the act of deception: How tragically painful it had been for Elizabeth, who still did not know what had transpired. Kate still did not know if she had done the right thing or not, but at that moment it had seemed the right thing to do. She rested her head on the back of the coach seat and remembered.

"I don't owe you an explanation!" Emily had screamed at her. "Now get out of here and shut the door behind you."

Kate stood her ground. "Charles," she asked, "would you like to explain this?"

He blushed a deep red. No words could have compromised him as much as the look of shame did. He shook his head no and mumbled, "I think this is fairly obvious."

Kate let out what sounded like a laugh, but in reality it was a noise created by the collision of disgust and pain. "I thought I was coming home to a wedding between Charles and Elizabeth. I see I'm mistaken."

Emily calmly got up from the bed and strolled around the room, still naked, looking for her night gown to put on. When she found it in a corner, she picked it up and slipped it on before coming back to face Kate. She looked her younger sister in the eyes as she said, "Charles will not marry into this family." The triumph in her voice vas unmistakable.

"I thought it was the ranch you wanted," Kate said. "I didn't think you were out to destroy everyone's happiness while you were at it."

Emily's hand shot up and smacked across Kate's right cheek. "You'll not talk to me like that," she said.

Kate smiled, a message glowing in her eyes that Emily read too late. Kate balled her right hand into a fist and swung it around in an arc. Although Emily tried to move out of the way, the fist still managed to catch her just under the left eye, toppling her over backward onto the bed. "And you'll not strike me again," Kate said.

Charles Hollingsworth was horrified. Not only had he let himself be compromised, not only had he cheated himself out of what would have been a perfectly good marriage, he now found himself in the middle of a mess that might spill out into the community and destroy his reputation. He hurried from the room.

Emily sat on the edge of the bed, a hand cupped under her chin. A trickle of blood from her nose ran into the palm of her hand. "How dare you," she said.

Kate felt someone close by. She whirled around to face Margaret, who appeared ready to grab her from behind. Face to face with Kate, the servant backed off. "And this must be Margaret. Sweet, innocent Elizabeth has written all about you. I wonder if she has the slightest idea of what her description portrays?"

Emily jumped to her feet. "I don't suggest you pursue that if you know what's good for you," she said.

The two women standing together were intimidating. Kate backed from the room, the suspicions raised by the letters confirmed as she saw the two side by side. Years in Paris had taught her much about the kinds of relationships formed by people as they tried to meet their needs.

"Elizabeth has to be told," Kate said.

Emily seemed to pale. "No," she said. "Leave it to Charles to make the break with her. Whatever he tells her is all she needs to know."

In the hall Kate stood her ground. "And what is it she needs to know? What was it that possessed you to do this?"

"This was the only thing I could do to protect Elizabeth," Emily said. Lying was the one thing she did well, and she knew it. Even her sisters had trouble catching her in a lie. "Charles wasn't interested in her; he was just interested in her money."

That was where it stood. The truth was entangled somewhere in the lies, but Kate could still not tell when Emily was lying so she had no hope of finding out what motivated her sister to seduce Charles. Whatever it was did not seem to alter the relationship between Emily and Margaret, which suggested to Kate that there was a conspiracy much deeper than she could imagine.

Kate stared out the window of the train and watched the countryside flash by. She would like to forget Elizabeth's devastation, coming so soon after the delight of finding that her younger sister had returned home. Charles, so quick to leave, also proved quick to tie up loose ends. As Kate and Elizabeth embraced on the front porch of the house, Charles gunned his motor car back up the driveway.

Kate would remembered the moment for the rest of her life, as she remembered many like it when disaster seemed to unfold before her eyes while she could do nothing about it. Elizabeth danced around the porch, squealing that Kate had come back for the wedding, and Charles slowly climbed the steps with that look of defeat stamped on his face.

He stopped in front of Elizabeth and waited for her to quiet before he said, "I know you'll never understand this completely, and maybe that's the best, but I can't go through with the marriage."

Elizabeth stood still, half a smile frozen on her face as she searched Charles' eyes for the joke he must be playing on her. When she could not find it, she asked, "Why are you saying that?"

Charles misread her question. He thought she wanted an explanation. "I do not wish to spend the rest of my life bound by Emily's whims. Although we might be husband and wife, Emily always would be our mistress. I can't live that way."

The half smile slid from Elizabeth's face as his words began to sink in. This was no joke. Emily had somehow found a way to ruin this for her. "But you love me," she stammered

To his credit, Charles looked absolutely miserable. "I'm afraid that's become the least significant element in all of this."

"Charles," she said, reaching out to him. "You can't mean this."

"I'm sorry," he said. He turned and walked down the steps of the porch, neither lifting his eyes from the ground until he reached his auto, nor looking back as he drove away.

Elizabeth was frozen in her pose, one hand still reaching out for the man who was now disappearing from view down the road. Although tears rolled down her cheeks, she did not sob.

Kate gathered her sister in her arms and hugged Elizabeth tightly. They stood that way for several minutes. Elizabeth pushed away from Kate and wiped her tears on the sleeve of her dress. Calmer than Kate would have expected her to be, she said, "I knew she'd ruin it for me. I'm surprised she let it get this far before she stopped it."

Kate Baker didn't think she had much romantic notion left in her after her years in medical school and the months she had spent treating the wounded of war, but she knew she was wrong at that moment. She wanted Elizabeth to get angry; she wanted her to cry, scream and carry on; she wanted her to fight back. But Elizabeth would not do these things. These were only the romantic actions that Kate imagined for her. In truth Elizabeth was incapable of such things. In reality Elizabeth was always one to be led, and one to accept it as her fate when she was led astray.

Kate did not stay long after that. To be on the ranch was to be at war with Emily. Convinced that Emily was no more or no less dangerous than before, and that Elizabeth was no more or no less in danger than she had been, Kate packed her bags and returned to Europe. She had invited Elizabeth to go with her, but the middle sister declined the offer. With remarkable clarity, she explained that as long as she was on the ranch, she was a wealthy woman, and perhaps that fact would finally tempt a man who was strong enough to buck Emily.

Becky Muldoone interrupted Kate's thoughts. "I can't swear on it," she said, "but I'd say that was an ocean I just saw."

"I hope so," Kate said. "I'm anxious to get back to work."

A week later Kate was back to work in a military hospital overflowing with Serbian wounded and a plague epidemic.

Man, woman, doctor, nurse: there were no differences here. When Kate was not in surgery, she was attending the patients, giving baths and emptying bed pans. In the operating room she was just another surgeon behind the mask she wore. When there was a moment when neither surgery nor patients called, Kate was on her hands and knees, scrubbing the hospital from one end to the other with the rest of the staff. Whatever medical science could not cure, soap and antiseptics would have to.

Kate kept the events at the Baker ranch to herself. She sensed that something was terribly twisted in the relationships of her family that reached back to Silas Baker or beyond. Isolated from other families at the time, she did not realize that something was wrong in their household. Now, having been out in the world, she knew differently. She had escaped it for now, but she was smart enough to know that whatever dynamics that were at work in the family had molded most of her life, and that someday she would have to deal with the twisting that these dynamics might have done to her. For now, though, she was content to lose herself in her work.

And it was dangerous work. German, Austrian, and Bulgarian soldiers pushed against the Serbs, each time weakening their defenses and sending more casualties to the military hospitals. Serbia was on the brink of collapse. The volunteers who worked in the hospitals were in danger of being over-run by the enemy and taken prisoner.

One day, in the middle of May, with the sun shining so brightly that it seemed to defy the horrors of war that were obvious inside the hospital, Kate slipped outside and stood against the brick walls of the building, absorbing the warmth of the sun in hopes of easing the chill of death that still lingered in her after a morning in the operating room. That morning she had saved four men and had lost three. After lunch she had lost another three. She knew it was dangerous for a doctor to try to keep score, and she normally didn't, but when the losses out-distanced the wins, she had to escape for a moment. She shut her eyes and let the sunshine caress her face.

She only got a moment of rest before a booming voice shattered it. "If it isn't the most beautiful doctor in the world. If you would just marry me, we would make the most handsome doctor couple this world has ever seen."

Despite the depression she felt, Kate smiled. She only knew one man who was this audacious. She opened her eyes and greeted Doctor Angelo Ferrano. "Doctor Ferrano," she said, "do you mean you have actually taken time out from the night life in Paris to join us at the front? How unlike you."

He stopped in front of her and swooped into a low bow. As he sprang back up, he defended himself. "I've not been in Paris for months. In fact, I have been on the front lines for a month."

"I'm sorry," Kate said, smiling apologetically, "I was making a poor joke. I've seen the good work you have done with patients who've been brought to us."

For a moment they stood and stared at each other, a remarkable contrast. Doctor Ferrano was dressed immaculately in a dark suit, and, despite the brilliant sunshine, he wore a cape draped over his shoulders. European ancestry had modified his Italian features. Although his hair was dark and wavy, like many Italians, his complexion was much lighter than most of his countrymen, and his eyes were an emerald green. His facial features were soft and round, almost effeminate, so much so that other men were uncomfortable in his presence. On the other hand, many women found him irresistibly handsome, a fact that he used to his advantage. He was a man known for his seductions.

At twenty-five, Kate was more beautiful than she had ever been, although at this moment few would recognize that. Having stepped out of surgery, she still wore an apron splattered with blood, and her long hair was tucked under a surgical cap so that only a few strands escaped, plastered against her forehead, victims of the sweat that rolled down her face while she operated. Suddenly conscious of how she must look, she pulled her cap from her head and let her hair fall loose. A shake of her head spread the hair around her face and turned her once again into a beauty.

She did not wear make up. She had no need for it. Her complexion was already golden so it took little sunshine to give her skin a healthy glow. Dark eyelashes and eyebrows accented her sky-blue eyes. Her full lips were naturally rosy. Her hair, of course, was a thick, rich blonde that came down to the middle of her back. Dr. Ferrano was not immune to her beauty. He stepped back so he could better see her features.

"I think we should at least put diamonds around your neck, even if we cannot dress you in the best of gowns on the battlefield. Diamonds would be a nice touch," he added.

She smiled again. "Is it possible for you to walk past a woman without making advances?" she asked.

He threw his head back and shook it, making a sharp sound by sucking air through his front teeth. "Maligned," he said. "I'm only a man... Perhaps more so. Why do you criticize me for doing only what comes naturally to men?"

"Because," she said, laughing, "I could just imagine what would be said of me if I were to do the same thing. Would they say of me I was only a woman, only more so?"

With his head still back, he stopped shaking it and looked down his nose at her. "I have not thought of it like that."

"Some have suggested your hormones do not allow you to think."

He lowered his head. "How unkind of them."

"How unkind it is to break hearts," she said.

"Heartbreaking is a two-way street, as is love in any shape or form. I wonder why I'm always the one to take the criticism. Oh, well," he said, shrugging, "I suspect I won't be breaking your heart."

She pushed herself away from the wall, suddenly feeling the tug of the operating room pulling her back inside. "I don't predict the future. Right now, I need to return to the operating room."

He offered her his arm. "Delightful. I've come to join you. We shall make beautiful surgery together." They walked back inside the hospital.

Becky Muldoone thought of Doctor Angelo Ferrano as being a time bomb. Walking together from the ward to the cafeteria, Becky made her case one more time. "You know what the good doctor is interested in, and it's not your medical ability," she said. "I've pushed you toward some marvelous men in the past. How can you be so foolish as to show an interest in this one, the last man I would hope for you to love?"

Kate dismissed this plea with a wave of her hand. "I'm not in love with anyone. Doctor Ferrano is amusing company and nothing

more. You don't need to worry. I'll not be one of his conquests."
She walked several steps before she added, "Unless I want to be."

"Kate," Becky moaned in exasperation, "don't let him pull the
wool over your eyes."

Kate smiled "I don't think it is my eyes that you're worried
about."

The meal they were served in the cafeteria line was skimpy again,
lacking in fresh vegetables and meat for the fourth day in a row.
They were given a thin soup, a boiled potato, and a slice of bread
that was stale. Neither complained. They were being fed the same as
the patients and better than the troops in the field. The enemy's ad-
vance had cut off supply lines to the farms in the country so that
food was scarce. Once they had sat at a table, Becky observed, "We
won't be here much longer if the food is any indication. If the Germans and Austrians are close enough to cut off our food, they're
close enough to take the hospital."

None of this was new to Kate. She and Doctor Inglis had discussed
the situation at length. Their hospital was so overcrowded with
wounded that many had to wait treatment outside in the courtyard.
To complicate matters, the spread of typhus was always a danger.
The volunteers were just holding their own. Doctor Inglis felt that
any less of an effort would doom many of the wounded to death.
She was sure that the advancing troops would not provide sufficient
medical treatment to the Serbs. Together, Kate and Doctor Inglis had
made a decision.

"Becky," Kate said, cautiously because she knew that what she
was to say would test their friendship. "I know that you're looking
forward to leaving here, and that you are only here because I am,
but I have some bad news for you. Despite the Germans, I've decided
to stay on and treat the wounded."

Becky was just about to take a sip of soup from her spoon. She
lowered the utensil back to the table and sagged back in her chair.
"And I thought Doctor Ferrano was my greatest fear in life. No,
stupidity seems to have taken his place. Do you have any idea of
what the enemy will do to us in case we are captured?"

"Do you have any idea how many of the men in this hospital will
die if we don't stay to care for them?"

Becky was not going to give in. She was no match for Kate in an argument, but she would have her say. "That's a foolish thought," she said, trying to be patient. "You're not going to be doing these men much good locked away in the German officer quarters satisfying their fancies. At least you'll get officers. I'll be lucky to get the infantry."

"That's a risk I'll have to take," Kate said. "You won't have to worry about it. I'm sending you back with the others who'll be leaving."

"So that's it," Becky said, shaking her head in disgust. "If I don't do it your way, off I go. Our friendship must not mean much."

"This sounds like too serious of a conversation for me. Perhaps I should try another table." Both women turned to look at Doctor Ferrano who stood behind them, tray in hand. He sat down next to Kate, showing no inclination to seek another table. "What is it that has us all so grumpy?"

Becky explained to him the disagreement between herself and Kate.

Angelo pushed around the soup in his bowl with his spoon, examining its ingredients. Convinced that nothing seemed harmful, he tasted it. He made a face and pushed the bowl away from him, turning his attention now to the potato. As he sliced it, he said, "If the wounded need us, I don't think there's much of an issue. It means we all stay."

"It doesn't mean any such thing," Kate said.

"Certainly it does," Angelo corrected her. "Becky can't leave you. She's your best friend. I can't leave you because without my protection you'll be a ripe plum ready to pick."

"Don't be foolish," Kate said. "I'm willing to take my chances, and I have no intention of dragging you into this with me."

"Well, your decision has done that. You forget I've been on the front lines and know what the Germans will do. But they're reasonable men, and they know the power of Italian nobility, even in the time of war. I shall throw over you my blanket of protection."

Both women looked at each other. Becky spoke their thoughts. "Italian nobility? What are you talking about?"

"I'm not your average, beautifully handsome and marvelously gifted doctor," he said, giving them each a dazzling smile, "I'm also from a wealthy family with a glorious blood line. Would you believe it, I'm even related to the Kaiser?''

It would take all of Angelo's blood line and even more of his talents to keep Kate out of the clutches of the Germans over the next two months. Her beauty stirred the passion of too many men who thought they had a right to the spoils of war.

TWENTY

ALONE IN the Baker mansion, he found the solitude overwhelming. Unlike the house on Shady Lane that was surrounded by the muted sound of a busy world swirling around it, the house was far enough removed from highway, valley, and neighbors to be in a cocoon of quiet. He sat in the parlor of the house for an hour and listened to the building. It was, in the end, silent.

He was afraid to leave the parlor. To leave it was to move to the study to confront the safe. When he let his mind drift to the safe, the image of its dial spun in his head, stopping on each of the sets of numbers until the doors sprung open. He did not want to think about the safe.

His thoughts turned to Pam Livingston. He smiled. Her beauty stirred him, perhaps in a way he had never been stirred before. She made it clear to Paul that she was attracted to him, and that she would like to have a deeper relationship with him. He had the safe to think about. He had Beth to think about. He did not want to think about Pam.

He thought about the sisters. He tried to feel their presence in the house. He strained to hear the echoes of their long-lost conversations. His efforts met with silence. How could he hear them? Kate was in Europe. Elizabeth and her sister did not communicate. Emily and Margaret's words were muffled by closed doors. How could he feel them? He still did not know what drove them. He sat in the parlor, in a stiff, uncomfortable winged back chair, his hands clasped between his knees, and saw the dial spinning. The stay in the Baker house was supposed to be a test of his feelings for Pam Livingston. Instead, he was discovering a test of his feelings for his girls, the Baker sisters. He saw the dial spinning. He sat and stared at the floor.

The dial spun.

He was running out of information. He could take Kate through the war and that was it. He knew nothing about Emily and Elizabeth after the wedding plans were canceled. He either got more information or he quit.

The dial spun.

How could he wrap up the book with the information he had? He had set out to find out why the girls had never married. He still did not know. In Europe Kate Baker stayed on at the hospital in Serbia, tending her patients even after the country was over-run by the enemy. Ferrano stood up for the women, and perhaps even saved them from being ravaged because of his bloodline to the Kaiser. More than likely the women were left alone because neither the Germans nor their allies wanted to worry about running a hospital to care for the Serbian casualties. They had their own to worry about. The fact that Kate was an American did not hurt much, either. America had still not entered the war. Bloodline or no, Ferrano was imprisoned. Kate and the other women stayed until nearly the end of the year, and then they were evacuated to a hospital in Krusevac, Hungary. In February of 1916 they were escorted out of Hungary under guard, and then went first to Belgrade, and then to Vienna and London. That was where the story ended.

The dial spun.

Lateral thinking. A problem that has no apparent solution might be solved if it is approached from a different direction. If you can't go up the middle, try an end run. He assumed that if he opened the safe he would violate a trust, and, worse, find information in it that would commit him to the Baker book. He realized now that there was another possibility. He might open the safe and find nothing inside. The journey could come to an end, and he could go back to Hollingsworth, satisfied that he had given the Baker sisters his best shot. The idea cheered him.

The dial spun.

He got up.

He may as well have been a thief in the night. Every soft rustle of sound, every whisper of wind, every creak of board was a sign that the interloper would be caught. Something or someone was sure to sound the alarm to warn the police. Pam had never trusted him alone in the house and had left behind a spy. The girls themselves, apparitions now, would stand over his shoulder, watching as he spun the dial on the safe.

What would they think? Would they collectively focus their powers upon him to stop the safe from being opened? Would they rejoice, knowing that now the truth would be told? Would they be indifferent, having learned something in the nether world that made their time on earth seem insignificant? He might muse about such things, but the sweat rolling down in big drops from his temples and the number of times he got wrong the combination suggested that he did not feel like laughing.

After five tries he got it right and the doors of the safe swung open. The groan of hinges long unused seemed to thunder through the house, and he nearly slammed the doors shut, fearing that some-one would hear. He held his breath and listened. No alarm rang. No one came running. No sirens wailed in the distance. He let out his breath and turned to the contents of the safe.

It was nearly empty. Nearly. But there were three books on the center shelf of the safe, neatly placed side by side. He did not have to pick one up to know what they were. Together they represented his worst fears. He knew they would be there. Lateral thinking was deception. It was an excuse for him to throw open these doors and get his hands on these diaries, one for each of the sisters. All of them, Kate included, might go unsung, but none could bear the thought of going to the next world unnoticed. The diaries had had to be in the safe, waiting for him, waiting for the one who would not be satisfied with the empty monument on the hillside and the questions that seemed to have no answers.

He left the doors of the safe open. He carried the books upstairs like an altar boy might carry a host to a priest, with great care and great dignity. He knew he would open each and read from it, but he must do it in a sacred place. He shut the door to Kate's room behind him and walked to the bed. Here and only here, he could stretch out and be one with the three sisters.

TWENTY-ONE

SHE WOULD LIKE TO HAVE had a photograph of that moment. When Margaret opened the door and recognized who it was, her face became quite severe. Behind her, pausing in mid-step halfway down the staircase was Emily, one eyebrow raised slightly above the other. In the doorway of the front room stood Elizabeth, her arms flying out and her face stretching into a look of joyful surprise. Kate turned around to see the expression on Becky Muldoone's face. She was curious to see how her friend would react to her first sight of the sisters.

Becky took it in stride. Months of working together under great pressure left few secrets between them. Ever calm, capable Kate could not keep inside her feelings for her family. And, after her last visit home, she could not return alone. She needed Becky's strength to face Emily again. Becky was happy to go. Like Kate, she had seen enough battle service for the moment and needed a rest. She hoped she was not moving into a different kind of battleground.

"So, the prodigal child returns," Emily said, staring past Kate to Becky.

Elizabeth was in Kate's arms before she had a chance to respond. Unlike the last time when Kate couldn't keep her sister still, Elizabeth buried her face in her sister's neck and stood quietly, sobbing softly. Kate looked up at Emily and said, "Prodigal? Hardly."

There was a long, awkward moment when nothing happened. Margaret stood frozen, refusing to let the women into the house. Her hand rested on the edge of the door, as if she was getting ready to slam it in their faces. Becky took charge of the moment. She picked up the luggage from the porch and pushed past Kate and Elizabeth. She dropped the bags at Margaret's feet, saying, "I'm sure you'll know what to do with these."

Margaret stared at Becky, dislike apparent on her face, before looking back at Emily. Over her initial surprise, the oldest sister took command of the situation. In a tone that was meant to cut, she asked,

"Will your friend be sharing a bed with you, or will she be staying in the servant's quarters?"

Kate separated herself from Elizabeth and moved to the bottom of the stairs. "I'm sorry to disappoint you, Emily, but no one shares my bed, and certainly not a servant if she were one. Becky is an outstanding surgical nurse and a better friend. She'll be staying in the guest room."

Emily colored slightly. "She can't," she said.

Elizabeth moved to Kate's side and filled in the rest. "She can't because Margaret's got the guest room."

Kate looked back at Margaret, who still held the door open, and smiled. "I'm sure Margaret won't mind moving back to the servant's quarters. Will you?"

Kate was enjoying every moment of this. She liked storming in and disrupting Emily's little empire. Emily's power was diminished with Kate there to push the legal terms of the will and her relationship with Margaret would have to be suspended. Emily might do what she wished under Elizabeth's nose, but she did not dare do the same with Kate. To show any weakness to Kate was to imperil her dynasty.

Emily succumbed quickly. She was a woman who needed time to scheme, and she didn't have enough of it now. To Margaret she said, "Go on upstairs and move your things into the servant's quarters."

Kate admired the way that Margaret handled what must be a reversal for her. She showed absolutely no expression and immediately shut the door and turned toward the stairs.

"Take our bags up with you, Margaret," Kate said. There was just a slight twitch of the shoulders this time, but when Margaret turned her face toward Kate she showed no hint of her feelings. "She must be a very good...servant," Kate said to Emily.

Emily would remember this moment as one of the worst of her life. She had to hurt the woman she loved to appease a sister she hated. Only then, at that moment, did she realize the position she was in. She had given Kate leverage, and now she would never quite have the control over her sisters as she had had before.

"Yes," Emily said. "She is quite good." Suddenly she spun around and ran up the stairs.

Elizabeth was shocked. That was the first time she had perceived a weakness in her sister. The knowledge would do her no good, she knew. She didn't have the slightest idea of how to take advantage of somebody else's weaknesses. Besides, she had much graver concerns.

To Kate she whispered, "Your arrival is God-sent. I need to talk to you as soon as I can."

Kate searched her sister's face for a clue to that message. She saw nothing there that suggested the matter was pressing. "Certainly," she said. "But first, Becky and I both need a hot meal and a long bath. We plan to stay for several months so we will have a great deal of time to talk."

She wasn't ready for talk right now. Six years of study and battle had taken much out of her. Dr. Englis had wanted Kate to stay in London and help organize another unit to aide the Serbs. Kate had declined. She needed a rest, although once the units were organized and ready to return to the front, Kate had promised that she would return.

The next morning Kate was up early, rising at dawn before the others had stirred. To her this was the first sign that the Bakers were getting soft. Before she left for medical school, the routine on the ranch had been much different. Elizabeth had always been up before first light to supervise the kitchen duties. Emily rose shortly after that to meet with the ranch foreman and outline the tasks for that day.

Not so today. Elizabeth and Emily both slept in. The cook was up before Kate, preparing breakfast, but by the leisurely pace that Kate had observed, it was apparent that the meal would not be on the table for some time to come. Outside the ranch was in full operation. Crews were filtering out from the barn area below the house to the orchards and fields.

Kate drew her long robe tightly across her and stepped outside into the chilly morning air. Thick, slowly tumbling gray clouds rolled over the valley, indicating another day of rain. In exchange for mild, nearly snowless winters, this country got heavy rain in the spring. The Rogue River Valley needed the heavy downpours to build reserves of water to carry through the hot, dry summers.

She walked to the edge of the front lawn where now a rough iron fence had been built to separate the yard from the steep slope to the valley floor. Beyond that one change, Kate did not see anything else that looked different to her. The ranch seemed to be frozen in time and that disturbed her. The equipment in the barnyard looked old and the buildings needed painting. Emily was sacrificing the upkeep of the ranch for what?

"You're up early."

Emily crossed the yard and joined her sister at the fence. She, too, wore a dressing gown, and her face was still puffy from sleep. She put both hands on the railing of the fence and stared out across the valley.

"This isn't early for me," Kate said. "A doctor during war doesn't have hours, only emergencies. Sometimes the emergencies blend together so they do not have a beginning or an end, and day and night become meaningless."

"I can't imagine you doing something like that," Emily said. Her tone today was quite different from last night, although it would not be mistaken for friendliness. Emily presented to people degrees of hostility. Last night she leaned toward armed combat; today she seemed prepared only for skirmishes.

"We haven't seen much of each other in the last eight or nine years. I don't suggest we prejudge each other from past experiences. We're old enough now that our accomplishments should speak for themselves." She turned her head to hide from Emily the tight smile that was on her face.

Emily felt the first flush of anger but kept it in check. The success of the Baker ranch should be Emily's accomplishment that would speak for itself, but it did not. The ranch had been in a steady decline for several years, and she did not know what to do about it. Kate's fortunes, on the other hand, had risen in the last few years. Since it was clear now that America would be involved in the war in Europe, the local community took an interest in the happenings overseas. Kate's exploits had been followed with fascination, if not with approval.

"The ranch hasn't been doing well," Emily said, grimly facing up to what had to be said. "With so many men getting ready to go off to war, the price of labor has gone up, yet prices of crops have continued to fall."

Kate understood that well; had even predicted it at one time. The monopoly of produce that the Bakers had enjoyed for years was sure to be broken once the railroad system expanded. Midwesterners could produce wheat more cheaply than they could, and southwesterners could raise beef for much less. Once the transportation cost for produce dropped, the Baker ranch was sure to be in difficulty.

"What have you done about it?" Kate asked.

"What can I do about it?" Emily asked, frustrated by the question. If she had known what to do, she would have done it.

Again Kate turned her head to hide her smile. Of course Emily would not know what to do, and, because it was her nature to dominate, she would not hire people who would know what to do, either. If she hired someone smart enough to change the direction of the ranch, she would have to give up a great deal of power. She couldn't do that. In fact, the admission that the ranch wasn't doing well must be killing her.

The first drops of rain began to fall but neither of the women moved. Both of them knew that the survival of the ranch was essential. The Bakers had invested too much of themselves in this land to lose it now.

"I'll take a look at the books, and then I will take a look at the market," Kate said. "If labor's short, we'll look for a low labor crop. If the market doesn't want what we offer, we'll plant what they do want. If we change the emphasis from ranching to farming, we can streamline the operation and unload land we don't need. People will always have to eat. There's no reason for a spread this size to do poorly." The last statement was a direct criticism of Emily. Kate thought to soften it, and then she changed her mind. Emily would need a lot more than an overbearing personality to excuse herself from the mistakes she had made.

Emily nodded. She didn't care what went on between them, as long as it was not shared with a third party. A third party was on her mind this morning. She asked. "Just what exactly is this Becky Muldoone to you?"

"A good friend," Kate said. "What's Margaret to you?"

Emily's hands tightened their grip on the iron railing. "A good friend," she said.

"I'm glad you have a friend." She turned now so that Emily could see the smile. "But," she added, "don't mistake Becky's friendship for one like Margaret's."

The lines were drawn. Each knew now what the other needed. Each knew where the other stood. Emily could have her Margaret, but she was not to assume that the sisters were the same as their oldest sister. Kate would save the ranch, but Emily would have to run it. Kate needed her freedom, and she needed to be assured that Emily would not be at home trying to sabotage her while she was away. They walked back in the house together.

LATER, AFTER BREAKFAST, Elizabeth walked with Kate down to the office in the main barn where they still kept the ranch's records. They walked in awkward silence. Despite what others might say, time and distance did not suddenly melt away for the sisters. Kate was twenty-six and very much her own woman. Elizabeth was thirty and set in her ways. Being sisters did not negate between them the things that they had become, and it did not allow them the security of being strangers, and yet they were expected to love each other blindly because they were sisters—one of the idealistic lessons taught to them by their mother.

They strolled slowly, side by side, with their hands locked behind their backs and their heads down. Emily had made her report and now Elizabeth would make hers. Between the two of them, Kate was sure she would find out most of what had been happening while she was gone. For some reason she did not expect the news to be bad; home was supposed to be the rock that one returned to, that safe harbor in the storm; but the financial conditions of the ranch put into question the safety of the harbor.

Elizabeth reaffirmed that. "Emily has been more interested in Margaret than she has the ranch. The two of them are always going to Portland or San Francisco together. Supposedly Emily is taking care of business for the ranch, but I know that these are just outings so they can do whatever they do without raising eyebrows."

"I'm sure that has been a burden for you," Kate said. "It sounds like you have had to manage both the household and the ranch at times."

"It wasn't so hard when Rodney was here."

They turned from the drive onto the road to the barns. Several seconds of silence passed while the name Rodney was held suspended between them. Kate waited patiently for an explanation. Elizabeth waited for a sign, some little movement to tell her it was all right to talk about this man.

Kate gave the sign. "I think you're going to have to tell me about Rodney," she said. "You have a gentleman caller?"

This was the hard part for Elizabeth. Father's desires were to be taken into account, and mother's dictates. Rodney Ryan may have met with the approval of one, but certainly he would not have pleased the other. Elizabeth blurted out, "He's not exactly a gentleman."

If Kate stiffened, it was ever so slightly, so little so that Elizabeth did not notice. As much as she hated the thought, she knew that she subscribed to her mother's desire that each of the girls marry a fine, upstanding man of privilege; anyone less was sure to take advantage of the sisters. In her own way, Emily had exposed that side of Charles Hollingsworth. If nothing else, Margaret was a safe choice because she did not threaten the family fortune.

"He sounds intriguing," Kate said, trying to encourage her sister to speak while fighting the sinking feeling in the pit of her stomach.

Elizabeth opened up the floodgate and let it out. Rodney, it turned out, was far from a gentleman of means. He was one of the ranch hands. Unable to communicate well with Elizabeth when Emily was gone, the ranch foreman sent Rodney to the main house for directions. Beneath the glorified description of the young man, Kate pieced together the portrait of a simple soul, much like Elizabeth, who seemed kind and decent, earthy. Rodney was not fettered by a gentleman's upbringing, nor did he sound graced by innocence.

"He's gone to fight the Germans," Elizabeth said, a hint of pride in her voice.

They stopped outside the door to the office. "How long has he been gone?" Kate asked.

"Oh, Kate, you just missed him by weeks. He's in training now. He hopes to get home one more time before he's sent overseas."

Kate left Elizabeth outside the office and spent the day with the books. In the quiet of the room she had time to think about the things she had learned since she had been home. The books confirmed that the ranch was in danger. The way that Elizabeth talked about Rodney confirmed another kind of danger.

She could form a plan of action for the first, but she didn't know what to do about the second. A simple man of the soil like Rodney was a threat to the Baker estate. He was the kind of man who could move in and take over. He was the kind of man, once in control, who could cut out the three sisters. He sounded very much as if he was a man just like their father.

After years of stress in school, and then the stress of war, the leisurely pace of the life on the ranch suited Kate well. During her stay she visited with friends, including Doctor Hollingsworth, the senior, and she researched the crop market, often dragging Becky along when she visited neighbors or rode into town. She did not limit her research to concerns of the ranch. Kate also took an interest in Rodney Ryan.

She didn't like what she found out. He was much younger than Elizabeth, only twenty-two. And he had nothing else going for him, either, as far as Kate could tell. He had dropped out of school to work on his father's farm, and when his family had lost that, hired himself out to work for others. He seemed to have little ambition beyond farming, and little education that would benefit him in the future. At this point in time there was no way of telling whether or not he was interested in Elizabeth for herself or for her share of the ranch. It was obvious to Kate, though, that he was unlikely to own land of his own unless he married into it.

Armed with information about the crop market, Kate brought Emily and the ranch foreman together and outlined a plan of action that they were to follow, no matter what happened. Kate was convinced that with America becoming involved in the war, certain food products would be in high demand and short supply. Wheat would be essential, as well as non-perishable crops such as nuts.

Kate also decided that the valley land had become too precious for just cattle grazing. Both Jacksonville and Medford now pushed up against their land in several spots, to the point that a crisis could unfold. Desperate enough, both towns would find a way to get what they needed by passing ordinances. Since most of this was pasture land for the ranch, Kate convinced Emily that it was to their advantage to sell it to the developers for top dollar before it was taken away from them at low dollar. They could purchase good grazing land in Eastern Oregon for a tenth the cost of their own land and move their herds over. That would nearly double for them the amount of land they had in the valley for money crops.

She worked out the transaction herself. When she was done she had not only doubled the acreage owned by the Bakers, but she had doubled their cash reserve. She used some of that money for the painting and repair of the ranch buildings and fences, and for the replacement of worn-out equipment with new, more modern pieces. The new equipment helped to reduce their labor needs, a point Kate thought vital because she was sure that many of the young men in the valley would follow in Rodney's footsteps and go off to war.

Satisfied that she had done what she could, she devoted the final weeks of her stay to relaxation. Unfortunately, she wasn't going to get much of it—which became apparent the morning that Elizabeth slipped into her room and crawled into bed with her.

Kate could not help but smile. After all, they may have done this as children, but that was years ago. There was something ungainly now about the way Elizabeth crawled into bed. It certainly was not with the bouncing exuberance of youth that she slipped between the sheets.

"You've rolled away the years," Kate said.

Elizabeth snuggled up to her sister and put her head on Kate's shoulder. She was quiet for a moment and then broke the silence. "I think I have a problem," she said. "I haven't bled in some time."

The smile disappeared. Kate was a doctor. She knew immediately the implications of the statement. She waited until she could speak calmly before she answered, saying finally, "It appears that your relationship with Rodney was more serious than I suspected."

Elizabeth buried her face in Kate's shoulder and said in a muffled voice, "I know it was wrong but you know what happened the last time I said I wanted to marry a man. I love him so much and I'm not a child."

Kate stroked her sister's hair. She could not be angry with Elizabeth. Her sister didn't need anger from her. She needed help.

"What do you want me to do?" Kate asked.

The muffled reply was, "I want Rodney to marry me."

Fulfilling Elizabeth's dream was not as easy as it seemed as Kate found out later when Rodney returned home on leave. Just because he was young and poorly-educated did not mean that Rodney was either naive or stupid. The news that he was to be a father was very good news to him, indeed. He knew he would never lay claim to Elizabeth Baker if her sister Emily decided against it. A pregnancy out of wedlock placed all the cards in his hands.

Kate gave Rodney and Elizabeth a few days together before she pulled the young man aside to talk to him. She wanted to take his measure before she gave him his choices. In the end, when she called him down to her father's office for a visit, she had decided that his measure came up short. He was a crude man who could just barely make himself presentable when he had to. He seemed no more devoted to Elizabeth than he was to his fellow ranch hands, already choosing the latter for company when he was home. Kate wasn't sure how Elizabeth and Rodney got along because the little time that he did spend with her was away from the house. Kate was sure that Rodney was far more interested in the benefits of a marriage to Elizabeth than he was in her sister. Their visit quickly confirmed that.

Rodney walked into the office without knocking. His close-cut military haircut was not becoming. He was not a handsome man to begin with and the haircut left his ears sticking far out from his head and made his mouth seem bigger than it was, the lopsided grin on it more appropriate for an idiot than a man who wanted to marry a Baker heiress. He strolled over to Kate's desk and plopped down in a chair opposite from her. He let his eyes wander over Kate, finally resting them for an uncomfortably long pause on her breasts. Kate had spent the last two years of her life surrounded by men, and she knew what it was to be admired by them. She also knew that his stare went beyond admiration.

She got to the point quickly. "Knowing Elizabeth, I'm sure she has told you that she's pregnant and you're the father."

The grin remained on his face, but the eyes lifted to hers. He winked. "That's right."

She almost expected him to deny it. If it weren't for Elizabeth's wealth, she was sure he would. "What do you intend to do about it?" she asked.

He slid down in his chair and threw his head back and stared at the ceiling. "That depends," he said.

"On what?"

He lifted his head to look at Kate. "No need to be hostile," he said. "It's not you I made pregnant, although I wouldn't mind giving it a try."

Kate let the first rush of blood surge through her body before she attempted to answer him. Sure that she was in control of herself, she said calmly, "You'd be dead before a finger touched me."

He laughed, throwing back his head again to share his mirth with the ceiling. He stopped suddenly and sat up straight, leaning slightly toward Kate with that grin on his face, saying, "That's what *she* said at first, too. For a woman so opposed to a man touching her, she sure loved it when she got it."

"What do you want?"

He swung his right arm in an arc. "I figure we'll take the land from here to Medford, plus maybe the section over by Jacksonville. Then I expect a house to be built for us and some money to start up ranching on our own." He turned the lopsided grin into a pleasant smile. "You didn't think I wanted it all, did ya?"

Kate folded her hands on the desk top and looked down at them, smiling herself now. "The best you will get is to share Elizabeth's bedroom with her, and a one third cut of the ranch profits each year, which isn't going to be enough to build you a house unless you save it up over a few years. Of course, Elizabeth is free to leave the ranch and take with her a modest allowance."

The smile dropped from his face. He leaned forward in the chair until his arms rested on the desk top. "That's bullshit," he said.

Kate lifted her head so he could have a good look at her smile. "That," she said, "is all that mother's will allows her. Of course, without Emily's blessing, the question of compensation is pointless. If she doesn't approve of you, you and Elizabeth will not be able to live on the ranch or share in its profits."

She expected an angry response to that from him. She was surprised when he smiled again. "Emily's not going to stand in my way, and I'm going to get what I want."

"And what makes you so sure of that?"

"I'm sure this town would have a good laugh if they knew that Elizabeth was fat with baby. Most people think it's about time the Bakers had their come down. Course, what I could tell them about Emily would be the pudding in the pie. The Bakers would never be able to lift their heads again by the time I was done."

Kate wanted to deny what he was saying and to stand up for her sisters, but she recognized the truth in what he said. Their father had made sure the valley would hate the Bakers. None of them had ever done anything to change that. But she wasn't about to let him have his way. She said, "The folks who are willing to believe the truth are just as willing to believe a lie. It wouldn't make much difference to them what you told them. There'll be enough who won't believe you, no matter what you say."

"Once they see Elizabeth fat with my baby, they'll believe me," he responded.

"Not if she is sent away," Kate said.

"You forget how much she loves me," he countered.

"You ask the impossible," she snapped back, aware now of just how messy all of this could be. For a moment she wished to drop the whole matter and leave it in Emily's hands. She had a war to return to; she had a life of her own. Emily would have to work it out.

But Emily couldn't work it out. Kate knew, and Emily knew, and now Rodney knew that Emily's compromising relationship with Margaret made her powerless. Either Kate handled this problem, or Rodney got everything he asked for.

"You Bakers have used that will as an excuse to do as you damn well please. You use it as a threat against each other and you use it as a reason to keep men at bay. It's about time you quit hiding behind it. The truth is you can do as you please and as long as you agree not to challenge each other in court, the will is meaningless."

She saw her mistake now. She had assumed that he was stupid because he hadn't finished school. He wasn't stupid; he was ambitious. If he left school it was because he saw an opportunity. Elizabeth must have had opportunity written all over her. He read her right. He read all the Bakers right. Getting Elizabeth pregnant was just the move he needed to get what he wanted from them.

"We've room to negotiate," she said. "You won't get everything you want."

He winked. "You won't regret it," he said. "You women need a man around to look after you. You've been without one too long."

He disgusted her, but it would do no good to let him know that. She said, "It is nice of you to be so concerned, but it looks like neither one of us will be around. We've both got a war to return to."

"A war?" he said. "Heavens. I never intended to go to war. I plan to be married within a week and be discharged shortly after that.

Going to war was a nice thought, and it certainly made Elizabeth cling to me, but people get killed in war.''

"Is that how you seduced her? 'Poor Rodney could be dead tomorrow, Elizabeth. If we don't do it now we may never get the chance.' That's an old, old line," she said.

He stood up and leaned over the desk, his face close to hers. "It worked, didn't it? We'll have a lot of time together in the future. I'm sure I'll find just the line that works with you, too. Unless, of course, you share Emily's taste in women.''

His face was too close to hers. He didn't have time to pull it out of reach before her right fist snapped his teeth together. He reeled back from the desk in surprise, rubbing his jaw. "That'll cost you," he said. Then he wheeled around and laughed as he walked out the door.

IT COULD NOT BE considered a family council because Elizabeth was not there in spirit. She spent most of the time pouting in a chair in the corner of the parlor, upset because both Emily and Kathleen were being abusive to Rodney. She had a feeling they were conspiring to ruin her love life, just as Emily had undermined her engagement to Charles Hollingsworth.

Elizabeth's estimate of the meeting in the parlor was not far from the truth. Kate and Emily were conspiring about Rodney.

Emily summed up the frustration that both sisters felt. "So he thinks he's got us over a barrel, does he?" she said. "Well, we'll just see about that." The words may have sounded brave, but they certainly didn't offer much comfort to her. She paced in a tight circle around the room, pausing once or twice to stare at Elizabeth with a look of disgust on her face. Finally she stopped and vented her feelings. "How could you have been so stupid?" she screamed at her sister. "You've practically handed that idiot boy the ranch on a silver platter and made us powerless to stop him.''

Elizabeth looked defiantly up from under her dark lashes and said, "You've been jealous of my ability to get a man, and you've always tried to ruin it for me.''

Kate stepped between them. Accusations would not solve the problem. They had to agree to what they would do, an agreement that would be satisfactory to each. She said, "Let's try to solve the problem, not make it worse. Elizabeth is old enough to marry if she wants, and she has a right to some of the property. The pregnancy and mother's will make it pointless to argue those issues. The question that must be answered is one of dowry. Rodney has asked for far more than is fair, and he has threatened to destroy the Baker name if he doesn't get what he wants. That's what we have to deal with.''

Emily threw herself down on a settee near the fireplace. She was angry; she was frustrated; she was stymied. Years ago this combination of feelings in her would have been explosively dangerous. Since Margaret had come into her life, she had mellowed. The force that would have enabled her to deal with this situation seemed to be dead in her.

Kate watched her oldest sister. Each time she caught another glimpse of Emily's weakness, she was surprised by it. Her sister had changed a great deal. Besides this new indecisiveness in her, there was a physical difference as well. She was still a beautiful woman, but she didn't care for herself as well as she had in the past. She had gained a little weight, and her complexion wasn't as clear as it had been. It was as if she no longer felt the need to stay beautiful now that she had someone to love her.

On the other side of the room, in the chair, Elizabeth sat like a rose in full bloom. She had finally aged enough so that she no longer looked like a little girl. Her skin was softer now and her body a little more rounded. For that reason alone Kate felt that they had to take Elizabeth seriously. They could not use the childishness of her nature any more as an excuse to ignore her. She was a woman.

"What do we do, Kate?" Emily asked. She was a tired woman who did not want to face these kinds of problems. She had managed the Baker estate for nearly twenty years and now she wanted peace; she wanted foremen who could do their jobs without direction; she wanted sisters who could take care of their own problems; she wanted outsiders to leave them alone; she wanted to spend the rest of her life with Margaret, no questions asked.

"The first thing we do is not make any hasty decisions," Kate said. "Rodney plans to be discharged from the military. I suggest he do that first before marriage plans are made. If he can't get discharged, it means he'll be sitting in some army camp until America decides to get into the war.''

"Rodney's very brave and he wants to fight the Germans," Elizabeth said proudly.

"That's nice," Kate said, "but if he wanted to make sure he was going to fight the Germans right away, he would have joined up with the French or the Italians."

"America could go to war at any time," Elizabeth countered.

"That's true," Kate said. "Or they might not go to war at all," she added. "I don't suppose it dawned on you that Rodney might have joined the military to put pressure on you to marry him?"

"No," Elizabeth snapped. "I never considered it at all because it is a stupid idea."

"No, obviously you didn't consider it or you wouldn't be pregnant. But it doesn't matter now," Kate said. "Tell Rodney that those are our terms. He's welcome to marry you as soon as he is discharged from the military."

Elizabeth sat up straight and began to plead, letting slip again the fact that she was subservient to her sisters. "What if he says no? Don't make him say no."

Kate walked over to Elizabeth and put her hands on her sister's shoulders and squatted down so that she could look into her eyes. "Listen to me," she said. "If we let Rodney have it all his way, there'll be no end to it. He'll run your life, and then he'll try to run ours. He's already asking for the heart of the ranch and most of our wealth. You might be willing to give it all to him, but we're not. He's got to compromise with us or there'll be no marriage at all."

"I'll run off with him," Elizabeth said.

"He'll never run off with you, Ellie; he wants the ranch."

"That's not true," she said, something in the way she said it suggesting that she didn't believe her own words.

"He's threatened to tell the world that you're pregnant, and he's threatened to tell about..." She let that go unfinished. The relationship between Emily and Margaret was still something that they did not talk about openly, even among themselves. "He's trying to blackmail us into giving him the best of the ranch."

"That's not true," Elizabeth whispered.

"He doesn't love you, Ellie," Kate said.

"Please, don't say that," Elizabeth cried softly.

She hated to do it, but she was sure if she pressed the issue Elizabeth would face up to the truth. Facing the condemnation of the valley was nothing new to the Bakers. It would be worth it to keep this man out of the family. Before she could press the point one more time, a sudden explosion of sound was followed by the parlor doors flying open as wood splinters showered through the room. Rodney stood in the doorway, drunk and unsteady on his feet, a crooked grin on his face.

"Didn't I tell you they'd try to do this to you, doll? Lucky for you old Rod's been outside the door the whole time."

Elizabeth rushed across the room and wrapped her arms around the man she loved. He was glad for the support. Kate and Emily stood together in the center of the room, both a little frightened by the man they had underestimated one more time.

Rodney pushed Elizabeth away from him and staggered into the room. "There'll be no selling me out behind my back," he said. "I'm going to marry your sister and then I'm going to take over the operation of the ranch. The two of you have conspired to cheat her out of what's rightfully hers for years. Now she's come to collect her due."

Kate looked past the ugly expression on Rodney's face to the one on Elizabeth's. There, she read the truth. Elizabeth did not object to Rodney's words. She did not jump to her sister's defense. She did not hear the greed in Rodney's voice nor see the lust in his eyes. She was deaf and blind, not because of love, but because of vengeance. On her face was the self-satisfied, smug expression of one who truly felt that she had been abused and was now about to get even. The loss of Charles Hollingsworth had been a greater blow than Kate had imagined. And, the fact that they had underestimated their sister and had spent years being condescending toward her was about to be rewarded. For the first time Kate realized that it was Rodney who was the pawn.

"Look at him," Emily shouted. "See him for what he is. He's a greedy, drunken lout who doesn't care about you in the least."

"Oh, really?" Elizabeth asked, folding her arms across her chest and leaning against the door frame. "You mean he doesn't care for me enough to steal my fiancé away from me, to ruin my plans for marriage, to humiliate me? He doesn't care for me enough to treat me like one of the servants? He doesn't care for me enough to abandon me for years on end, only to rush back into my life on occasion to tell me what I can and can't do?" She stepped forward into the room. "Well, I'm sorry to disappoint you, but he does love me. He loves me enough to want to make sure my sisters don't continue to cheat me of the life that's owed me."

Emily stood frozen in the middle of the room, her mouth stuck open, too shocked to respond to this outburst from her weakling sister. It was so unexpected, so uncharacteristic that her brain could not grasp what Elizabeth had said.

Kate was less shocked. If anything, she was surprised by her own naiveté. Emily was the product of two gentle people. She had been made tough by circumstance, not by breeding. Elizabeth, on the other hand, was a mix of hard and soft. It had been a mistake to believe that she could not be hard, just as it would have been a mistake to think of Kate as soft.

"You don't need Rodney to get your due," Kate said.

Rodney swaggered up to Kate and stopped in front of her, hands on his hips. "I'd be happy to show you how much of a man I am," he said, leering at her. "I figure you've been hiding from men all your life, and now it's time to show you what you've been missing."

"Did you choose him because he likes to bully women?" Kate asked, not taking her eyes from Rodney.

"I chose him because he's not afraid of the two of you, like all the other men in this valley."

"Not the least bit afraid," Rodney said, reaching a hand out to touch Kate's hair.

She brushed away the hand and said, "I wouldn't do that if I were you."

He laughed. "Tough until the end," he said, reaching out again to touch her hair.

Two years of being surrounded by men had taught her a great deal about them. It had taught her about their strengths, and their weaknesses. She had been a good student. She brought her knee up sharply between Rodney's legs and dropped him to the floor, a writhing mass at her feet.

Kate took Emily by the arm and led her from the room, leaving Elizabeth to comfort her fallen lover alone. In the hall Emily was the first to speak. She said, "I underestimated her all these years. I never thought she could be so strong."

"She's a poor mix," Kate said. "She can be strong, but not without someone like Rodney to help her."

"What are we going to do?" Emily asked. "If she marries the man, I don't know that I can handle him alone."

"Then we have to make sure she doesn't marry him," Kate said.

That night behind locked doors plans were discussed and strategies were made. Kate and Becky measured each of the options, considering particularly how the law might be used to benefit the estate. Down the hall, Emily and Margaret contemplated force. Could the other ranch hands be enlisted to help oust Rodney from the grounds? If he could be kept away from the ranch physically, she was sure she could control her sister.

In Silas' office in the barnyard, neither Rodney nor Elizabeth were considering the impending victory over the sisters. They were too busy making love on the sofa where years before Silas Baker had made love to Chin.

The discussions went on into the night, and then again deep into the day. Rodney and Elizabeth were at a slight disadvantage because he had passed out early in the morning, and when he did wake in the afternoon he was not in the mood for talk. Still, somewhere in the deep of the night, a plan emerged that was to be put into action. They would marry as quickly as they could. As soon as the wedding vows were complete, they'd challenge Mary's will in court. If the sisters protested too violently, they'd let the truth be known about Emily. They'd get what they wanted one way or another.

By late afternoon reality had begun to seep into the discussion. Emily, better than any of them, knew the terms of the will. If the two married, she couldn't keep Elizabeth and Rodney from the land. Given the choice of sharing the house with them, or building a new one for them, she'd prefer to build. If the profits of the land were split, the Baker ranch would suffer. It took most of the money the ranch earned to keep the giant operation moving smoothly, and whatever extra money there was needed to be set aside to cover them in case the crops should be poor the next year. The Bakers were rich only if they sold out everything and split the proceeds, or if the ranch was run as one giant operation. Anything in-between would be disastrous. Since they were forbidden by the will to divest themselves of a healthy ranch, what Rodney and Elizabeth proposed could crumble the empire.

While Emily was well-versed in the terms of the will, it was Kate who best recognized the economic implication of the marriage to the operation of the ranch. The will would stop Elizabeth and Rodney from parceling the land, but nothing could force them to invest their third of the profits back into the ranch. They could live on the ranch for free, bleed off their share of the profits until the ranch went under, and then take their wealth and run.

There was an irony in that. Kate and Emily would still be able to salvage some of the Baker wealth from a bankrupt ranch, but even that would have to be split equally among all three of them. Elizabeth not only had the ability to destroy the ranch, she also had the ability to be the one to come out of it the richest. When Mary had made the will she had believed that it was written in such a way that the sisters would be forced to work together to keep the Baker fortune. She must have recognized the weakness in the will, yet she probably thought that Emily was the only one of the girls who might betray the other two, and Emily was so much her father's girl she would never betray the ranch. Certainly Mary must have died in peace, knowing she had created a document that would keep both ranch and sisters tied together, and certainly she must now be turning in her grave, finally realizing the error in what she had done. If there was any chance to save the ranch, Kate would have to cancel her plans to return to Europe to do it.

Becky Muldoone felt the heartbreak when Kate Baker realized that she would have to stay to save the ranch. Her friend had worked hard to separate herself from the Baker name so that she could be recognized as an individual, and then she had struggled to make it in a man's world, doing a man's job, while still maintaining her identity as a woman. If she had to return to the ranch, all of that would be lost.

Down the hall in Emily's room, Margaret contemplated another kind of loss. Emily needed the Baker name and the power of the ranch behind it. As long as she had those two things, Emily could stand tall with her head up in a world that despised her for her success. Take away the power of the ranch and tarnish the Baker name and this woman she loved so dearly would crumble like a dirt clod in a firm grip. The death of the ranch, she was sure, would be the death of their relationship, for she knew Emily's weaknesses well by now, and she knew that without her support to give her strength Emily could not overcome the shame she felt for loving another woman.

IN SILAS' OFFICE, where Rodney had stayed since his return, the two lovers planned their triumphant moment. At the dinner table that night Elizabeth would announce that they would marry by the end of the week. It was agreed that Rodney would not attend the dinner because his presence so upset the women. But, as a consolation, Elizabeth agreed to let him move into the den in the main house in the morning, and then into her room as soon as they were married. Beginning the next morning, his presence would be felt every minute of the day until they had what they wanted.

There was tension at the dinner table. Elizabeth let them get through the silent dinner before she made her announcement. "We're to marry this week," she said. "Rodney will move into the house in the morning and into my room as soon as the vows are complete. I'll arrange for the minister tomorrow. I think a small dinner celebration would be nice."

Neither of the sisters looked up from their plates. They had examined all the possibilities and had decided that this announcement was the most likely.

"The least you could do is congratulate me," she said, teasing a little now. She enjoyed the discomfort of her sisters.

Neither sister responded. Their thoughts were elsewhere: Emily's probing the future; Kate's lost in Europe.

"Your silence won't do the least bit of good," Elizabeth said. "I'm going to have my way and you're not going to stop me."

Again there was no answer. Again the other two women stared at their plates and let their minds wander into the night.

"Rodney's really not so bad when you get to know him," Elizabeth said, cheered by the thought of her husband-to-be. She had never believed that she would find a man who could make her secret desires a reality.

There was a muffled sound from outside.

Elizabeth might not have noticed it except her two sisters responded to the noise, lifting their heads so that their eyes could meet. A message seemed to pass between them, but it was not one that Elizabeth could read.

"I wonder what that was," Elizabeth said.

"You know how sound carries in the valley," Emily said. "It could have been anything, almost anywhere."

Kate started to say something, and then thought better of it. She returned her attention to her plate.

Fifteen minutes later, as the last of the dinner dishes were being cleared from the table, the ranch foreman slipped into the room and stood uncomfortably at the end of the table, the rim of his hat circling through the fingers of his hands.

"Excuse me, ladies," he said, "I'm afraid I've got some bad news."

The blood drained from Elizabeth's face. "What is it?" she asked, sure in her heart that she already knew the answer. Her sisters had always been too strong for her. What had ever made her believe that might change?

"It's Rodney, Miss," he said. "He seems to have had an accident."

Elizabeth slowly rose to her feet. "What kind of an accident?" she asked in a whisper.

"It appears he was getting ready to clean the shotgun in your father's office. He must have dropped it or something. It discharged."

Elizabeth started for the door, but he quickly stepped in front of her. "You don't want to go down there, miss. It's not a pretty sight."

Kate stood up. "I'll go," she said. "I'm a doctor."

The foreman shook his head. "He doesn't need a doctor, Miss Kate. He took the blast in the head."

Elizabeth slowly began to settle to the floor. The foreman had just enough time to grab her before she had a nasty fall. Kate moved to Elizabeth and checked her pulse.

"She's fainted," she said. "Would you help us get her to her room?"

THAT NIGHT Elizabeth recovered from her faint, but once again faced with the devastating news of Rodney's death, she responded to it physically. She miscarried. A week later, while she was still bedridden, it was discovered that Rodney had left her one other gift. She suffered from syphilis.

TWENTY-TWO

"OH, SHIT!" he said.

He gave the back door to his house a shove, and it swung open. Someone had jimmied the lock. Paul stood in the doorway and listened. No sounds came from inside.

Common sense told him that he should get back in his car and drive to the nearest phone booth to call the police. If someone was still in the house, it would do neither one of them any good to have a confrontation. That's how people got killed.

Almost any emotion tended to cancel common sense. In his case, the emotion was worry. There was a computer, a television, and a video recorder ripe for the picking inside the house, none of them covered by insurance. He never thought about renters' insurance until he pushed open the back door.

He reached inside the doorway and flipped on the laundry room light and the porch light. He stepped through the door and walked cautiously to the kitchen entrance. He reached inside and turned on the kitchen light. Again he paused to listen.

Everything was as he had left it on Friday. He moved to the dining room. He could see the computer's silouette by the light filtering through the French doors. For a moment he felt relieved, until he realized that the reason the computer was still there might be because the thieves were still there, too. He flipped on the dining room light.

Paul was confused now. The light from the dining room illuminated the living room enough for him to see both the video recorder and the television set. It did not appear that anything was taken. Perhaps he had scared off the intruders when he drove up the driveway.

He was even more confused by the time he came back downstairs. Not only did everything still seem to be in place, but each of the windows was locked from the inside and the chain locks were in place on the front door and the French doors. Whoever came in the backdoor, went out the backdoor. If they had been in the house when

he came home, he was sure he would have seen them running out
the backdoor when he drove up. But if someone had broken into the
house earlier in the weekend, why hadn't they taken something?

He took a flashlight from a drawer in the kitchen and went outside
to carefully search the grounds. Because it was late and dark, a moonless night, he spent nearly fifteen minutes looking around the yard.
Again he came up with the same answer. Nothing was missing. He
returned to the house, trying to figure out what had happened. He
examined the backdoor. He was sure that the lock had been jimmied.
The marks on the lock and the door jam were unmistakable. He
walked back inside.

Somewhere between the backdoor and the dining room it hit him.
One thing he hadn't checked. Because of his own security system,
he didn't worry about it. He knew he was protected. He walked
around the table and stared at the computer. Now that he knew what
was taken, he was surprised he hadn't noticed it in the first place.

He had several file boxes on the desk in which he stored the disks
for the computer. Each of them was empty. The research documents
he kept on the table were gone. The computer printouts were missing.
He found the same thing in his bedroom. The file in the closet that
contained his backup copies of information was empty. Even his
operating system disks and word processing programs were gone.
They had cleaned out his software. They had stolen all his research.
They had both incomplete manuscripts, the one about Hollingsworth
and the one about the three sisters.

He fought down the panic that was building up inside him. There
were several unopened boxes of disks in the closet and several neatly
stacked reams of tractor-feed computer paper. He picked these up and
carried them to the dining room table. He had another fleeting moment of panic when he stuck his car key into the trunk lock, but that
disappeared as soon as the trunk lid opened and he saw the box of
disks inside. Every scrap of usable information they had taken from
him was backed up on these disks.

Once, when he was in high school, someone had vandalized his
little MG—slashed the top, poured coke in the gas tank, and scratched
the paint. It had taken him all weekend to do it, but on Monday he
drove the car back to school, the damage done to it no longer apparent. He had sewn the cuts, rubbed out or repainted the scratches,

and drained and cleaned the fuel tank and fuel lines. He would not let the vandal have the satisfaction of seeing his handiwork in the light of day.

That same kind of determination drove him through the night. First he made a copy of each of the disks that he kept in the car, including the program disks for the computer. After that, he began making a printed copy of each of the disks. He still wasn't done when the sun came up.

He paused to let the printer cool and to eat breakfast. At noon he stopped again to take a shower and then to have lunch. Late in the afternoon, he returned the disks to the trunk of his car. By five, when Pam Livingston's car drove up the driveway, he had just finished organizing the printer readouts on the dining room table. As soon as he heard her car, he quickly gathered up the materials and moved them to his bedroom.

Over coffee in the kitchen, Pam asked, "Did you enjoy your two days in the Baker house?"

He leaned his back to the kitchen counter and considered how he would answer the question. He could cover up the break-in and leave it at that, or he could throw it out and see how she responded to the news. He wasn't sure he wanted to see her reaction.

He said, "I enjoyed my stay. I could almost suspend reality up there and imagine myself in the house at the turn of the century. Unfortunately, every time I achieved that mystical state a jet plane would fly over and ruin it for me. And, unfortunately, while I was there someone broke into my house."

"You're kidding," she said, looking genuinely shocked. "Was anything taken?"

He watched her carefully, searching for the smallest of clues. Nothing suggested that she was anything other than surprised by the news. "Yes, they took all my research and manuscript material."

"Have you called the police?" she asked. "Oh, God, how do you put a price tag on something like that? You must feel devastated."

She seemed sincere, he thought. Still, doubt floated around in the back of his brain. "Other than the materials I had with me this weekend, I lost everything."

"Why on earth would anyone want to steal your research?"

"I thought you might know the answer to that."

"Wait a minute," she said, her face flushing red. "You don't think I had anything to do with this? I know that I've been trying to discourage your research of the Baker sisters, but I'm not the kind of person who would stoop to something like this."

He had never seen her angry before, but there was no doubt that she was angry now. "I'm sorry," he said. "I wasn't accusing you; I just thought you might have an idea of who would steal my research."

She accepted his apology, but her feathers were ruffled and it took her a minute to smooth them. When she calmed down, she said, "I don't know who would take them. I'm the last Baker on my side of the family, and, of course, the sisters left no heirs. It might have been one of the Hollingsworths or it might have been someone else who's been researching the same thing. I'll have the district attorney nose around and see what he can stir up. Have you called the police?"

"Not yet," he said. "I was afraid an investigation might embarrass someone I don't feel like embarrassing."

"You mean like me."

"No," he said, "I was thinking more like Nora Ryan."

She shook her head, saying, "No, no, no. Nora's many things, but she's not a thief. Don't bother with the police. I'll talk to the DA in the morning and then get back to you." She left shortly after that without offering to be kissed.

That night he slept like a man in a coma. If he dreamed, the dreams were so deeply buried beneath his sleep that he had no hint of them. In the morning, he rested on his back in the same position he had assumed when he crawled in bed. The covers around him were hardly disturbed. Although he was awake, his brain was far removed from the light of day. It hovered on the edge of sleep, ready to plunge back in. He pushed himself. The best way to handle a sleep deficit was to get back to normal sleeping patterns as quickly as possible. He crawled out of bed. Two good eight-hour sleeps and he would be okay.

He was doing the lunch dishes when the phone rang. His hands were still wet with dishwater when he answered it.

Pam's voice had in it a tone he had heard before, once when they first met. It was the tone she used for business. "Paul, I'm quite concerned," she began. "I think there's been a breach of faith."

"What are you talking about?" he asked.

She got directly to the point. "Your research and manuscript material was left at my office yesterday. I have just finished going over it."

"Oh," he said, cautiously. "Who left it?"

"I don't know," she said. "It was in a box near the front door when the secretary came to work. How it got here is not the issue. What's in the material is the issue."

"Then there's no issue at all," he said. "I've obtained all my material by legitimate means."

"I would take issue with that," she said. "I also take issue with the content of your material. I believe that much of what you say about the Bakers is speculative and libelous."

"Since you're dealing with unedited material and since the Supreme Court looks down on prior restraint, I don't think there's a hell of a lot you can do about it. Should I finish that book, and should I find a publisher for it, you're welcome to sue me. In the meantime, I would like my materials returned to me."

"Your materials won't be returned to you. We'll let the courts decide about the manuscript. In the meantime I am seeking a restraining order to keep you from continuing to research or to write this unauthorized biography of my relatives."

He was becoming aggravated by the tone in her voice. He had made love to this woman. Where did she come off talking to him like this? "How does a charge of receiving stolen goods sound?" he asked. "I've got some rights here, too. If you try to use that material in court, a good lawyer will put you on a line and hang you out to dry."

"We'll know the answer to that in two or three years, won't we?" she said.

He knew he didn't have two or three years. In that time she could authorize a sanitized biography of the sisters and kill the market for him. He didn't want her to know that he had a copy of the material, so he said, "If I found the information once, I can find it again."

"But you won't use it."

"Like hell I won't, Pam," he said. "I don't give a piddly shit about your desire to protect your relatives, will or no will. They're historical figures, I've documented my research, and I've identified speculation when I speculated. I'm within my rights.''

"If you persist, I will tie up the Hollingsworth book in the suit and you won't be able to meet the terms of your grant to write it.''

"Hey," he said, "I just have to deliver the manuscript by a certain date to meet the terms of the grant. Publication of the work is their problem.''

"You won't earn a penny from it if it doesn't get published,'' she said.

"The grant was the appeal of this project," he said "I doubt that a book on Hollingsworth is going to pay for very many of my meals.''

"You're forcing me into something I don't want to do, Paul. I humored you about this Baker book because I didn't think you would find the material to write it. I didn't know how good of a researcher you were, so now I have to deal with the reality of the book. The Bakers didn't want anything written about them. I have to honor that, so I have to stop you any way I can.''

"I don't see that you have much chance of doing that in the long run," he said.

"While you were in the Baker house a silent alarm went off, indicating that you got into the safe. Fortunately for you, I informed the police that you would be staying in the house over the weekend, so they didn't respond to the alarm. Unfortunately for you, they have a record of the alarm. I think I can put together a good case for breaking and entering.''

He kept waiting for the joke, for the laughter. This was Pam he was talking to. Or was it? It wasn't the Pam he had taken to bed. "That still might be hard to prove.''

"I had prints lifted from the safe," she said.

"Circumstantial unless you have an eye witness.''

She hit him with the crusher. ''There's a video camera in the house that's wired to go on when the safe door is opened. We have pretty pictures of you opening the safe and removing material from inside it.''

"How long has that been there?" he asked.

"Since last week.''

"This is beginning to smell like a set-up," he said.

"I've been following your research since you came to town. It became apparent some time ago that I would need to take unusual precautions if I was going to protect the sisters' wishes. I never dreamed that you could get in the safe, but I wanted to take precautions anyway."

"I see," he said, not really seeing at all. This seemed like an incredible effort on her part to protect the wishes of women long dead and long removed from the harm his book might do to them. "What are you asking for, then?"

"I want the book on the Bakers stopped, I want the material you took from the safe, and I want anything that you have written in addition to the material I already have."

"According to you, you've stopped the Baker book already. As far as the material in the safe is concerned, your video tape should show me putting it back. And, I've only written one more chapter." He quickly outlined the last chapter, being careful to delete any implication that Rodney was murdered, suggesting instead that he had indeed had an accident. "That's all there is," he concluded. "You may not believe this, but I was actually hit by a bad case of guilt. I put the diaries back in the safe without reading in them any further than I have written. I decided that your friendship was more important than my research."

"And that sounds like bullshit," she said, her professional voice suddenly lost in a blast of anger. "I want to know what else you found out, and I want that information right now."

"I'm sorry, Pam," he said, "but that's the truth."

"We'll see about that," she said, and hung up the phone.

He didn't have long to contemplate the meaning of the phone call before he got another one. Again he was confronted with a professional voice. "Mr. Fischer, this is District Attorney Charles Owings. Pam Livingston has filed a formal complaint against you for breaking and entering. Upon hearing the charges against you, I believe that we might save the court system some time and money by working out an agreement of some kind. If you will be in my office by ten tomorrow morning, I won't feel the need to issue a warrant for your arrest and have you picked up and jailed immediately."

A speech as precise as that had two immediate effects on Paul. It set off a string of caution lights in the back of his mind. First he agreed to meet with the district attorney in the morning. And then he got madder than hell.

That evening he went into the workshop in the garage and rummaged around in the boxes of odds and ends left there. He found several items he thought would be useful and put them in a burlap sack.

He was not one taken with spy novels nor was he practiced in the craft of burglary. Instead, he was a writer with imagination. Over the weekend he had stood at the iron fence in front of the Baker house and imagined how he might circumvent the security system that protected the house. From that viewpoint he saw clearly how to do it.

Instead of driving his car to the road above the estate, he drove to one below it. If he had not looked down on the valley from the house, he would not have noticed the connecting links of highway, gravel lanes, and dirt ruts that led to the concrete retaining wall below the yard. After one or two wrong turns, he managed to park his car near the base of the wall just as the sun was beginning to set.

The dirt road was the remains of the drive that led to the barns when they still existed. Now it was a seldom-traveled maintenance road, used to check the condition of the wall and to bring in equipment to plant and harvest the fields and tend the orchards that were still in existence to buffer the estate from the surrounding urban development.

Security at this point was lax. The perpendicular wall discouraged most would-be intruders. The alarm system in the house stopped anyone who could get past this point. Besides, a thief would need a large truck to take anything of value from the estate, and a truck would have to get past the elaborate security system above the house.

Getting up to the yard was ridiculously easy. On the third toss he looped a length of rope over several points on the iron fence. He was then able to pull himself up to the lawn.

He made his apologies to the row of graves in the corner of the yard as he climbed over the fence. He was past having a guilty conscience at this point. He was too angry with Pam Livingston for trying to thwart him and for selling short his integrity as a writer. He wasn't out to embarrass the sisters; he was out to set the record straight. He couldn't hurt them now, but he could give some meaning to what appeared to be wasted lives.

Even in the dark, the climb up to the roof of the house was less difficult than it looked. From the porch he climbed on top of the railing to shimmy his way up a support post. Using the grooves in the siding as a toe hold, he pushed himself up onto the roof of the porch. From there it was an easy climb to the cupola, and from there a short crawl to a third story window, the smallest in the house and the one he had left unlatched.

Yes, he had replaced the diaries in the safe only partly read. He had not lied to Pam when he said his own guilt got the best of him. But he also knew that it was a nagging curiosity that plunged him into the research of the Bakers, and he knew he could not simply walk away from that without remorse. So he unlatched the window in the attic and disconnected the alarm to it, and he planned a way to get back into the house. Convinced he could get back to the diaries if he wanted to, he had left them unread, and in the safe.

Five minutes after squeezing through the attic window, he was standing in front of the safe. He didn't make the same mistakes twice. Using a flashlight to see by, he searched the edges of the safe until he found where the alarm system was located. The device was crude, nothing more than two contact points that came together when the safe doors were closed, completing an electrical circuit. When the doors opened, contact was broken, and the alarm sent its silent signal to the police and to the camera.

From the burlap sack he removed a pair of pliers, a reel of insulated wire, and a tube of liquid solder. Within a few minutes he had each end of the wire attached to the contact points. He spun the dial, worked the combination, and opened the door of the safe. The insulated wire stretched straight but maintained the electrical circuit. The alarm did not send out its signal.

With the diaries safely in the sack next to him, Paul closed the safe and removed the wires. He scraped away the solder, wiped off his fingerprints, and made sure he didn't leave a clue behind. Twenty minutes later he was in his car on his way back to the house.

At home he had moved everything into his bedroom, including the phone, and began pouring over the diaries as quickly as he could. He was determined to get as much done as he could before he saw Owings.

He was interrupted once, just before midnight. When he answered the phone, he heard Beth's voice say, "I miss you." And then she hung up.

TWENTY-THREE

KATE BAKER and Becky Muldoone traveled for five days by train before reaching New York, and two weeks by boat before arriving in London. During that time Rodney Ryan's name was not mentioned once, yet it was suspended between them like a great cloud of poisonous gas. They both knew that Rodney had been murdered.

No word was ever said and no word was ever written that would identify the murderer. The sisters sat at the dinner table together the night Rodney was killed, but that did not absolve them of guilt. A word was spoken, or a hint was given that ended Rodney's life. Who pulled the trigger was secondary to who gave the command to fire. The sisters never discussed the issue between them, and they never left a clue behind.

Kate and Becky stayed in England until the end of August. With the financing of the London Suffrage Society, Dr. Englis was able to organize two units of 80 women to help the Serbs. They sailed from Liverpool on August 31. Nine days later they reached the White Sea, and then they anchored in the Dvina River for two weeks before traveling by train across Russia to Odessa on the Black Sea. From there it was a short journey to the Rumanian front.

Kate and Becky were weary when they arrived, but their spirits were lifted when they were invited to the staff mess for tea with the other women. Two hundred men rose to cheer as they came in. The cheering was short lived. The next day they moved to the hospital tents at Medgidia, near Dobruja. For Kate Baker this was the beginning of a long nightmare.

Wedged between the Central Powers of Austria-Hungary, Bulgaria, and Turkey, Serbia and Rumania saw some of the bloodiest fighting of the war. Like any theater of combat the battles here produced dead, permanently wounded, wounded, and a lucky few who went through it unscratched. Kate Baker was one of the permanently wounded. The horrors of war left their marks on her. At first it was the sleepless nights. She would return from the operating room exhausted after a sixteen-hour shift, only to crawl into the bed and lay awake, each incision made and each cut sewn running through her mind on a non-stop reel.

Soon it was more than that. She could just barely tolerate the hot blood that soaked through to her skin during surgery, but when it turned cold against her body she could no longer stand it. She would have to rush from the operating room a half a dozen times a day to change. Finally Becky found a rubber apron for her that solved the problem, but the feel of the cold blood on her skin haunted her restless sleep, cutting it shorter than it had been.

A woman who could not sleep and who was obsessed by the feel of blood was not likely to eat. Three weeks after her arrival in Medgidia, when they all had to make a mad dash for their lives, she weighed twenty pounds less than she had when she left England.

They evacuated the wounded the best they could. As the enemy pushed at the city limits, trucks hauled those who could survive the journey to the train station. The train pulled away from the city, leaving it in the hands of the Central Powers.

For Kate the four-day journey to Braila was the worst experience yet in the war. Enemy planes swept over the train, strafing its length with machine gun fire and dropping bombs that rocked the cars on their tracks. When the attacks persisted the train was stopped, a convoy of trucks was gathered together, and the wounded were transferred. In their haste to escape the enemy guns they left dozens of dead onboard the train. The steam engine was stoked with coal and the train was left to lumber down the tracks unattended, a worthless target full of dead soldiers waiting for the next flight of enemy planes.

When the trucks ran out of petrol, they were replaced by carts. More of the staff became victims of the war. Kate suffered shrapnel wounds twice in the legs. Becky was hit by a bullet that broke her left arm. Kate dragged herself from cart to cart to attend the wounded, her legs in great pain. Becky assisted her with one arm.

They reached the Danube and for awhile escaped the immediate threats of war, but not the reminders. An old steamboat took them to Braila, passing in its journey hundreds of bodies floating down the river. Onboard the boat Kate set up a crude operating room and began to deal with the freshly wounded. She sat on a stool while she operated to take the pressure off her wounded legs.

They stayed in Braila for a month while seven doctors attempted to care for 11,000 wounded. Pressure from the enemy forced them to move to Galati, where Kate operated for 35 hours straight before she collapsed and had to be carried from the operating room. Again they were forced to move, this time to Reni. The pattern of Kate's life repeated itself, only this time one thing was different: Dr. Angelo Ferrano caught up with her in Reni.

Ferrano was not a bit player who traveled with a second-rate theater group; he was a major actor who had yet to find a major role. In one capacity or another he had been at war since 1912. Nationalistic by nature, he was also a doctor by intellect. Intellect dominated emotion. Because of that he had been a doctor for the British, the Germans, the French, the Austrians, the Serbs, and the Russians, depending on the circumstances. He was often a prisoner of war because he did not like to leave his patients behind when his hospital was over-run by the enemy.

Because he was such a good doctor, and so kind, he won the trust of the people he served. That made it easy for him to escape when the time came for him to move on. When he heard that Kate was back in Europe, he worked his way in her direction, twice allowing himself to be captured to facilitate his journey.

The first thing that Angelo did when he settled into Reni was to reset Becky Muldoone's broken arm, and to treat Kate's still painfully infected leg wounds. The rest of the staff and patients at Reni knew Kate to be a strong-willed woman and a dedicated, skilled doctor. Everyone came before her own needs, which was the main reason why her wounds went poorly treated; therefore, her friends were more than a little surprised when Kate gave in to Ferrano's command to take bed rest while her wounds healed.

Becky Muldoone was not surprised. She had seen the expression on Kate's face when she had told her friend that Ferrano had arrived. The hospital was set up in a large school building and Kate and Becky shared a small book room together on the top floor, the books getting more of the space than the two of them.

Becky had walked into the room and shut the door behind her, leaning against it. No longer on the move, Kate went back to her old habits, which meant little sleep for her and only a few casual moments alone, usually with her nose buried in a book. Kate was lying on her cot, reading.

"Guess who's here," Becky said.

"The Germans and the Austrians," Kate said, not looking up from her book. "They've been every place else we've been."

"Close," Becky said. "Only you're too far north. Try the Italians."

Kate put down the book. "You mean somebody on our side actually showed up?" she asked.

Becky could not keep from smiling. "Not exactly the Italian army," she said.

Kate sat up. "Ferrano?" she asked, unconsciously reaching up to straighten her hair.

"The one and only," Becky said. "Mr. Romance said he followed your essence here."

Kate blushed. "That idiot," she whispered. Louder, she said, "He's going to get himself killed."

"He wants to see you," Becky said.

Kate smiled. "I want to see him, too."

When she did see Angelo Ferrano that afternoon, she was surprised by what she saw. Years of doctoring in combat zones had finally caught up with him. His tall frame now had a slight stoop to it, and his hair was sprinkled with gray. Angelo had not yet reached forty years of age, but he looked as if he had.

There was something in his demeanor that had changed as well. Kate noticed it the first time he spoke. She was trying to stand on her sore legs when Becky let him into their room. He was abrupt and a little rough with her when he noticed the injuries.

"What is this?" he asked, rushing into the room and pushing Kate on the bed. She was wearing a pair of men's pants, a habit she picked up early in the war. She needed her freedom of movement and dresses did not provide it. Angelo rolled up her pant legs and looked at her wounds. "You're a doctor and you let your body do this to you," he said. "Shame on you." He stood up and shook his head.

In her own defense Kate said, "We've just been too busy to worry about ourselves. We have so many wounded and so few doctors."

"We will still have many wounded and fewer doctors yet, if I do not do something about those injuries. I'm surprised that gangrene hasn't set in." To Becky he said, "Take off that sling and let me look at your arm."

Becky did as she was told. She had always liked Angelo, although she didn't trust him when it came to affairs of the heart. He was a brilliant doctor, but as she jokingly told Kate, he was an even better heart surgeon. He could break a woman's heart and she wouldn't even know it was broken.

He examined her quickly, causing a little pain as he twisted it around. Finally, he said, "I'll have to re-set that. If not, you will have a bend in it you don't want and some problems with pinched nerves for the rest of your life. I'll get to it just as soon as I operate on Kate."

"Just a minute," Kate said, getting off her bed. "You're not going to operate on me. I've too many patients to care for."

"I'll take care of your patients. I may not be as pretty to look at, but I'm just as good of a doctor as you. Besides, if I don't remove the shrapnel from the legs, you'll risk complications."

She knew that was true. As it was her wounds were not healing because she could not give them time to heal. If the shrapnel was left in her legs, it would cause her pain for life. Worse, a piece of metal could work loose and do more damage than it already had.

"I was waiting until we reached a safer location," Kate said feebly.

"This is as safe as it's going to get," Angelo said.

There were no illusions in this war. The Serbs and the Bulgarians were being walked over by the Central Powers. The fact that the British had put on a strong show and that the Russians were too concerned with their own internal problems were the only reason these two countries had survived this long. If the United States, the sleeping giant, finally stirred and jumped into the war in force, there was a small chance these countries might be saved, but even that was a big if.

"We'll be safe here for awhile," Angelo had said. "Keep an eye on the bear to the north. How Russia goes, we go." One of Angelo's finer qualities was his ability to see the overview of the war. Most people were so caught up in their fight for life that they did not see beyond their immediate horizon. Life to them was the shadow around the corner, the gun on the hill, the bayonet poised over their bodies, or the scalpel about to slice open their skin. Countries, governments, ideals, rights, wrongs: these were the words to ponder for those select few who were well fed and safely protected behind the combat lines.

Both Kate and Becky accepted Angelo's opinion. He was famous for the time he spent behind enemy lines. He was known for his ability to sweep across the heart of Europe, despite the war. His forays into enemy territory to dine with princes and princesses, dukes and duchess, and counts and countesses were legendary. If there had been no war, Angelo would have toured Europe in grand style, moving from one wealthy circle to the next, always a welcome addition to the party because of his great wit and charm.

Angelo Ferrano had become a doctor because a young man of a wealthy, titled family must become something to prove his worth. Of course, he never would have *practiced* his craft if it had not been for the war. His family had too much money for him to need to work. In fact, he would have been an embarrassment to his family if he had actually gone to work. But, war, of course, changed all that. It was acceptable to serve, even if Angelo did carry it to an extreme.

In the beginning Angelo was concerned about the social implications of war. He would have preferred to live the free and easy life of a privileged bachelor, than to practice his skill as a doctor. As war spread across Europe he became resigned to the changes in his life that it brought. But somewhere along the line his attitude changed. He stood ankle-deep in blood too often; he had seen life slip through his fingers too many times; he saw too much suffering. Gaiety was gone from his life. He was looking for something substantial to replace it. He was looking for Kate Baker.

Both Becky and Kate became patients, locked away in their room while they recovered from their operations. Becky was the first to get out of bed, but there was little she could do. The pain from the reset fracture was too much, and the medication it would take to relieve the pain was needed for the severely wounded. Until she could take care of them both, Angelo watched over them between his stints in the operating room.

One afternoon he came into their room carrying a tray. He had covered the standard fare of soup and bread with a white linen, and he had added a vase with a rose in it to cheer up the bland meal. He set it down on a stack of books next to Kate's bed that served as a night stand.

"Well, my precious patients," he said, "Angelo has brought you another fine meal, once again proving that this war is just a minor inconvenience."

Kate lowered her bandaged legs over the side of her bed and sat up. She was not in as much pain now, but her legs were stiff and weak. "Would you walk with me up and down the corridor?" Kate asked him.

"What, and miss this great meal? After how I slaved over it?"

"It tastes the same hot or cold," she said.

He laughed. "Bad," he said. "Here, take my arm. You are right, you do need the exercise and I'm afraid the mounting casualties make it impossible for you to sit around much longer."

They walked slowly in the hallway, she holding on to his arm and leaning a little on him for support. He was a solid, strong man, handsome and intelligent. She thought at first that he was egotistical, until she realized that the Bakers, too, had been raised like that, to think that they were superior to others because of who they were. Only now both of them had seen too much war. In their hands had died men of privilege and men of poverty, men of rank and men without it, men of beauty and men of brawn. Not much remained superior in the face of war.

"I'm a very tired man," Angelo said.

"In a day or two I think I'll be ready to give you some relief. As always, you have been trying to do the work of three men." It felt good to be next to him.

"No," he said, "I am talking about a different kind of tired. I think I am weary of soul."

When she glanced up at his face, she knew what he meant. This was not the same man she had met two years before. It was as if a shadow had been cast across his features and had made a permanent change in them. The circles under his eyes were deep and dark. He had a hollow in his cheeks. A little shine had gone from his eyes. War could temper even the most spirited of men.

"Is there anything I can do?" she asked.

He chuckled. "At another time I would have had a lecherous answer for you," he said. "But that was another time. Today I would settle for being held instead of loved."

She stopped, bringing him to a stop as well. Carefully, because she was still in pain, she wrapped her arms around his waist and placed her head on his chest. He rested a cheek on the top of her head and pulled her gently to him. They stood that way for several minutes before he said, "Thank you."

"Such a little thing can mean so much," she said. And then, softly, to herself, she said again, "Such a little thing." She closed her eyes tight for a moment and then she asked the question she thought she would never ask of a man. "Sometime, when for a moment we can leave the operating room behind us and forget the war, will you make love to me?"

She was afraid of how he might respond to that. She would never forgive him if he laughed and kidded her about being the iron maiden the rest of the staff thought her to be. Or worse, if he slipped back into that lecherous Italian playboy image he so loved to present to the world.

He was very quiet for a long time, his heart beating slowly next to hers and his breathing even and shallow. When he did speak, his voice was quiet and firm. He said, "I think we should both give that idea careful consideration," he said. "If I make love to you, it will be a commitment to you. More than anything now, I need something of permanence. Anything less might shatter a man who has become very fragile. If you cannot make a commitment in return, then, no, I do not want to make love to you."

If falling in love can be marked by a single moment in time, then Kate Baker fell in love at 2:16 on the afternoon of December 11, 1916, in the hallway of the top floor of the Breshka High School, in Reni on the Danube.

THAT QUIET MOMENT together did not come for another two months. With the Americans on the way and the Russians fighting an internal revolt, the Central Powers were trying to consolidate their positions before the war heated up. Kate and Angelo were simply too exhausted from long hours in the operating room to think of their own passions.

Their weekend together near the end of February was a gift from the Americans. Troops poised to crush the Serbs and the Russians had to be pulled from the battlefield to meet this new threat from abroad. The hospital staff was able, finally, to handle the new casualties coming in from the front and still get time off from work.

Angelo arranged, as only he could arrange, for the use of a hunting lodge for a weekend. He did not give Kate the details of the arrangements, but it was understood that the lodge either belonged to someone he knew or someone he was related to. Angelo's bloodline stretched like the Rhine, the Elbe, and the Danube Rivers, across Europe.

That was to be their only time together. In March, 1917, the Russian Revolution broke out, making it too dangerous for the women to remain in Reni. They were sent back to London. Angelo stayed behind, determined to doctor his way across Europe and meet Kate in England where they would make their plans for the future.

In the end there was to be no future for Angelo. One of those ironies of war caught up with him: he was captured in Russia by the Red Army. This time his charm did not serve him well. He was accused of being related to the Czar and was summarily executed by firing squad. He was in no way related to the Czar, although his bloodline could be traced to Vladimir Lenin.

TWENTY-FOUR

A MAN SITTING IN the electric chair shouldn't be worrying about next year's income taxes, Paul told himself, but it didn't change anything. Despite the tension in the room and the uncomfortable silence around it, his mind was thousands of miles away in another time and place.

When he wrote it, he knew it wouldn't do. He had found the key event that explained all that was the cornerstone for the life that the three sisters would build for themselves, and he failed to give the moment its dramatic due. They went away for a weekend. He died. Why had he handled it so poorly?

"You haven't answered my question, Mr. Fischer," Chuck Owings said. Owings leaned across his desk, resting his weight on his elbows. To his left, deep in one corner of the office, Pam Livingston sat, brooding, a silent figure whose eyes did not leave Paul. Paul ignored them both.

He read all three diaries to the end, and now he knew why these three women had lived out their lives as they had. The information, instead of being liberating, was a heavy burden on his conscience. He had been touched deeply by the convolutions of their lives, directed by their fate of being children of Mary and Silas Baker: she the disillusioned romantic and he the lover of land.

He would be able to write this book to the end now. He had all the information he needed. Pam Livingston's betrayal had given him the motivation to do it. The threat of legal action by the district attorney was sure to make the book a hot property. But he stopped himself. Kate Baker's diary had told him in near poetic terms about that weekend with Angelo Ferrano. It told of a gentle man finally ready to fall in love; it told of a woman who had saved herself for just such man. The words painted a portrait of romantic perfection: the fire in the fireplace, the tender word shared, the cautious physical union, the great passion unleashed. He needed to say nothing himself, only let Kate's diary speak for itself. But he couldn't. To do that, he knew, would betray this woman who, in the end, had suffered enough.

"Mr. Fischer?" Chuck Owings pressed him again.

Paul looked in the corner at Pam. Their eyes met in a long, cold embrace, and neither of them blinked or smiled to lessen the impact of the contact. With his eyes still on Pam, he asked, "What's going on here?"

Chuck Owings started to say something, but Pam cut him off, asking, "What do you mean?"

Paul sat up in his chair and turned to Owings. "Pam and I had a pretty good relationship," he said. "I think that she and I could have talked about this without having to bring it to the attention of the DA. So what's going on?"

Owings answered. "The security people brought this to my attention. I told Pam about it. I'm the one who suggested that we have this formal meeting to make sure that her interests are protected."

"Meaning what?" Paul asked.

"Meaning that if a complaint is filed, she has a legal means to stop you from using any information obtained during your search of the safe," he said.

"I told you," Paul said, "I put everything back in the safe."

"After you read the diaries," Pam said.

"As I said, I didn't finish reading them." Technically he was not lying. At that time he had not read the diaries all the way through.

"We don't believe that," Pam said.

"Believe what you want to believe." He was becoming a little exasperated, although he know he was to blame for it. He wanted them to believe the truth, but, of course, it was only the truth for that moment. They weren't about to accept that. He was becoming angry because they wouldn't believe him, while at the same time admitting to himself that they had every right not to believe him.

Owings tapped his desk with a pencil and then looked at Paul with cold, blue eyes. At that moment he did not look like the loud, friendly man that Paul had first seen in Pam's office. He looked, instead, tough and unbending. "Let me lay it out for you," he said. "I think I can get a five thousand dollar fine and six months in jail for an unlawful entry. I think I can hold on to all the material that Pam Livingston had dumped on her doorstop. And, I think I can stop publication of any material related to the Bakers, no matter how you obtained it.''

"That sounds like a hell of a lot for one man to be able to do," Paul scoffed. "I'm betting a good lawyer can get unlawful entry thrown out of court. After all, I was just playing with the safe dial when the door fell open. And you're welcome to hold onto any papers if you don't mind a receiving-stolen-property charge. Then, once those two things are resolved, you won't be left with squat to stop publications of a book dealing with the Bakers." He turned to Pam. "Anyone for hardball?" he asked.

"You can laugh your way through this, Fischer," Owings said, tapping the pencil hard enough to break its point, "but you're in much more serious shape than you think. I've convinced a judge that we have just cause, and I have been granted a search warrant for your property. Right now your house and your car are being searched. We'll see if you're still laughing when my men are done."

"I'll laugh at you right now," Paul said, smiling and leaning forward in his chair. "I know you're not going to find a darn thing you think you're going to find." And he did know it, too. All of the material he had kept in his car was now in a locker at the local bus station, and the key for that locker was in a hefty garbage bag, buried in the orchard next to the house along with the three diaries. When he smelled a rat, he started to take precautions.

Owings glanced at Pam. She flushed red and stood up. This was the second time Paul had seen her angry. "I want that material, Paul. I don't want any games played, or lawsuits, or charges brought: I simply want all the material you have."

"Why?" he asked, forcing himself to stay calm. She looked like she wanted him to say something cute so she could pounce on him.

"None of your damned business," she shouted.

"Calm down, Pam," Chuck said.

Her glance snapped toward him and then back as she said, "You keep out of this. You haven't helped one damned bit."

"Wait until we see what the search warrant will turn up."

"You still haven't answered my question," Paul said.

"Look, the only answer you're going to get is this," she said, still angry, "you took something that belongs to me and I want it back."

"Have you looked inside the safe?" he asked. He knew such a

question might incriminate him, but he also knew he needed to know the answer.

"I can't get in the fucking safe," she snapped.

She was standing in front of him with her hands on her hips, breathing hard, the frustration carved on her features like the etchings on a coin. At that moment she looked much older than she was. He leaned back and stared at her face. There, he thought, was the answer to his question.

He said, "You mean that in a legal sense, don't you."

"You know I do," she said.

"He knows no such thing," Owings said, the words apparently some kind of warning. Pam immediately retreated to the chair in the corner.

Paul looked from one to the other. He had an idea now of what was going on, but it seemed too ridiculously absurd and complicated to be real. Still, it would explain one hell of a lot.

"I think I remember the combination. I'd be glad to open the safe for you," he said. The answer to this question would tell him just how wild of an idea he had.

She turned her head to the side and clicked her tongue in disgust. A warning look from Owings stopped her from saying anything. Neither one of them jumped at his offer.

"I see," Paul said.

"And just what do you see?" Owings asked.

"A lot of murky water. Do you plan to file charges?"

"Yes," Owings said.

"No," Pam countered.

They stared at each other for a moment, while some angry message passed between them. Owings turned away from her, saying as he did, "Not right now. I'll wait to see what the search warrant turns up."

Paul stood up. "Are you sure you don't want to tell me what's going on here?" Neither responded to his question. "Okay," he said, "then I'll be on my way." He started for the door.

As he shut the door behind himself, he heard Chuck Owings' booming voice growl, "Dammit, now you've fucked it up."

HE FOUND Nora Ryan in the museum's storage room, sitting at the computer terminal while she scrolled a lengthy document on screen.

She did not hear his call for her in the outer office or the noise he made when he pushed open the door to the back room.

He stood over her right shoulder and read along with her. If it hadn't been for the meeting with Pam and Chuck Owings, he might have been surprised by what he saw on the screen. "Why, Nora," he asked "what are you doing?"

He didn't realize that an old lady could move so fast. She sprang from the chair and whirled on him. Then, as quickly, she turned around and turned off the computer. The writing on the screen faded away.

Finally, with a hand clutched to her chest, she said, "You frightened me."

"I bet I did," he said, smiling. "Why did you clear the screen?"

"I was done," she said, pushing past him and walking back to her office. "Why don't we move in here?"

He stared at the computer. He knew if he booted the disk back into the computer, he could bring this whole issue to a head, but he also knew that if he pushed Nora to the wall he'd get nowhere with her. He wanted her cooperation.

She was sitting at the roll-top desk, looking disgustingly handsome for a woman her age. If he was thirty years older, he would be tempted to spend a lot time with her, but only with that thirty years of experience behind him. So far she'd been quite good at taking advantage of his inexperience.

He leaned in the doorway of the back room and asked, "Are you going to be the one to tell me about it?"

Her eyes grew big behind her round glasses, and she blinked them innocently. "What do you mean?"

"I got this peculiar feeling this morning," he said, "I was being used for some reason. This beautiful woman who most certainly was in love with me only days ago seems to have turned on me viciously. And, to top it off, the district attorney is trying to throw me in jail. Now, as best I can tell, the only thing I did was to get ripped off. You wouldn't know anything about that, would you?"

Nora smiled. "I love the part about how innocent you are," she said.

He laughed. "The safe opened by itself," he said. If he was guessing wrong, then Nora wouldn't know what he was talking about.

She laughed, too. "How'd you get it open?" she asked.

"I found out the combination," he said. "You'd be surprised what kind of information you can get out of a computer."

She shook her head. "No," she said, "I wouldn't be surprised at all. When I got your letter telling me that you had received the grant to research Hollingsworth, I figured you'd be the one to get into the safe."

"Are you telling me that I was set up?"

"I'm not going to tell you anything."

"That's my research material on your computer. It could get embarrassing if I brought the police in to ask you where you got it."

"My, my," she said, "you must have left it here when you were using my computer."

"Won't work," he said. "The stuff you had up on the screen was gathered long after I last used your computer."

"Oh," she said. "Then, maybe someone left a box outside the museum door."

He chuckled. "Do you really think that will work twice? I think a good investigation might show that someone, Nora, entered my house and removed my research material. That someone loaded all the material onto your computer before sending the originals over to Pam Livingston's office."

"That might be a heck of a thing to prove," she said. She turned back and forth in her swivel chair, not taking her eyes from his face or losing the smile on her own.

"Am I going to get a straight answer out of you?" he asked.

"I'll tell you what I'll do," she said. "I'll answer your questions if you'll answer mine. I'll go first. Have you written any more since your house was broken into?" she asked.

He considered the proposal. There were a few questions he was not ready to answer, but this was probably the only way he would get information from Nora Ryan. "Okay," he said. "The answer to that is yes, I have written more, and no, Chuck Owings didn't find it. My turn. Was I set up?"

"'Set up' is such a nasty phrase," she said. "The Bakers were brought to your attention with the hopes that you might take an interest in them. Now it's my turn. Are all your of questions about the Bakers answered?''

He liked the way she phased the question. She didn't ask him if he had read the dairies, which, of course, he would have to deny. "Yes," he said, "I'm satisfied. Now, was it Pam's idea to use me?''

"Again, you're being nasty. Pam has taken an interest in your research for some very good, material reasons. By the way, did you prove that Pam's directly related to the sisters?'' She stopped swinging in her chair and leaned forward. The look of expectation on her face explained a lot to him. This, obviously, was the question she wanted answered. "I'm sorry," he said. "I can't give you the answer to that.''

"Can't or won't?'' she asked.

"I mean, if that's the information you're after, you're not going to get it from me,'' he said, moving from the storage room door to the one exiting the office.

She followed him, talking to his back. "I knew from the first you'd be a darned good researcher. You passed by my best efforts the first week you were here. I can't believe you didn't get it all. I can't believe you didn't read the diaries when you had the chance.''

"Believe what you want," he said, walking down the front steps.

"Don't be a fool," she said. "There's a hell of a lot of money in this.''

He stopped listening. He still wasn't sure what was going on, but it was obvious now that he was in the middle of it. He'd been set up from the beginning to research the Bakers, and Pam was in on that. He wasn't sure if he wanted to know any more than that. The truth, he was sure, wasn't going to be nice at all.

TWENTY-FIVE

NEWS DOESN'T TRAVEL FAST during war, unless it is bad news. Kate Baker had been in London for a little over a month when the first rumors of Angelo's death reached her. Two weeks later his death was confirmed, as confirmed as any death could be. Eye witnesses claimed...

In her heart she knew it was true. She had not heard from Angelo since the evacuation. He was not a callous man who would have an affair and then disappear from it. Some kind of word would have come from him if he was alive—some kind of farewell if he planned not to see her again.

Spirit is a fragile commodity, broken if pressed too hard, spent if not conserved. Kate Baker, so stubborn in youth, so strong as a woman, had spent her spirit into a deficit. When she was sure that Angelo was dead, all the forces that had channeled her life for so long were no longer enough. She didn't want to stay in England. She did not want to be a part of war. She did not want to be a doctor. She wanted to retreat into the shadows and nurse a very painful wound.

She took with her memories good and bad. She would treasure her years with Becky and her precious moments with Angelo, but she would still wake in the middle of the night and feel the cold blood against her body, and she would be haunted day and night by the vivid images of war. And, she took back home with her one more thing. Deep in her womb stirred the four-month-old fetus that was the product of her weekend with Angelo.

She was met by the ranch foreman at the train station in a flatbed truck. Her bags were tied on the bed of the truck, and she was given a silent ride back to the ranch. She didn't mind. She was in no mood to talk.

The foreman stopped the truck under the carriage port of the house just as the dining room doors swung open and Emily stepped onto the covered porch. She stood there, her arms crossed, and waited for

Kate to climb the steps. She did not smile. She had no reason to. Just two weeks ago she had received the telegram saying that Kate would be home, without any further explanation. In the year that she had been gone, Kate had not written to either sister, nor had she indicated in any way that she planned to return home soon. Emily had assumed that when the war ended, Kate would decide what she was going to do with her life. Whatever that was to be, she hadn't expected Kate to do it here on the ranch.

Kate climbed the steps to the porch and paused long enough to give Emily a brief hug. Inside the house, on the dining room table, she put down her hat and gloves before walking to the parlor. A girl she hadn't seen before followed behind her, first picking up the gloves and hat and then waiting for the cape thrown over Kate's shoulders. Kate gave her that and then asked for tea to be served in the parlor.

Emily came into the parlor and shut the doors behind her. She leaned against them, waiting with a look of curiosity on her face. She was a little in awe of this baby sister of hers who had defied her for so many years and then had proven herself so adept at so many things.

"How does it look?" Emily asked.

Kate had slumped down in a chair. The combination of travel and pregnancy had been tiring, but that was just the surface weariness of a much deeper exhaustion that ran through her body. War and grief, grief and war: how they ate away at the foundation, how they threatened to topple the house.

"What's that?" Kate asked.

"The ranch," Emily said.

Kate shook her head. "I didn't notice."

"You didn't notice." She was hurt. As stupid as it seemed to her, when she learned that Kate was coming home, she had an overwhelming desire to please her. "The house and all the buildings have been painted. New fences have been put up. You rode in one of three new trucks we bought. In the barn are two new tractors and dozens of accessories to go with them. In one year we have more land, more cattle, and more harvest than before, and to top it off, we'll have a substantial profit at the end of the summer. The things you did when you were home were a stroke of genius."

Kate nodded. "They were things that needed to be done," she said. "Where's Elizabeth?"

Their eyes met, the ghost of Rodney Ryan passing between them. "She's taken to bed."

"Is she sick?" Kate asked.

"Like Mama," Emily said. They were interrupted by a knock on the door. The new girl came in with a tea tray and served the two sisters before quietly departing, closing the door softly behind herself. The women were silent while the girl was in the room.

Once the girl was gone, Kate said softly, "Like Mama. That doesn't surprise me," she added. "I always thought that Elizabeth's one flight to freedom would be a wing-breaker. How long has she been there?"

"Months."

She nodded again. "And the syphilis?"

"The doctor thinks it's still there."

Kate nodded again. She knew what happened when people became broken both physically and mentally. If Elizabeth still had syphilis, it would show up again in five or ten years, devastatingly so.

She said, "The perfect Protestant disease—one indiscretion and a lifetime of misery." How ironic, she thought. Elizabeth's one venture led to disease. Emily's one venture was an act of vengeance. Kate's one fling had left her pregnant. None of them seemed to have gotten it right.

"I'm worried about her," Emily said. "She's getting crazy like mother was."

Kate nearly laughed. This was the woman who had spent years idolizing her mother speaking such blasphemy. Was she beginning to see it too? Their father's land and their mother's values were to be their curse. They had not been taught to function like normal human beings, and they had been given this great refuge from the world around them. It was so easy to escape back to the Baker Ranch. No other place in the world could be as secure. She laughed aloud. And other people envied them.

"I'll look in on her later. I assume my room is empty," she said.

"The guest room is empty, too, if you want to move in there," Emily said.

"Oh, you mean Margaret didn't move back into it? Her exile wasn't meant to be permanent."

"Margaret is no longer here," Emily said. "I sent her away."

She could have asked questions, and Emily would have answered them, but Kate decided not to. The affair with Margaret had made Emily vulnerable and powerless, an unthinkable state for her. Margaret was destined to go eventually.

Kate moved back into her own room. She felt secure in that long, narrow room with its bank of windows across the back of the house. She knew its drafts in winter. She knew how to circulate its stagnant air in summer. The Morris chair next to the fireplace was still there to be curled up in at night with a book to read. The window seat was there for her when she felt like sitting for hours to stare outside. As soon as she had unpacked and slid her empty suitcases under the bed, she felt at home again. And then, after years of hardship and pain, after too many deaths and too much disaster, after too little gained and too much lost, she let it out and sat on the window seat and sobbed late into the night.

The next morning, when she was finally ready to face Elizabeth, she walked into her sister's bedroom. Elizabeth was propped up in bed, surrounded by white linen and bedding. Heavy drapery covered the windows so that little light entered the room. Elizabeth waited for Kate with her arms crossed under her breasts and a look of defiance on her face.

"Hello," Kate said as she eased herself down on the foot of the bed. "I'm home."

"How wonderful," Elizabeth said, one word a knife thrust and the other a twist of the blade. "Baby sister's back." Pointing a finger toward Kate's face, she added, "Don't try to change a thing. I'm not coming out of this room again, ever."

Kate looked at her sister with the eyes of a doctor. She saw a face white and puffy, a body bloated with extra weight. According to Emily, Elizabeth had not left the bedroom for six months.

"You'll only harm yourself staying in bed," Kate said.

"I can't have anything that's not good for me," Elizabeth said, mimicking Kate's voice. "Charles wasn't good for me, so Emily took him away. Rodney wasn't good for me, so the two of you took him away. Now you want to take away my bed from me."

"Staying in bed won't bring either Charles or Rodney back," Kate said.

Gesturing dramatically, Elizabeth said, "If bed was good enough for mother, it is good enough for me. Try to take me out of this room and I'll kill myself." She folded her arms across her chest and tilted her head majestically.

Too weary to deal with this now, Kate said, "I wouldn't think of it. Mother seemed happy enough in her room."

Elizabeth nodded triumphantly. "I knew you'd see it my way." Frowning now, she asked, "What are you doing back?"

"I'm back for a rest," Kate said.

"Well that's just exactly what I need—rest. So get out! Send the maid for me. I want to be tucked in."

Kate rose slowly and turned away so that Elizabeth could not see the sadness on her face. "I can do that," she said as she left.

That evening, in her room, Kate sat by an open window and smelled the luscious flavors of the warm summer night. In the air was a tinge of death as the grass began to die under the summer heat, but for the most part it was free of the sickly odor of death that she had been breathing for years.

She knew why she came home. She could have had the baby in England, surrounded by women sympathetic to her, but she'd had enough. Compared to the rest of the world, the Baker Ranch was paradise. Sharing the ranch with her sisters was a minor inconvenience compared to the benefits of being insulated from the outside.

She heard a tap on the door. "Come in," she said.

Emily pushed open the door with her foot. She was carrying a tray with a serving of tea on it. "I thought you might like a snack before bed," she said. "I've some toast and honey and tea."

Kate made room for her on the window seat. When they were settled and sipping the tea, Emily asked, "How long are you going to stay?"

"I don't know," she said. "Six months. Maybe longer."

"Good," Emily said. "I have some chores I'd love to turn over to you. You know how I hate to keep the books, although I've been pretty good at it this last year. I was afraid we might get into financial difficulty."

"We won't get into financial difficulty. If war's taught me anything, it has taught me the value of gold and silver. I think we should turn all the profits we have into precious metal and keep it stored in the safe of the ranch. Paper money and paper investments become nearly worthless in a time of crisis. If we do that, we'll never have to worry, no matter what happens."

"I'll leave that to you, then," Emily said. "That certainly would make it easy for me to pick up the finances again should you decide to leave."

Kate had not planned to tell her about the baby right away. She figured she still had a month before Emily would notice the growth, yet, now, with Emily being so pleasant, was a perfect time. She had no guarantee that they would get along so well in another month.

She began by saying, "I want to tell you about a man I met." She told the story of Angelo Ferrano from her point of view, one that was surprisingly more objective than others who had known him as well or better. "Angelo was a handsome, noble, wealthy man who attracted to him many women. He never knew if it was his looks, his nobility, or his money that made women putty in his hands, so he became cautious with them. He loved, and then he gently extricated himself from them.

"Women were his second love. Being a doctor was his first. He blessed the war because it allowed him to be a doctor without bringing disgrace to his family name. Ferranos did not work. They were too wealthy even to consider it. To have a son who insisted on working as a doctor would have been an embarrassment to the family. Of course, during the war, it was noble and patriotic to serve one's country, so Angelo was encouraged to practice medicine.

"He knew he would have to stop when the war ended, so he did the unthinkable. He practiced medicine for everyone, regardless of the side they were on. When a prisoner, he treated the enemy. When free, he treated his own troops. Whenever possible, he slipped from the hospitals to serve the medical needs of the civilians. Few people knew how dedicated he was to healing.

"In the end he died because he could not separate himself from his family name. If he could have walked out on his family years before and lived his own life, he would have been a happy man, but too much nobility was engrained in him."

In conclusion, she said, "In many ways he was a Baker through and through. Unfortunately, and unfairly, it killed him." She paused a moment to see how Emily was taking in all of this. Her sister had never asked her about her life away from the ranch. Kate did not know if that was because of anger, or jealousy, or disinterest. To her surprise, Emily seemed to have devoured eagerly every word Kate said.

Kate continued. "He was a marvelous man. I loved him deeply. I feel fortunate to be carrying his child."

Emily did not comprehend at first. When she finally did understand, she stood up, sending tea cup and saucer flying across the room. "You're going to have a baby!" she shouted.

"Yes," Kate said, startled by her sister's response.

"Why, that's marvelous." Emily bent down and gave her a quick hug. "That's absolutely marvelous."

This was not the reaction Kate expected. "I'm glad you're delighted," she said, laughing a bit, "but if you don't keep it down the whole world will know."

Emily whirled in a circle. "I'll be glad to tell the world that there will be an heir to the Baker fortune. Daddy would be delighted to know that the ranch will stay in the family."

"All of that's nice," Kate said, "but let me remind you that I'm not a married woman. I'm afraid that fact won't do the Baker name much good."

"A little fib here and there will take care of that. We'll let it be known that you were married in Europe and that your husband was killed shortly after that. Not everyone will believe it, but they'll have a time proving that it's not true."

"I suppose you could tell that to the help," Kate said, "but I'd just as soon keep things quiet. I'll stay out of sight until the baby is born so we won't have any talk."

"You can't keep something like this secret," Emily said. "You will need a doctor."

"I know, I know. I am a doctor," Kate laughed. "I want Dr. Hollingsworth to deliver the baby."

"Charles?" Emily asked, a horrified look on her face. "Not Charles!"

"Not Charles," Kate said. "His father. I want him to deliver my baby. We know we can trust him."

Details were settled that night. The Bakers, very much people unto themselves, would stay that way. The help was told the story of Angelo Ferrano and was told of the wedding that never took place. They were then instructed to keep quiet about Kate's pregnancy. As Emily explained it, Kate did not want, in her grief, to be burdened with the sympathy of the community as well. She simply wanted to have her baby in peace while she tried to put her shattered life back together.

The final months of pregnancy were difficult for Kate. In Europe she rarely had the opportunity to eat well, and she almost never had the chance to rest. She came back to the ranch a too-thin, anemic woman, not at all in the best shape for having a baby. At home she rested, exercised often, and ate properly, but she was trying to fill a bottomless well. The baby sucked up what Kate did for herself and demanded more. Inside her the fetus grew healthy while the mother grew more tired and more weak.

The first time old Doc Hollingsworth came to see her, his bushy white eyebrows pinched together when she met him at the door. This was not the beautiful young girl he had encouraged to go off to Europe to become a doctor. She was so happy to see him that she wrapped her arms around his neck and buried her face in his shoulder.

He patted her on the back and said, "Don't be silly. Now get away, get away." He gently pushed her from him, shaking his head and clucking his tongue. "I've got an excuse for looking the way I do, but you don't. What have you done to yourself?"

He was old now, and bent and stooped, his hair long gone and his face deeply wrinkled. He might have aged more gracefully if he hadn't heard too many stories from his patients like the one Kate told him. He felt their pain and he lived their agony, until it took a toll on him too.

When Kate finished telling him the story of Angelo, he nodded a few times and then said, "I wouldn't have expected less, not at all."

She did not know what that meant, although she suspected that the doctor had many opinions of the Bakers he did not express. She said, sincerely, "I'm sorry if I've disappointed you."

"If you have to apologize for something, you shouldn't have done it. I suspect you don't feel that way at all, so don't apologize."

She laughed "You're right. This is all that Angelo had to leave to the world. I could have aborted the baby, but I felt I owed it to him to give birth."

"That doesn't sound like a woman committed to motherhood," he said.

She rested her hand on her stomach, feeling for the first time the bulge that was beginning to grow. "I'm not sure," she said, "if the world needs another Baker."

Need it or not, the world got another Baker in January of 1918 in a scene reminiscent of the one that took place twenty-eight years before when Kate was born. And with similar results. A strong, healthy baby's wail cut through the night while the mother began a desperate struggle for life.

She was a spectator of her own tight rope walk, watching as her arms circled in the air in a frantic attempt to keep from falling. Below her was an endless drop through the outreaching arms of a thousand people she knew, all of them dead now. At the other end of the rope were the desperate cries of a little bundled baby left abandoned and helpless. Her heart reached out to the baby, while something in her longed for the drop below. In the end, she inched toward the baby's cries until finally, with the dawn of another day, she opened her eyes.

"Water, please," she said, but nobody heard the hoarse whisper that slipped through dry, closed lips. She tried again and managed a croak that caused someone in the room to stir. A hand rested on her forehead for an instant.

Doc Hollingsworth felt Kate's brow and mumbled to himself. She was cooler than she had been, but still not cool enough. "I wish you Bakers would learn to have babies without scaring everybody half to death," he said.

Kate could not smile. She ached too much to do that, but she did manage to whisper, "Let's see you do better."

"Humph," he said. "If men had to have babies, there wouldn't be any more babies. How do you feel?"

"I hurt," she said.

"You've got every right to hurt," he said. "What makes man so precious is the pain it takes to get him here."

"There's a lot of pain in the leaving, too," she whispered. "The baby?" she asked.

"Weak women, iron children," he chuckled. "Happens every

time. I thought I lost Mary three times to get you here, and now look at you.''

No, if she looked the way she felt, she didn't want to look at herself. "A girl?" she asked.

He poured her a glass of water from a pitcher on the dresser and then lifted it in the air as a toast. "Silas finally got his boy. You'd think that Emily has never seen anyone finer in her life.''

Kate closed her eyes and let the news sink in. Doc Hollingsworth held her head up and let her sip from the glass of water. With her lips moist, she was finally able to smile. "That makes it easier," she said.

"And just what does it make easier?" he asked, looking less concerned now than he had an hour earlier when he was sure he was going to lose Kate.

"I want you to do me a favor," she said. "I want you to send for Uncle Tim."

Harry Hollingworth's mouth dropped open. In all the years he had known the Bakers, never once had he seen them have anything to do with Silas' brother. When Tim had come west years before, Silas had done little more than stake him to a claim. From that fact grew a deep resentment between the two men. Tim had moved to the hills on the other side of the valley and started a ranch in a poorer location and on poorer ground. He did okay for himself, but his success paled next to his brother's.

"Why on earth do you want to do that?" he asked, not caring whether or not it was any of his business to know.

"I've some family affairs to take care of," she said. That was all she would say. If she were to tell Harry the truth, then he might thwart her efforts that would in the end betray Angelo, her sisters, and, of course, herself.

TWENTY-SIX

As PAUL DROVE back to the house after treating himself to dinner and a movie, he tried to figure out the puzzle.

The picture he had now still did not have all the pieces in place. It had not been hard for him to make the connection between Nora Ryan and Rodney Ryan, the uncle she had never known, her father's brother who had been killed before her birth. He was thrown off track at first because he knew Nora had been married, and he could not make the connection between her married name and Rodney, but then he discovered that she had returned to her maiden name after her husband's death.

Beyond that he had to guess. He doubted that Nora began her research with the Bakers. Although they were interesting enough when all the information was in, Nora had very little of that material available to her. She would have found much more interesting people to write about. No, more than likely she started out looking into the life of her uncle, and the research had led her to the Bakers, and something she found there hooked her up with Pam Livingston.

The connection between the two seemed logical enough, but he still didn't understand where he came in. Nora had said a lot of money was tied up in this, but he hadn't seen any of it. If money was to be had, Pam would know more about that than he would. And, since she was a lawyer, if she had the chance to get her hands on the money, she'd know how to do it. So why did they need him?

True, he had gotten into the safe, and he was pretty sure that neither of these women had seen the diaries. Still, a smart lawyer could find a legal reason for having the safe opened. It seemed as if they wanted him to get the diaries for them. But why? What was it that he was suppose to prove that they couldn't prove themselves?

He parked the car behind the house and cautiously walked through the dark to the back door. He thought he had left the porch light on, but perhaps it had burned out. He would have to check that in the morning. He let himself in and walked into the kitchen. He never had a chance to switch on the light before he was spun around and slammed into the refrigerator.

He was too stunned to react. Any action on his part would have been useless because he was quickly driven through the door into the dining room and driven to the floor. For a second he was free. He struggled to his hands and knees. That was as far as he got before a foot caught him in the ribs and drove him back to the floor. A knee was placed in the small of his back and a hand grabbed a handful of hair and pulled his head back as far as it would go. A long, pained moan escaped from Paul's lips. He didn't know which hurt more, his ribs or his back.

He braced himself on his elbows and tried to roll over and force the man from his back. As soon as he began to struggle, the knee came off his back and his head was shoved back to the floor. This time he didn't bother to get up.

The man moved to the living room and threw himself into a chair. He breathed heavily for a moment before he spoke. When he did, Paul recognized Chuck Owings' voice. "We turned this place tonight while you were out," he said. "I had a good team go through it from top to bottom. I'm amazed at how clean it is. If I'd found half the stuff you have on the Bakers, I wouldn't be so suspicious. But to find nothing... You don't know how that pisses me off. I know you have it, and I want it."

Paul rolled over and sat up. Despite the pain he had felt just moments before, now he didn't hurt at all. Owings was good, he thought. He bet he wouldn't have a mark on his body by morning. He also knew he didn't want to press his luck, so he stayed on the floor as he said, "I've quit the Baker story."

"Yeah, and I'm not going to run for state representative the first chance I get. Let's try another story."

"You know," Paul said, "for such an ambitious man, this doesn't seem like such a good career move."

Owings stood up and slowly walked into the dining room. Paul braced himself. This time he didn't strike out, but instead Owings lifted his hand to the light coming through the French doors so Paul could see the gun in it. "Let me make this clear," he said, leaning over Paul, "I could plant your body in the orchard next door, clean out every speck of you from this place, and leave your car mysteriously abandoned on a fire road in Northern California. When the cops try to figure out what happened to you, not one of them will think of asking me about it. I hope I'm getting through to you.''

Paul put his head in his hands and rubbed his eyes. He knew he should feel afraid, but he didn't. Something that made so little sense simply did not seem real to him. Chuck Owings had proved himself to be stronger than Paul, but both of them already knew that. The gun was nothing more than a stage prop. Owings could easily intimidate him without it.

''Just exactly what is it you want to know?'' Paul asked.

''I want to know what you found out about Pam in the diaries.''

Paul didn't get a chance to answer. Both men were suddenly frozen by the dining room light flicking on. Pam Livingston stood in the doorway of the kitchen. Owings reaction was to try to hide the gun behind his leg. Paul's reaction was to jerk the gun out of Owings' hand and toss it into the living room. The district attorney froze, not sure whether he should go after the gun or Paul.

Pam settled the issue. ''I told you I'd handle this,'' she snapped. She added, softer, soothingly, ''Chuck, I want you to leave.''

Owings' shoulders seemed to sag. ''You know he's got the stuff,'' he said, the intimidation completely gone from his voice.

''I want you to leave,'' she said.

''I need to get my gun,'' he mumbled.

''I'll get your gun for you and give it to you later.''

He nodded several times, and then he shuffled past her and left through the kitchen. In that moment, Paul saw what he might have been in the hands of Kate Baker—as subserviant as Chuck was to Pam.

While she went into the living room and retrieved the gun, Paul struggled to his feet. She walked by him into the kitchen and turned on the light. He followed. She poured water into the coffee pot and put it on of the stove.

He leaned against the counter, waiting for her to finish. When she turned back to him, she was every inch of Kate Baker caught in the soft light of the kitchen and framed by the darkness of the windows beyond. He hated this moment. He knew that she was as close to Kate Baker as he would ever get, and he knew that after tonight he would lose Pam.

"I deserve an explanation," he said.

Pam nodded. She said, "No one ever appreciated Kate Baker in the valley except for her beauty. She never practiced as a doctor again after she returned to the ranch. She had considered opening a practice with Doc Hollingsworth, but he was too old to take care of many patients, and not many were willing to come to a woman doctor in those days. Doc Hollingsworth died in nineteen twenty, and Kate let her plans rest." She stopped and smiled to herself. "You know," she said, "she really was a terrific doctor. Nora showed me the material you gave her. It only confirmed what I had found out myself. She was one of the first truly gifted women surgeons in the world, and nobody around here knows that."

She leaned back against the stove and stopped for a moment. A hint of tears welled up in her eyes. Paul was surprised that she would have this much feeling for Kate Baker. She continued. "She was a genius when it came to money. In the nineteen twenties she turned the substantial profits of the ranch into gold. When the market crashed at the end of the decade, she was one the few ranchers in the valley not hurt by it at all. She could have ridden out the Depression on the gold reserves, but she didn't think that wise. Profits were down because of the poor economy. She was afraid that they would use up the gold and then have nothing left when things did turn around. So she hedged her bet. Like Joe Kennedy, she bought up a lot of stock for practically nothing and then sat on it."

That was new information to him. He couldn't resist a question. "What kind of stocks?"

"A little bit of everything. G.E., railroads, airlines, oil; whatever she could get at a good price. I don't think she picked a bad one. Each returned a small fortune. Collectively, they added up to a large fortune." She turned off the boiling water and fixed them a cup of instant coffee.

While she worked, he said, "Nora Ryan said that a lot of money was involved in this."

She handed him a cup of coffee. "Nora Ryan is a greedy old lady." She laughed as she said it. "She was the first one to see all the money in it. If it hadn't been for her, I wouldn't have gone looking and wouldn't have found where Kate had stuffed it all. I found a safety deposit box crammed full of bonds in one bank, over

forty-two pounds of gold in deposit boxes in three other banks. I
converted the gold to cash at six hundred thirty-two dollars an ounce
and I invested it at fourteen percent. The bonds on today's market
were worth six million dollars. The estate still owns forty acres of
prime residential land in the valley and six thousand acres in eastern
Oregon. She left a fund for over two million to maintain the estate.
The whole thing came to just under thirteen million. And Kate gave
away millions more before she died."

He nodded. He knew that Silas was a millionaire in his day. As
sharp as Kate was with money, it did not surprise him that she had
taken Silas' fortune and dramatically increased it.

"How does Nora Ryan figure into this?" he asked. "I know Rodney was her uncle, but she's got no direct or indirect claim to the
estate. Why would this mean money to her?"

"That was one of the things you were suppose to prove," she said,
glancing down into her coffee and then coyly glancing up to see how
he would take the news that he was indeed being used. When he did
not respond, she said, "Nora's mother was adopted. Her mother was,
of course, the illegitimate daughter of Silas Day and Chin. Here you
have the indirect link to the Baker fortune and the explanation for
the dollar signs in Nora's eyes."

"And what is it that puts the dollars signs in your eyes?" he asked.

"You already know the answer to that," she said. "You *know* that
I'm Kate Baker's granddaughter. The money belongs to me."

"Maybe so," he said, nodding. "Since you're a pretty good lawyer, you shouldn't have trouble proving that."

"It's nice of you to think so," she said, a sad smile lingering on
her lips. "But I'm no match for Kate. You'd be surprised by the
legal knots she used to tie up the estate. Even though I found all the
money, even I couldn't find a way to touch it. Nor can I find a way
to prove that I am an heir to the estate which will meet the terms of
the will she left."

Again he nodded. "So I was to prove it for you. If an independent
researcher came along and showed that you were the rightful heir to
the estate, you would have the ammunition you needed to break
Kate's will? You must have seen sucker written all over me when
we first met."

She shook her head no. "This wasn't personal. Nora and I came up with the idea to offer a grant to write about Hollingsworth. We're the ones who picked you from the applicants over the others. We thought you'd be the best of the lot, and we weren't wrong."

Another piece of the puzzle fell into place. "And how does Chuck Owings fit into this?"

"We were engaged to be married," she said. "That kind of got put on the back burner when *we* made love."

He was surprised he didn't feel more angry than he did. Of course she had deceived him. Maybe even as many times as he had deceived her. "What do you want from me now?"

She looked him in the eyes. "I want you to make my case for me. I want you to prove without a doubt that I'm Kate's granddaughter and that the fortune belongs to me. If you do, I will make sure that both you and Nora are financially rewarded."

"What makes you think I can do that?"

"Because you read the diaries and know it's true."

"And if I refuse to help?"

"One way or another, I'll get the money. With your help, you'll get some of it, too."

"And what about Kate's will and wishes?"

"She's dead. Her wishes don't count anymore."

"I'll think about it," he said.

She glanced down as she asked, "Would you like me to spend the night?"

He admired her coyness. "No," he said, "I couldn't come to an objective decision wrapped up in your arms."

"Can I take that as a compliment?"

He took both their cups and put them on the counter, and then he took her by the hand and led her outside to the car. There he kissed her good night. The kiss was long and hard, and she shoved her body against him and stirred up his passions, but he was still able to push her away gently.

When she was in her car, he asked, "How much?"

She smiled, the look on her face saying it all. She knew money would bring him around. "You can write the book and keep the profits. As soon as you can prove the money belongs to me, you'll be a millionaire." The knowing smile stayed on her face even as she pulled away.

He did not return to the house. Instead he walked down the gravel driveway to a hammock he had stretched between two cedar trees. The night was moonless, yet clear skies allowed starlight to illuminate the yard in a soft glow. Now that his eyes had adjusted to the night, he could see everything clearly.

In the hammock he stared overhead through the branches of the trees at the stars beyond. Up there, eternally written, were the answers to questions that man could not find written on earth. In an invisible script stretched between the thin points of light he hoped to see what he was meant to do, to see what he owed Kate Baker, to see what he owed Pam Livingston, and to see what he owed himself.

TWENTY-SEVEN

"NO!" SHE SHOUTED. "You can't do it. Oh, please, Kate, don't do it."

The argument had raged from one end of the house to the other after Emily discovered Kate's plan to give the baby boy, Oliver Angelo Baker, to Tim Baker. Kate's mind had been set since talking to Uncle Tim, but that didn't keep Emily from trying to change it.

She caught up with Kate at the top of the stairs and began again. "He's a Baker, Kate. He belongs on the ranch."

Kate walked resolutely back to her room. She would not give in to this barrage of pleading from her sister, no matter how much it surprised her. She had never expected Emily to be so emotional about a child.

"He'll be on a Baker ranch," Kate said, "but not this one. Uncle Tim is a hard-working, God-fearing man who has raised three fine daughters of his own. He'll bring the boy up right, and he's delighted to finally be getting a son."

Emily followed her sister into the bedroom, saying, "Uncle Tim is a jealous old man who always envied father his land and his success. He'll use the boy to try to get the ranch."

Kate whirled around. "It's not to your advantage to compare Silas and Tim. Our dear father does not hold up well in the light. It was Silas who turned his back on his brother. It was Silas, even when he was filthy rich, who never thought to offer his brother a penny. It was Silas who severed the bonds with his family because he didn't want to be bothered. Uncle Tim, on the other hand, didn't need us. He's got a good ranch and a good income, and he has three daughters who adore him. And, he's offered to take Oliver simply because he is a Baker. That's all I need to know to make this decision."

Emily shut the bedroom door and leaned her back against it. "Tim will never live long enough to see him grow into a man. Who'll raise him then? That child the foolish old man married?"

The child to whom Emily referred was actually forty years of age.

She was Tim Baker's third wife. His first wife had worked with him shoulder to shoulder in the fields, helping turn the poor land into something that would support a ranch. She wasn't strong enough for the task, so weakened by overwork that the first modest fever of a colder-then-normal winter took her life. Tim was heartbroken. He didn't remarry for another ten years, this time to a robust woman who gave him three girls and twenty years of happiness before she, too, succumbed to the stresses of a hard life. Just recently, well after his sixtieth year, Tim had married Clara Higgins, the spinster daughter of a local minister who was known for her goodness and charity, if not for her good looks. She had never been attractive enough to attract the kind of man she could have loved, and she had never been desperate enough to take anything less. Tim Baker, even at sixty, proved to be the man she wanted. He was a hard worker and a devoted father, and, when the demands of the farm decreased after the harvest was in, he was a devout, church-going Christian for about six months of the year.

Kate sat down and stared out the window, focusing on a distant point to keep the tears from falling. She could not let Emily see her cry or she would never win this argument. She said, "You know as well as I do that Tim has raised marvelous children. You also know that Clara Baker is the kindest person in the world. And, furthermore, you know as well as I do that Tim thinks that this ranch has been cursed by the devil, and he wants nothing to do with it."

Emily came to the window seat and kneeled at her sister's feet. "Kate, Kate," she said. "He's your blood. How can you give him up?"

She bit the inside of her cheek to keep the sob from escaping her lips. "Because I love him," she said. "I won't have him raised here."

Emily shook her head vigorously. "That's foolish," she said. "Who could give him more love than we could?"

Kate took Emily's face in her hands and whispered harshly, "Look at us! Just look! Our mother was a fine woman from the east, a servant girl who actually thought she was much too good for everyone, but oh so moralistic and refined, except that she had a long affair with her doctor and took to bed in middle-age and willed herself to die. And don't forget father. Not only did he and mother team together to drive a poor servant girl to suicide, he used Chin like his own personal prostitute for years while doing it. The only thing he cared about was land and money, and only about money because he knew he could turn it into land.''

"Don't say such things, Kate," Emily sobbed, her head twisting back and forth in her sister's hands.

"I have to say them," Kate said. "I have my boy to think about."

"But it's all over now," Emily said. "They're both gone."

"But they're not," Kate insisted. "They're here, in this house, right now, embodied in each of us. Do you think we could escape them so easily? Look at Elizabeth, already taken to bed, already more than half crazy. Mother's gotten into her. Mother's pulling her into hell."

"No, no, Kate," Emily moaned, slapping her hands over her ears. "Don't say such things."

She pulled Emily's hands from her ears as she said, "And father's in you," Kate continued. "He's obsessed you with land, money, and greed. I know you fight it, but you're losing the battle. They've left us only two choices: If we're not Silas, we must be Mary. I don't want that for my boy."

Emily grabbed both of Kate's hands in her own. "How can you be so cruel?" she cried. "How can you say those things?"

"Think of Chin, think of Charles, think of Margaret. What drove you, Emily? What possessed you? You hated us. You wanted us dead. Why? Our parents molded us, and twisted us, and corrupted us, and finally, they ruined us. I will not pass that heritage on to my son."

"Okay," Emily said, pleading again. "Let Tim raise the boy. But we'll leave the ranch to him. He'll be the heir to the fortune."

Kate shook her head vigorously. "Never," she said. "Don't you understand? The land is cursed. Uncle Tim is right. Baker blood and power and wealth do not mix. Oliver will be better off if he doesn't know we exist."

Emily broke away from her sister and stood up, anger turning her face flush. "I'll fight you on this," she shouted. "I'll see to it the boy knows who we are, and I'll see to it that he gets the ranch. You won't stop me."

"You're wrong," Kate said, speaking softly because she knew it would do no good to get into a shouting match with Emily. "I will stop you at every turn. He's my son."

When Uncle Tim came for the boy, Emily was locked in her bedroom and watched through a split in her curtains, feeling the familiar boiling hatred that she thought she had put to rest. To see the little bundle handed from Kate to the plump arms of Clara Baker was more than she could take. A great sob escaped from her lips, and no longer was she able to see through her tears. She stumbled to her bed and threw herself on it. After all these years, she knew now that Kate had finally taken her revenge.

TWENTY-EIGHT

PAUL BEGAN WORK just as the sun edged over the distant mountains. First he spread a sheet of plastic on the grass next to the spot where he made the deep cut with the kitchen knife. Carefully, so not to kill the roots, he rolled back the section of grass he had freed from the earth, exposing a square of moist soil beneath it. Using a garden trowel, he began digging a hole in the ground, placing the loose soil on the sheet of plastic.

The sun was clear of the mountains by the time he was done. His last two finishing touches were to roll the section of grass back into place and then to take the excess dirt on the plastic sheet and dump it over the fence. He walked around his project several times, inspecting it from a variety of angles. Satisfied that no one could spot the area where he had worked, he gathered up his few tools and returned to the fence. He made his descent, retrieved the rope, and climbed into his car. It wasn't until he was back on the road again that he considered the morality of his act.

On one hand his conscience was clear. He had just returned the diaries. He had to smile at the gall of such a thought. He hadn't exactly returned the diaries to the safe where they belonged. No, instead he had returned them directly to their rightful owners. The hole he had dug was behind Kate Baker's headstone. He had carefully wrapped each of the diaries and then placed them in a water-tight plastic box. He had buried the box about two feet down in the ground.

He turned onto Hanley Road before he considered what the other hand represented. His conscience was not so clear about this. He knew that he had effectively killed any chance that Pam Livingston would have to claim the Baker fortune. Without the diaries, she would not be able to prove her case.

Although he knew it wouldn't comfort Pam any, he had not done this to hurt her. Seeing that she received the fortune might be the easiest thing for him to do. Like she said, he would get a lot of good things out of such a deal. Doing was one thing, he told himself, living with it was another.

Ten minutes later he pulled into his driveway and spotted as he did the tail end of Pam's Mercedes sticking out from behind the house. He glanced at his watch. It was only seven in the morning. He hadn't expected her quite so early.

He stopped the car and got out, making sure the plastic and the trowel were well hidden under the seat when he did. She was waiting for him at the back door.

"Hi," she said. "I made a fresh pot of coffee." She held open the door for him.

Two cups of coffee were poured and waiting for them on the kitchen table. He slid into a chair in front of the one without cream and said, "You're both very efficient and up very early."

She sat down across from him. "After you called me last night and said you wanted to talk, I couldn't sleep. I decided the sooner we talked, the sooner I'd get back to normal."

Even a sleepless night did not distract from her beauty, he thought. The dark circles under her eyes might even add to it. Looking at her made him wonder if he wasn't being a fool. She had made it clear to him on the phone that a long-term relationship was available to him.

"I guess I made you wait anyway," he said, referring to his absence when she arrived at the house. He had expected her to ask him about it. When she hadn't, he got the uneasy feeling that she might have known where he had been.

She laughed. "I have to admit I was curious. When I found your bed empty, I thought you might have left town."

"I just ran down to the little market to get something to eat for breakfast, but, of course, it wasn't open yet," he said. This was a safe lie because he didn't have much left in the house to eat and the market wasn't open when he drove by it earlier.

"I must have just missed you, then," she said. "I got here about fifteen minutes ago."

He relaxed. If she had arrived any earlier, she might have wondered what took him so long just to run down to the store a short distance away. He leaned back in his chair and wrapped his hands around the warm cup. To start each morning with a cup of coffee and this beautiful woman might be as close to heaven as he would get—if he didn't know all the things he knew.

He knew he must sacrifice heaven, though, and he said, "I'm not going to be able to help you."

The expression on her face changed only slightly. She still looked pleasant, but a little of her smile was gone. She said, "That will kill any chance of you writing a book about the Bakers."

He sipped from his coffee cup, and then he said, "I've decided not to write about the Bakers. I'll still do the Hollingsworth book."

Although she didn't appear to be angry, the smile left her face. She asked, "And?"

"I fly back home tomorrow," he said, watching her face closely.

"I see," she said, softly. "Is there anything I can do to keep you from going?"

"No," he said. "Legally you might try some tricks, but I've gotten rid of all the material pertaining to the Bakers that I'm not using in the Hollingsworth book." That was mostly true. Carefully wrapped to protect them from the elements were a set of disks buried with the diaries.

She nodded. "Are you going back to your wife?"

Impulsively he leaned forward and took one of her hands in his. He wanted her to understand even if he believed she might be incapable of it. "I don't know anything about you, Pam, that isn't tainted by my knowledge of the Bakers. I don't know how many times you've been in love. I don't know how many times you've been hurt. I don't know how committed you've been to another person. Because of that, I don't know if you can understand what I am going to say. For me, for my wife, I have to go back. I've got to bring to a close this thing between us, no matter how it ends. Without that, whatever comes next will be built on a faulty foundation."

"And if she still doesn't want you back?"

"I don't know."

Tears rimmed her eyes before she could fight them off. "I must be a real loser," she said, "if millions of dollars can't keep you here with me."

"You've flattered me," he said. "I'd like to go home thinking I had seduced one of the most beautiful women I had ever known. But I won't. I'll go home wondering if it was me or the money."

"It couldn't be both?"

"I don't think so."

She squeezed his hand. "I'll still get the money," she said, the tears gone now and winter in her voice.

"Maybe," he said.

She pulled her hand from his and sat up, every bit the lawyer now. "What made you decide to give up on the Baker book? Certainly not to keep me from getting what rightfully belongs to me."

"Do you know how the sisters lived out their lives?" he asked.

"I only know about their lives from the legal trail they left behind," she said.

"They lived a hell that only Jean Paul Sartre could have conceived. Each took turns keeping the others from having what they wanted. Elizabeth died from syphilis. Kate and Emily lived a silent struggle, each determined to out-live the other to shape the final will. Emily was doomed from the start. She had to spot Kate eight years. Kate didn't live much beyond Emily. She made sure no one would get the Baker fortune, and then she departed quickly an unhappy life."

"Then why did she leave that house up there on the hill like a beacon to draw me to it?" Both anguish and anger were in Pam's words.

"In the end, none of the Bakers were very strong. Not Silas, not Mary, not Elizabeth, not Emily, and especially not Kate. She blamed it on the corruption that came with the land and the money. In her own words, she said in her diary, 'I want the house to be kept as a monument to the futility of our lives. I want people for years to come to see that lovely, empty house and say to themselves, what a waste. Only then will they begin to understand in the least part what our lives have been...'"

"My life would not be a waste," she said.

"You're over thirty, Pam, and what have you got to show for it? A life dedicated to a quest. I don't know if you can love anyone, anymore than Silas or Emily could love someone unless it led to an end."

She stood up, insulted. "You bastard," she said. "Just go the hell back to where you came from. I don't need you." She rushed from the house to her car.

He stood in the doorway and watched her get into the car. She sat in it for a minute without starting the engine. She opened the door and slowly got out again, looking at him over the roof of the Mercedes. "You destroyed the diaries, didn't you?"

"Don't count on them in your plans," he said.

She laughed. "I have more plans," she said, "just in case you didn't pan out."

"I thought you might."

She stared him in the eyes, apparently determined to make him believe what she was about to say. "I could love you, even without the money. You kept seeing me as Kate, but I'm more Elizabeth than the other two."

"A Baker nonetheless," he said.

She smiled. "A Baker nonetheless. Will you let me know what happens between you and your wife?"

"I still have six months left on the lease. I'll be back—with my wife, or without her."

"I'll have to make plans," she said, laughing to herself as she got back in the car.

As she drove off, he said to himself, "I bet you will."